PRAISE FOR
The Forgery of Venus

"Tantalizing . . . exhilarating. Retains power from the first chapter to keep readers desperate for the suspenseful, addictive fix of every succeeding one. *The Forgery of Venus* is a highly intelligent novel that entertains and educates."
—*USA Today*

"Ingenious. . . . The author owns his subject matter and packs it with well-researched details, making this . . . a successful, suspenseful examination of insanity, forgery, and reality."
—*Chicago Sun-Times*

"[An] imaginative novel of psychological suspense."
—*Boston Globe*

"Michael Gruber's new thriller, *The Forgery of Venus*, is as layered as a luminous portrait by an old master. A tour-de-force combination of suspense and characterization as well as a primer on the world of art and art forgery."
—*Seattle Times*

"Gruber writes passionately and knowledgeably about art and its history—and he writes brilliantly about the shadowy lines that blur reality and unreality. Fans of intelligent, literate thrillers will be well rewarded."
—*Publishers Weekly* (starred review)

"Irresistible. Fast, frightening, and, as usual, richly imagined."
—*Kirkus Reviews* (starred review)

"Gruber writes thrillers for smart people. This novel is about art and creativity. That sounds lofty, but Gruber gives it humor and heart by handing the narration over to the fast-talking, appealingly crass Chaz Wilmot. The ensuing drama, involving a forgery believed to be the work of Diego Velázquez, keeps you on your toes."
—*Arizona Republic*

"Gruber is on a roll. Not even a year after *The Book of Air and Shadows*, he delivers another terrific art-historical thriller. . . . Gruber incorporates historical scenes into this very contemporary tale; we could call it formula, but it's far tastier than that. Mixed in with the plot twists and suspense—mostly psychological this time—are both fascinating details about art forgery and thought-provoking conversations about art and morality. It's a tale within a tale within a tale, a perfect place to get lost for a few days. Once again, Gruber mines a popular vein and strikes gold."
—*Booklist* (starred review)

"Smart and literate. Gruber approaches art with obvious appreciation, and has woven a clever story with plenty of detail." —*Wichita Eagle*

"A quick and sharp romp through the art world. Downright delicious."
—*Seattle Post-Intelligencer*

"Gruber writes with a deft hand, creating a fallen hero who is likable despite his faults." —*Library Journal*

"Gripping. . . . Absorbing suspense well garnished with history and a dollop of high culture." —*Salon.com*

"This is an art lover's dream. Mystery and obsession are textured with art history in a plot that explores not only the shifting nature of art but also the complex nature of identity." —*Milwaukee Journal Sentinel*

"Michael Gruber's large and growing number of fans won't be disappointed with his sixth novel, a thriller in the art history vein. He's woven a tale within a tale within a tale, all filled with marvelous twists and turns that build suspense and heighten the mystery until the satisfying conclusion."
—*Fort Worth Star-Telegram*

"This terrific art thriller has history, thieves, insider snippets, and a convoluted plot to keep you guessing." —*Toronto Globe and Mail*

"A dead genius, a sleuthing couple with romantic chemistry, and some bad guys. . . . It's a fun party." —*Entertainment Weekly*

"It has quirky, flawed characters, tricksy first-person narration, some knowing references to the cinematic nature of its own plot, and nimble, witty prose—a dash of Nabokov and a dollop of Amis. Gruber is the real deal." —*Salon.com*

"Very good. . . . Ingenious and suspenseful." —*Maclean's*

"Entertaining. A wild ride." —*Charlotte Observer* (Best Books of Summer)

"Smart and irreverent." —*Arizona Republic*

"[An] intoxicating mix of fact, fiction, secret codes, and ancient conspiracies. . . . Well-written and cleverly told. A terrific thriller." —*Edmonton Journal*

"A crackling whodunit. Characters [with] rich inner lives that transmute genre fiction into literature." —*Dallas Morning News*

"[An] entertaining thriller with *Da Vinci Code* appeal but far better writing." —*Ventura County Star*

"Finely honed prose, ambitious structure, and captivating characters. . . . This is a whip-smart adventure that surpasses its competitors with dexterity." —*Rocky Mountain News*

"Another one of [Gruber's] patently intricate thrillers." —*TheMorningNews.com*

"Gruber is no ordinary writer." —*Milwaukee Journal Sentinel*

"A gripping literary thriller. A taut novel that offers ingenious puzzles plus murderous threats along the way." —*Seattle Post-Intelligencer*

"Michael Gruber pulls out all the stops [in] an elaborate game of cat and mouse." —*Newsday*

Nina Subin

About the Author

MICHAEL GRUBER has a Ph.D. in marine sciences and began freelance writing while working in Washington, D.C., as a policy analyst and speechwriter for the Environmental Protection Agency. Since 1990, he has been a full-time writer. His novels include the *New York Times* bestseller *The Book of Air and Shadows, The Forgery of Venus, Night of the Jaguar, Tropic of Night,* and *Valley of Bones.* He is married, with three grown children and an extremely large dog, and he lives in Seattle.

ALSO BY MICHAEL GRUBER

The Book of Air and Shadows

Night of the Jaguar

Valley of Bones

Tropic of Night

The Witch's Boy

THE
FORGERY
of
VENUS

MICHAEL
GRUBER

HARPER

NEW YORK · LONDON · TORONTO · SYDNEY

HARPER

A hardcover edition of this book was published in 2008 by William Morrow, an imprint of HarperCollins Publishers.

An excerpt from the poem "The Rokeby Venus" by Robert Conquest appearing on page ix is reproduced with permission of Curtis Brown Group Ltd, London, on behalf of Robert Conquest. Copyright © 1955 by Robert Conquest.

HarperCollins books may be purchased for educational, business, or sales promotional use. For information please write: Special Markets Department, HarperCollins Publishers, 10 East 53rd Street, New York, NY 10022.

FIRST HARPER PAPERBACK PUBLISHED 2009.

Designed by Jessica Shatan Heslin/Studio Shatan, Inc.

The Library of Congress has catalogued the hardcover edition as follows:

Gruber, Michael, 1940–
    The forgery of Venus: a novel / Michael Gruber. — 1st ed.
        p. cm.
    ISBN 978-0-06-087448-3
1. Painters—Fiction. 2. Art forgers—Fiction. 3. Painting—Forgeries—Fiction. 4. Extortion—Fiction. I. Title.

PS3607.R68F67 2008
813'.6—dc22   2008002363

ISBN 978-0-06-087449-0 (pbk.)

09 10 11 12 13 OV/RRD 10 9 8 7 6 5 4 3 2 1

FOR E. W. N.

So with the faulty image as a start
We come at length to analyse and name
The luminous darkness in the depths of art:
The timelessness that holds us is the same

As that of the transcendent sexual glance
And art grows brilliant in the light it sheds,
Direct or not, on the inhabitants
Of our imagination and our beds.

ROBERT CONQUEST, "The Rokeby Venus"

THE
FORGERY
of
VENUS

"I'll lay a bet," said Sancho, "that before long there won't be a tavern, roadside inn, hostelry, or barber's shop where the story of our doings won't be painted up; but I'd like it painted by the hand of a better painter than painted these."

"Thou art right, Sancho," said Don Quixote, "for this painter is like Orbaneja, a painter there was at Ubeda, who when they asked him what he was painting, used to say, 'Whatever it may turn out'; and if he chanced to paint a cock he would write under it, 'This is a cock,' for fear they might think it was a fox."

—Miguel de Cervantes, *Don Quixote*

Wilmot showed me that one, back in college; he'd written it out in his casually elegant calligraphy and had it up on the wall of his room. He said it was the best commentary he knew about the kind of art they were showing in New York in the eighties, and he used to drag me to galleries back then and wander through the bright chattering crowds muttering in a loud voice, "This is a cock." A bitter fellow, Wilmot, even back then, and it should not have surprised me that he came to a bad end. Whether the story he tells is merely remarkable or literally fantastic I still cannot quite decide. I would have said that Wilmot was the least fantastic of men: sober, solid, grounded in the real. Painters have a rep, of course—we think of van Gogh and Modigliani flaming out in madness—but there's also stodgy old Matisse and, of course, Velázquez himself, the government employee and social climber, and

Wilmot was always, even back in college, on that zone of the spectrum.

Did this all begin in college, I wonder? Were the lines of relationship, envy, ambition, and betrayal set that early? Yes, I believe so, or even earlier. Someone once said life is just high school, on and on, and it does seem that the great of the world are only familiar schoolyard figures—the obnoxious little shit we recall from ninth grade becomes the obnoxious little shit in the White House, or wherever. There were four of us then, thrown together by chance and by our mutual dislike of dorm life at Columbia. Columbia is technically an Ivy League school, but it is also neither Harvard, Yale, nor Princeton, and has the additional misfortune of being located in New York City. This tends to make its undergraduates even more cynical than undergraduates tend elsewhere to be: they're paying all this money and yet they might as well be attending a suburban community college. And so we were cynical, and affected also a paint-thin coat of sophistication, for were we not New Yorkers too, at the center of the universe?

We lived on the fifth floor of a building on 113th Street off Amsterdam Avenue, across the street from the great futile mass of the unfinished Cathedral of St. John the Divine. I roomed with a fellow named Mark Slotsky, and in the other apartment on the floor were Wilmot and his roommate, a reclusive, pasty pre-med whose name I had forgotten until reminded of it somewhat later in this tale. Aside from the pre-med, the three of us became pals in the manner of students, deeply, but provisionally: we all understood that school was not real life. This was perhaps unusual at the time, the waning days of the great patriarchy, and there was still floating around in the air the notion that this experience would mark one forever, that one would always be "a Columbia man." This none of us bought, which is what pulled us together as a group, because it would have been hard to find three young louts with less in common.

Slotsky's parents only appeared at graduation, and I sensed that he might have excluded them then had he been able. They were actual refugees from Hitler, with dense accents, almost parodically overdressed, noisy and vulgar. Mr. S. had made a modest pile as a soft-drink distributor and loudly wondered what items of the college's property his money had paid for. They seemed, to my eye, oblivious to their beloved college boy's desire to stay as far away from them as possible, indeed to be mistaken, by reason of dress, speech, and comportment, for another scion of Charles P. Wilmot, Senior.

The name of C. P. Wilmot (as he always signed himself in a thick black scrawl) is not as famous now as it was then, but he was at one time considered the natural heir to the throne occupied by Norman Rockwell. He'd made a rep as a combat artist during the war and had flourished as a delineator of American life in the mass-circulation magazines of the fifties, and at the time of our graduation it was not at all obvious that his profession and livelihood would utterly vanish in the succeeding decades. He was rich, and famous, and happy with his lot.

I should add that upon this graduation day I was an orphan, parents killed on the road when I was eight, only child, raised by a responsible but distant aunt and uncle, and so forth, and therefore I always had my eye out for appropriate father figures. During the various graduation ceremonials I found myself staring at the elder Wilmot with filial lust. He wore on that occasion a soft cream-colored double-breasted suit, with a foulard bow tie and a Panama hat, and I wished I could stick him in a shopping bag and take him home. I recall that the dean came by and shook his hand, and Wilmot told an amusing anecdote about painting the portrait of both the president of the university and the president of the United States. He was much in demand as a fellow who could paint into the faces of world leaders a nobility of spirit not always apparent in their words and deeds.

After the graduation was over, the great man took us three friends and our families to Tavern on the Green, a place I had never been to before and which I then regarded as the pinnacle of elegance rather than what it is, a sort of higher Denny's with a terrific location. Wilmot sat at the head of the table, flanked by his son, and I was down by the foot, with the Slotskys.

During lunch I therefore learned a good deal about the distribution of carbonated beverages and what little Mark had liked to eat as a child, but what I chiefly recall about the afternoon (and it's amazing I can recall anything, so generously flowed the champagne) was the senior Wilmot's voice, rising witty and mellow above the restaurantish murmur and clink; the laughter of the company; and once, the sight of Chaz's face, illumined by a chance bar of sunlight from the park outside, and its expression as he regarded his father, a look that combined worship and loathing in equal measure.

Or perhaps I am interpolating this based on what I later learned, as we so often do. Or I do. But there can be no doubt about what I am now to relate, and this bears more directly on the veracity of Chaz Wilmot's remarkable, horrible tale. He was one of those sons who, looking upon their father's profession and finding it good, set out to match or surpass the old guy's achievement. He was therefore an artist, and a surpassingly good one.

I first met him in our sophomore year as I was moving in. He happened to be going out while I was struggling up the filthy marble stairs with an enormous suitcase and an over-full grocery carton, and with hardly a word, he pitched right in and helped me with my things and afterward invited me into his place for a drink, which was not beer, as I had expected, but a Gibson, made in a chrome shaker and served in a chilled stemmed glass. My first ever, and it went to my head, as did the appearance somewhat later that afternoon of a lovely girl who removed all her clothes so that Chaz could paint her. I was reasonably experienced in that area for an undergraduate, but this was for me a new and expansive level of the louche—Gibsons and naked girls in the broad light of day.

After she was gone, Chaz showed me his work. His room had the street-side windows and for a few hours a day the light was fairly good and to obtain this light he had agreed to occupy the smaller of the two bedrooms, even though he was the lessee. There was an immense professional easel in it, a ratty pine table smeared with paint, a junky student desk, a brick-and-board bookcase, a plywood wardrobe, and a beautifully made antique brass bed, this last brought from home. One wall was covered with pegboard, from the hooks of which depended an astounding variety of objects: a stuffed pheasant, a German lancer's helmet, a variety of necklaces, bracelets, tiaras, a stuffed beaver, an articulated human skeleton, swords, daggers, odd bits of armor, a large flintlock pistol, and an array of costumes representing the last half millennium of European dress, with a few tastes of the Orient thrown in. This collection, I soon gathered, was a mere overflow from his dad's, who had a virtual museum of paintable objects installed in his studio at Oyster Bay.

The place stank of paint, gin, and cigarettes; Chaz was a heavy smoker—always Craven A's in the red cardboard box—and you could see the yellow nicotine stains on his long fingers even through the omnipresent blots of paint. I still have a little self-portrait he did that year. I watched him do it, in fact, entranced: a few minutes staring at himself in a dusty mirror of a Broadway saloon and there he was—the pall of coarse black hair falling heavily over the broad forehead, the elegant straight nose, the long jaw, those remarkable large pale eyes. When I expressed appreciation he ripped it out of his sketchbook and handed it to me.

On that first afternoon, however, I woozily stood in front of his easel and caught my first sight of his work, which was a smallish painting of that naked girl done against an ochre ground. Without thinking I gasped and said it was terrific.

"It's shit," he replied. "Oh, it's alive and all that, but overworked.

Anyone can do a figure in oils. If you screw up, you just paint over it, and who cares if the paint is half an inch thick. The thing is to catch the life without trying, without any obvious working. *Sprezzatura.*"

He said the word lovingly, with a roll; I nodded sagely, since we were both being formed into little Renaissance manikins by the Columbia great books program and had both read Castiglione's *Courtier,* with its admonition to achieve excellent results without showing obvious effort. One was languid, therefore, one whipped out brilliant papers at the last minute, one despised the sweaty grinds in the pre-med program. I should mention here that Chaz rather set the tone of our little community, which was as aesthetic as all get-out. The three of us were in the arts: Chaz painted, of course, and I was acting seriously at the time—I had some off-Broadway credits, in fact—and Mark had a Super 8 camera and was making short films of intense existential dreariness. In memory it was a lovely era: bad wine, worse marijuana, Monk on the record player and an endless stream of lanky girls in black tights and heavy eye makeup with straight hair down to their butts.

Strangely enough it was something Chaz did that knocked me out of acting for good. This was at the start of junior year, and they had brought in a visiting professor, a real Broadway director who was mad for Beckett. We did a series of his plays and I was Krapp in *Krapp's Last Tape.* Chaz went to all three performances, not, I think, to support me, for we sold out the Minor Latham Playhouse straight through, but because he was genuinely fascinated with the idea of taping one's whole life—of which more later. At the cast party I got into a drunken argument with some frat boy gate-crashers and there was a modest spasm of violence. The police were called, but Chaz hustled me out through the restaurant kitchen and back to our building.

We sat in his room and we drank some more, vodka out of the bottle, I recall, and I talked and talked until I noticed that he was looking at me peculiarly and I asked him what was wrong. He asked me whether I realized I was still in character, that I was using the querulous, middle-aged voice I had devised for Krapp. I tried to laugh it off, but the realization generated a deadly chill that penetrated through the booze. In fact, this happened to me a lot. I would get into a character and not be able to get out, and now someone else knew about it too. I changed the subject, however, and drank even more sincerely until I passed out in Chaz's armchair.

And awoke to dawn and the sharp stink of turps. Chaz had set up a large canvas, maybe five feet by three, on his easel. He said, "Sit up, I want to paint you." I did so; he adjusted the pose and began to paint. He was at it all day, until the light was gone, pausing only for the necessary toilet breaks and a Chinese meal delivered to the door.

I should say that although I had scrubbed the theatrical makeup off my face, I was still wearing powder in my hair and my Krapp costume of collarless white shirt, baggy dark trousers, and waistcoat with watch chain; and I'd grown a three-day beard to add to the seedy effect. I believe I said "Holy shit!" when at last he allowed me to see what he'd done. I'd taken the obligatory history of art survey course, and the apposite name popped into my head.

"Jesus, Chaz, you're painting like Velázquez," I exclaimed, with a peculiar combination of feelings: astonishment and admiration at the feat of art, and an absolute horror of the image itself. There was Krapp, with the impotent lust and malice playing on his face and the little lights of incipient madness around the eyes; and beneath this mask there was me with all the stuff I thought I had successfully hidden from the world staring out, naked. It was like the picture of Dorian Gray in reverse; I had to make myself look, and smile.

Chaz regarded it over my shoulder and said, "Yeah, it's not bad. A little *sprezzatura* working in there, finally. And you're right; I can paint like Velázquez. I can paint like anybody except me." With that he snatched up a brush and signed it with the black colophon he would use throughout his career, the "CW" with a downward pothook drooping from the "W," to indicate that it was Wilmot *Junior* who'd done it. I have the thing still, rolled up in a cardboard tube on the top shelf of a storage closet in our house, never shown to anyone. A couple of days after he made the painting I went to my advisor, dumped all my theater courses, and switched to pre-law.

I should say here a little something more about myself, if only to frame, as it were, the story of Chaz Wilmot. My firm is one of those anonymous outfits denoted by three capital letters, and we specialize in insuring the entertainment industry, broadly speaking, everything from rock concerts to film locations, theme parks, and so on. Still in showbiz after all, I like to say. We have offices in L.A. and London, and for about twenty years I was based out of town in those places. Currently, my domestic arrangements are ordinary in the extreme and related to my business life, in a way, for I married my travel agent. Someone in my position necessarily spends a good deal of time on the phone with the person who arranges flights and hotels and so forth, and I developed an attachment to the voice on the phone, so helpful and accommodating at all hours, so unflappable in the many emergencies, blizzards and so forth, that afflict the traveling man. And I liked her voice: Diana is a Canadian, and I grew accustomed to those long vowels and the perky little "eh?" she appended to her sentences; I found myself calling her number late at night with pretended routing changes, and then we dropped the pretense. We have been, I suppose, happily married, although we see little of one another, except on vacations. We have the canonical two children, both now in college, and a comfortable house in Stamford. I am not rich, as wealth is calculated in these imperial times, but my company is both successful and generous.

Chaz and I were fairly close up until our senior year, and then I went off to law school in Boston and we lost touch. I saw him for about twenty minutes at our fifteenth college reunion, when he walked off with my date. She was an arty type with a wonderful name—Charlotte Roth-schild—and I seem to recall that they eventually got married, or lived together or something. As I say, we lost touch.

Mark kept in touch, being a keep-in-touch kind of guy, active in alumni affairs, always a call for the annual contribution. He tried his hand as a screenwriter in Hollywood for a season, got nowhere, then got his parents to set him up in a downtown gallery when SoHo was just taking off, and he flourished at it, but not before changing Slotsky to Slade. I got invitations to all the Mark Slade gallery openings and we occasionally went to them.

We didn't discuss Chaz much on those occasions, and I gathered that he was working as an artist with some success. Mark mainly likes to talk about himself, somewhat tediously, if you want to know the truth, and in any case I am not terribly interested in the art scene. I own only one original work of any distinction, curiously a painting by none other than C. P. Wilmot, Senior. It's one of his wartime paintings—the crew of a gun tub on a carrier at Okinawa, the antiaircraft cannons blazing away, and hanging in the air in front of them like a hideous insect is a kamikaze on fire, so close you can make out the pilot and the white band wrapped around his head, and there's nothing they can do about it, they're all going to die in the next few seconds, but the interesting thing about the picture is that one of the crew, a boy really, has turned away from the oncoming doom and is facing the viewer, hands outstretched and empty, with an expression on his face that is right out of Goya, or so I recall from my liberal education.

In fact, the whole painting is Goyesque, a modern take on his famous *The Shootings of May Third 1808*, with the kamikaze standing in for those faceless Napoleonic dragoons. The navy did not approve, nor did the magazines of the time, and the painting remained unsold. Thereafter, it seems, Wilmot was more careful to please. Chaz had it on the wall of his bedroom all through college, and when we were packing up just before we graduated he gave it to me, casually, as if it were an old Led Zeppelin poster.

As it happened I had just flown into town the weekend Mark threw a party at the Carlyle hotel to celebrate his coup in acquiring the painting that has become known as the *Alba Venus*. I'd followed the saga of the painting's discovery with more than my usual interest in things artistic, mainly because of Mark's involvement, but also because of the value of the object. They were quoting crazy figures for what it was expected to bring at auction, a couple of units at least, a "unit" being a movie mogul term I like to toss around for fun—it's a hundred million dollars. I find that sort of money very interesting, whatever its source, so I decided to stay at my firm's suite at the Omni for the evening and attend.

Mark had rented one of the mezzanine ballrooms for the party. I spotted Chaz as soon as I walked through the door, and he seemed to spot me at the same time—more than spot, he seemed to be looking for me. He stepped closer and held out a hand.

"I'm glad you could come," he said. "Mark said he'd invited you, but your office told me you were out of town, and then I called later and they said you'd be here."

"Yeah, Mark really knows how to throw a party," I said, and thought it was strange that he'd taken all that trouble to establish my whereabouts. It's not like we were best buddies anymore.

I looked him over. Pale, with what seemed to be the remains of a tan, and waxy looking, with his bright eyes circled with grayish, puffy skin. He kept glancing away, over my shoulder, as if looking for someone else, another guest, perhaps one not so welcome as I. It was the first time I'd ever seen him in anything like what he was wearing then, a beautiful gray suit of that subtle shade that only the top Italian designers ever use.

"Nice suit," I said.

He glanced down at his lapels. "Yes, I got it in Venice."

"Really?" I said. "You must be doing okay."

"Yeah, I'm doing fine," he said in a tone that discouraged inquiry, and he also changed the subject by adding, "Have you seen the masterpiece yet?" He indicated the posters of the painting that hung at intervals on the ballroom walls: the woman lying supine, a secret, satisfied smile on her face, her hand covering her crotch, not palm-down in the traditional gesture of modesty, but palm-up, as if offering it to the man revealed smokily in the mirror at the foot of the couch, the artist, Diego Velázquez.

I said I had not, that I'd been out of town during the brief period it had been on public display.

"It's a fake," he said, loud enough to draw stares. Of course, I'd seen Chaz drunk often enough in college, but this was different, a dangerous kind of drunk, I realized, although Chaz was the mildest of men. The taut skin under his left eye was twitching.

"What do you mean it's a fake?" I asked.

"I mean it's not a Velázquez. I painted it."

I believe I laughed. I thought he was joking, until I looked at his face.

"You painted it," I said, just to be saying something, and then I recalled some of the articles I'd read about the extraordinary scientific vetting of the painting and added, "Well, then you certainly fooled all the experts. As I understand it, they found that the pigments were correct for the era, the digital analysis of the brushstrokes was exactly like the analyses from undoubted works by Velázquez, and there was something about isotopes . . ."

He shrugged impatiently. "Oh, Christ, anything can be faked. Anything. But as a matter of fact I painted it in 1650, in Rome. It has genuine seventeenth-century Roman grime in the craqueleur. The woman's name is Leonora Fortunati." He turned away from the posters and looked at me. "You think I'm crazy."

"Frankly, yes. You even look crazy. But maybe you're just drunk."

"I'm not that drunk. You think I'm crazy because I said I painted that thing in 1650, and that's impossible. Tell me, what is time?"

I looked at my watch and said, "It's five to ten," and he laughed in a peculiar way and said, "Yes, later than you think. But, you know, what if it's the case that our existence—sorry, our consciousness of our existence at any particular *now*—is quite arbitrary? I don't mean memory, that faded flower. I mean that maybe consciousness, the actual sense of being there, can travel, can be *made* to travel, and not just through time. Maybe there's a big consciousness mall in the sky, where they all kind of float around, there for the taking, so that we can experience the consciousnesses of other people."

He must have observed my expression, because he grinned and said, "Mad as a hatter. Maybe. Look, we need to talk. You're staying in town?"

"Yes, just for the night, at the Omni."

"I'll come by in the morning, before you check out. It won't take long. Meanwhile, you can listen to this."

He took a CD jewel box out of his inside pocket and handed it to me.

"What's this?"

"My life. That painting. You remember Krapp?"

I said I did.

"Krapp was crazy, right? Or am I wrong?"

"It's left ambiguous, I think. What does Krapp have to do with your problem?"

"Ambiguous." At this he barked a harsh sound that might have been a laugh in another circumstance and ran his hands back through his hair, still an abundant head of it even in middle age. I recalled that his father had such a crop, although I couldn't imagine Mr. Wilmot wrenching his tresses in the way Chaz was now doing, as if he wanted to yank them out. I had thought it merely a figure of speech, but apparently not.

"Great," I said, "but if you don't mind me asking, why are you handing this to me?"

I can't describe the look in his eyes. You hear about lost souls.

He said, "I made it for you. I couldn't think of anyone else. You're my oldest friend."

"Chaz, what about Mark? Shouldn't you share this with—"

"No, not Mark," he said with as bleak an expression as I'd ever seen on a human face. I thought he was going to cry.

"Then I don't understand what you're talking about," I said. But I sort of did, as a queasy feeling cranked up in my gut. I have little experience with insanity. My family has been blessed with mental health, my kids went through adolescence with barely a blip, and the raving mad, if you except the people who make movies, are not often found in the fields where I have chosen to work. Thus I found myself tongue-tied in the presence of what I now saw was a paranoid breakdown of some kind.

Perhaps he sensed my feelings, because he patted my arm and smiled, a ghost of the old Chaz showing there.

"No, I may be crazy, but I'm not crazy in that way. There really are people after me. Look, I have to go someplace now. Listen to that and we'll talk in the morning." He held out his hand like a normal person, we shook, and he vanished into the crowd.

I went back to the Omni then, poured myself a scotch from the mini-bar, and slipped Chaz's CD into the slot in my laptop, thinking, Okay, at worst it's eighty minutes, and if it's just raving, I don't have to listen, but it wasn't just a recording. It was a dozen or so compressed sound files, representing hours and hours of recorded speech. Well, what to do? I was tired, I wanted my bed, but I also wanted to find out if Chaz Wilmot was really around the bend.

And another thing. I have sketched my life here, a singularly bland existence strung around the cusp of the century, and I suppose I wanted a taste of, I don't know, extravaganza, which is what the life of an artist, which I had declined in terror long ago, had always represented to me. Perhaps that's why the Americans worship celebrities, although I deplore this and refuse to participate, or only to a slight degree. But here I had my own private peep show, and it was irresistible. I selected the first file and clicked the appropriate buttons, whereupon the voice of Chaz Wilmot, Jr., came floating from the speakers.

Thanks for listening. I realize this is an imposition, but when I heard Mark was throwing this party and he said he'd invited you, I thought it was perfect timing. There's other stuff I want to talk about, but that can wait until I see you again. It's a shame you haven't seen the actual painting—those posters are shit, like all reproductions—but I guess you've read the stories about how it was found and all that. These are lies, or may be lies. Reality seems to be more flexible than I'd imagined. Anyway, let me set the stage for this.

Did you ever do any acid, back in the day? Yeah, now that I think about it, I believe I gave you your first hit, blotter acid, purple in color, and we spent the day in Riverside Park walking, and we had that conversation about seagulls, what it was like to be one, and I seem to recall you transmitted your consciousness to one of them and kited along the Hudson, and then later we spent the bad part of the trip in your room in the apartment. It was just before spring break our senior year. When I asked you how you liked it after, you said you couldn't wait for it to be over. Oh, yes.

And that's my point—it implied that you knew you were doping, knew you were hallucinating, even though the hallucinations might have seemed totally real. One time—did I ever tell you about this?— I was tripped out on acid and I happened to have this triangular tortoiseshell guitar pick on me, and I spent half the night staring at it, and all those little brown swirls came alive and showed me the entire history of Western art, from Lascaux cave painting, through Cycladic sculpture and the Greeks and Giotto, Raphael, Caravaggio, right up to Cézanne, and not only that—it revealed to me the *future* of art, shapes and images that would break through the sterile wastelands of postmodernism and generate a new era in the great pageant of human creativity.

And of course after that I couldn't wait to trip again, so the next weekend I got all my art supplies lined up and the guitar pick in hand and I dropped a huge fucking dose, and *nothing*. Worse than nothing, because the guitar pick was just what it was, a cheap piece of plastic, but there was a malign presence in the room, like a giant black Pillsbury Doughboy, and I was being squashed and smothered under it and it was laughing at me, because the whole guitar pick event was a scam designed to get me to trip again so this thing could *eat* me.

You remember Zubkoff, don't you, my old roommate? Pre-med? The guy who stayed in his room studying all the time. We called him the Magic Mushroom? I heard from him again, out of the blue. He's a research scientist now. I joined a study he was doing on a drug to enhance creativity.

Did you ever wonder how your brain worked? Like, say, where do ideas come from? I mean, *where* do they come from? A completely new idea, like relativity or using perspective in painting. Or, why are some people terrifically creative and others are patzers? Okay, being you, maybe the whole issue never came up.

But it's always fascinated me, the question of questions, and even beyond that I desperately wanted to get back to the guitar pick, I wanted to see what's next. I mean, in Western art. I still can't quite believe that it's all gurgled down to the nothing that it looks like now, big kitsch statues of cartoon characters, and wallpaper and jukeboxes, and pickled corpses, and piles of dry-cleaning bags in the corner of a white room, and "This is a cock." Of course you might say, well, things pass. Europeans stopped doing representational art for a thousand years and then they started up again. Verse epics used to be the heart of literature all over the world and then they stopped getting written. So maybe the same thing has happened to easel painting. And we have the movies now. But then you have to ask, why is the art market so huge? People *want* paintings, and all that's available is this terrible crap. There has to be some way of not being swamped in the ruthless torrent of innovation, as Kenneth Clark called it. As my father was always saying.

I mean, you really have to ask, do we love the old masters because they're old and rare, just portable chunks of capital, or do we love them because they give us something precious and eternally valuable? If the latter, why aren't we still doing it? Okay, everybody's forgotten how to draw, but still . . .

Drifting here. Back to Zubkoff. He called me up. He said he was running a study out of the Columbia med school, lots of funding from the government, National Institutes of Mental Health, or whatever, to explore whether human creativity could be enhanced by taking a drug. They were using art students, music students, and he also wanted to get some older artists in on it, so they could check if age was a variable. And he thought of me. Well, free dope. That was never a hard sell.

Anyway, I volunteered, and here we all are. And I'm sure you're wondering now why, after however long it is, old Wilmot is dropping all this on me. Because you're the only one left, the only person who knows me and who doesn't care enough about me to humor me if I'm nuts. I'm being blunt, I know, but it's true. And while I'm being blunt, of all the people I've known, you're the one with the solidest grasp of what the world calls reality. You have no imagination at all. Again, sorry to drop this on you. I'm dying to know what you think.

Setting the stage, interesting phrase, that, like our life is a drama, act one, act two, act three, *curtains*. So let's start with me at twenty-one, just out of college. Did you ever wonder how I graduated? How could I be an art major and flunk three art courses? This my advisor asked me. Well, sir, the reproductions make me sick, I can't look at them and I can't write about painting, the words seem like jokes. It took me three years to learn how to fake it, and if it wasn't for Slotsky I would've failed the other courses too. A genius at doing art papers, Slotsky; if they hung twelve-hundred-word art papers in museums, Slotsky would be one of the great artists of our generation.

I was home in Oyster Bay, home sweet home, and all I could think of was how to get out of there before I killed myself or him. My dad. I don't think I ever mentioned this to you, but Dad had a little problem.

He was chasing Kendra the maid again, although she's practically deformed. How could he? Maybe he stopped seeing them as they are. It was worse before Mother started hiring the maids, not that she cares anymore, but we kept losing maids, and of course she needed a maid by then, she could hardly function by herself.

I remember you invited me out to your aunt's place one summer, and you might have wondered why I never reciprocated. Well, Dad's problem is one reason; maybe he would've behaved himself with guests—always a sense of decorum in public—but I didn't want to risk it. Another reason: there are nude portraits of my mother on every fucking wall in the house. Interesting progression though, from Pre-Raphaelite sylph (my favorite, if that's the word, she's maybe a couple years older than I am now: naked, hair shoulder-length, leaning against a wall, looking out at all of us—am I not beautiful?), to classical Venus, to the Titian version, finally to Rubens, and then he stopped painting her, or maybe she stopped posing. I wonder what she tipped the scales at that summer, four or even five hundred, I couldn't look anymore, but she got even with him in a sort of Dorian Gray self-destructo way.

Anyway, you have to imagine me skulking around that huge, echoing house, wishing I had the balls to join a cult, the kind where you get a tattoo on your forehead, and other stupid thoughts, and decided I was never going to play into his hands, I was never going to wreck myself to get even like she did. Why didn't she leave him? I never figured that out. It's not like she didn't have any money.

Her dad had plenty, made it in switching equipment for the railroads. All that complicated electromechanical machinery that relayed current to the right switches in railyards and out along the line. There used to be something called a Petrie junction that got some use in telephone exchanges too. Westinghouse bought him out right after the war for something like thirty million, which was serious money in those days. He died when I was seven or so, but I knew my grandmother pretty well.

Grandma Petrie was a character, a beautiful, stupid woman, always concerned about whether her hair was right. She lived with us for twelve years after the old man died, becoming dimmer by the year and increasingly concerned with the Church and her place in the next world. A little Dickensian drama here on the shore of the Sound, or one of those other guys, a lavender-scented breath from the previous century. Dad, of course, smarming around, phony as hell about all the religious horseshit, entertaining fat monsignors right and left, making sure we were all raised in the Church, Catholic schools and all, Charlotte to Sacred Heart, of course, and me to Columbia only because the old man went there, instead of the decent art school I should've gone to. Grandma didn't much like me. Charlotte was her favorite. They used to sit for hours, saying the rosary or looking at her thick, leather-bound photograph albums. I would ask Charlie how she could stand it and she'd say it was charity, a lonely old woman needing companionship, and after a while I learned not to tease her about it, and I took it as natural that my sister could be two completely different people, the quiet little nun-in-training and the tomboy in shorts and a T-shirt, palling around with me down on the beach, in our boats, always covered in sand, tracking it through the house.

When she died, I mean Grandma, it turned out that all the smarm was for naught. She left the bulk of the estate to the Church, with life grants to me (small), Charlotte (larger), and Mother. Mother got the house. In the will she said she expected Charlotte to pursue her vocation and enter religious life.

That's a scene etched into my brain, the bunch of us sitting around listening to the lawyer read it out, all of us in black, like it was 1880, and when that part got read I rolled my eyes and nudged Charlotte, who was sitting next to me, expecting her to give me the elbow back, but she didn't, she just turned and looked at me, and there was someone else looking out from behind her eyes and it fucking froze my blood.

Why he never left her, I guess, why he never had a real French-type mistress in a Manhattan apartment like he must've wanted. I remember looking at him when he realized he wasn't going to get a dime, that he was stuck with us more or less forever; he went white, like he'd been punched in the gut. Funny, because his income was pretty high then; he was at the peak of his fame as a second-rate Rockwell, he could've split then, but he didn't, he just kept grabbing the maids and the locals, waitresses and cashiers.

But he loved her once; you couldn't paint a woman that way unless you did, or I couldn't anyway, and there are photographs, God, are there photographs! They met in the last summer before the war, they were both at the Art Students' League, he was an instructor, she was a student for her bohemian summer before she got serious and started settling down with a good Catholic boy, and I think he just blew her away with sheer talent. The Petries must've loved it when she dragged him home that summer, a heathen with no money, no family. But

Mother was a hardhead when she wanted to be, and she was Daddy's girl, the only child, a bit of a disgrace there in a fine Catholic family, only one kid, what's wrong with them? And he converted, naturally, more Catholic than the Pope after a while; he could be charming too, charmed the old guy, but never Grandma, as it turned out. I bet she was praying that a Jap bomb would solve her problem, but he came back and they got married and he got famous, and then came Charlotte and then a set of miscarriages and a little girl who died of polio at age two, and then me, and that was it.

There it is, the sad story, for the record, this record, or at least what I've been able to gather. Not that anyone actually ever sat down and told me the truth. I get versions. Who to believe? More to the point, how to avoid it?

I finally settled on a plan to go to Europe—the geographic cure, always attractive at that age. I didn't have enough money of my own and I thought he'd never give me any of his, although he spent enough of it on himself. I guess he assumed that I'd stay here, he had the stupid idea that we were going to be a father-and-son thing like the Wyeths or the Bassanos, a little atelier here in the cultural desert of Long Island. He was talking about how I could do the lesser portrait commissions, or maybe the liquor ads. But as it turned out he sprang for the whole thing. That's what was so maddening about the bastard, you thought he never considered another human being besides himself, and then he goes and does something like that; he said, take as long as you want, you're only young once, and remember to use condoms.

Of course I'd asked my mother for it first, and she'd said, ask your father. I couldn't believe it, standing there in her room, trying not to gag from the smell of the disinfectant and her rotting feet. Her mouth drawn down from the stroke, her eyes almost invisible in the pads of flesh: ask your father.

Which I didn't, no, I got drunk instead, a half bottle of bourbon, and passed out in the downstairs bathroom in a pool of puke, charming, and he found me there and cleaned me up. What was he trying to prove? That in the end he loves me more than she does, that he won the war of the Wilmots? Anyway, he wrote me out a check for five grand the next morning, and we talked about what I had to see and we sat there in his studio and talked about it, about the museums, London, Paris, Madrid, Rome, Florence, the same trip we did together when I was nine, when I got to look at the European collections for the first time.

That first time with Dad we stayed at the Ritz—God, he could throw money around in his flush years—everyone was real nice to me there, and I thought it was because I was such a terrific kid before Charlotte set me straight, incredible embarrassment, though I never admitted it to her. She hated that part, and now that I think about it I guess it was then she started visiting churches and convents, insisted on going up to Ávila to see St. Teresa.

When I made the European trip by myself in my twenty-first year, I skipped the Ritz and stayed at a one-star *albergo* three flights up on Calle de Amor de Dios at the corner of Santa Maria, an address Charlie would no doubt approve of and about a ten-minute walk to the Prado. I hadn't been to the place since I was nine, but it seemed like I just stepped out for a minute, the pictures all in the same place. But my eye had been polluted with art history courses, and I knew that I'd never recapture that fucking explosion when I first saw it, because it was one of Dad's ploys never to have art reproductions in the house, no coffee-table books spoiling the golden eye of young Chaz. My father took me into the big room through the back way, through the dreary mediocrities of the later seventeenth

and eighteenth centuries, fussy brown paintings, and then Room Sixteen and there's the *Surrender of Breda*, the first big Velázquez I ever
saw. I wanted to spend my life looking at it, that Dutch soldier glancing casually out of the picture plane—how did he even *think* of doing
that—and the lances the way they were, just perfect, but he wouldn't
let me stay, he grabbed my arm and pushed me past the famous portraits and the prophets in the desert with that wonderful black bird
suspended in real air and through the grand room, the center of the
cult, Room Twelve, and we hung a sharp right and there was *Las
Meninas*.

The school of painting, Manet called it, and my father's opinion
was that taken all in all, it really was the best thing anyone had ever
done in oils. He told me, and I can believe it, that when I first stood
in front of it my mouth dropped open and I held my hands up to my
cheeks, like a version of Munch's *The Scream*. It was so wonderful at
first sight, like the Grand Canyon or the Statue of Liberty, but more
so, because I had been hearing about it for my whole life and I'd never
even seen a postcard of it. And so I stood there trying not to disgrace
myself by crying while he talked.

Nine-year-olds are not supposed to have that kind of reaction to
paintings, but I suppose I was a kind of twisted prodigy. Can I even
remember what he said? Maybe it's been layered over in my mind by
all the formal art criticism I got in college. There wasn't much historical material, just a working painter's admiration for a genius. He made
me look at the light coming in through the window on the right, the
way that light shines on the painted wood of the window frame. Vermeer made a whole career out of light shining on painted surfaces,
he said, and never did anything better than that, and Velázquez just
tossed it in as something extra.

And the playing with visual reality in a way that wouldn't appear
again in Western art until the mid-nineteenth century. In fact, he

said, Manet got all that business of flat tonality and bold clean out-lines from this painting, and there wouldn't be anything like the blurred treatment of the lady dwarf until the twentieth, it was like something out of de Kooning or Francis Bacon.

And the perfect, doomed little girl at the center, the most impor-tant little girl in the whole world, the heartbreaking look of pride and terror on her face, and the two attendant *meninas*, one superbly painted like her mistress, the other blocked in angular planes like a wooden doll, a little Cézanne *avant le lettre* (why? He didn't know, a mystery) and the whispering nun and the waiting figure in a glory of yellow in the far doorway (terrifying! Who knew why?) and the unimportant king and queen in the dusty mirror, and every move-ment and gesture in the whole vast thing directing the eye to the guy with the mustache and the black tunic with the cross of a knightly order on it, standing calmly in the midst of it with his palette and brushes. He's saying I made this all, my father told me, he's saying I have stolen this moment from time, this is how God sees the world, each instant an eternity, and when the dwarfs and the dog and the nun and the courtiers and the royal family and their maids are for-gotten dust, this will live and live forever, and I, Velázquez, have done this.

I recall the expression on his face as he said it, and I guess I thought he was talking about himself, because at nine I thought my father was in the same class as Velázquez, the greatest painter in the world. No, not really true; I think after that trip to Europe, after really see-ing the masters, even at nine I could tell the difference, and I think he could see that I could. Over the next year it made him increasingly cranky, more demanding, more authoritarian. He was the master; I was the student and always would be. But the fact is I'm better than he was, maybe not as far above him as Velázquez was above his own master, Pacheco, but a discernible gap. Not that I could actually say that or claim that, even to myself, and I wonder how Velázquez handled it. Of course Pacheco wasn't his father, just his father-in-law, but still.

All that crap came flooding back when I stood in front of *Las Meninas* for the second time and I realized that's what I've always wanted from art, the ability to stand apart from the domestic whatever, the whispers, the favorites, the little cruelties.

And, my friend, you'll see that, in a strange and unexpected way, I have succeeded. But also you may be thinking, hey, isn't this supposed to be about the painting? Why is he giving me all this crap about his sad life? Because it's not just about the painting. It's about whether my memory has anything whatever to do with what really happened. Figure that out and the painting is explained one way or the other. Therefore I spread my memories before you as with a trowel. Are there inconsistencies? Impossibilities?

Pay attention, please.

The following day I met Suzanne Nore in the Prado.

I never pick up girls in museums, I can't see them when I'm in my art head, but there she was, looking at Velázquez's equestrian *Baltasar Carlos*, and I couldn't take my eyes off her, that mass of red-gold hair down to her butt. I waited until we were alone in the room and then I just started talking like a maniac about the painting, the unbelievable mastery of technique, the paint so thin that it runs, the weave of the canvas showing through, all done in one go with practically no corrections, look at the damn background, it's like a sumi-e painting or an aquarelle, and the texture of the costume, he taps the brush here and there and your eye reads it like gold embroidery, and look at the face, it's practically a sketch but the whole psychology of the kid is stripped bare, and so on and so on, I couldn't stop, and she started to laugh and said, you really know a lot about painting, and I said, yeah, I do, I'm a painter and I want to paint you. I almost said I wanted to paint you naked, but I didn't.

She was a singer, or wanted to be; she went to Skidmore, she was on a junior year abroad taking lessons at the Paris Conservatory, and she'd hopped the train down here for a long weekend. I took her through the museum, talking nonstop like some kind of nutcase; I thought she would disappear if I shut up. We were there until it closed, and afterward we went to a little bar I like on Calle de Cervantes and drank wine and talked until it got dark and it was time for tapas, and we ate and drank some more. We closed the place and I walked her back to her hotel by the Plaza Santa Ana, very respectable, and I kissed her there in the doorway, getting dirty looks from a couple of Guardia Civils—no public kissing allowed, Franco didn't like it—and I thought, This wasn't supposed to happen, I wasn't set up for this, *love* or whatever it is. Crazy.

I spent the next couple of days with her, every minute. She talked a blue streak, funny as hell, jokes about everything, wandering around the city. She made up a fantasy about us being in a war movie because of the soldiers in the Nazi helmets marching around everywhere—we're hiding from the Nazis!—and it started to get real, it's hard to explain. But the next night after we closed the tapas place again, and back at her hotel, I kissed her like before, but longer, and when I said good night like a dope, she grabbed my belt buckle and dragged me inside and up the stairs.

So, that was it, all the stuff the movies teach us about passion, all those scenes where the actors tear their clothes off standing up and the actress jumps up and impales herself on his dick, we're supposed to believe, and they fall on the narrow bed. I always thought I was a cool guy, in control, but this was a whole different kind of thing. I lasted about two minutes, and I was opening my mouth to apologize but she wouldn't stop, she told me what to do, she worked on me with her hands and her mouth, and all the time she kept talking, telling me just what she was feeling; I never heard a girl say stuff like that, I couldn't believe it was happening. "Insatiable" is probably not the right word, I don't know what the right word is, but we did it until we were raw, we would've started hemorrhaging if we hadn't fallen asleep. And laughing, giggling. I remember thinking, This is too good, there's got to be something wrong with this, some punishment to come.

We stayed in bed almost all the next day. I staggered out for food and beer once, and then when night fell we got up and cleaned ourselves off, sneaking down the hall to the bathroom together and doing it again under the weak stream of the shower in the tin stall. We went out late like the Spaniards do and she knew clubs—this was all underground stuff, she had addresses from musician friends of hers—and there were kids there playing music. They had no records; rock and roll was banned by the government, so all they knew was what they could pick up on shortwave from the U.S. Armed Forces Radio, and they'd invented their own version, a weird combination of flamenco and Hendrix, incredible music. And I had my drawing stuff and I just drew like crazy, making portraits of the musicians, and her, of course, blazing away on a homemade electric guitar, drawing in ink and putting the gray tones in with spit and wine, ripping the sheets off and handing them out to anyone who wanted them. I thought, Okay, it doesn't get any better than this, this is life.

When she had to go back to Paris, I went with her. She said we'll always have Madrid, like in that movie, and so now we have Paris too. I have to say a huge relief leaving fascism behind, it was getting old, that sense of people taking down what you were doing, and the Guardias in their shiny hats on every corner giving you the eye like you're thinking about bringing down the state.

We stayed in her place off the Rue Saint-Jacques near the Schola Cantorum, third-floor walk-up, filthy bath down the hall. Her room was incredibly messy; I was the fascist in the relationship. She took voice classes at the Cantorum every morning, not the Conservatory, or maybe I got it wrong. *La vie bohème*, left bank, student demos, everyone in black, pretentious, smoking and drinking and doping like mad. While she was out I hit the museums and the galleries. Paris was dead as far as painting went at the time, all political shit and wannabe New York School.

But I went to an exhibition at the Orangerie, it was Weimar art: Dix, Grosz, and some people I never heard of before, like Christian Schad, Karl Hubbuch. Some terrific stuff, the style was called *Neue Sachlichkeit*, New Objectivity. So these guys were in the ruins of Germany after the first war and everywhere abstract modernism was the thing to be doing—Picasso, Braque—and there was Dada and Futurism cranking up, and these guys tried to rescue representational art from kitsch and they did it, especially Schad, a technique like Cranach's, wonderful depth and structure, and shocking penetration. Look at the world you made, you bastards, this is what it looks like. I recall thinking, Can we do that now? Would anyone be able to see it? Probably not, and the world hasn't changed that much, except we stick the war-wounded behind the walls of hospitals so we don't have to look at them, and the rich are now thin instead of fat. But even if you did it, the rich shits would buy them up: oh, you have a *Wilmot*, appreciating very nicely, thank you, not as much as de Kooning but a good return on investment. Everyone is blind now, except if it's on TV.

I was going to stay in Europe for at least a year, but I came home that fall, to find some interesting developments. Mother had been moved to a care facility because of her worsening diabetes and the effects of the new stroke, which is probably a good thing considering more parts of her were turning black and falling off, and no one wants that around the house. They had to take the door off her room, and the frame too, and move her out through the French windows and the garden. My prayer is she had no brains left at the time. She loved that garden.

The wreckage from this demolition was still apparent when I returned, but Dad seemed disinclined to do much about it. Charlie left the day after Mother did, off to her novitiate somewhere in Missouri. She was going to be a missionary sister and help the far-off poor. She didn't write or leave a note for me; I mean, I knew she was talking about, it but I didn't think she was just going to leave, like sneaking off while I was gone. I used to tell her when she first started to get serious about it, I told her, you don't have to do this, Charlie, we can run away together, we can make a life, but she just looked at me in a kind of holy blank way she's developed and said, it's not that, Christ was calling her and so on, and I didn't believe her. She was never that religious when we were growing up; I always thought it was a girl thing, like being crazy about horses. For a while I thought it was because he did something to her—you hear about shit like that all the time, even families around here in Oyster Bay, Daddy and Daddy's little girl—I should have asked her, but I couldn't, the one time I went to see her, not in a convent parlor, and I have to say, I never really believed it. He's a monster, but not that kind of monster.

I missed her. I never thought, I mean I always thought we would be together, or close, anyway, my big sister, Chaz and Charlie together forever. I thought charity began at home, but I guess not. Dad was by that time boffing the lawn guy's daughter, Melanie, a conventionally cute brunette with a face unlined by suffering or complex thought. She was about four years older than me, just a little younger than Charlie, and I actually went out with her a couple of times myself, which is really weird, even for chez Wilmot. He wasn't painting much then, although he was anticipating a big commission to do a fresco in a seminary dining hall out on Long Island. He wanted me to help, part of his fantasy that I was his student and artistic heir.

You'll want to know why the fuck I came home.

Yeah, a long pause there; but basically, it was Suzanne. When I said good-bye to her at the station in Paris before she got on the airport bus, and right, it was rainy and gray, and we were hugging and kissing there and she was crying, she said I was the love of her life and she'd never forget me and she just knew she'd never see me again, it was too good for her. What I was thinking, I'm ashamed to say, was, Whew, I'm glad to have a break from this consuming girl, and so long, darlin', see you around.

So she left, and there I was with plenty of time on my hands, and it turned out all the movies and the popular song lyrics were true. Whatever sensible-Chaz thought—that she was too much to take on at this stage of my life, that I didn't need the aggravation and grand opera that were part of the Suzanne package, that I had work to do, you know, defining myself as a painter and all that crap—whatever, there was a part of me that just ached for her. I would pass a street corner where she used to sing sometimes with a group of scruffy French kids, American folk songs and standards, for tossed coins, and I'd see them singing with some other girl and I'd feel my heart clench up.

I kept her room, which was probably a mistake; I should've packed up and gone to Berlin or something, but I stayed on there, not doing much, while her smell gradually faded from the room. I found a miniature bottle of shampoo she'd left behind, with only a little smear of it left, and I kept it and opened it every night and sniffed it and remembered what her hair smelled like. Did I try other girls? Oh, yeah. It's not hard to get laid on the Left Bank when you're twenty-one and you can draw. Everyone wants to be immortal, and maybe I'll be famous someday, I could practically hear them thinking.

But, God, you know? I couldn't figure it out, why none of that was any good. I mean, I'm out with my pad, doing tourist sketches on the boul, just for something to do, and then the girl sits down and you make her look a little prettier than she is, and she's blown away by it—these are not French girls, oh, no, they're Americans, Brits, Danes—we're speaking English here, and then some smooth talk, a date for a drink, and yeah, you have a terrific body, I can tell, and then up to the apartment where they take off their clothes and there you have it, a fling with a genuine Paris artist, and as far as I'm concerned I might as well be using someone else's dick.

And then my work started to go downhill, I mean it was like there was a scrim over everything, my eye had no penetration, and the paint wouldn't behave itself, it wanted to go to mud; it's hard to describe, but there was no doubt about it. I'd rented a piece of a studio after Suzanne left, going to do some serious work now that I had more time, and I thought I'd try to work on the kind of psychological portraits that I'd seen in the Orangerie, with a little Eakins precision thrown in, but even though I worked like fury, everything I did was garbage. I got frenzied, I broke brushes, I threw fucking canvases against the wall, but nothing came. And after a couple of weeks of this, the word "muse" started to float up through my mind, something I always thought was complete bullshit, but now I thought, Well, there was Rembrandt and Saskia, and van Gogh and his whore with the earlobe, and Picasso always had a short stack of girls on hand, and I thought, Okay, I found Suzanne and she's mine, however that works, I needed her. And as soon as I started thinking that way, I saw that the stuff I'd done while she was there was the best stuff I'd ever done, it was vital and passionate, and I remembered what *I* was like with her, my base temperature was ten degrees higher, and you could see that in the lines of the drawings, especially the drawings of her.

And there was the sex, too: boy oh boy, screwing tourist girls— thin wine after that hundred-proof brandy. I mean, there's a kind of sex you have when you're floating off somewhere, kind of watching yourself have it, and the girl is too, who knows what they're thinking, and you know that you'll have nothing to say to them after, and even if the girl is cool and pretty there's a moment when you can't wait to see the last of her and you have a sense that she feels that way too. But Suzanne demanded the full presence, she held on like it was the end of the world, like this was the last fuck before the bomb went off, the last fuck in history, talking through the whole thing, narrating it, and her body never stopping, clenching, and totally *there*.

So I came back and we met and it was the same in New York as it was in Paris, couldn't get enough, and the first thing I did was rent a loft on Walker Street, a hundred bucks a month, five flights up, an old wire factory, full of scrap and filth, and that was where we stayed, on a big slab of foam I bought on Canal Street. We'd turn the lights off and light dozens of thick plumber's candles and afterward wash up in the tiny workman's toilet. I decided to turn it into a living loft; I would dump the scrap out the window into the air shaft or carry it down. I would paint it white and put in a sleeping platform and lighting and partitions and a kitchen, and we would live there and be happy.

In the meantime I stayed in Oyster Bay with Dad, keeping out of his way as much as I could. He had some idea that we were going to be a family again—were we ever that kind of family?—the pair of us and Melanie, the girlfriend. The stepgirlfriend? And he kept going on about this church fresco, how it's going to be a gigantic revival of that great art, with Wilmot *père* and *fils* as the ringleaders.

When I happened to run into him I could barely stand it, those affectations, that straw sombrero he wore, and the walking stick, and the cape, strolling through the increasingly ragged garden. Maybe the gardener was not that delighted his daughter'd shacked up with a client thirty years older than her, or maybe it was just the lack of money. Mother's entire income went to the luxurious madhouse she was in, and he was living on whatever commissions he could wrangle. *Collier's* was long gone by then, and the *Saturday Evening Post* and the others. His main business had become fat cat portraits and selling originals of his old work, but this fresco was going to make everything okay again.

J ust before I moved out I had a conversation with his girlfriend. I was sitting on the living room sofa watching a fire I'd just made and thinking about my sister and how that was one of our favorite things to do in the winter, make a big fire and watch it burn and throw in stuff we hated—bad photographs of us or toys we'd outgrown, anything that wouldn't make an actual stink or explode, but occasionally that stuff too—and Melanie came in and plopped down in the leather armchair where my father usually sat. After a while I realized that she was staring at me. I stared back a little and then I said, "What?" and she started in on why was I being so cold and cruel to my father, who loved me so much and was so proud of me and all that. And I said, "You know, for someone who just walked in the door you have a lot of opinions about the nature of this family. For example, they just dragged my mother out of here with a crane. That might have something to do with how I feel about my father."

"You think that was his fault?"

"I don't know," I said. "He's been screwing nearly every woman and girl around this place since practically day one. That might have an effect on a woman's self-esteem, might make her inclined to excessive eating and the use of drugs. Who knows, if you stay here long enough you might get to see what it's like."

This produced a shrug that made me want to reach for the poker. She said, "He's a great artist. Great artists play by different rules. If she couldn't handle that . . . I mean, I'm sorry for her and all, but . . ."

I said, "He's not a great artist. He had a great talent. It's not the same thing."

"That's crazy—what's the difference?"

"Oh, you want an art lesson? Okay, Melanie, just wait here. I'll be right back."

With that, I went to the racks in the lumber room where he kept all his old stuff, the salable and the unsalable carefully divided, and from the latter section I removed a portfolio and went back to the living room. I threw the portfolio open on the coffee table and fanned out the contents.

I said, "When I was a little kid, starting from about age six through about age eleven, my father would take me out to our dock or down the beach, nearly every day when it wasn't raining or freezing, with watercolor sets and portable easels and canvas chairs, and we would paint together. I had a set just like Dad's, with Winsor and Newton colors and sable brushes, and we used expensive cold-pressed D'Arches watercolor blocks, twenty-four by eighteen. My father doesn't believe in cheap materials, even for little kids. And we painted together, for an hour, two hours, depending on the light. We went down at different times of the day, so we could catch all the varieties of light and what the light did to the water and the sand and the rocks and the sky. In the warm weather we painted figures, people on the beach, and boats out on the Sound, and in the winter, we just painted the beach, the sea, and the sky, the same view, over and over again. It was our Mount St. Victoire, our Rouen Cathedral. Do you know what I'm talking about?"

"Not really," she said.

"No. But anyway, what do you think of the paintings? These are his, by the way. I used to tear mine up afterward because it made me so mad that I couldn't do what he did with a brush."

"They're beautiful."

"Yes, they are. This one, for example, a fleshy woman and a child sitting on the beach, early in the morning. Look at the heft and presence of the figures, all done freehand with a loaded brush, ten strokes and there they are. And look at the sweep of the wet sand! That perfect color, and the white of the paper showing through just enough to make it shine. And this one: winter on the Sound, and three seagulls made out of the white of the paper, just chopped in against the gray sky, and they're perfect and alive. Do you have any idea how hard it is to get those effects in aquarelle? This is not the kind of kitsch you buy in resort souvenir shops, it's nearly as good as anything Winslow Homer or Edward Hopper ever did in the medium. You get that word, 'nearly'? I use it because that's the story of his life as an artist—'nearly.' He didn't ever take it that extra foot into greatness. He checked at the fence. And it wasn't just that he was an illustrator. Homer did illustration, Durer, for Christ's sake, did illustration. No, there was something missing, or maybe, yeah, something stifled in him. That's why he put these away, he doesn't want to be reminded of how close he came. You need more than talent to be a painter. You have to take risks. You have to not give a shit. You have to be open to . . . I don't know what it is—to life, God, truth, some kind of *other* stuff. It's a business, art, but not *just* a business.

"And you know what the really horrible thing is? He knows it. He *knows* it. He knows what kind of gift he threw away, and that knowledge made a poison in this house, a curse, and that sad, ruined woman they just dragged away knew it too and she took it all in, she tried to absorb the poison, she fucking *carried* it, so that he could still be jaunty C. P. Wilmot, with his little straw hat and his romantic cape, traipsing about her house and chasing cunt. He's a vampire: perfect manners, charming, beautiful clothes—come *innnn*, I only vant to suck your *bluuuuhd*. I can see he's got his fangs into you too, darling. He's given you the line about how he needs a woman who understands genius, about how the rules that regular people have to follow don't apply in his case, how he'll make you immortal with his brush . . ."

And so on and on. She looked at me like I was a traffic accident, one of those mashed-beer-can ones with blood on the glass, where you can imagine what happened to the people inside, but you can't take your eyes away. She jumped to her feet while I was still yapping away and walked out of the room without another word.

The strange thing about this little encounter was that while I was talking it came into my mind why I was so reluctant to leave Oyster Bay. Looking at those pictures—it was like a concentrated elixir of my childhood, the beach, the flats, the water, the boats, my mother wrapping me in a sweater on the beach on a cool evening, and Charlie's hand over mine on the warm tiller of her little sailboat the summer she taught me how to sail. And the smell of low tide, and always the sparkle and play of light on the water; I used to lie facedown on the dock and stare at it like a mystic stares at a mandala, the door to a higher existence. I was born there, I never really lived anywhere else but there and in the city during school, and even then I'd come home every summer.

After Melanie walked out I went up the back stairs to the widow's walk, and stood out in the breeze, and looked at the lights on Lloyd Point and Centre Island, and the channel markers, red and green, and beyond the black Sound the glow of Stamford on the Connecticut shore. Charlie and I used to sneak up here at night when we were kids, we'd stand by the railings wrapped in blankets and be pirates and explorers until Mother came up and yelled us back to bed, but not much of a yell because she used to do the same thing when she was a girl, and now Charlie's entombed and

Mother's entombed, rotting alive, and he's still trotting around like nothing's wrong, with his new honey, although he's probably in a deeper tomb than either of them, when you think about it, but not me, I said to myself, I'm not going to be buried alive, not here, not anywhere. It fucking broke my heart, but that day I performed a homectomy on myself, without anesthesia, and left and never lived there again.

I seem to recall you had a car and helped me move out, or maybe it was someone else, and I started living in the ruined factory on Walker Street. I worked like a bastard for five weeks, throwing out a ton of trash, tangles of wires, rusted machinery, then putting down tile on the splintered floors, wiring the place, hauling cabinets up five flights of stairs, plus a stove, a kitchen sink, and the hot-water heater. If I'd known what it would be like, I probably wouldn't have started. A hot-water heater up five flights of stairs by myself!

The only thing I had help on was the drywall. The guy on the second floor took pity on me, Denny Bosco, another painter, he saw the ton of drywall stacked on the sidewalk and told me I should hire some guys from the labor exchange on the Bowery to haul it up, and I did: who knew? And he helped me with the drywall too, one thing it's real hard to do by yourself, you can't hold a panel up over the baseboard and nail it in unless you have three hands. He was the Oldest Inhabitant around there, been living in the building since SoHo was a decaying industrial neighborhood; you had to have an AIR sign outside the building, "artist in residence," so that if there was a fire the firemen would know to look for a charred corpse. He said he used to sit up on the roof at night—this was back in the late sixties—and look out toward Canal, and except for the neon glow from Chinatown, which was a quarter the size it is now, you could see nothing but blackness and a few little lights from the lofts of the pioneers. He told me that it was going to get worse, that the parasites were moving in, like they do anytime the artists generate a little life in a neighborhood—the rich come to suck at it and make it dead again. A prescient guy, Denny, as it turned out.

A week later I rented a paint sprayer and masked the windows and my face and sprayed the whole interior white. The paint was barely dry when, as we'd arranged, Suzanne showed up with a U-Haul full of furniture. I was glad to see her and I carried the stuff up in a pretty good mood, although it was mainly really heavy pieces from her parents' house, and I thought it would be a nice day, moving into a place we were going to live together in, but I noticed she was in one of her dark phases; she sat on a chair smoking, and didn't really respond when I started joking and playing around about where we were going to put the different chairs and dressers and all, like I was an interior decorator. Really the place looked kind of grungy still, despite all my work, and I thought that was what was bringing her down, she was disappointed.

But no. She said, "I'm pregnant." And the usual, are you sure, yeah, almost two months late, and she's had the tests and all, and how did it happen, I thought you were on the pill, and she sort of lost it then, like, oh, I knew you'd say it was my fault and my life is over, and my career is just taking off. Which was mainly that she sang on open mike nights in a couple of clubs in the East Village and there was a guy who said he was from a record company and gave her a card, but I didn't mention that. And I said, well, what do you want to do? She was crying by then, and I hugged her and said I loved her and whatever she wanted was okay with me, abortion or have the baby, we'd manage.

The girl gets pregnant and either you get rid of it or you have it and your life flows into a different channel than you thought it would. We went back and forth about it quite a few times; first she wanted to abort and I didn't, and then she didn't and I did, and I guess the Catholic thing is still there, but not only that, it's something about the flow of life, it makes me crazy to think of the hole you'd have to live with for the rest of your life, and that can't be good for a relationship. But what did I know? Charlie always said go with life, love your fate. *Amor fati* is the expression. I'd have given anything to be able to talk this through with her, but when I called the number of her society they said she was en route to Uganda.

And so was my life set on a false course, which is another reason why I'm telling you all this ancient matter. For lust will languish and its heat decay, says Petronius Arbiter, you'll recall that from the class we had on Renaissance translations from the Latin masters—one of my rare B grades, I think—and it's so true. By the time I marched up the aisle with Suzanne my attachment was more than half guilt, but I thought I could fix that somehow, through fidelity, through affection, and somehow lay the curse my father had passed on. Unfortunately, it turns out the habit of self-betrayal tends to spread. It pollutes the other parts of life, in my case my painting, and it acts as a marker for others, like those cruel experiments where they paint a monkey green and the other monkeys tear it to pieces. If you're false to yourself, I think, other people find it easier to be false to you. I mean, there's no one there to begin with, so what's the big deal?

It's a shame, in a way, that I didn't actually tape my life like old Krapp did. The present effort is not an adequate substitute because—how should I put this—I'm not entirely sure who I am anymore. Maybe that was Beckett's point in his play, that none of us are *anyone* anymore, we're all hollow men, heads filled with straw, as Eliot says in the poem, colonized by the media, cut off from the sources of real life. Why art with any soul in it is grinding to a halt.

So let's run through my life from then, quickly, because it's not much fun for me, and also, I have to say, because it may or may not be my life. But stay with me here.

Okay, the girlfriend's pregnant, we go to visit the parents in Wilmington. Max, the dad, is a big, jovial slab of beef; Nadine, the mom, is a slightly withered Southern ex-belle. They are not pleased with the catch, I detect, but they're resigned, whatever the little girl wants. Max takes me aside, asks how I'm going to support Suzanne in the manner to which she's become accustomed, and I say I intend to work as an artist, and he goes, lots of luck, sonny, I hope you intend to be a commercial artist, because you're buying into a high-maintenance package, don't be fooled by the bohemian styling.

We got married anyway and lived in the loft and had the baby, which was Toby. The fact is me and Suzanne should have been three hot weeks in a Spanish hotel room, not a ten-year marriage, although you can build a lot of plans on guilt. It was going to be great, I thought, the opposite of my parents' marriage, or her parents' marriage, and we were going to be artists together, that was the basis, really, a life together in art. Then it turned out that for whatever reason I wasn't going to be the hot young painter of the season and she was not going to be one of the defining singer-songwriters of that decade, and the funny thing is, despite our mutual mediocrity we both made a shitload of money for a while, which muffled the pain, as it often does. I could barely keep up with the ad work, and she had one of her songs covered by the thrush of the moment and it was a Top 40 hit for a while. Terrible song, I still hear it now and then if there's a radio tuned to an oldies station, all her songs anodyne and slightly sappy, tinkly, no real juice, easily distinguished from Joni Mitchell, Neil Young, etc.—like my painting, unfortunately.

Then, because she said you can't raise a kid out of a loft in SoHo, we bought a house in the country, a four-bedroom in Nyack on three and a half acres, with a barn; God alone knows what it's worth now, but way back then those big houses were going for a hundred and a half, two hundred, which seemed like a lot of money, and I started to work all week in the city, and I should have been the one to have affairs, I mean come on, I was rich in New York and that was the era for it, but I never did, not once, guilt again, probably—no, yet another example of schmuckhood. Mark was burning up the bedsheets during that time, and he used to invite me along to the meat markets down-town, but no, I was the opposite of Dad in that respect. I was just like Mom. It actually took me years to catch on about what Suzanne was doing; I thought I had an okay marriage until one evening she got drunker than usual and set me right with the list of guys.

Somewhere in those years she gave up music, decided clay was more her thing, then printmaking, then book design, then video, then back to clay, but at a higher level, she wrote a play too, and film scripts, an all-around artistic type, Suze, no focus in any of them, just a desperate desire to be in a scene, be noticed.

Or so I think, but I have no idea who she is. "Late for the Sky," that Jackson Browne song, from the days when we thought rock lyr-ics held the key to all mysteries, I still think about her when they play it on the oldies. I have to say, I can't carry the freight for the breakup of my first marriage. I don't have it in me to be the complaisant hus-band; I might have looked the other way for a long time, like they do in Cheever stories, sophisticated and all that, cool, but she brought the guys into the house, into our bed, and they were universally scuzzballs, bartenders, drifters, arty fakes, lawn guys with rusted-out pickup trucks. I'd come home on Friday after a week in the city and there'd be some gap-tooth skinny asshole on my deck drinking my booze, her new friend, and one week I just didn't bother coming back and that was it. I guess my first marriage was based on a secret deal: I would take care of her and she could do what she wanted, and I would always be there when she got tired of it, but in the end I couldn't; and the reason, I have to say, was I just didn't care for what she produced. The sad fact is that only the great artists have different rules, and the patzers have to live like everyone else or settle for being pathetic.

As for Toby, all there is now is a kind of helpless sorrow, although why I should feel sorry for someone who's doing a lot better than his dad, a pillar of the community and his church, three lovely children he's never introduced me to—no, I don't think I want to go there. Although, it was really amazing, as soon as he developed a personality he rejected everything I was, I mean he actually broke crayons deliberately, snap snap snap, and left good drawing paper out in the rain, and ruined the expensive German markers I bought him, and he fixated on my first father-in-law.

And Max just took him over and raised him according to his strict principles, which hadn't taken all that well with Suzanne but did for her son, and the kid went out for football in high school and was a quarterback and went to Purdue just like granddad and was a star there just like, and became an engineer, ditto. Each year I get a dutiful Christmas card with the beautiful family depicted thereupon, a pleasant-looking group of strangers.

So then back into wonderful singlehood, until I met Lotte and we got married and we had Milo and Rose and then split up. For a while, I thought Lotte would save me, because I could speak to her in a way I could never speak to Suzanne, and I thought I could store the real Chaz kind of *in* her, like a constant mirror. She has a Memorex-like memory, never forgot a conversation or a dream or one of my many fuck-ups, maddening actually when I think about it, you can't do that to another person, however much they might love you. No substitute for the true self. Making this recording, together with what remains of my memory after all the dope I sucked into my system while I was with her, and what happened with Zubkoff and later, I have to admit what I did to her. Basically, I walked whistling into my father's tomb, just like I said I was never going to do, ha ha, and it broke her. The poison leaked into her the way it leaked into my mother. I think it's why she betrayed me in the end, the most honest and decent person I ever met. And right she was to do it too.

I'd never really understood what she wanted from me. Self-expression? It can't just be that. I used to do paintings for her all the time, pure self-expression if you like, and the best thing I ever did for her when we were married sent her into a shit fit. It was our fifth anniversary and we'd been fighting on and off for a couple of weeks, and I wanted to make it special for a change. What we'd been fighting about was this goddamn magazine cover I'd done for *New York* about Giuliani's wedding, the one to Judith Nathan.

They wanted the obvious pastiche, van Eyck's *Wedding of John Arnolfini*, so I did that, in oils on a real oak panel just like the original. I got the arrogant hypocrisy on the face of the man and the Persian-cat self-satisfaction on the face of the woman, and I used the convex mirror behind them to paint in the wedding party, all the pols and celebs, all grinning like skulls, and also I used the ten little lunettes around the edge of the mirror to illustrate scenes from his career and the breakup of his two previous marriages. I mean, it was good. It was a real painting, not a cartoon, and it had some of the authority of the original.

I brought it home after the magazine was finished with it and she went ballistic, her usual business about how could I do this to myself, like my talent was like a god that had to be worshipped in a certain way, and how all the bozos at the magazine had no idea what I was doing, the details wouldn't even reproduce, and all the time I was wasting on crap like that, my only life. That was one of her phrases—how can you spend your only life this way? But I didn't see her spending *her* only life making the kind of money we needed for Milo, I mean it wasn't like she was maximizing her talent in that little gallery, when any of the big guys would've hired her in a heartbeat, she was that good—no, that was down to me, thank you, and around then was when I started in with the amphetamines, to get more work out in my only life and bring in the cash.

Anyway, about mid-May that year, a Sunday, it was, one of the first really nice days we had, maybe a month before our anniversary, I was making coffee or something in the kitchen and I heard this sound of giggling and laughter coming from our bedroom and I went to the door, which was open just a slit, and I looked in. They were on the bed, Lotte and Milo, he must've been around four then, and they were playing some kind of tickling game. She was in a white batiste nightgown and he was in Spider-Man pj's, and it just knocked me out, the sunlight streaming in and lighting them up on the white duvet and the brass of the bed glinting. It was like I was in on some secret, the kind of semierotic play that mothers and sons get into at that age, and for a second I almost remembered—like a sense memory, not like something in my head at all—doing the same kind of thing with my mother.

And that afternoon I went to the loft and stretched and primed a biggish canvas, maybe three feet by five, and I started painting what it was like. I made the boy slightly turned away from his mother, with an expression of delight on his face, and I had the mother sitting up in the center of the bed braced on one arm and with her other arm extended, touching his head, her index finger barely wrapped in a dark curl of his hair. And I got lost in it and for the next few weeks it was like a refuge; I'd grind out my daily bread and then turn back to it, and it was fine, everything was working right, the child's mouth rendered with three quick strokes, perfect, glistening with the juice of life, and the same with the flesh tones of the mother's skin I knew like my own, showing through the translucent fabric of her gown in the morning light, pink and pearly, you could almost breathe in the bed-scent of a woman.

And it could've been just a genre piece, but it wasn't; the painted surface was alive and really existent, like it is in serious painting, not mere image at all, and I made the white duvet into what I really have to say was a gorgeous blizzard of the innumerable shades that white can take in morning light. And the vital line of the mother's arm connecting her to the child, and the set of her haunch on the bed, and the other, supporting arm—perfect, sculptural, vital. I couldn't believe it.

And I wrapped it up and I was so happy and I thought she'd be too. But when she took the paper off she just stared at it for a long time, as if she was stunned, and then she ran into the bedroom and burst into weeping, just sobbing her heart out, and when I went to her and asked her what was wrong she said something crazy, like, you're going to kill me, you're going to kill me. And it turned out that she didn't get that I could do stuff, I mean in painting, for love that I couldn't do for money, and she seemed to calm down, and we hung the damned thing in the bedroom, but she wouldn't talk about it and it was like a bad fairy gift in a fairy tale: instead of bringing us together like it was supposed to, it drove us apart. So after that I didn't do anything but commercial work.

Which would have been fine, except around then Photoshop came in and art directors who wanted pastiches of famous paintings could just buy the rights from Bill Gates or whomever and pop in new faces, and they even had tools to give that impressionistic effect or craqueleur, and there went half my business. So I had to work twice as hard, especially after we found out that our Milo had those bad lungs, familial pulmonary dystrophy, a disease not attracting much research attention and barely controllable by means of a set of drugs that might have been compounded of powdered diamonds if you looked at the damned bills. And naturally I had to up my own dosage, and one night I lost it and wrecked our house and apparently I slugged Lotte and they had to come and take me away. I say "apparently" because I can't really recall any of it.

I went into rehab like a good boy and did my program, but when I got out she said she couldn't live with me anymore, she couldn't carry the weight of the demons. I moved back into my loft then, and since then I've been living from check to check, magazine work mainly, newspapers, a few ads, never enough, sinking ever deeper into plastic hell, IRS hell . . .

Maybe.

That brings us up to last summer, a day in June; I was at *Vanity Fair* that day talking to Gerstein, the art editor, about a project they wanted to do, a series of pieces on the great beauties of the day illustrated with oil portraits in the manner of the great masters. They got the idea, of course, from the movie *Girl with a Pearl Earring*, Vermeer and Scarlett Johansson, that was the hook: Madonna by Leonardo (ho ho!), Cate Blanchett by Gainsborough, Jennifer Lopez by Goya, Gwyneth Paltrow by Ingres, Kate Winslet by they hadn't decided yet. And he thought of me, naturally, and he went on and on about how he had to fight management to get to do them as real paintings rather than Photoshopped photos, and I asked him had they agreed to pose, and he looked at me funny and said of course they're not going to pose, you'll work from existing photographs. I argued with him for a while but it's impossible to get anyone, especially a magazine fart director, to understand the difference between a posed portrait and one cocked up from photographs, and he knew I needed the money, so we shook on it, $2,500 per, a bargain. I suggested Velázquez for Kate Winslet and he said great idea. I called Lotte and told her about the sale, just to hear her happy with me for once, and she was. I could practically hear her mental calculator clicking over the phone.

There was a fairly short deadline on the project, and by the time I got back to the loft I was thinking about painting and trying not to think about where in the bottomless money pit I was going to stuff that twelve and a half grand. Since I turned whore I have all the art books, and it's kind of cool to look through them and summon up the originals I've seen. The funny thing is I know that when I actually have the palette set up and brush in hand I won't give a shit what the finished product is, I'll be stoned off the process of painting.

Lotte, in her art gallery head, used to calculate that I made about eight bucks an hour with the kind of work I put into a project, and I could never explain to her why I do it, why I have to work like that in order to get out of bed every morning, because I knew what she would say. She would say, why don't you paint then for yourself, Chaz, and give up this *connerie*? Then I'd get mad and say, how the fuck are we going to pay for Milo's goddamn pills, five grand a month at least, and are you going to pull that out of your little gallery? And then she'd say, but I can sell your work, your work is wonderful, people would love to have your work. And there it would sit, like a fresh turd on the table, the thing that busted us up, Chaz Wilmot's principled refusal to paint real work for the commodity market. So I would storm out to the studio and work on a magazine cover or a record album and smoke dope until everything seemed just peachy.

I was just sitting down with a book of Ingres portraits when the phone rang and it was a secretary asking me if I would hold for Dr. Zubkoff, and my belly dropped because I thought it was one of Milo's docs with more bad news. So when he came on and I figured out who it was and found out what he wanted, I was so relieved that I would have agreed to practically anything.

The next day I took the subway up to the Columbia medical school campus and walked to the building I'd been told to find, a four-story brick-and-glass structure on St. Nicholas Avenue at 168th Street. Inside, the usual medical smell, the over-cooled reception room with the tattered magazines, the white-coated receptionist behind her little window. They were expecting me. I filled out a medical form, lied about my drug use and my smoking like everyone else, and was turned over to a nurse in pale blue scrubs who took me into a little room and told me to get into a gown. They said they wanted to make sure I was totally disease-free before they let me into a major drug study, so if I had a prior condition I couldn't come back at them with an accusation that their drug messed me up.

A couple of hours later, I found I was healthy, despite my lifestyle, still sound as a bell, apparently, just like Krapp. It was an impressive medical workup, bloods, scans, the whole nine yards, and after it I had an even greater sympathy for my poor kid.

After all the tests were done and I was dressed again, they led me to a small conference room with the other guinea pigs and I saw Shelly himself, now a far cry from the pale slug he was in college, a man with a tan and longer hair, with the flossy rich-guy cut they all have and that aura of authority they must bolt on when they give out the med school diplomas. A dozen or so people in the room, all arty types, about evenly divided between the sexes, mostly younger than me. It looked like Sunday brunch at any hip place in Williamsburg.

Dr. Z took us through a PowerPoint show about salvinorin A, the drug we were about to pollute our bodies with. On the screen a picture of some dusty Indians sitting around in a circle, Mazotecs from the deserts of Oaxaca, who used a plant called *Salvia divinorum*, the diviner's sage; their shamans used it to break loose from time and see the future and the past. Silly them, because according to Shelly it was all happening in the damp meat of their brains, like everything else we perceived. Over the last few decades, researchers had extracted the active principle of the Indian herb—salvinorin—and discovered that it was not an alkaloid like most of the psychoactive drugs, but a much smaller molecule, a diterpene, and unique in that respect. It was a kappa opioid agonist, I recall that, something to do with the control of perception. The drug had a variety of different effects, we learned, and these varied considerably between users. Of particular interest, though, was its ability to create the illusion that you were reliving a portion of your earlier life. Dr. Z said he thought that since the retention of childlike wonder and freshness of perception was widely considered to be a central element in the creative process, maybe salvinorin might enhance it, which was why he'd selected his subjects from artists and musicians. Then there was some technical stuff about how if they got psychological effects they would use tracers and so forth to try to pinpoint the areas of the brain that did creative stuff, and then he closed with assurances that while the drug was extremely potent, it appeared to be quite safe and nonaddictive.

Then the usual questions from the floor, which Shelly handled, I thought, with a smoothness that had not been apparent in him as an undergrad, and the meeting broke up. I went up to him afterward and we shook and did the whole small world thing, and he invited me for a private chat in his office. Which was very nice, golf clubs in the corner, all kinds of awards, blond wood desk and chairs, flat-screen monitor, framed kids' drawings on the walls and a small amateur oil of flowers in a vase, maybe by the wife, a happy family man it seems, good for Shelly. No talk about old times; he boasted and I listened. His great career, his beautiful family, his house in Short Hills. He said he saw my stuff in the magazines all the time, he thought it was great. He thought I was a success, just like him.

He said he particularly wanted me in this study because it was really going to penetrate to the roots of creativity and even lead to ways of augmenting it. I thought that if he wanted to do that he better bring his lunch, but I didn't say anything; why rain on the guy's parade? I was happy for him, the poor schmuck, and it was a hundred bucks a session to me.

After that he turned me over to Ms. Blue Scrubs and I had my first dose of salvinorin. They've discovered that the best way to ingest it is via the oral mucosa. They can heat the drug and shoot you the fumes, or they can give you a surgical sponge soaked with a solution of the drug and you have to keep that in your mouth for ten minutes. The first way brings on an intense reaction in a few seconds but it fades in half an hour. The sponge works best; the reaction lasts for a full hour, more or less, and then drops off over the next hour. It's a way to provide a controlled dose but still imitate chewing the leaves, which is what the Indians down in Mexico do.

She took me to a little room, like an examination room, with a low-slung recliner and left me with an observer in a white coat, name-plate HARRIS, young woman, all business, notebook, tape recorder, and a comfortable chair to sit in, like psychotherapy. I made a joke to that effect, minimal response. Message: this is serious research. She opened a plastic tub marked with a numbered label and extracted a damp surgical sponge with plastic tongs. She stuck it in my mouth and told me to chew on it for ten minutes starting *now*— clicked her watch—try not to swallow, and then she dimmed the lights.

I chewed on the cloth and kept the liquid it yielded in a cheek pocket, like a country-boy pitcher on the mound. Faintly herbal, a little like turkey stuffing, not unpleasant. After ten minutes I was allowed to expel the wad. Then nothing for a while. I thought about the *Vanity Fair* project, about money, the usual sad, self-pitying thoughts about how essentially and irreparably screwed up my life was, floating mind-crap. After a while I felt a certain relaxation, like I was looking at Chaz thinking this shit and finding it amusing; I guess I actually laughed a little then. Next a feeling of vague physical discomfort, like my muscles were starting to cramp, that claustro coach-class airliner feeling, and I got up and went for the door.

Harris said I couldn't leave, so I sat down, got up, sat down, paced back and forth, energy flowing through my body, electric, vibrational and crunching over gravel and dead leaves, the air chill and damp and I'm just drifting, not really sad, but somehow feeling a déjà vu as we're walking toward the grave site at the head of a column of mourners, quite a few of them, more than I had expected really, my sister in her nun's head-scarf, they'd dumped the black clothes by then, holding on to my arm. I stopped and stumbled a little from the force of the disorientation and she asked me what was wrong. I told her and said I'd never had a déjà vu that strong, and she said no wonder, it's not every day you bury your father, and we walked along and the rest of the funeral played out.

Charlie and I got a little drunk later and she told me she was thinking about leaving the religious life. She liked helping the starving millions in the world's nasty places, but the good they could do seemed so paltry compared to the extent of the evil. Yes, it was good to give twenty girls a year a convent education and keep them from being raped by older guys, but there were hundreds and hundreds they couldn't help, the mothers would bring them to the school in Kitgum, crowds of women and girls begging for admission, knowing it was hopeless, but what else could they do? And somehow now that our father was gone a lot of the reason for it (as she now admitted) was gone too, and she felt she wanted to move into the world, not to leave religion exactly, but to be of some greater service. We talked about that for a while, what different orders of sisters did, and she asked me how my painting was going and did I think I would start painting for myself now and not just to piss the old man off, and I laughed at that.

We stayed up late talking, just like we'd done in the old days when we were kids, and she kissed me good night and then I went up to my old room. It hadn't changed at all, the Indian blanket on the bed, my old hockey stick on the wall next to the painting of my mother, and that damp wicker smell from the old furniture. I got out of my clothes and was going to go to bed but remembered I hadn't closed the French doors leading to the terrace and if the wind shifted in the night the rain would ruin the carpets, so I put my old blue plaid robe on and tried to open the door. The door wouldn't open, and I rattled the knob and pounded and kicked at it, and there was a hand on my shoulder, which scared the shit out of me because I was alone in the room, and I turned around and this woman was there in a white coat with HARRIS on the tag and I was back in the drug study.

Now, you absolutely have to understand that this was *not* a reverie or a dream, nothing like that at all. I was *there*. I was back in time twenty-two years, inhabiting my younger body, talking to my sister in the living room of my father's house, full color, stereo sound, the works. I said, holy shit! And my knees gave way and I had to lie down on the couch, and Harris was all over me about what had happened. It was hard to reply at first. It wasn't that I felt drugged, or dull, or extra sharp like on coke or speed, but more detached, a very subtle variation in consciousness, and there was a beating in my head, a pulse like a kitten licking my brain four or five times a second, *thnick thnick thnick*, in just that delicate way.

At the same time I felt both extremely focused and detached, as if experiencing my life for the first time without the blurring of worry and regret. Not in the least like hash and the furthest thing from acid. She asked me a bunch of questions she read off a printed sheet, and I answered them as best I could, yes, I attended my father's funeral; no, I can't guarantee that what I experienced was a memory and not a fantasy. It seemed perfectly real, just like talking right then to the silly woman seemed real, although if you informed me that I was still in my room on the night of the funeral and that this interview was a fantasy I would have said sure, right.

She kept me for another hour. The kitten licking faded after a while and I returned more or less to normal, although at that point I was no longer sure what normal was. On the way out I lifted from the reception room table a tattered old *People* magazine with a story about Madonna in it. Back at the loft, I set up a small gessoed wood panel and dug through the chests until I found an old theatrical costume that would do, plum colored, with gilt threads and a straight, high bodice—some Juliet must have worn it in the Edwardian age, stank of mothballs, but in good shape. I hung it on my manikin, propped her in an armchair, arranged the lighting, pinned Madonna's face up on the wall nearby, and got to work.

I drew it out in charcoal, a figure from the waist up with her arms demurely folded, pale hair in ringlets falling to the neck, showing against a cloudy background and a little city with walls and towers back there. Underpainting in warm gray-ochre, mixed a little Japan dryer in because I'm a commercial artist, can't wait for the paint to dry, and who cares if it cracks and blackens in fifty years? So when the *imprimatura* was touch-dry, I built up the masses, laid on glazes, and then the fall of the drapery, and it went terrific, I painted for hours, it got dark outside, I got hungry, I ignored the phone ringing. Was it different? I guess. I can often get lost in the act of painting and forget for a while that what I'm doing is essentially commercial crap, but this session was even more so, I was totally into it, with my body, just letting the paint flow out onto the fresh white surface, magic.

My stomach was growling by then and I wanted to give the underpaint a chance to dry, so I took a break and walked over to Chinatown for some noodles and took the *People* with me to read and study Madonna some more. Her face in the cheap printing showed the mere mask of the celebrity, and the job was to find the interior behind it, and of course you can't do that from a photo, that's the point, the handlers want to control the star's image, revelation not wanted, so I knew I'd have to imagine it. And naturally I thought about Suzanne, a singer at a vastly lower level of celebrity but a face I knew well, and I worked with that. The *People* photo was a typical lowering Madonna shot, the overbit mouth pouting and a little downturned, the eyelids at half mast in a way meant to be read as sexual according to the conventions of beauty shots.

When I got back to my place I opened her mouth into a little gape of astonishment and put into her eyes the deep loneliness and insecurity of the famous performer. And the not-so-famous, as I knew from experience.

And the bambino. They hadn't asked for one but I thought it added the right touch. So I pulled out an old baby picture of Milo and painted it in freehand. Milo had a kind of sly expression, you know the kind, the secret and unknowable joy of the pre-articulate child.

I glazed the underpainting all night, and when I looked at it by daylight it was certainly a credible Leonardo, no sharp outlines, everything smoky—*sfumato*, they called it—and the background is pretty good. I threw in some of those flat-looking quattrocento trees, which I always thought were an artistic convention until I went to

Italy and saw they had taken them from life—I never learned what kind of trees they were, I always call them quattrocento trees. Amazing really; I would have futzed around with something like this for weeks, and so if Shelly thought the drug enhances creativity, I have to say yeah, it does.

And it got better. I did five paintings in five days, by far the most productive period of my life, I mean without coke and speed. And it was nothing like the frenzy I used to have when I was drugged out, it was just like . . . shit, I can't say what it's like. Being supernormal, maybe, not getting distracted, total focus, total pleasure in the work. When I was four or around there I could sit forever in my father's studio while he worked, with big sheets of newsprint on the floor, drawing with my crayons or painting with watercolors. Time stopped, or flowed at a different pace, and there was nothing but the moment before I made a mark; and the making the mark; and looking at the mark afterward. And again. That week was just like that; for some reason all the shit that usually runs through my brain—worries about money, about the wives and kids, about what I'm doing—all seemed to take a little vacation, leaving a stripped-down Chaz who just painted. Wonderful!

A couple of days later I went back to the med school for another session. They took a blood sample, and I got a quick physical; I told them I felt fine, great in fact, even if I did lose almost ten pounds, and I had to fill out a form about how I fared the past week. Interesting the stuff they were checking on—paranoid ideation, sleepwalking, violence, convulsions, catatonia, hallucinations, uncontrollable laughter, excessive urination, no urination at all, reverse ejaculation, eating unfamiliar foods, priapism, impotence, paralysis, dyskinesia, and there's a section for changes in creative process, where you can rate your creative functioning on scales of one to ten, and I gave myself all tens. Unless *that* was a hallucination. How could you tell?

Then the same little room with Harris, she said, we're going to try a slightly lower dose, and she hooked me up to various meters, including a brain-wave device. Chewed my wad. Same as before, one second I'm in the little room, the next I smell the cologne my mother always used back when she was alive, lily of the valley, and I'm in her lap on our deck looking over the Sound, a gray day, it must be early autumn, and she has me wrapped in a brown velvet throw; Charlie is away somewhere and Mother's lovely and I am perfectly happy.

She's telling me a story, always the same story, about the brave little boy whose mother is kidnapped by an ogre and taken to his castle, but the brave little boy fights through many dangers and drives the ogre out of the castle, and the brave little boy and his mother live happily ever after in the ogre's castle.

Okay, the same as before, I'm there, it's real, and now something happened that was even more weird. I'm sitting in her lap, and then the scene darkens and the smell of the water and of her perfume fade, and they're replaced by heavier smells, meat cooking and scorched feathers, and a sweet/sour smell like sewage and lavender fighting it out, and I'm still on a woman's lap, but it's not my mother, and I'm not me.

But I also know she's my mother, and I'm also me in a strange way, as if the two little boys are the same boy, both the same age, one on a deck overlooking Long Island Sound and the other in this room. A familiar room, familiar comforting sounds and smells. My mother is wearing a black velvet dress that smells of lavender, and there are other women in the room moving about and my mother is talking to them, discussing domestic affairs, how to cook a chicken, the need for more beans. I am wearing a dress too, of some stiff fabric, bloodred, with a lace collar. The room is small, with a low beamed ceiling, and dim—the light comes through a narrow casement window made of round lenslike panes.

My mother puts me off her lap and stands, and another woman grabs me by the hand and leads me out of the room into a courtyard flooded with strong light; overhead is the hot sky of some southern region. This too is all familiar, a fountain lined with blue tiles playing in the center of the courtyard, and I am fascinated by this blue and how the water changes the color of it. I splash my hand in the water and the sensation is real, actual; I look at the blue of the tiles and the blue of the sky and I think that this has some importance but I don't know what it is. From outside I hear the noises of the street, vendors' cries and the snort of horses and creak of cart wheels. A dark-skinned woman comes in through the gate with baskets of flowers, red carnations. I stare at the flowers and I conceive a desire for them, I want to hold the perfect red of them.

But someone shouts, and the flower woman darts away and does not latch the gate, and I slip out into the street, although I have been warned not to, warned the Jews will steal me. I follow the flower lady through narrow streets; she knocks at doors, enters or is shouted away. While I wait I play with a stick; I poke a dead cat into the sewer that runs down the center of the street. I am careful with my shoes, I am not to get them wet with the filth.

The flower seller leaves the narrow lanes of the neighborhood and enters a broader street. She walks faster and I have to trot to keep up with her. She no longer knocks at doors. Now we are in a plaza full of carts and animals, and many people; most of them are shouting out the names of foods and other things. The flower seller has disappeared.

Some men are looking at me, talking, but I don't understand what they are saying. They are dark men, wearing unfamiliar clothing. One reaches out to grab me, but I am suddenly afraid, and I dart away. I am lost, I run through the crowd crying. Maybe the Jews are following me, they will steal me and drink my blood, as Pilar the nurse has often assured me that they love to do.

I run blindly, tripping and bumping into people, I knock over a hen coop, and then I am swept up off my feet and held, a man in black, a broad hat and a cassock, a priest. I beg him not to let the Jews get me, and he laughs and says there are no Jews anymore, little man, and who are you, and why are you crying, and I say my name, Gito de Silva, and my father is Juan Rodríguez de Silva, of the street of Padre Luis Maria Llop, and he says he will take me home, and I am glad to be saved but also terrified that I will be beaten and so I struggle in his arms. The priest says, hey, take it easy, buddy! And I find myself struggling with a UPS man in a brown uniform.

I still had the EEG leads trailing from my head and I'd lost a sneaker. I managed to croak out the lie that I was all right, that I was fine, and the man said I had dashed out the door of Shelly's building and run into him full tilt. Like I was blind, he said. We were at Haven Avenue and 168th Street and he'd been en route to making a delivery at the Neurological Institute. In a minute or so, Harris came running up and apologized to the guy and led me back into the building.

She had me down on the recliner and was taking the leads off my head when Shelly Zubkoff popped in, looking a little ruffled. Apparently, without warning, I had jumped off the bed, knocked Harris away when she tried to stop me, and somehow got out of the building, where I'd bounced off the delivery man. Shelly apologized and observed that I was lucky that the man hadn't been driving his truck. I had no memory at all about this. One second I was a kid in some other age struggling with a priest, and the next I was out on the street with the UPS guy. Disorienting is barely the word.

He made me stay for an hour, for observation he said, although

I felt perfectly okay, really good, calm and kind of blank, and again without the usual internal dialogue going on, the crap that constantly fills up our heads, and it turns out, you know, that without that script running, you can really focus down on the world around you, and if you do that everything is really interesting. Everything.

There's a feeling you get on crank or cocaine where you think you have super powers: anything seems possible, and worse, sensible, which is why you get people painting six-room apartments with a one-inch brush or doing mass murders. But what I felt when I left Zubkoff's office wasn't like that at all. I felt perfectly myself, but more so, like there were forces behind me, encouraging me, stroking me. Again that kitten-licking sensation in my head. It was exactly like being a well-beloved child, it was *that* kind of omnipotence, at home in the universe (a book title I've always liked), and everything was just as it should be and everything was interesting.

Right, I keep saying that, "interesting" is the word, because as I rode downtown on the subway, the car crowded with the end of rush hour, ordinary people going home to supper and their lives, I couldn't help staring at the faces and the patterns of the people in random juxtaposition, but it wasn't random at all—everything was loaded with meaning, and you could point that out with art, I saw, you could make sense of it. I cursed the hours I'd spent being bored and pissed off and getting high because real life wasn't quite perfect enough for me, and I was nearly crying with the desire to paint these faces and this choir of people arranged for me and paint everything so that people would look at it and say oh, yeah, that's true, it all makes sense. This vibrating moment.

I won't say it was an epiphany, because God wasn't involved, but I knew there was something *else* going on, that time itself is the real hallucination, that the material world isn't all there is of existence. I could see divine stuff peeking through the cracks, I felt supported by Creation and it was flowing through me stronger than ever, and I thought, Okay, this was what Fra Angelico must've felt like all the time.

I was home and in bed before it occurred to me that I hadn't thought about that other thing that had sent me running through the streets, the little boy in the red dress and the house with the strange smells and the girl with the carnations, and when I started thinking about it I realized that the people were all speaking a language I didn't know, like Spanish but not quite, but I could understand it just like English. And who the hell was Gito de Silva? What was he doing in my head?

The next week was fairly rotten, even for my life, because I got a call from *Vanity Fair*. Gerstein was real apologetic, but his editor didn't like the paintings, and they weren't going to use them. They thought they were too spooky and weird, he said, and they didn't look enough like the stars, he said, and I controlled my temper and I said they looked *exactly* like the stars, as those stars would be seen by the five old masters concerned, which I thought had been the fucking point of the exercise, and we went around the barn for a while on this, and what it turned out to be was they really had no idea that anyone had ever seen things differently from the way they do now. They thought that the current view of everything was the stone *reality*, that this week stood for all time.

And I guess if you're running a style magazine with cultural pretensions, that's the way you have to see the world. Such an enterprise can't really handle much penetration. If people looked and thought deeply they wouldn't read magazines, or at least not magazines like *Vanity Fair*. I have to say they were generous; they paid me a kill fee of a grand per painting and said I was free to sell them elsewhere.

I was pretty calm, compared to what I would have been at another time, and I couldn't help wondering whether that was a side effect of the salvinorin, a kind of tranquilizer thing, although I didn't feel in any way dulled out, really the opposite in fact. A kind of acceptance, maybe, of what I've been fighting my whole life, that I can do something extremely well that has absolutely no exchange value as artwork.

People can see that quality in the old masters, or at least they write about seeing it, but not in something made yesterday.

So my work's a complete fucking waste of time, at least where money is concerned. I used to think I'd been born out of my proper era. I mean, it'd be like a major league pitcher being born in 1500. His ability to throw a small ball at a hundred miles an hour through any sector of an arbitrary rectangle is totally unsalable, so the guy would spend his life shoveling shit on some estate, and the only time he does his thing is at the fair, hey, guys, look what Giles can do! But basically it's not all that interesting, not even to Giles.

Meanwhile, there was over seven thousand bucks I would not be seeing, and I dreaded going around to the creditors I'd promised it to and having to eat shit, again. Mark Slotsky had left a message on my cell phone, which I hoped was about money, and I called him back, but his phone said I had to leave a message.

Later that day, I went into Gorman's on Prince Street, the only place in SoHo where I still have credit. Clyde the bartender has a soft spot for artists. Behind the bar is a painting of mine, the original of a cover I'd done for *New York* magazine a couple of years back, Mrs. Senator Clinton as Liberty leading the people in the Delacroix painting with her breast hanging out. Clyde had loved it, and I gave him the painting in exchange for my bar tab and a year of free drinks. Gorman's used to be a cop saloon when the police headquarters was still in that palace on Centre Street, and then it was artists for a while, until most of the painters moved out when the rents went up, and now it is all retail people from the boutiques and the galleries. This is fine with me. I don't have much to say to painters nowadays; I can't stand the hacks and the serious ones make me ashamed of myself. I'm a little isolated, actually, all alone in the big city, a cliché, but there it is. From week to week the only people I see are Lotte, Mark, and a guy named Jacques-Louis Moreau, who, as it happened, was sitting at the bar in Gorman's when I walked in. He usually is, with a glass of wine and the French papers and a cell phone.

I wouldn't exactly call Jackie a pal of mine, he's actually more Lotte's friend, a fellow diplo-brat, been to the same schools in various capitals and here in the city. Whether they'd ever been an item I don't know, she would never tell me. Although after we broke up she'd been seeing a lot of him, and I had the mixed feelings you have about a guy who's sniffing around your beloved even when she's not exactly yours anymore. He's a big guy, a soccer player, with that roundheaded neat French look, close-cropped dark hair and a ready smile. Our relationship consists mainly of drinking at Gorman's in the afternoons and bitching about our hard lives. Maybe that's why I went into the bar that day.

Jackie's a painter too, but unlike me he yearns for gallery success. Unfortunately, while he has all the technique in the world he has no creativity at all. Ever since I've known him he's been pursuing the fashions, always a little too late. He started out doing big splashy abstracts and then, in turn, op art, color fields, pop art, and now he's into conceptual. One winter a few years ago I walked into his loft on Crosby Street and found him feeding big Warholian-wannabe canvases into the Ashley stove he used to heat the place. No loss, that, but he seemed curiously cheerful about it, and I recall being a little envious that he honestly didn't give a shit about his work. He thought the whole art scene was a scam and that sooner or later he'd hit it right and cash in.

Anyway, when I came in he waved me over, and I ordered a martini and unloaded about the *Vanity Fair* fiasco. He commiserated and, unlike Lotte, didn't ask me why I didn't do the gallery thing, which was restful at least, and then he said he was leaving New York for Europe. Yeah, some rich guy wanted some paintings done, a variety of styles, money up front.

"This is hotels?" I asked him, but he got a sly look on his face and said, "For private customers, yes, you know, yachts and beach houses, and this man I am working for, he says he'll represent me on the European market, all these Russian billionaires now, they want paintings, so it will be very big."

I asked him what Mark had to say about that, because Mark's his gallery and I happen to know that Mark had been carrying him for a while, but he said, "No, it was Mark who turned me on to this. It is partly his idea."

So fine, I was happy for him and I figured that if I wanted to bitch I could use the bartender. Or the back-bar mirror.

I walked out of there with a couple of martinis in me easing the pain and strode up to Prince Street and Lotte's gallery to pick up the kids, it being my night for them, and to tell her that there wouldn't be quite as much money as expected this month. I received a lot less sympathy than I'd just had from Jackie, but when I showed her photographs of the rejected paintings, she thought they were terrific and she said she was sure they'd sell, if I wanted, and I did want, I couldn't stand the sight of them. She let out one of her famous sighs, the meaning of which I perfectly understood—the insoluble, neurotic business about why I mind selling this stuff to people for their walls, as opposed to a magazine. It's totally irrational, selling is selling, but still . . . I think it's because the buyers won't see what's there either, they'll say, oh, I *love* Kate Winslet, and they'll buy it as a kind of kitschy joke, like it was the same as Andy Asshole's silk screens of Marilyn, a pure pop object, and that brought up the thought that maybe it is, maybe I'm just kidding myself. I'm a joke too, after all, like I said, but a poor one.

The kids are fine with self-entertainment in my loft, all kinds of stuff for them to play with, cut themselves with, poisons galore, and nothing's ever happened, not a scratch; is it luck or just growing up around a non-childproof environment? While the two of them messed around with paints on the floor I went to my old Dell and Googled some of the weird stuff I'd experienced in that second drug session. I drew a blank on "Gito de Silva," but I had a hit on "Calle Padre Luis Maria Llop," which it turns out is a street in the old quarter of Seville, in Spain. I brought it up on Google Earth and zoomed down as far as it would let me. A tiny little street, and I could see the route he (or I) took from his (or my) house to the plaza. I told myself that I was in fact a tourist in the old city of Seville once, age nine, with my father, and therefore it was some kind of dredged-up residual memory.

Had a good time with the kids, our usual drawing contest, we all sat around and drew each other and Rose won by popular acclaim like always. She's pretty good for four years old; maybe she'll be a famous artist like her daddy, God forbid. Milo can draw too, but I think he's mainly a word guy. Walking down the street behind them, I almost had to cry. Milo is so frail and Rose is such a sturdy little truck, and she worships him, it's just going to tear her apart, when . . . Another thing I have to talk to Shelly about; he's a research guy, maybe there's some program I can get Milo into, or move to a country where you don't have to be rich to live. But what he needs is a new set of lungs.

After they were asleep I went out on the fire escape and smoked some dope and had a funny little reverie about my first and only gallery show, and it was interesting because of the contrast between it and what I'd experienced on the salvinorin. Or maybe the salvinorin was somehow enriching the experience in some neurophysiological way. Anyway, I recalled being late because I'd decided I had to drop some stuff off at an ad agency in midtown, and then I had to have an after-work drink with a couple of people from the agency. A couple three drinks or so, and then I called Suzanne from a phone booth and told her to go on without me, I'd be there soon. The show was in Mark Slotsky's gallery on West Broadway off Worth Street, and she got all steamed at that, was I nuts, this was my big break and I was screwing around with some crappy ad, and didn't I know who'd be there, Mark had called in all these chips to get a good crowd and had spent a fortune on the spread, not shitty wine and cheese but catered from Odeon and so on and so on. What it was, she wanted to make an entrance with the star, and now she'd have to just walk in like everyone else.

I remember walking down West Broadway and feeling like I was going to my execution. I was still wearing my work clothes, paint-smeared, not that clean, a hoodie and jeans and really awful raggedy-ass sneakers, and I felt embarrassed, like I had *wanted* to look like this to impress all the art lovers that I don't give a shit about.

And I arrived, the place all lit up and people spilling out on the sidewalk, chattering and holding flutes of champagne. They looked at me, and I felt like the skeleton at the feast, but then I was recognized: Mark shouted out my name and he and Suzanne came running over to me, my wife dressed in a black spaghetti-strap outfit that would have been racy underwear in my mother's day, and I collected slaps on the back and kisses, and they were all beaming and happy, because the show looked to be a hit, there were little stick-on red dots on many of the paintings, they were sold, I was *selling*, this is success. And then I had to meet the buyers, the art hags, women in black with ethnic jewelry hanging from neck and ears, and chunky gold and diamonds like fetters on their wrists, and I was trying to be happy like them, and I heard how wonderful it was for them to have paintings that *look like something*, and Mark was talking a mile a minute about appreciation, he means appreciation in value, a good investment, they were getting in on the ground floor with Charles Wilmot, Jr.

And while this was going on I was chugging champagne as fast as I could grab the flutes off the silvery trays; the bubbles brought up a froth of bile from my stomach and I wanted to vomit. The paintings on the white walls were unbearable to look at, the paint looked like shit, muddy and dull, and all the avid faces around me looked like birds of prey, carrion beasts. Yes, neurotic, self-destructive, I know it, and I was wondering why I thought about that show just then. It's a memory I don't treasure, except that was the night I first saw Lotte Rothschild, although I was able to turn that into shit as well.

The next day I took the kids off to their school and I came back to my place and borrowed Bosco's van to take my rejected paintings from the magazine offices in the Condé Nast Building over to Lotte's gallery. The place was empty and we had a nice talk, almost like old times, so much so it made my heart hurt. And then I recalled that fire escape reverie and I said, "Do you remember my first show?"

"When we met," she said. "Why do you ask?"

And naturally I was not going to tell her about sitting out on the fire escape doing dope while the kids were with me, so I said, "No reason, really, but I was just thinking about it last night and I remembered how I felt, the sensation of . . . I don't know what you'd call it, terror, revulsion."

"Yes, you seemed miserable. And I couldn't understand why; you were selling out the show and the paintings were wonderful." Here her face fell a little. "Our old tape. Do we have to run through it again?"

"No. But I remembered how I noticed you in the crowd. You were wearing a green velvet jacket with glass buttons, a lace blouse, sort of very pale ochre, like parchment, and an ankle-length skirt, in some rustling material. And red boots. Everyone else was all in black."

"Except you. You looked like a derelict or an 'artist' in quotation marks. I thought, Oh, no, make him not a poseur, he's too good for that."

"I noticed your eyes too. *Les yeux longés*. Wolf eyes. You used to say you fell in love with me through my paintings first."

"I did used to say that," she answered, looking straight at me, those beautiful eyes, huge and slanted and gray as clouds, but without the warmth I often used to see there. "What a pity you never did any more like them."

I pretended I hadn't heard this, and added, "And then I didn't see you for years afterward, and Suzanne and I broke up, and then Mark dragged me to the college reunion, the fifteenth, and there you were, dating a friend of mine—"

"Don't remind me!"

"How did you ever meet up with him? I forget."

"I forget too."

"And I stole you away from him right there in the Hilton ballroom. We eloped to that club on Avenue A, one of those black basements, and we danced until three in the morning and I took you back to my loft."

Saying this, I grabbed her and led her through a few steps, but her body was stiff as a manikin, not like it used to be.

"Chaz, what are you doing?"

"Oh, nothing, just thinking about old times. I've been spending a lot of time on memory lane recently, you know, bullshit about my life, how things could have been different, if only . . ."

"Yes, but that's something you have to work on yourself. I can't get into that with you. I tried once, if you recall, and it nearly killed me.

So, you know, you can't come around here and be all sweet and loving and expect me to leap into your arms." Looking bright darts of flame at me.

A little moment of heartbreak here, and then she pulled away and said, "So let's see what these look like."

We stood the paintings up against a wall. Paintings always look so helpless and wan against a white gallery wall, like they're crying "save me!" but she thought they were terrific and decided right then to combine them in the show she was planning to open that Friday, guy named Cteki, from Bratislava, does Hopperesque alienation scenes from central Europe, empty cafés, rusting factories, people in shabby overcoats waiting for the trolley, not my idea of something for the living room, but he can draw at least, proud to have my crap on the same wall as his crap.

"They should fly off the walls," I said lightly. "Everyone loves a celebrity."

She ignored this and stood in front of Kate Winslet, staring for a long minute, and then the same with the others, shaking her head.

"My God!" she said. "Do you know, I can't think of another contemporary painter who could pull this off, this incredible bravura."

"You like them?"

"Honestly? Aside from their commercial value, I hate them. This is what's between us, do you realize that? That you can do this, that you can take something that comes from God almighty to maybe three people on the whole planet and treat it as a big laugh. Kate Winslet! Madonna!"

I said, "I don't see what the difference is between that and painting princesses in the seventeenth century or plutocrats' daughters in the nineteenth."

"That's not the *point*, as you know very well. These are pastiches. But the paintings I saw that night at your show, I remembered them all those years later. And when you showed up in that hotel it was the memory of them that made me fall in love with you, leave the very nice businessman I was with, and run off with you like a different kind of woman than I thought I was. Because those paintings were not pastiches. They were *you*. Not Velázquez, not Goya: Charles Wilmot."

"Junior," I said.

"Yes, and in a junior way you've let your gift curdle and turn to acid and eat away your heart, just like your father, as you never stop telling me."

"Except not as rich. Well, dear, I'm sorry I didn't become a famous, wealthy artist for you—"

"Oh, *fuck* you!" she shouted. "Fuck you and damn you to hell, you sucked me into this again, you bastard! Get out of here! Go on, scram! I have work to do. And don't forget you promised to take the kids on Friday."

With that, I was out on the street, feeling like shit, and then drove back to Bosco's to drop the keys off and paid for the van use as usual by listening to his political rants and art theories. Most people know his work, life-size, anatomically correct stuffed cloth figures, giant rag dolls, with smooth, white, blank faces upon which he projects video loops. The effect is uncanny; despite the abstraction you read the doll as having a talking face. Some of them are animated by internal motors and pushrods, so that our president, for example, is seen having dog-style intercourse with a large stuffed pig as he gives a speech about Iraq. Given the politics of the art community in New York and L.A., Bosco sells a lot of this work.

Denny bent my ear about Wilhelm Reich, a current hero of his, and showed me an orgone box he built for one of his dolls, a lush beauty in shocking pink, but with the white face, and she's lying on a cot in the box and there's a mechanism that makes her writhe and move her hand against her crotch. He paid a couple of dozen girls to make videos of their faces as they masturbated to orgasm, and we had a beer and watched as he ran them in a loop against the face of his boxed odalisque. With the accompanying cries and squishy noises, of course.

An interesting experience. We discussed the faces, whether you can tell acting from feeling, and about what warped desire for exhibitionistic fame would compel obviously middle-class young women to participate in such a project. Bosco said it was because none of them wanted to be president of the United States, which seemed to be the only restriction on behavior nowadays.

Then we talked about his next project, which involved dust from the 9/11 attacks. All of us living in lower Manhattan were showered with the gray cloud on that day, but Bosco had collected a whole barrel of it, consisting of pulverized buildings, computers, firemen, terrorists, bond traders, etc., and wanted to use it in a project that would piss all over the cult of 9/11 in the most offensive way possible. Most artists nowadays have made their peace with the bourgeoisie, the class from whence they arise and the class that pays their bills, in return for which they supply a little frisson of outrage, usually of a sexual nature, but Bosco still believes in the power of art and thinks that anarchy is the only proper politics for a conscious artist. He considers me a neolithic reactionary and accuses me of Republican sympathies. You're a fucking fascist, Wilmot, he always says, in everything but the lust for gold and power. You're like sex without orgasm—sweaty, uncomfortable, expensive, with no payoff. You're a sellout who never collected the check.

We've been friends for twenty years, ever since the day of the drywall—nice guy, wouldn't hurt a cockroach, two grown kids, been married for decades. Lives in a big Dutch Colonial house in Montclair, New Jersey, a perfect phony and a happy man.

And speaking of phony, after I got finished with Bosco I went over to Mark Slade Downtown to see what Slotsky wanted; it was lunchtime and I figured he'd spring for a meal. The girl in black said he'd gone out but she expected him back soon, nice-looking kid, and I thought I recognized her from one of the orgasm clips, although Bosco said that since he collected the vignettes he's been thinking that every woman between eighteen and forty he sees on the street is one of the ones on the doll's face.

Slotsky was showing a kid named Emil Mono, big square tricolored abstracts in the loose dramatic style of Motherwell. One ground color, a blob of another color, and some blobs and streak of a third color, perfectly respectable work, suitable for corporate lobbies, hotel meeting rooms, and the Whitney Biennial. I really have no problem at all with work like this, in most cases a kind of wallpaper, anodyne, meaningless, or rather announcing the fact that meaning no longer inheres in painting.

Pretty colors, though. I recall once when I was in Europe a dozen or so years ago, in the Prado as a matter of fact, and I got caught in one of the endless corridors they've got stuffed with barely distinguishable academic painting, all brownish remakes of Rubens and Murillo, and I felt like I was drowning in sepia. I practically ran out of the place and walked down the Paseo to the Reina Sofía modern art museum and into a cool white room, and there was a Sonia Delaunay that was like a little girl singing on some bright terrace, lovely and fresh, just some watery stripes and numerals and letters, and it cleaned my eye, the way the art needed to have its eye cleaned around the tail end of the nineteenth century. And God bless them all, the nonfiguratives, but I can't do it myself, I am chained to the world as it is; but, yeah, it's a way to paint, and Cézanne is as good a daddy as anyone. Art is a universe in parallel with nature and in harmony with it, as he famously said; true enough as long as you keep a grip on the harmony-with-nature part. I just find 95 percent of it as exhausting to look at as those miles of brown, slick academic pap.

I hung around for forty minutes or so, drank some free coffee, and was just going to leave or strike up a conversation with the girl, maybe about *art*, when Slotsky came in. He was dressed for uptown, double-breasted suit, handmade shoes, he's always reminded me of my father in his good clothes—maybe an actual model there, his own father did not dress like that. He seemed glad to see me, a hug, not a shake, that's a newish affectation, Mark always trendy that way, and ran me back to his office behind the gallery.

He looked reasonably well, I thought, or as well as a short, pudgy fellow with floppy lips and white eyelashes ever looks. He still has his Harpo mop of yellow curls, now a little tarnished with age, but still his logo, as it was at school. Mark no longer wears all black. Since he started selling old masters some years ago he has adopted the English squire look, which suits him rather better, since combined with his features and general carriage his former all-black costume inevitably recalled the Hasidim rather than urban sophistication, although he doesn't look much like an English squire either. For example, he'd left the last button on the sleeve of his suit jacket partially open, so that knowledgeable people could tell that he had real buttonholes, and therefore that the suit had been custom-made. I don't know any actual English squires, but I kind of doubt they do this.

We took a cab to Chez Guerlin, the place du jour, I guess, not the kind of joint I would ever go to but sort of interesting in a natural history way. They seated us at a banquette table, right side front, which is the supreme place to be in this particular beanery, a fact he related to me shortly after we sat down. He then told me which famous people were dining with us, cautioning me not to stare, which I was in any case not inclined to do, except I stared at Meryl Streep. Mark's shamelessness is a legend and is part of his charm.

There followed a good deal of tedious business with the captain, who came by to pay his compliments, and a discussion with the waiter about what we should eat and what wine was drinking well this week, to which the two of them gave not quite as much discussion as Eisenhower held with his aides on the subject of D-day. I let them order for me. This done, Mark gave me a rundown on his business and dropped a dozen or so boldfaced names, which were largely lost on me, although when he observed this he helpfully provided the identifying surnames for the various Bobs and Donnas and Brads so dropped. Business was apparently booming. The art market was going nuts again: the sixteen-thousand-square-foot houses that people of a certain standing now require have lots of wall space that cannot be left blank, and since the rich are no longer paying taxes, money was squirting through New York like a firehose and a lot of it was going into high-end art.

Then we talked about his current artist, young Mono; he asked me what I thought. I told him wallpaper of a superior grade; he laughed. It's his pretense that I'm opposed to nonrepresentational art on principle, like Tom Wolfe—I've never been able to explain to him why that's not the case—and he spent a while bending my ear about the dynamic values and hidden wit of his kid's wallpaper. Asked me how I was doing, I told him about the *Vanity Fair* fiasco but left out the part about the show at Lotte's—he's always trying to get me in with him in a business way and I won't do it, don't ask me why.

I admitted I was in deep shit, no shame in that, maybe fifty grand in the hole, and he said he'd just gotten back from Europe, buying pictures, talked about hotels, the luxe life, a completely insensitive guy, yeah, but I know him a long time now. I asked him what he'd bought and he said he'd gotten a nice small Cerezo and a couple of Caravaggisti I'd never heard of, and some Tiepolo drawings almost good enough to be genuine—laughed here, just kidding, but you have to be a shark over there, everyone wants to sell you a missing Rubens, and I said it sounded like a perilous life.

Then he asked me if I could work fresco and I said I hadn't in a while, not since I'd done the St. Anthony seminary out on the Island with my father when I was a kid, and why was he asking, and he said he had a nice little project for me if I could get away to Europe, an Italian zillionaire he'd met in Venice had bought a palazzo with a Tiepolo ceiling in bad shape, ruined really, and he might be able to get me in there, and I said I wasn't interested, and he said, you didn't ask how much.

So I asked, and he said a hundred and fifty grand. He had a "gotcha" look in his eye that I hated, and I said I might be interested but it couldn't be for a while, after Christmas really, because I was committed to participating in a drug study being run by Shelly Zubkoff. When he heard the name he laughed and we did the whole "small world" thing that people do in New York, and he asked about it and I told him the story of what had gone down while I was on the drug. He pumped me pretty dry on the subject, which I thought was a little funny because Mark mainly likes to talk about himself and *his* experiences. He said it sounded a little scary and I agreed that it did, but I still wanted to go on with it because of the effect it was having on my painting.

So we ate minuscule portions of pretentious food, the sort of stuff that Lotte calls gourmet cat food, and drank a lot of expensive Chambertin, and he filled me in on the gossip of the art world, who was up, rising, falling, or down, and while he talked I could not (as he'd obviously intended) get out of my mind the prospect of earning a hundred and fifty grand for a month or so of work.

I said, "Okay, you got me, tell me more about this palazzo job."

And he did, and it turned out that the palazzo had been vacant for a while and the roof leaked and the ceiling had essentially collapsed, so it wasn't a restoration job exactly but more like a reproducing job. Which kind of pissed me off, because it was getting into the forgery zone, but he said, "Not at all, no way, not only do we have a photo of the ceiling, but we even have Tiepolo's original cartoons for the thing, you'll be one with the masters, except with electricity."

"You know this Italian guy personally?" I asked.

"Castelli," he said, "Giuseppe. He's big in cement and construction, builds airports, bridges, like that."

"But do you know him?"

"Not as such. I met him at a dinner Werner Krebs organized in Rome. That name mean anything to you?"

"No. Should it?"

"Probably not. He's an art dealer. Old masters. Very big in Europe, private sales, multimillion-dollar level."

"Well, that lets me out of his circle, being a young master myself."

"Yeah, you could say that. You know, Wilmot, you're a fucking piece of work. You're always broke, you do shit magazine work for peanuts, and all the time you're sitting on a million-dollar talent. Christ, you could be another Hockney."

"Maybe I don't want to be another Hockney."

"Why not, for crying out loud? Look, you want to do representational? You think I can't sell representational? There are people dying for representational work. They only buy the conceptual and abstract shit because they think they should, because people like me tell them to buy it. But they hate it, if you really want to know the truth; what they'd really like is an old master, or a Matisse, or a Gauguin, something where they don't have to read the artist's statement to know what's going on. I'm talking people who have a million, a million and a half to spend on art. It's a huge fucking market. Why aren't you getting rich off it?"

I finished my glass of wine and filled the glass again. "I don't know," I said lamely. "Whenever I think about doing another gallery show it makes me sick. I want to get drunk, dope myself into oblivion."

"You ever think about seeing someone about that little problem?"

"A shrink. Yeah, oh, Doctor, save me, I can't participate in the corruption of the art market! Vermeer had the same problem, you'll recall. He did about one painting a year, and when he could bring himself to sell one, sometimes he used to go and try to buy it back. Then his wife would take the painting back to the buyer and beg him for the money again."

"So he was a nut. So was van Gogh. What does that prove? We're talking about you, the Luca Giordano of our age."

"The who?"

"Luca Giordano, the painter, Neapolitan, late seventeenth century. Hey, you're an art major. You took Italian painting in the seventeenth."

"I must've been out that day. What about him?"

"Fastest brush in the west, and he could imitate any style. They called him the Thunderbolt, or Luca *Fá Presto*, Luca Go Faster. Interesting guy, a major influence on Tiepolo, as a matter of fact. Never developed a real style of his own, but that didn't matter, because if you wanted a sort of Rubens, or a sort of Ribera, Luca was the man to see. He once did a Durer that was sold as a genuine Durer, and then he told the guy who bought it that he'd done it."

"Why would he do that?"

"Because he wasn't a forger. The client took him to court for fraud, but Luca got off when he showed the judge that he signed the painting with his own name and covered it with a layer of paint, and also that he never personally stated it was a Durer. He left that to the so-called experts. The judge threw the case out of court. After that it was balls to the wall for Luca; he imitated just about every famous artist of his time, and the previous generation too: Veronese, the Caraccis, Rembrandt, Rubens, Tintoretto, Caravaggio—especially Caravaggio. And always with the hidden signature, so he could skate on any forgery charges. When he was court painter to Carlos the Second in Spain, he forged a Bassano from a private collection, a picture he knew that the king wanted, and after it got bought he told the king it was a fake and showed him the hidden signature. The king cracked up, he thought it was terrific and complimented him on his talent. I mean, the guy was a rogue, but a genius with a brush."

"So are you paying me a compliment with this comparison?" I asked. "Or is it a put-down?"

"I don't know," he said slyly. "However you want to take it. Meanwhile, I'm sitting here with a guy who could make literally millions off his talent and he's pissing it away with hack work, and when he finally does a show, hallelujah, he does it at his ex-wife's low-end gallery. It offends my professional dignity, is what it is, like if I was a theatrical agent and I went to a coffee shop every day and there was Julia Roberts or Gwyneth Paltrow slinging hash. What is this gorgeous woman doing here, I'd ask myself, and I'd want to do something about it. Not to mention you're an old pal."

"How did you know I was having a show at Lotte's?"

He shrugged. "I have my ways. Very little goes on in the art world in the city that I don't get to hear about. Anyway, I don't want to be a bore about it, but if you ever want to get your hands on some serious money . . . for example, did I tell you my idea about almost–old masters?"

I said he hadn't and he told me.

"Let's say you're a guy who's clearing, say, ten million a year in, I don't know, real estate or Wall Street, whatever. There're fifty thousand guys like that in the city, right? This guy's got everything, the apartment, the house on the Island, the car, his kids are going to the top schools, he's got a small collection of important pieces, modern stuff, but appreciating pretty well—"

"Which he bought on your recommendation, of course."

He laughed. "Of course. We stipulate the guy's sharp. So what this guy can't buy yet is major art: Cézanne, van Gogh, Picasso, they're all out of range, not to mention Rembrandt, Breughel, the old masters. It's a gap in his self-image. Also, let's say his wife likes traditional furnishings. He can't hang a Butzer or a Miyake up there, it'd look like shit. But what if I can sell him a nice little Cézanne fake, a nice almost-Reni madonna, the gilt frame, the little brass light above it. No one but an expert can tell it from the real thing. Obviously, we're not going to do *Girl with the Red Hat* or the *Mona Lisa*, not at all. We're going to do obscure stuff, small but beautiful. The guests come in and they say, 'Hey, is that a Cézanne?' And our guy says, 'It may be. I picked it up for a song.'"

"These will be signed?"

He wrinkled his face disapprovingly. "Of *course* not signed! Jesus, that's all I need! No, it'd be exactly like, you know, fake gems, cubic zirconiums. A woman has a forty-carat ring, she doesn't wear it to the grocery store or the country club. It's in a vault and she wears a custom-made fake, which all her friends accept because one, they all do the same thing, and two, because they know she's got the real jewels. So our guy is demonstrating he's got taste, and also—and this is the big selling point—maybe he's got a *lot* more money than his pals thought, because look what's on the walls—Cézanne, Corot. What do you think?"

"I think it's a terrific idea, Mark. It's pretentious and false, yet at the same time completely legal. I can't think of another gallery owner who could have come up with it."

Mark sells a lot of irony but he has a little trouble actually getting it in real life. He gave me a big smile.

"You really think so? That's great. So, are you interested? I mean, in doing some pieces."

"Let me ask you something first: I ran into Jackie Moreau the other day and he said you'd set him up with a hot deal in Europe doing paintings in many styles, as he put it. Was that what you're talking about now?"

Mark waved his hand dismissively. "No, that was something completely different. I mean, Jackie's okay, but he's no you. So what do you say? Are you in?"

"No, sorry."

"No? Why the fuck not?"

"I just don't think I'd like the work. And . . . I've got some big projects I want to work on now and I might not have the time."

He swallowed this lie, or seemed to, and shrugged. "Okay, man, but if you ever want to make some serious cash, give me a call. Meanwhile, I'll set up this Castelli thing. Who knows, it could turn into something for you."

"Who knows, indeed," I said, and then the waiter bustled up and we had to have a conversation about dessert. Over this, Mark wanted to know more about salvinorin, so I gave him the short version of what Shelly had given me, and then he asked me why I thought I'd stopped visiting my own past and started visiting what seemed to be the past of someone else, and I said I didn't know, but the sense of it was like being inside a baroque painting, maybe late cinquecento, and then I mentioned that the place I was in was a real place and that I'd looked the address up on Google, Calle Padre Luis Maria Llop, in Seville, and his eyes bulged out when I said that. Slotsky's a fucking encyclopedia of art history, and he asked me whether I knew what the kid's name was, and I said yeah, he said it was Gito de Silva, and Mark said, "Holy shit!"

So I go, "Oh, you heard of this guy Gito de Silva? I mean, he's a painter?"

And he goes, "You could say that. 'Gito' is a short form of 'Diegito,' 'little Diego.' He was born in Seville at number one Calle Padre Luis

Maria Llop in 1599," and when he said that I swear there were sparks coming out of his eyes. And he goes on, "His father was Juan de Silva, just like you said, but because it was the custom in Seville to use your mother's name professionally, when he started painting he called himself Diego Velázquez."

So, okay, I'd been painting like Velázquez recently and I must have had him on my mind and that's where that came from. I explained that to Slotsky and he said, "Yeah, but you didn't know all that stuff until I told you about it; where did *that* come from?"

I said, "I must have read it somewhere, what other explanation is there?"

He shook his head. "No, you're really going back in time, you said yourself that it was real, not like a vision or a fantasy, your dad's funeral and all that; maybe you're in some psychic contact with Diego Velázquez."

And I said, "I didn't know you believed in that shit," and he said, "I don't, but it makes you think, maybe your mind is preparing you to paint like Velázquez."

I said, "My mind would do something like that, one more thing to fuck up my life and get me to produce even more unsalable paintings." So we had a laugh about that and he bugged me a little more about selling my stuff through him until he saw I wasn't paying attention.

Well, that was an interesting day, followed by a restless night. I couldn't fall asleep. I had a strange sort of vibrational energy, like my life was going to change radically, and I'm resisting the urge to fight it, to take a pill, for example, a couple of pinks out of the trove of Xanax I had from my rehab days. I'd made a damned fool of myself at Lotte's, and afterward I was thinking maybe it would be different if I had some real money, because the plain fact is that for all her business about the purity of art, Lotte hates being poor, especially because of

Milo and the medical expenses. So it was kind of strange that just then up steps Slotsky with this offer.

So I thought then that this thing with Slotsky could be the solution—if I could just get a little ahead, get free of this crazy rat race, maybe then I could, I don't know, get back to that place again, when I was painting for love; maybe that's the place to start.

That Friday—I remember it was October first—I had the kids for the weekend again so Lotte could do her show. No smoking around the kids, so I was covered with nicotine patches, and it wasn't the same; they made me slightly sick all the time, and there was none of the good stuff about smoking, the taste and the look of the smoke curling upward that mysteriously unlocks the creative process.

After dinner, I called my sister Charlie at her place in Washington. She always likes to talk to the kids, and after they'd had their chatter, I got on with her. She asked me how I was doing and I said fine, and she said, you don't sound fine, she's using her "sisdar," as we used to call it, and I kind of gave a nervous laugh and said yeah, something's happening. And I told her about the drug trial and seeing her again at our father's funeral and Mom again when she was young, and I asked her what she thought was going on, Charlie always my gateway into the strange, and she asked me what she'd said when we talked back then (or just the other day, depending on how you looked at it). I told her we'd talked about her life and how she was thinking about leaving her order and doing something else, and she said, yeah, I remember that conversation, it was an important conversation, I was really confused about my vocation and talking it out with you really helped, and I said, I didn't recall it at all until it happened again.

Then I asked her what she made of the Velázquez stuff and she asked me what Velázquez meant to me, and I said, he was a great painter, you know, Rembrandt, Vermeer, Velázquez . . . and she said, "No, what he means to *you*, what he represents."

I said, "What, you think it's some kind of Freudian thing, I'm fantasizing being Velázquez because I want a substitute father, my father didn't love me enough?"

"I don't know what I think yet, although I'm a little concerned you're playing around with your brain, given your history with drugs."

"It's not the same thing at all—this is a perfectly safe experimental drug under medical supervision."

"Well, they would say that, wouldn't they? Anyway, you had plenty of love. You were everyone's golden child."

"You always say that, but I never felt it. I always felt like the prize in a grab bag or the ball in soccer. I think they spent a lot of time competing for me. I thought you were the one they loved."

"Oh, please! Plain, gawky Charlotte, who could barely finger paint, in a house where beauty and talent were the be-all and end-all? And Mother actively disliked me, if you recall."

"I must have missed that. Why did she?"

"Because I was the thing that trapped her into her marriage. She didn't have the guts to face the social death that would follow ditching a kid, and besides, I worshipped Dad. Hopelessly, of course. Why I fled into the Church, or so I tell myself. I think I probably warped you more than they did, the way I doted on you. Your total slavey. Spoiled you rotten for a normal woman, may God forgive me."

"Yeah, I remember *that*," I said. "I used to think we would grow up and get married. You remember that time when you explained to me that it didn't work that way? I must've been six or so, and I went wailing away. We were on the beach out at the point and I got lost."

"Oh, yes, I couldn't forget that. You got cosseted and I got a whipping for losing you. As I say, spoiled rotten."

"Of course, now that there *are* no more rules, maybe we should try it. The kids love you, anyway . . ."

Raucous laughter, she's got a big booming laugh like a man, like our father, in fact, and it went on for a while, and then she said, breathless, "I'm sorry, I was just imagining myself in the archepiscopal palace: 'Um, Archbishop, I know we just got through the process of releasing me from my formal vows, but there *is* one other little thing . . .'"

"So it's a possibility?"

Another hoot. "If it were, my lad, I wouldn't have you on a plate. You're far too hard on the girls."

"I beg your pardon—I happen to be nice as pie."

"In your dreams, bozo. You're exactly the kind of wonderfully decent guy who somehow manages to totally destroy any woman he gets involved with. How do you do it? It's beyond me, unfamiliar as I am with the ways of men, but you know, I always thought you and Lotte were going to last."

"Oh, Lotte! I thought we were sort of making up, but now she hates me again."

And I told her about our fight in the gallery in some detail and she went, "You said *what?*"

I said, "Well, you know, she was going on about how I never got to be the rich and famous artist that my so-called talent warranted, like she always does—"

"That's not what you just said at all. You said she was talking about you ruining your gift, so it curdled, not about being a success and famous."

"What's the difference?"

"Oh, Christ Jesus, give me strength! What's the difference? The difference is the heart of life, you dunce! Don't you understand, that woman would scrub floors, she'd do anything short of whoring on the street so you could paint what you wanted to? Don't you understand anything about love at all? I'm surprised she didn't brain you with a hammer."

"I don't understand," I said.

"Yes, I know, but I have some work to do and I haven't time to explain it all just now—not that you'd listen, not that you listened the last fifty times I tried . . ."

"Work? It's nighttime."

"Not in Uganda it isn't."

"As usual, blowing me off for the distant poor."

A long sigh. "Oh, Chaz, you know I love you and you take terrible advantage of it. If I'm sharp it's a form of self-protection. And also, when you spend time with desperate, starving, brutalized people who pass their short, shitty lives wailing over dying children, you tend to lose patience with brilliant neurotics who can't seem to find a way to be happy. Good night, baby brother."

"What is this, you stop being a nun and that gives you a ticket to be extra mean? You used to be nice."

"The nice got all burnt up in Africa. God bless, kid."

She hung up. I'm always strangely invigorated when Charlie gives me a spanking. Probably part of our sick quasi-incestuous relationship. But that was the last time I talked to her for a real long time.

On Saturday afternoon I took the kids to MoMA; Milo asked for an audio guide and wandered off, and I took Rose and was her audio guide myself. She wanted to know what the pictures were *really* about, and I had to make up a representational story for each one. I think that shows something about what we want in art. She didn't whine once, a patient kid, an art lover maybe, but I think mostly it was having a monopoly on Dad for a couple of hours, looking at art. Oldenburg was of course a favorite—who doesn't like gigantic silly everyday objects—but also Matisse and Pollock. She tells me Pollock's big *Number 31* is *really* about a little mouse, and a story went with this appreciation, pointing out the various places where the mousie had adventures in the tangled grass; I wish I could have got it down, it would have revolutionized Pollock scholarship.

After that, lunch and went to watch Buster Keaton movies. Rose announced afterward she is going to be an artist like me, but better, watching my face for signs of dismay, which I provided, then she held her thumb and fingers up barely separate and said just a *little* better. Milo did his Steven Wright jokes on the street and subway, he has the timing and the deadpan down cold. Terrible to love your kids this much, and this mixed with guilt because of the mess I made of Toby—maybe if I'd spent more time with him, but I had to work like a demon in the city to keep up the damn house and all that, which we bought in the first place so he could have a happy childhood among the birds and bunnies.

Around eleven that night Lotte called from the gallery and said three of the five actress paintings had been sold, for five grand apiece.

"Mark bought the Kate Winslet Velázquez three minutes after he walked in the door," she said. "He insisted on taking it off the wall right then and paid us extra for the trouble. I had to wrap it in brown paper and he walked out with it clasped to his chest like a girl with a new dolly."

"That's strange," I said. "Mark usually plays it fairly cool. He must've had a customer in mind. Or we'll see it in his gallery marked up two thousand percent. Who bought the others?"

"Some media mogul and his girlfriend. This is wonderful, Chaz, you know? Everyone loved them!"

I tried to be enthusiastic for Lotte's sake. The money's nice, but not so nice the thought that I could paint these things forever, maybe add a male line, Cruise and Travolta by suitable masters, and wouldn't that solve all my money problems? I could go back on dope too, really crank the fucking things out, and I looked at Milo and listened to him drag each breath in while he slept and thought, How can I be such a selfish piece of shit, not to fucking burn myself to a crisp to buy him absolutely top-of-the-line medical care. I don't understand anything.

Except that in between my little domestic and parental tasks, and despite my obsessional shit about making money, I was boiling with ideas, filling page after page of my sketchbook. I was practically nauseous with the flow of creative juice; it started with those silly paintings, images of fame. I mean really, what is the world now? I mean visually. Image after image on the screen, but the kicker is we aren't allowed to see them, I mean actually study them long enough to derive meaning, it's all quick cut and on to the next one, which essentially destroys all judgment, all reflection.

By design, I think. I mean, what does the president *actually* look like, what does anything actually look like? You can't get it in a photograph, or only a hint, and so there was opened up to me a whole potential universe of realistic, penetrating, analytic painting, picking it up where Eakins left it, but adding all the stuff painting's done since. You'd have to push it, but not like Bacon did, or Rivers, or that new kid, Cecily Brown, not so obvious, not the screaming Pope, not so on the nose—what if you pushed it from *inside*, up from the hidden structure of the painting? So that it worked subliminally almost, like Velázquez, it would be devastating, yeah, if you could bring it off, you could light up this whole blighted era. *Neue Neue Sachlichkeit*. If anyone can still see.

On Sunday morning I took the kids over to Chinatown for dim sum, and in the restaurant Milo started coughing. I thought he had something caught in his throat, and I got up and he threw his head back with his tubes all shut down and started to go blue around the lips, and I dropped him down and did CPR until the paramedics came. His face was gray by then, and matte, like a bag of lint. Then at the NYU Medical Center when they heard I didn't have health insurance they were going to ship him over to Bellevue after they got him stabilized and I said he had familial progressive pulmonary dystrophy and he'd been treated here before, and I made the stupid woman call Dr. Ehrlichman and she took my credit card grudgingly—she'd have been even more grudging if she knew it was blown. I called Lotte from the hospital and before I could say anything she told me I'd sold out, little red dots on all five actresses, and this time I didn't even pretend I gave a shit and told her about our boy. So she came to the ward and we waited until we knew he was going to survive this one, and she stayed and I took Rose back to my loft.

After Rose was asleep I sat out on the fire escape in my parka chain-smoking and thought about being the kid Velázquez—funny what the mind constructs, another thing to talk with Shelly about. After smoking my throat raw, I went back through the window into the loft and sat at my desk and calculated my riches: twenty-five grand for the actresses plus the kill fee Condé Nast promised makes 30K, enough to pay off the really embarrassing debts, and Slotsky's job in Italy will fix everything for the indefinite future; I'd have to stick Lotte with the whole child-care load for a while, but what else can I do? She won't mind if there's serious money involved, she's got the nanny. I thought I could finally get even with the fucking medical bills and have a chance to take a breath.

Two days after that the magazine sent the kill fee: amazingly fast pay, they must feel guilty as hell. Lotte deposited the checks for the paintings, so I was flush for about twenty minutes before I started writing my own checks. The IRS ought to get nearly half of it, both for back taxes and this year's estimated, but I couldn't bear to pay it. Let them come and get me. Instead I got up to date with Suzanne— my more present parasite—then the rent, phone, and paying down the four credit cards, laden with medical bills, Milo's plastic lifeline, and then around town with a stack of cash for all the people who let me have a flying hundred never expecting to see it again.

And Milo was out of the hospital, looking like old oatmeal. I spent some time with him, trying to cheer him up, and of course, he cheered *me* up, which is the usual case with us. He cheered up Ewa the nanny too, who has a tendency to Slavic depression at the best of times, but thank God for her anyway. Ewa from Kraków, one of the rare Polish maidens who, applying for a job as a child-care worker in America, actually obtained such a job rather than a slot in one of the slave brothels that seem to be one of the more common features of globalization.

I don't know what it is about a sick kid that's so hard for us moderns to deal with; it's that core of irony that makes real grief almost impossible, you think, oh, how banal, like your life was a novel and this was a cheap literary trick, and of course we don't really have religion anymore, or I don't. I recall reading something that Hemingway wrote, to the effect that if your son dies you can't read the *New Yorker* anymore. It's grinding, grinding, I have these demonic thoughts like wishing he was a little piece of shit instead of the most perfect kid in the world, beautiful and talented and good, just stone decent all the way to the center of him, so it wouldn't rip me up like it does, but maybe the parents of awful kids don't feel that way, you see moms of serial killers weeping for their babies in the courtrooms. Where does he get it from, that cheerful grace? What is it, the booby prize from God almighty? You only get to live for twelve years, sucker, so here's an extra helping of the Holy Spirit? Another topic I planned to discuss with Charlotte.

After I dropped the kids off in Brooklyn I took the subway up to the med school. When I checked in the secretary said Dr. Zubkoff would like to see you before you go in for your session, and pointed the way. Shelly was in his office; he motioned me to a seat and brought out a file. The usual small talk, and then he said, "Let's talk about these past-life hallucinations you're having."

I said, "Yeah, if you want to call them that."

He said, "What would you call them?" in that patient doc tone of voice.

"I relive the past," I said. "It's not me, as I am now, having hallucinations. I'm really *in* my former self, reliving a moment, whether I can recall the incident now or not. It's a real experience."

"I see. How is that different from a vivid dream, or a waking hallucination?"

I said, "You tell me, you're the doctor. How do I know *you're* not a hallucination? How do I know I'm not locked in a rubber room somewhere, fantasizing all this? You remember what Hume said about the limits of empirical observation."

The doctor was not amused. He said, "Let's just take it as given that the world is real, and external to us, and that we're both sitting here. And I understand the vividness of the salvinorin experience. It's been reported extensively in the literature. What I'm a little concerned about is this most recent run, where according to your report you experienced what seemed to be someone *else's* past."

It turned out this was not a normal reaction to the drug and he was hot to pump me about it. I told him what I went through last time and what Slotsky had said about the probable identity of Gito de Silva, and added that I was in the middle of the lushest creative run of my entire life.

This got him all excited and he gave me a lot of neurological information that I couldn't follow, but the main point was that he thought that it was all a matter of various brain regions responding to the chemical stimulus and that I was constructing the past experiences as a result. It was like dreams, he said, the actual stimulus for dreaming is just random brain noise, and we interpret this noise as imagery and events.

"Yeah, that might explain me reliving my own past," I said, "but it doesn't deal with me reliving the past of Diego Velázquez."

He gave me what I thought was a strange look and said, "We don't know a lot about the subjective effects of the drug. That's the point of the study."

"Not much of an answer," I said, and he sort of withdrew a little behind the professional Kevlar and said, "Well, you're a painter, and you're having a kind of fantasy about being a famous painter. It's merely an enhancement of what we see every week on *American Idol*."

"You think it's a wish-fulfillment fantasy?"

"What else could it be?" he said, and he had me there. "But let's lower the dosage, shall we? You seem to be particularly sensitive to the drug."

Then he had to go do something and he handed me over to Harris, who ushered me into one of the little rooms.

I lay down on the couch. She arranged her tray of little beakers, selected one, and said, "Would you mind if we put you in some light restraints? It's for your own safety."

I said I didn't mind at all, and after I had chewed my wad, she placed Velcro bands around my wrists and across my chest. Then the usual floating sensation, and then I'm standing at a table grinding massicot into a fine powder using a stone mortar and pestle. The four casement windows of the room were lately barred with shutters, but now the fighting in the city has died away and there is light again to do this work. I feel the grit of the bright yellow powder with my fingers. It isn't fine enough, so I keep grinding. The old man will not beat me if I don't do it right, but that doesn't matter. I must do it right, I must please him, because it's my duty, and the honor of my family demands it. Honor is like a constant pressure, sometimes between my eyes, sometimes in my gut, like a live thing, like life itself.

The fighting was about the Immaculate Conception, which means the Blessed Virgin was born without original sin. I believe this, and it gives me an almost physical comfort even though I don't really understand the theology. I know that some in the city deny the Immaculate Conception, and that's why there was a small war here. I saw beaten and dead people on the street, and I wished that I was a man so that I could fight for the Blessed Virgin too and kill the bad people who deny her glory in this way. Mary's honor and my family's honor and my own honor are all tied together into that solid feeling in my center.

I am a hidalgo, a son of someone, I am noble on both sides of my family, of pure Christian blood, and this thought is a constant undercurrent of all my thoughts, like my name, or my family's history, or the positions of my limbs.

I finish the grinding and place the pigment carefully in a stoppered jar. I go into another room, where there is an elderly man staring at an uncompleted painting: my master, Old Herrera. I tell him I have finished grinding and say that if he has nothing else for me to do I would beg his leave to go out drawing in the plaza. He waves me away. He is no longer interested in me, because he knows I can already draw and paint better than he can himself and that I will not ever work for him so that he can profit from my skill.

I put on my hat and cloak and call out for my servant, Pablo. In a minute or so he comes out from the kitchen, smelling of smoke and grease. He is a boy a little older than me, dark skin, greasy black hair, wearing my cast-off clothes, which are too small for him. I feel a kind of affection for him, but also I feel that he is not really a person like I am, more like a superior kind of dog, or a donkey. I understand also that there are those, the grandees, who feel the same way about me, and this thought is like an intolerable itch. I wish to rise in the world.

I order Pablo to pick up the box and portfolio I use for drawing, and we go out, him following behind me at a suitable distance. We go to the plaza. It's a market day and the stalls are full of tradesmen and women selling vegetables, fish, meat, leather, and household goods. I sit down on a keg of salted fish in the shade of a fishmonger's awning. I open my box, set up my inkhorn, and point a reed pen with my penknife. I draw piles of fish, cockles, oysters, an octopus, the fishwife. Later I tell Pablo to adopt different postures and make faces, and I draw these too. The local people are used to me doing this, but often a stranger will pass and look at what I have drawn, and sometimes there will sound a soft oath from behind me. Sometimes a woman will cross herself. Many people find what I can do disturbing, it is too much like God, they think, to make things that look like life itself. But it is from God and the Virgin that I have this gift.

And I am painting the Virgin now, the first large painting I have been allowed to do, and I stop, my brush stutters, and I am struck with a memory from my days with Herrera, of grinding paint and then going out to draw in the market. It is very strange; I have not thought of him for two minutes since I became Don Pacheco's student, and suddenly this burst of fresh memory. It has been nearly five years I've been with him, and this painting will be my masterpiece for entry into the painter's guild of Seville. Of course it has to be a religious painting for that. The memory vanishes in a flash, like a street magician making a bowl of fruit disappear with a flourish of his cloth, and I shiver as if someone has walked on my grave.

I resume painting. The thing is not bad, better than anyone else in Seville can do, but not entirely satisfying. There is a stiffness in the figure that I don't care for, but this is how it is done with Virgins, and she stands on a globe, which is unnatural to begin with, so perhaps the stiffness is part of what the good sisters at the Shod Carmelites expect. I've made her hair like that of Don Pacheco's daughter. There have been hints this year that she would not be adverse to a proposal. I think it will happen. It's important to have friends, and my master knows everyone who paints in Seville and even in Madrid, and he has connections with powerful people. A man he knows, Don Juan de Fonseca, has been chaplain to His Majesty. What could be more wonderful and full of honor than to wait upon the king himself!

I step back from the painting to examine the balance of the masses. More clouds on the left, I think. The face does not look *too* much like Juana de Miranda de Pacheco, that would be impious, but it is the same kind of face, and a real woman's face too, not the doll face you see painted by the religious artists of Seville.

I load my brush with lead and lay in more clouds, blending the white into the ochre of the background. Already I am thinking of my next piece, a John the Evangelist for the same convent. Don Pacheco has written that John should be an old man, but I am going to paint him as a young fellow. I will use as a model a market porter of my own age, a man I've used before in my *bodegones*. I think the nuns will like to look at a young man. In any case in a short time I will be my own master and can paint what I like.

And now I have a strange feeling, the room is somehow too small, there is a tightness across my chest, I have to escape from my clothes, and a woman's voice is calling out, "Relax, relax, it's all right!" and I was struggling against my restraints as the room and the couch I was on seemed to toss around like a boat in a gale.

"It's all right," said Harris repeatedly, and after a while, "Are you okay now?"

"Drink," I croaked. My throat was clawky with the taste of the drug and an intolerable dryness. I asked for water and she unwrapped my hand and gave me a plastic pint bottle, which I drank dry.

"How long was I out?"

She checked an electronic stopwatch. "Eighteen minutes. What happened?"

"Nothing. I was painting something."

She untied me, gave me the usual clipboarded form, and asked, "What were you painting?"

But now I found myself unwilling to share the details of my experience with these people. I mean really, they were trying to determine the effects of the drug on creativity, and I was perfectly willing to go on about that and fill out their tests and forms, but this stuff was really none of their business.

"It was just a painting, Harris," I snapped. "What the fuck does it matter what it was? You can't buy and sell it—it's all in my head."

"You're feeling aggressive," she said in that clinical tone.

"No, aggressive would be if I broke this goddamn clipboard over your head. And yeah, I'm being a pain in the ass because we artists are often a pain in the ass. If you wanted docile you should've brought in a bunch of kindergarten teachers. Now get out of here and let me finish this shit so I can go home!"

She flushed bright pink, started to say something, but turned and left the room. I finished the form and then I noticed that she'd left the tray full of little beakers with the gauze sponges in them, and there was a large covered jar on the tray with some code numbers on it.

I opened it, and for some reason I pulled out a couple of the damp sponges and stripped out a latex glove from a dispenser and shoved them inside it. I don't know why I did this; maybe it was Shelly saying he was going to cut my dosage. I didn't like that. Something about being Velázquez was—I won't say *addictive*, but compelling. I wanted more of it, not less.

I left the lab with the kitten-licking feeling under my skull more intense than before—maddening not to be able to scratch it—also hyped, energetic, like speed coming on, but without that jaw-grinding thing; I felt fine, spring in my step and all that. For a while after I got off the subway I wandered through Chinatown, drawing the markets, the piles of fish and fruits. I was trying to recapture the feeling I'd just had as the boy Velázquez and it was great, and when I got back to my loft I stretched a big canvas, over five by seven feet. I sized it with glue mixed with carbon black, and when it was dry I put on a thin layer of iron oxide, red lake, and carbon black, mixed with powdered lime-stone. Paint like Velázquez, prep like Velázquez. This took all day and into the evening. I was hungry, so I went out and got something in Chinatown and then came back and put on my lamps and stared at the vast thing for a while. I looked through my recent sketchbooks, but the ideas I thought I'd had seemed to have vanished. I kept feeling Lotte peering over my shoulder, expectant, ready to offer love again if I would just be true to the real Chaz. That or make a lot of money, I thought, hiding behind the cynicism.

I paced, I filled an ashtray with butts, a couple of times I picked up a charcoal and stood in front of the thing, waiting for the power to kick in, and after a while I got impatient and took one of the sponges from my rubber glove.

I lay down on my daybed and chewed it, and no out-of-body experience this time, nothing freaky, except the colors seemed to get a little sharper and brighter, the edges between patches of color sort of glowing, and that kitten-licking thing in my head, and I was sitting in psych class, late spring in my sophomore year in a classroom in Schermerhorn Hall, warm breezes in through the windows and the professor gabbing on about how human existence was just a lot of operant conditioning, the mind was an illusion, and the rest of that tedious and fallacious story, and I was ignoring him and concentrating on drawing a girl sitting across the aisle from me, terrific neck, like Nefertiti, and her hair piled up on her head, streaky blond, with bright little pennants from it tossing in the breeze from the open windows, a slight overbite to the mouth, very nice, pale eyes, she knows I'm drawing her and she's holding the pose. I'm working with a soft pencil on cartridge paper, using my thumb to blend it in; the chin's a bit weak, but I'm correcting that, the magic of drawing, it's what she wishes she looked like, but still a fair likeness, as the professor drones on, though now his voice slips into a lower register and he's reading from the lives of the saints, St. Cecilia, whose day it is, and I'm drawing the king of Spain.

The friar reads on and from a distance sounds the plashing of a fountain; I'm in a room in the Alcázar. To one side is a lectern at which stands the Dominican reading, in front of me His Majesty and a tall canvas I have primed with glue and black-lime mixture, and over that a priming of red earth, *tierra de Esquivias,* as they do here in Madrid. I am painting his face. His Majesty wears a suit of black, as is customary at court, with a narrow white ruff.

The friar comes to the end of his chapter and looks up to see the king's pleasure. His Majesty tells him to retire, for he wishes to converse with this painter.

So we speak. I am speaking with the king of Spain! I find I must grip the brush hard and my stick is trembling against the canvas. His left hand at hip, weight on left leg, an easy pose, a paper of state in his right hand. He graciously asks me of my home and family, of Don

Pacheco, of Don Juan Fonseca, and how things pass in Seville. Then we speak of paintings: the king wishes to have the finest collection in Europe, surpassing that of the king of France, and we speak of which painters are best for which subjects. I believe I do not make a complete fool of myself, nor yet vaunt myself about my station. He is younger than I by three years; I think he is not eighteen.

A courtier enters, whispers to the king. He says he must leave me and says further he has enjoyed our conversation and looks forward to the next time he sits for me. And smiles. Then, coming around to view my work, he studies the painted face, which of course I have spent the most time upon, and he says, "Don Diego, I know what I look like. See you paint me as I am." And touches me lightly upon the shoulder. The king has touched me! I am all in a sweat as he leaves. The Dominican gives me a baleful look and sweeps out too. My shoulder tingles still, and I realized I had slumped down in my chair and the edge of the computer desk was cutting into my shoulder.

I checked the clock on the machine. I'd been gone eight minutes, although I'd experienced at least an hour in subjective time. So then I thought, Okay, I was drawing as Velázquez but my canvas is still blank, could I maybe make myself actually *do* a painting in the here and now while I was having a Velázquez hallucination? Maybe if I stood in front of the canvas with my brush in my hand and took some more salvinorin? And maybe the stuff was cumulative, maybe I'd get deeper into it.

Into the mouth with my other dose, ten minutes of staring at the blankness, and then I started to draw. It'd be a group scene, I decided, eight guys just sitting around a saloon, no, at an outdoor party, like a wedding, just a bunch of regular guys who liked a belt or two after work, and the drawing went very fast, no detail, just blocking in the relative positions of the figures. After I'd got that down I mixed up a big batch of flake white and added a little ochre and azurite to it to make a neutral gray, and then I blocked in the outlines of the figures.

They say I can do only heads, and this is my answer to them. Carducho and the other royal painters, they mock me as an upstart who knows how to imitate nature but has no conception of how to make a true painting with ideas, in the Florentine style. All of them, Carducho, Caxés, and Nardi, will never forgive me for having won the competition His Majesty ordered for a painting of the expulsion of the Moors, and I have heard they were joking that I only won because I am a Moor myself, being from Seville, where there is so much impure blood.

Yet I am painter to the king and I am usher of the chamber, and will rise higher still. If these calumnies on my blood reach the king, he will not hear them; besides, I am well in with his grace the count-duke of Olivares, and his word should sustain me against all slanderers.

I finish the outlining and return to my apartment. I am short with Juana, as I always am when I am on a new painting and I go to bed early. Again these strange dreams of hell, monsters of noise and light that's neither from sun nor candle, infernal light that warps all colors into impossible shades. I go to mass early and pray that these dreams may cease, and then back to work, this time with models.

I have Antonio Rojas today, a mason, and I give him as much wine as he wants. He grins like an ape at me and I take his likeness quickly and then dismiss him with a clap on the back and fifty maravedí. Then comes in a butcher from the royal kitchen who I paint as my Bacchus.

When he has left me I look at the unfinished painting. There is something wrong with it, but I don't know what it is—perhaps the figures are too crowded together in the foreground, as if they were all sitting on a rail. I have tried to correct the composition, but it is still unsatisfying. The faces and figures are from nature and full enough of life, but the space they're in is not real space. There is a secret here

I don't know, and none of the fools who paint in this kingdom can advise me. Not that I would ask. Yet, God willing, His Majesty will like it, I think, and it's still better than anything Carducho ever did.

A boy comes in with a message from His Majesty and I must leave this and change my clothes to be fit for his presence. I believe he must have decided on the portrait of his late father that he mentioned on Friday last. That arm is not right either.

I came out of it walking down Canal Street in a cold rain, wearing a T-shirt and jeans and no shoes. When I got back to my loft I was not surprised to see my canvas was full of *Los Borrachos*, or *The Feast of Bacchus*, by Velázquez, not the completed painting, but the underpainting and two almost completed faces, the Bacchus and the guy in the middle with the sombrero and the drunken grin. The paint was still a little wet and you could see where he, or I, had repainted the peasant on the extreme right, giving him a new head, and where the figure in the back had just been painted in, in a failed attempt to give the whole thing more depth. I could see what he meant about Bacchus's arm—it was set into the shoulder a little wrong and the foreshortening was off a hair. The face was terrific, though.

I took a shower, changed my clothes, and carefully made myself a Gibson with my dad's silver shaker. Pearl onions are among the only foodstuffs in my refrigerator, those and olives, because sometimes I prefer a martini.

Thinking back, it occurred to me that I must've spent a couple of days at least in Velázquez's life this time, given the work on the painting, and so I was curious to see how much time I had actually spent in . . . can I still call it real time? The little screen on my answering machine told me that approximately thirty-four hours had passed since I had set up the canvas, something my belly was starting to confirm, and the Gibson was having an unusually powerful effect on my brain and balance. There were fifteen messages on my machine, said the little lights, and I ran through them and answered the one from Mark Slotsky.

"Where've you been, man?" he demanded when he answered his cell phone, before I could say my name. This still annoys me, that technology tells us who's on the phone, another little erosion of the social. There were saloon noises in the background. "I've been leaving messages," he added. "You heard I bought Kate?"

"Yeah, thanks. I presume you have a Winslet fan you're going to shop it to."

"A Velázquez fan, actually. Terrific piece of work."

"Yeah, right. Listen, can you come over now? I have something you ought to see."

"Now? I got Jackie Moreau here. We're at the Blue Orange. What've you got?"

"More Velázquez. Really, you need to see this."

He agreed and twenty minutes later the two of them came in, both antic with drink, but they quieted down when they saw what was on the easel.

"Jesus, Wilmot, what the fuck is this?" Mark said.

"What does it look like?"

"It looks like Velázquez's *Feast of Bacchus*, about a third finished." He looked around for a pinned-up reproduction, and when he didn't find one, he said, "You're copying it from *memory*?"

"I'm not copying it at all. I took some salvinorin and I was back in 1628 and I was *him*. Painting it, I mean, and when I came to this was on the easel. Pretty neat, huh?"

"It's incredible," Mark said, and leaned close to the painting, touching it tentatively with a fingertip. "Have you ever seen the radiographs of this thing? I mean the ones published in the literature."

"No," I said. "I'm not a scholar like you. Why do you ask?"

"Because what you got here is an early version, without the penti-menti. You know, if it wasn't fucking insane and impossible, I'd almost believe you were telling me the truth."

Jackie said, "Can you be other people too? Because if you were Corot or Monet you could have yourself a nice little business with this."

And we laughed, and then Mark stopped laughing and said, "What'll you take for it?"

"It's not finished," I said, "and it's not for sale."

"No, really. What'll you take for it?"

"Ten grand," I said, meaning it as a joke, but he whipped a check-book out of his jacket and wrote a check with a gold Montblanc the size of an antitank round.

I stared at the yellow slip of paper, stunned. "You think there's a market in unfinished old master copies?"

"There's a market for everything. All you have to do is create it."

I didn't know how to respond to that, so I turned to Jackie, who, like the sweet guy he is, was grinning like a monkey, enjoying my good fortune.

"I thought you were going to Europe," I said.

"Tomorrow. We were having a bon voyage at L'Orange Bleu when you called. You were invited, but you did not return all these calls."

I said, "Well, let's continue the party."

"Agreed," said Jackie. "And the drinks are on you."

There were a lot of drinks, and we closed the place and poured Jackie into a cab after he'd given us more than one Gallic embrace, with kisses. Then Mark hailed a cab of his own and told me he'd have some people come by for the painting in a week or so, when it'd be dry enough to move. I went back home and when I got there I took it off the easel and turned it to the wall. It was starting to freak me out a little.

The next day I was awakened from the sleep of the sot by a pounding on my loft door, and it was Bosco; he wanted to show me something, his latest. Nice to see a guy still excited about art, so I went down to take a look. He's been talking about doing this for a while, using the barrel of 9/11 dust he collected back then, a major critique of what he called the fascist hysteria that enabled the Iraq war.

In his loft the masturbating girls were gone (sold to some rich creep in Miami, he said), replaced by a huge Plexiglas case that must have measured ten by ten by twenty feet. It was equipped with lights and TV projectors and peopled with his trademark rag dolls. He made me sit down in front of it and switched it on.

A great show, I have to say. He had video loops of Bush and Giuliani playing on the faces of dolls dressed in clown suits, and video loops of the planes striking the twin towers projected on the background. He'd made pneumatic models of the twin towers that expanded upward and collapsed in spastic jerks. At the foot of one tower he'd built a little trackway on which tiny figures made up as

Orthodox Jews escaped from the building before each collapse and vanished down a miniature subway entrance. The air compressor that operated the towers also shot gusts of air to blow little Styrofoam dolls dressed as cops and firemen and civilians up into the air to fall down again, these figures suitably charred and blood spattered, complemented with tiny amputated heads and limbs. And he'd filled the whole box with the actual gray 9/11 dust, which made interesting clouds in the space above the yapping dummies as well as ever-shifting drifts on everything in the box. The sound track was a densely layered mix of politicians speaking, newscasters casting, explosions, and screams of anguish; from a separate speaker came hysterical laughter. This speaker was embedded in one of those amusement-park chortling torsos that used to grace penny arcades back in the forties. He'd re-dressed it as a Saudi Arab.

"What do you think?" he asked after I had stared some minutes.

"I think you've outdone yourself with respect to sheer offensiveness. It's as if Duchamp had presented his urinal filled with piss."

"You think so? Well, thanks, but I really wanted to rig it with gas—you know, for real flames? But I was worried about the dust igniting and also the gallery was freaked about the fire insurance. Maybe I could use colored foils or plastic film—it would flap pretty good in the breeze in there, you know, for a fiery effect."

"I think it's perfect as it is, and besides, you have the video projection of the actual flames. Are you really going to show this in a gallery?"

"Yeah, Cameron-Etzler's giving me the whole of their SoHo space next month. It's going to be big."

I told him that I thought it would be and left for my place, trying without much success to keep the envy out of my heart. I looked through my recent sketchbooks and thought about what Chaz would paint if he were going to get big, recalling my recent subway thoughts, that notion of deep analysis of modern faces using traditional techniques. How to generate dignity and keep from descending into kitsch? *Man Ordering Pizza. Woman Looking for Metrocard.* Is it still possible? Not anything like photorealism, no, everything steel but the breastplates, the bumpers on the cars all phony, a copy of a Kodachrome slide flashed onto the canvas. Structure, weight, authority, the authority of the paint applied on a living surface: *sprezzatura.* Velázquez's dwarfs and grotesques, revive the *bodegones* but with what we've experienced in the past centuries added—it has to show on the faces. I smoked half a pack and filled my paper shredder with sketches, but nothing came, and after a while I gave up and went out.

The next three weeks passed in the same state of suspended animation. I did a little job for the *Observer,* Bush as Pinocchio with the long nose in the manner of Disney, with the other characters as current pols, and passed up a couple of other similarly distinguished jobs, living on the ten grand I'd gotten from Mark, hoping I'd have a breakthrough before I had to leave for Italy to do the fresco. But no dice; everything I did looked like shit, and someone else's shit at that.

To increase the torment, one Sunday I took the kids to the Metropolitan's American figurative painting show. Milo waltzed off with his electronic art critic pressed to his ear, trailing his little oxygen tank on wheels, and Rosie breathed God's own air but had only me to tell her about art. The place was jammed; everyone loves figurative painting in their secret heart, even mediocre pieces, although practically everyone makes the mistake of confusing the mere image with painting as art.

They had big posters up with remarks from the famous artists. Richard Diebenkorn had this to say: "As soon as I started using the figure my whole idea of my painting changed. Maybe not in the most obvious structural sense, but these figures distorted my sense of interior or environment, or the painting itself—in a way that I welcomed.

Because you don't have this in abstract painting. . . . In abstract painting one can't deal with . . . an object or person, a concentration of psychology which a person is as opposed to where the figure *isn't* in the painting . . . And that's the one thing that's always missing for me in abstract painting, that I don't have this kind of dialogue between elements that can be . . . wildly different and can be at war, or in extreme conflict."

I feel the same way, Dick. And Tom Eakins weighed in with: "The big artist does not sit down monkeylike and copy . . . but he keeps a sharp eye on Nature and steals her tools. He learns what she does with light, the big tool, and then color, then form, and appropriates them to his own use. . . . But if he ever thinks he can sail another fashion from Nature or make a better-shaped boat, he'll capsize."

We small artists capsize anyway. It would be so much easier for me if figurative painting was well and truly dead, dead as epic poetry or verse drama, but it's not, because it speaks to something deep in the human heart. What I would like is a drug that informs me why I can't just have a normal career as a modern figurative painter.

Again, I mention all this to show that my life was progressing as it has for years, whiny, discontented, blocked, occasionally suicidal, except the kids kept me from that. This was the life I had, these were all the memories I had, except for the memories of being Diego Velázquez, which, of course, I *knew* were being induced by a drug.

Anyway, we stared at the wonderful paintings along with the mob, and dear Rose asked me where *my* paintings were hanging, and I said they weren't, and she asked why, and I said that museums only hang the very best paintings and that mine weren't good enough, and she said that you should just try a little harder, Daddy.

Good advice, really, and then we went back to my place, and Milo played with the computer and I tried harder and Rose invented a new art form using shredder waste and a glue stick to make fantastical collages, multilayered weavings of colored strips, just the thing, if they were twenty-five feet long, for the Whitney Biennial. And watching her I thought about Shelly's theory that creativity sprang from the child self and that returning to that self under salvinorin might jump-start the process on a higher level, and I found myself looking forward to my next dose. I suppressed the thought that even in the drug state I was a pasticheur, that I wasn't mining my own past but that of someone else.

Then it was time for my next appointment at the lab, but when I arrived the receptionist, instead of handing me a clipboard, told me again that Dr. Zubkoff wanted to see me in his office.

I went in and he gestured me to a seat and gave me a grave look like there was a bad shadow on my CAT scan, which he probably practiced in med school and hadn't had much of a chance to use in his career. He said, "Well, Chaz, I have a little bone to pick with you."

"Oh?"

"Yes. You didn't tell us you had a history of drug abuse."

"I wouldn't call it a *history*—"

"No? Two commitments to rehab, one court ordered. I'd call that a drug problem."

"I sold some pills in a saloon, Shelly. It was a horseshit bust. I was doing a favor for a friend of a friend and he turned out to be a narc. That's why the involuntary—"

"Yeah, whatever, but in any case you can't stay in the study. It's a confounding variable."

"But I've been clean for years."

"So you say, but I can't be testing you for drugs every time you participate. The other thing is, my staff reports you're uncooperative and aggressive."

"Oh, please! Because I didn't describe a painting in a fantasy?"

"Right, you're supposed to tell us what you're experiencing on the drug. The accounts are part of the study."

And then he talked about the Velázquez stuff, which still disturbed him; that wasn't supposed to happen on salvinorin.

"So what is it?" I asked.

"Something else. Something confounding." He seemed to search for a delicate way of saying what he wanted to say. "An underlying psychological issue."

"Like psychosis?"

"I wouldn't go that far, but clearly something odd is going on with you that is unlikely to be related to salvinorin, and unfortunately we're not set up to give you the help you need. My advice is to check into the hospital here, run a full battery of tests, complete blood panels, EEG, PET scans, fMRI, the works, and make sure there's no underlying pathology. I mean, for all we know you could have some kind of endocrine imbalance or an allergic reaction to salvinorin, or, God forbid, a brain tumor."

I said I'd think about it. Shelly shrugged and we shook hands and that was it, out on my ear.

Then they asked me to sign some releases and I was officially expelled from the study, and I have to say I felt bereft. On the ride downtown I started thinking about where I could get some more of the drug. I recalled that it was one of the few psychoactive drugs that had not yet been made illegal and I figured I could get hold of it somewhere in town. Then I thought to myself, Don't be crazy, Chaz, that's all you need; if Lotte found out about it you'd never see the kids again. Thus my subway thoughts.

When I climbed out into daylight my cell phone said I had two messages: one from my sister, and the other from Mark, and he was all about his Italian gangster businessman wanting to get the palazzo ceiling done this fall, before the next rainy season in Venice, he was having the roof fixed and he wanted the work on the fresco to go on simultaneously, and could I possibly see my way clear to going early, he'd negotiated a bonus, 25K if I started the first of the month and another twenty-five if I finished before Christmas, and I called him right away and said fine, since I wasn't going to be in the drug study anymore.

My sister had left a voice mail saying she'd be out of touch for a period, she'd had an opportunity to go off to Africa to save babies or something, she had to leave instantly and she couldn't give me any details because she didn't know them, and also because she suspected that covert entry into an unnamed but nasty African nation was going to be part of the picture.

Then I went over to Lotte's gallery and told her I had to be out of town for maybe three months and why, and she bitched a little about it, but the money dangling there, maybe two hundred thousand, was an argument she couldn't really get past. I was real formal, not like last time, just a business relationship now, and she said, "Hey, did you see you got a review?"

In the main room of the gallery my actresses (except Kate) were still up there with the sacred red dots that said they'd sold, and there was a review from the *Village Voice*, framed and hanging nearby. It was not bad. The guy had actually got it that it wasn't just a postmodernist appropriation but a genuine effort to use the traditional means of painting to penetrate character, to pry up under the mask of celebrity. And he hoped I'd continue to do work in that vein. Unfortunately he closed with a little riff about how Andy Warhol had started as a commercial artist and look where he'd gone. Yeah, look.

I said, "Very nice. It's always a treat to be lumped with Warhol."

Lotte said, "Don't be ridiculous. It's a great review. I've had calls from some very big collectors; do you have any more work to show? This could be a very good thing for you."

I looked at her and I was about to say something cynical and nasty, which is what I usually did in these situations, but I saw she was really pleased—her face was positively shining with happiness and admiration—so I just nodded and, after an awkward moment of suspension, hugged her, and she hugged me back.

Then I said, "Well, good, but they're going to have to wait," meaning I had to do the Italian job first, and she was fine with that and was glad I was at least out of the magazine business for a while. I told her about some ideas I'd had for paintings, and my God, it was nice to talk with Lotte again about painting and real work, just like we were back at the start, and I left her with the hope that my work had turned a corner.

I went home, dreading the solitude that might require me to actually paint something. But as it happened, as I climbed the stairs to my loft I saw that the door to Bosco's loft was open, and when I looked in I found my neighbor examining himself in the dusty mirror that hangs next to the door. He was wearing an antique tuxedo jacket over jeans and a black Nine Inch Nails tour T-shirt, and I remembered his show and that I had promised to walk over to it with him.

Although Bosco has a perfectly serviceable wife and children, plus an agent, plus a gallery, he likes to have me or some other artist hang out with him when he goes to one of his openings. It's a tradition I'd always supported with my usual masochism, so we went out and made the short walk up Broadway to Broome. The gallery is west of Broadway and by the time we got to the corner we could see something was up. There were two police cars parked with their lights flashing at the junction of the two streets, blocking traffic, and when we turned the corner we saw that Broome Street was jammed with people, I guessed at least five hundred of them, and maybe twenty cops. A couple of TV vans rumbled and hummed near the gallery entrance and lit it with their glare.

"Man, what a crowd!" said Bosco. "And television. This is great!" He was grinning; his teeth went red then yellow as they alternately glowed in the cop light and the overhead crime-lights. He said, "Hey, let's get in there before all the champagne's gone," and strode off toward the crowd.

Or the mob, as I ought to call it. Even at half a block away I could tell that it wasn't a crowd of art lovers. I heard the sound of glass breaking and a scream, and then distant sirens. Behind me a large black van appeared from Broadway, halted near the patrol cars, and disgorged a squad of tactical police in black uniforms with helmets, face shields, and long batons. They started to form a line and I spun on my heel and ran away. Then I went calmly to a Chinese restaurant and ordered some take-out. Shameful, yes, but what could I have done?

When I got back to my place I sat down with my lo mein and turned on the TV. There was a woman anchoring the local news with the grave look and lowered voice suitable for portentous matters, and she was talking to someone offscreen; it was a breaking-news moment, and then the scene flashed to a guy with a microphone who was standing not far from where I'd last seen Bosco. Behind him you could see what remained of the gallery, its window smashed, its blackened smoking interior, and firemen walking through the ruins doing their usual after-fire cleanup. The reporter was saying, "No, Karen, we don't know the condition yet of the artist, Dennis Bosco, but witnesses say he was badly beaten and taken to St. Vincent's Hospital. We'll get back to you as soon as we have any more information."

Some more questioning back and forth about injuries and arrests, and then they showed some footage of Bosco's 9/11 piece and a tape taken earlier at the gallery, the stuff I'd seen the start of in real life, Bosco walking into the crowd around the front of the gallery and then being recognized and getting shoved and screamed at by a group of big guys and then going down in a flurry of kicks and blows, and the cops shoving through to rescue him, not very enthusiastically I thought. And then a trash can going through the window, and then the mob pushing through into the gallery and screaming art lovers streaming out and getting their lumps too, some of them, and then there was a blaze of fire that made the video go white and there were shouts and screams. The final shot was the tactical police finally moving in like imperial storm troopers and clearing the street.

I couldn't stop watching, even through the talking heads and the stupid street interviews, some of which had to have the obscenities bleeped out. Then later there was video of Bosco, his face a pudding of blood, on a gurney being loaded onto an ambulance, from which they cut to more interviews, every one of whom agreed that it was obscene to make fun of 9/11 and especially to use the actual ashes of that day, and that the artist had gotten what he deserved. There was a spokesman from the mayor's office who said the usual about free speech and our constitutional values and that the culprits would be prosecuted, but he didn't sound too enthusiastic about it either, and why should he be, since the affray was clearly the doing of off-duty cops and firemen. The whole thing was a work of art.

I tried to call Connie Bosco in Jersey, but the line was busy. Then I called St. Vincent's and found that Bosco was in surgery and they were only giving information out to family members. So I went to sleep.

I visited the hospital the next day but they wouldn't let me in to see him. The floor was guarded by three big cops, two at the nurses' station and one by Bosco's room, so I had to use my charm on one of the nurses; she agreed to take a message in to Connie, and after a while Connie came out and told me I could go back in with her. From what I overheard of the police conversation, I gathered that they resented having to guard him and would have liked to add some lumps of their own; ironic postmodernism has obviously not penetrated the consciousness of the police.

Connie Bosco is from Mexico and is a potter of some distinction. She seemed distraught and confused by what had happened to her husband. She understood getting your ass kicked by the cops—that's what the cops did in her native land—but she didn't get the part about them doing it for art rather than money. Bosco, however, got it just fine. He was as happy as a man with internal injuries, three busted ribs, and a smashed face could be. It hurt him to grin, he said, but he grinned all the same. This was what he'd wanted all his life—to get a rise out of society with his art. He'd tried pornography, he'd tried absurdity—ho-hum. But he'd finally located a sacred cow in the ashes of 9/11, and at last he was one with Monet, van Gogh, and Marcel Duchamp. A urinal moment, and to be savored.

"Apparently, the thing's gone," I said. "You heard there was a fire?"

"It doesn't matter," he said. "The memory will live on. Besides, I have a lot more ashes. I could build it again. Maybe I will."

"You do and I'll kill you myself," said his wife.

I left Bosco and took a sharp left onto Eleventh Street and into a sour depression. Okay, he'd found one of the last few sore spots in the culture and stuck his blade in there pretty good and paid the price. He'd literally suffered for art, which was supposed to be part of the deal, but it wasn't a deal I was ever interested in. What I wanted was . . . What I *wanted* was . . .

It struck me that I didn't know. That was strange. In the what-I-really-want section of my brain there was a dusty shelf with nothing on it. Instead there was a longing.

Thinking this shit and walking down the *via negativa* this way, I found myself in Gorman's, where I drank away the evening under my silly painting of Hillary. I fell into conversation with a fellow who said he was an unemployed philosophy teacher, and we talked about the nature of reality through a serious number of rounds and then staggered out into the glowing dark of the city. He needed a cab and said he'd drop me off at my place and he hailed one and . . . actually I can't recall the tail end of the occasion very well. I remember Wittgenstein and "the world is whatever is the case," and the cab, but I don't have any memory of getting out of the cab and walking up my stairs, which has often served to burn a lot of alcohol out of my system. I do remember waking up.

I wasn't in my bed but in a king-size item with sheets far finer and cleaner than mine, looking up at a ceiling higher and cleaner than the one in my loft. I had a brief and ridiculous thought that I'd been seduced by the unemployed philosopher. I called out; nothing. Whereupon I rose carefully, so as not to move the spiked thing in my skull, and cast around for the bathroom.

Someone had spent a lot of money here, all the latest European fixtures and a huge glassed-in shower enclosure, quite a gap between it and my old tin job up on stilts, with its mildewed curtain. I washed my face and opened the medicine cabinet, looking for aspirin; I found a bottle of Advil, took three, and checked out the rest of the stuff there. The usual, and I learned from the high-end makeup and face treatments that a woman also lived in this place, but when I examined the amber drug vials I got a shock: one of them was for amoxicillin, and the name on the label was mine.

I recalled that I'd had the vial for nearly a year, since the cough I picked up last winter, and yeah, it was the same vial, with about the same number of residual pills and the smear of blue paint on the cap. So the little quivers were starting up around the heart, and the higher brain parts were thinking explanations: maybe I lent it to someone and forgot about it, and he lent it to someone else, et cetera, and it ended up here. I put it back and went out into the loft and looked out the window. As I'd expected I was in Tribeca; I could see Greenwich Street and a slice of shining river, so I was probably in one of the elaborately gutted and rebuilt loft buildings catering to media stars and the upper crust of the art world.

Running along under the window was a long painted shelf full of family photographs, and I glanced at them casually, as one does with the photographs of someone else's family, and then looked at them again, and looked at them again, each one, and now my heart was really pounding, and fat drops of sweat burst out all over my face because it was my family in all the pictures, mine and Lotte's, my dad in his jaunty cape, and my mother when she was young with her two children in our best white outfits, and Lotte's parents and her grandparents from old Europe, all photographs I'd seen throughout my married life. And others were strange, for example me and Lotte, somewhat younger, on what was apparently the Great Wall of China, a place we've never been. That I can recall.

I went exploring on wobbly legs. Bedrooms for the kids, and in them I recognized a lot of their gear—although Milo had a better computer than he does in real life—and Rose's room with her stuffed animals and a big corkboard for her drawings.

The huge living room held a good collection of contemporary art on the walls, including one work by Wilmot, Jr., that painting of Lotte and Milo I'd given her for our fifth anniversary, plus comfortable, expensive furniture, a great black piano lurking in the corner, shiny, hideous; the kitchen all à la mode, granite counters, Sub-Zero fridge, with pictures of my kids, their school stuff magneted up there, the Vulcan range, Lotte's stained and worn cookbook on its stand on the counter.

So then I thought, This must be a drug thing, some strange reaction to the drug, like the Velázquez, but no, it was entirely different because in those I *was* Velázquez, at ease in himself, and here I was just me, pissing myself in terror.

But I had to see it all, so I followed my nose, chasing the turpentine scent to a door, and when I went through there was the studio, skylighted, spacious, with a big oak Santa Fe easel smack in the middle with the latest by the supposed me on it. I seemed to be doing groups now, a big one, maybe four by six feet. This was of four people, three women and a man, on a rose madder–colored velvet love seat, all slumped to one side, limbs entwined like they'd all stumbled and fallen down in a heap of beautifully painted and glazed pink limbs, slick Barbizon-style surface, invisible brushstrokes, good as Bouguereau any day. The faces were clearly recognizable: Suzanne and Lotte and my mother, all in the full bloom of their youth, and the man was Dad. It was unspeakably more horrible than the family photos. I ran out of there without another look.

Elevator down to the lobby, and this was indeed a fancy building renovation rehab because there was a real lobby, not the usual loft building hallway: it had potted plants and indirect lighting and a little desk for the doorman. Who greeted me cheerfully: "Hi, Mr. Wilmot. Looks like we gonna have a nice day."

He was a short, dark man in a gray uniform, labeled AHMED on a chromed pin. I approached him and said, "You know me?" and my tone and face must've been something else, because his formal smile jelled and he answered, "Sure, I know you. You're on the top front. Mr. Wilmot."

"How long have I been living here?"

"I don't know, sir. I been here six years and you were here when I got hired. Is there something wrong, sir?"

I left without responding to this inane question and took off, and in a little while I was running up Broadway and I didn't stop until I got to my loft building. The street door was propped open, which was unusual, but people sometimes did it when they were expecting deliveries. I ran up the stairs to my loft and stood in front of my loft door.

Only it wasn't my door. My door has the original battleship-gray paint with a universe of old chips and stains I know like the palm of my hand, and the door I was gaping at now was new and painted a cheery cerulean blue, and it had a brass cardholder and an engraved card stuck in it bearing an unfamiliar name. It took me a while to push my door key in the hole, my hands were shaking so badly, but in any case the key wouldn't turn. I pounded on the door until I skinned my knuckles, but there was no answer.

So I went down the stairs to Bosco's, not running anymore, but slowly, like if I moved fast now the world would shatter. Bosco's door was painted shiny red. Bosco was still in the hospital, but I knew that Connie had moved in so she could be in town while he was recovering. I knocked. The door opened and there was a tall, athletic black man standing there, looking at me inquiringly.

"Where's Connie?" I said.

"Who?" said the guy.

"Connie Bosco. This is her husband's loft."

"Sorry, there must be some mistake. This is my loft."

"No, Bosco's been living here for over twenty years," I insisted.

"No, you must have the wrong building. This is Forty-nine Walker."

"I know it's Forty-nine Walker, goddamnit! I live upstairs on five. I've been living there for years. What the fuck is going on here?"

The guy's face tensed up then, and he started to close the door. He said, "You need to take a break, boss. Patty Constantine lives up there, and I doubt you live with her and Yvonne. I don't know who you are, but you sure as hell don't live in this building."

He slammed the door. I pounded on it and yelled, "I'm Charles Wilmot!" a number of times, until my throat was sore and I heard the man threaten to call the police unless I left.

So I did. When I reached the street I was crying, just blubbering like a little lost kid. I was saying, "Okay, change back! Change back now! Change back!" but it kept on being the same merciless twenty-first-century New York, except that I'd been squeezed out of it like a zit and replaced by a painter who was doing just fine and was still married to the woman he loved and was painting just the kind of stuff I could've done and wouldn't.

Then I had my cell phone in my hand and I was punching Mark's private number, not Lotte, never Lotte, because she couldn't see me this way, she couldn't know about the drug or any of that, and what if she confirmed it, that we all of us lived in that beautiful rich-guy's loft together and all my memories of the last twenty years were false?

Mark answered and I jabbered, and he said he was with a client and couldn't talk but he'd try to break away, but for Christ's sake calm down. In fact, his voice through the tiny earpiece *was* calming, it was contact with someone who knew me, the real me. I took some deep breaths and felt the sweat start to cool on my face and agreed to meet him at Gorman's in half an hour.

The lunch rush was just clearing out when I got to the saloon, and I took a seat at the bar. "Where's Clyde?" I asked the young woman behind the bar. I'd never seen her before, and Clyde has been the day barman at Gorman's since the Beame administration.

"Clyde?" she said, clueless, obviously, and my insides started to wobble again and I ordered a martini to make them stop. I drank it and ordered another one and I noticed that my Hillary painting wasn't up on the wall anymore. It had been replaced by a framed vintage prize-fight poster. I asked the girl what happened to it and she said she didn't know what I was talking about, and I was about to give her an argument—in fact, I was yelling at her—when Mark came in and dragged me to one of the corner tables and asked me what the fuck was up with me.

I told him. I told him about the fancy loft and my key not working in my door and the guy in Bosco's place and it added up to . . . what? Someone had stolen my life and replaced me with someone else? And even as I said the words they seemed the very definition of crazy to me, a short step from conversations with space aliens and the messages from the CIA. But he heard me out and then said, "We got a problem, kid."

"We?"

"Oh, yeah. I just guaranteed Castelli you're going to do his ceiling and now you're having a nervous breakdown on me."

A little glow of hope here. "So the ceiling is a real job and I, like, wouldn't have taken a job like that unless I was a starving hack commercial guy, would I?"

"I don't know, Chaz. Maybe you needed a break. Maybe you're fascinated by Tiepolo. Who knows what artists will do? Hockney did all those Polaroids for years—"

"Fuck Hockney!" I said, louder than I had intended, and people in the bar looked our way. "And fuck you! What happened to my Clinton painting?"

"What are you talking about, Chaz? What Clinton painting?"

"That one, the one next to the bar that's been there for years, and the bartender's wrong—"

"Chaz! Calm yourself the fuck down!"

"Just tell me I'm who I am!" I was shouting now, and he replied, in just the sort of soothing voice that does more than anything else to inflame incipient madness, "What good would that do, man? If you're as nuts as you say, you could be imagining me saying just what you want to hear. Or the opposite. Look, let's get out of here, you're going to get eighty-sixed if you keep screaming like that."

He threw some money on the table, more than necessary to cover our tab with a generous tip, and hustled me out into the street. There he used his cell to call his black car, and in a few minutes it appeared and we got in. Which was fine with me at that point. Black car, Mark talking on his cell to some client, a normal situation—he wasn't particularly concerned with what had happened to me, so why should I be? Yes, crazy logic, but just then that was all the logic I had.

We pulled up in front of his gallery and got out. He had some business to transact; I could wait in his office, upstairs from the showroom. I was content to do so; I had no pressing engagements. I sat in Mark's big leather chair and closed my eyes. Maybe I could go to sleep, I thought, and when I woke up everything would be back to normal. No, that wasn't going to work, I was wired despite the drinks. Okay, I kept coming back to the idea that this had to be a side effect of salvinorin, something they hadn't figured on, some delicate system in my brain had collapsed and I was hallucinating an alternate reality as a successful painter of the kind of paintings I happened to despise.

Then I thought, Wait a second, I have a *life*, with all kinds of physical traces, bank accounts, paper trails, websites, I'll just check it out right now, and so I turned to Mark's computer and Googled myself. I had a website, it seemed, a beautiful one, all about my wonderfully slick nudes, and strangely enough it displayed some paintings, early stuff, that I actually recalled doing. The website I remembered, with my magazine illustrations on it, was gone.

I tried to get into my bank account online. My password didn't work.

I pulled out my cell phone and brought up my phone book. I had the name of every magazine art director in New York in that list, and they were all gone, replaced by a bunch of names I didn't recognize. But Lotte's name was there, and almost without volition I found myself ringing the home number associated with her name, a number I didn't recognize, a Manhattan number. It rang; then a message telling me that I'd reached the home of Lotte Rothschild, Chaz Wilmot, Milo, and Rose, and I could leave a message at the beep. I left no message.

No hope then, the hallucination was complete. The me I remembered no longer existed. Except for Mark. And now I was terrified of Mark. Mark was God now; he could erase me with a word. So I passed the time until he chose to reappear. I played computer solitaire. I cleaned my nails with my Swiss Army knife. While I had the knife out I carved my monogram into the side of his desk drawer, so in case this was a complete hallucination and I was really someplace else, I could come back and check. If I remembered.

It turns out that when you're going crazy it's probably better to be with a complete narcissist like Slotsky than with a caring person. Your agony is so trivial to him that in a strange way it stops being so all-consuming to you. Mark came bouncing in with a big smile, talking about some killing he'd just made on a painting. He was in the mood to celebrate and he just happened to have an invitation to a big opening at Claude Demme in Chelsea. Sushi from Mara was promised, and unlimited Taittinger. My little difficulty was apparently forgotten, and I was willing to pretend it was no big deal for the nonce, because I was waiting to wake up. One day at a time, as they say in rehab. It goes for the minutes too.

So I followed him out like a wooden pull-toy and we traveled in the black car to Claude Demme on West Twenty-sixth Street. It was a three-man show by guys who were fifteen years younger than me; their work was about what you'd expect, and the people too, art hags, Eurotrash, dealers, a couple of A-list celebrities. Mark filled a plate with pricey sushi and started his usual schmoozing and air-kissing. I air-kissed not and filled my belly with champagne. After half a dozen flutes I felt the need for air and strolled out down the street toward Eighth Avenue.

All the galleries were lit, and I passed them without much interest until I came to a large storefront with a plaque on the wall that said ENSO GALLERY in artful calligraphy, white on black, and stopped to stare at a large painting in the window. It was of a nude woman unusually well rendered, and she was clutching tenderly to her breast a miniature version of herself, another spasm of irony wrung out of the corpse of surrealism, although the guy could really draw. It took me a couple of seconds to realize it was in exactly the same style as the unfinished piece I'd seen in the fancy loft. I stopped breathing and looked at the window card. It read RECENT WORK BY CHARLES WILMOT, JR., and sure enough, there was my monogram painted in the lower right of the painting.

I went in, shaking all over. There were a few people in the small white space and maybe ten paintings on the walls. All nudes, a few men, mostly women, more than a few young girls. The technique was realistic: flat lighting, concealing nothing, a good deal of crotch hair depicted, a soft-core effect, a little Balthus, a little Ron Mueck, a little Magritte. I recognized some of the models, women I'd known; Lotte and Suzanne were there too. The prices were up in the high five figures and quite a few had been sold. I'd never seen any of them in my life.

I went up to the girl behind the desk, a pretty blue-eyes with extralarge round spectacles and gelled punk-black hair. She looked up and gave me a big smile: "Hello, Mr. Wilmot," she said, and I said, "What the hell is going on here?"

Her smile faded and she asked, "What do you mean?"

"You know me?" I demanded.

"Uh-huh." Carefully. "Yeah, you're the artist. Is something wrong?"

And I snapped.

The poor failed bastard I was in my every memory grew knuckle hair and tusks and shouted, "Is something wrong? Is something *wrong*? Yeah, I'll tell you what's wrong, darling: I never painted any of this shit."

I gave a yell and took out my knife and attacked the paintings, slashing through the beautiful, oh-so-salable surfaces, and my God, it felt good! The art lovers were screaming and running out and the girl screamed too and called out, "Serge!" and reached for the phone. I ran over to the window display and grabbed the card that had my name on it, and I was trying to slice it up with the knife when I was grabbed from behind by, I imagine, the Serge whom she'd called. The card with the knife still stuck in it fell from my hand as we struggled. I broke free and threw the first serious punch I'd let loose since the schoolyard, and he slipped it with an ease one doesn't really expect in a gallery manager and connected with a left jab, then a powerful right cross, and I went down and out.

I came to in the back of a patrol car in handcuffs. Dimly, I observed a cop in conversation with Serge and the gallery clerk on the sidewalk, and then they drove me to what I assumed was their precinct and took my ID, watch, belt, and the laces from my sneakers away from me and put me in a cell, where I puked Claude Demme's expensive champagne and some partly digested Chinese food all over myself.

Now I was officially a crazy person, and a dangerous one too. New York has a system for dealing with such emotionally disturbed people, as we are known, and I was now part of it. They are supposed to notify your next of kin, but when they asked I stayed mute. Many of us EDPs are similarly bereft, so it was no big deal. They shipped me to Bellevue with the vomit still caked on me, and there I was cleaned up, given a gown and a robe and paper slippers, shot full of Haldol, and left tied to a bed.

Some time passed. There was a painful swelling under the injection site on my shoulder, and I complained about it; they said they'd use the other arm if I needed another, but I was a good boy and didn't make any trouble. A couple of days later, they switched me to pills and then I had my interview, fifteen minutes with an intern half my age. He asked me who I was and I told him I didn't know. He asked me if I had someplace to go and I said I did. That was the magic answer, for it seemed that the Enso Gallery did not care to press charges. A little artistic misunderstanding, happens all the time. I got a scrip for olanzapine and a boot out the door, back into the world's largest open-air aftercare facility, the streets of Manhattan.

Once there I fished my cell phone out of the envelope with my personal effects in it and brought up my phone book. It was my old one, with the art directors on it. Oh, good, I thought, the Haldol has kicked in. I called Mark.

He wanted to know where I'd been, and I said the mental ward at Bellevue, and he said, "Well, that was probably for the best. Are you back to being you?"

I said I was.

"You're going to do my guy's fresco, right?"

I said I would. In fact, I wanted to leave that very day.

"Not a problem," he said. "I'll call you."

I went back to Walker Street, and my old door was there and my key worked. I looked around at the familiar environment, but it gave me no comfort. It was like I didn't fit into that life anymore; it's hard to explain, but I had the feeling that whatever happened I'd never live there again. I took a shower and dressed and packed a small bag. While I was packing, Mark called and told me I could pick up the tickets and the other stuff I'd need at his gallery that evening, and I did, and his black car took me to Kennedy and out of my old life.

They flew me to Venice on Alitalia, in first class. People complain about air travel a lot nowadays, but this was considerably better than being in Bellevue. I had a pint or two of Prosecco to start and the *gnocchi alla Romana* with a good enough Montepulciano. I was picked up at the airport as promised by a silent and efficient man who introduced himself as Franco, then taken by private launch to a boutique hotel off the Campo San Zaninovo, convenient to the palazzo, which is right on the Zaninovo Canal between the Ponte Storto and the Ponte Corona. I was just settling into my room when my cell phone rang, and it was Lotte calling. A renewed pang of terror and I refused the call. She left an angry message: according to her I should be in a psychiatric hospital and not swanning around Europe. She knew all about my recent craziness because someone at the gallery had used a cell phone camera to snap me being dragged from the gallery with blood all over my face, and it had made the tabloids, and she'd called Mark, who filled her in on the whole story, the rat. I didn't return the call.

After a day of rest in my lovely room, Franco took me to the palazzo and turned me over to Signor Zuccone, who is the major-domo of the place and responsible to the big cheese for this abortion. Well, you know, it's real *damp* in Venice, and the palazzo was built in 1512, and they probably spent fifty bucks on the roof since then, and when I looked up at the dining room ceiling I saw a sagging gray porridge, lightly smeared with angels and clouds. I told Zuccone that the whole thing had to come down. He didn't blink, and the next day the demolishers were at work. While that was going on I had a look at Tiepolo's cartoons. This was the actual working set, complete with the tiny holes and the marks of the red chalk pounce he'd used, miraculously preserved. So that was okay as far as the design went, which was an Assumption of the Virgin with angelic choir and saints, lots of lush clouds, no deep feeling, just pure gorgeousness. I loved it, and in a strange way it blew my recent identity problem right out of my skull. A consuming art project will do that sometimes, stifle the little voices of ego—or, in my case, madness—and let you exist in the realms of form and color when nothing's of concern except the next stroke of the brush.

It was, of course, not a restoration in any real sense. It was a forgery. I still loved it—how cheaply sold my long-protected virginity!

The first thing I had to do was to find someone who knew fresco plaster. I thought about my father and the St. Anthony job, his great fresco fiasco, on which a Mr. Belloto was our plaster guy. He looked about a hundred years old, the last man in America to wear a bowler hat, came to work in a suit and a tie with a diamond stickpin in it, changed into coveralls at the job site, kept the tie on. The deal was that some rich bastard son of the Church had given a dining hall to a seminary in Suffolk County and there was money to do a fresco of the life of the patron saint, and of course immediately Father was Michelangelo revived. This job was his bid for immortality, so the fresco had to be right, had to last for the ages, as long as Pompeii at least. I was the apprentice, so if the quattrocento ever rolled around again, I'd be set to cash in—crazy, of course, but thanks, Dad, it eventually came in real handy.

I spent the better part of that year—I was twenty-two—doing all the things that people do on a fresco besides the actual painting, under the hand mainly of Mr. Belloto. It's not like plastering the kitchen. The trick is that your slaked lime has to be really old. You don't want any unslaked lime in your mix because it might slake up on the wall and generate gas that'll bubble the surface.

Footnote: immortality, in this case, lasted around ten years. There were over a hundred seminarians in there when we started, a number that sank to around six not too long after the Second Vatican Council finished trashing the grand old Tridentine Church. So the diocese sold the barn to a nondenominational retirement home that didn't want scenes from the life of St. Anthony staring down at the crocks while they ate; they wanted the artworks of the residents up there, flowers and clowns and so forth, so they painted a nice peach color over the fresco. No great loss, as a matter of fact, it was typical Late Dad, beautifully drawn, utterly spiritless. I think even Mr. Belloto knew that; he used to grip my shoulder and sigh while viewing each *giornata*.

After asking around a little I found Signor Codognola, also about a hundred years old, and he said he had a trove of plaster from before the war—I think maybe he meant World War I. He was slow but good, worked with a couple of relatives, grandsons or great-grandsons, I don't know, took them a week to get the *trullisatio* in, the coat that sticks to the lath, and another week to adhere the brown coat to it, what they call the *arricciato*. I didn't even pretend to supervise; mainly I toured the city by foot and vaporetto, checking out all the Tiepolos I could find to pump up my sense of how he handled form and color. One of the great natural draftsmen, yeah, but almost over-slick. The famous comic book illustrators of the golden age were all Tiepoloesques. So I am right at home. But really, beautiful work with the small brush, used like a pen. I spent my time grinding colors and waiting for the brown coat to cure up.

Fresco work fixes your mind on a day at a time; all you think about is how you're going to handle the next *giornata*. Obviously it was a lot easier for me because Tiepolo marked his *giornata* right on the cartoon. You have, let's say, a section of fluffy cloud and a triangular chunk of blue sky between some clouds, and another lump of darker cloud, and that's about all you can do in one day's work—your *giornata*—on the wet plaster of the *intonaco*, or surface layer. We had modern scaffolds and lights, so no candle stuck on the head for Chaz. I just mixed my colors with lime water, set up the palette, and up I went. And Marco, or another one of the grandsons, helped pin up the cartoon and I pounced it with red chalk, and then we took off the cartoon and I incised the lines of chalk dust with a wooden stylus, and then they laid the *intonaco* and I painted on it wet, using the incised lines as guides.

It was like a gigantic paint-by-numbers, only in the style of Tiepolo; it looked clumsy from close up, but from the floor it looked like old Giambattista did it yesterday. It had that don't-give-a-shit ease in it, true *sprezzatura*, total authority laying down the paint, like I'd been doing Tiepoloesque frescoes every day of my life. In the center, the Virgin exalted, the most important part; I took the liberty of giving her Lotte's face, nice Jewish girl after all, or at least the Rothschild half, and why not, I'm sure Tiepolo stuck his honeys on ceilings all over Europe.

About three weeks into the project, say the middle of November, I got a surprise visit from my ex-father-in-law—I mean Lotte's father, not the side-of-beef one. He was in Venice for a conference. Interesting guy, pushing eighty now but still active, had a long career in the UN diplomatic service, then moved on to art scholarship. Calls himself an amateur, but he's written a lot, apparently quite respected in European art-history circles. Not one of *those* Rothschilds, as he likes to say, consequently went through a rough time as a kid, lost his family to the Nazis and survived by being sheltered in a convent in Normandy. Married an Italian woman; she had the one kid and then died, cancer, when Lotte was about twelve. He never remarried. Lotte had told him where I was and I sensed that this visit was in the nature of an inspection tour. I didn't mind; I kind of wanted to know how I was too.

We had lunch at a little hole-in-the-wall place he likes near the Palazzo Grimani, a slow Venetian meal.

I asked him how Lotte and the kids were. He said, "The children are wonderful as always. They miss you. Rose believes that Big Italy, as she calls it, is on the subway somewhere near Little Italy. She has her own MetroCard now and threatens to come and visit you when she feels like it. Milo . . . well, what can one say? He is melancholy after this last relapse, but he has a tremendous brightness and courage that keeps breaking through. He said he hopes to live long enough to see you again."

"Shit!"

"Yes, life is sometimes shit. Lotte is holding up despite . . . perhaps you haven't heard. Jackie Moreau is dead."

"What? Oh, God! How?"

"Murdered, in Rome. Stabbed and dumped in the river. The police believe it was a robbery gone wrong."

"Christ! She must be devastated."

"Yes. He must be her oldest friend, you know. As I say, life is sometimes shit, but we are obliged to keep living. Tell me about the work you are doing here."

I was happy to change the subject, and we talked about Tiepolo for a while; he said it was a shame I'd not had a chance to see the frescoes in the prince-bishop's palace in Würzburg, which were in his opinion the best things the artist had ever done.

"I suppose your next project will be something by the Guardis," he said with a smile.

"Why the Guardis?"

"Didn't you know? Tiepolo married Francesco Guardi's daughter. His sons, Giovanni Domenico and Lorenzo, both became pretty fair painters. One of the few cases where talent bred true, and isn't this one of the great conundrums of human existence? From whence it comes. I, for example, have a passionate love of painting, but it would never occur to me to try to paint, or rather it *did* occur to me, unfortunately. After the war I spent an unhappy year in art school, until it became clear that I would never amount to anything in that line. And Lotte too, as you know, tried her hand, and the antitalent was also inherited, poor child. And you of course are the counterexample."

"I'd say the counter-counterexample. I inherited a load of talent from a man who never used what he'd been given properly, and guess what? I don't use it properly either."

"You are blocked."

"I *am* blocked." At that moment I almost spilled it: the whole horror of what had happened in New York, the fancy loft, the Enso Gallery, the loft door that wouldn't open, the falsification of memory. Because of anyone I knew, Maurice Rothschild would have been the person most likely to understand it. But I didn't. Why not, Chaz? Why didn't you unburden yourself to this enormously charitable and knowledgeable man? Maybe there would have been a great vomiting out of the blockage then, he'd be my magician lifting the curse with a subtle word, but the truth is we love our dark stuff, we hug it to our inner hearts even as it corrodes our vitals. I confess it: just like with Slotsky, I was simply too fucking terrified to ask.

Instead I laughed a fake chuckle and said, "But what can I do? At least I'm making money."

"Not to be sneezed at," he said after a decent pause. "Let's have some coffee and a little grappa and then we'll go see your ceiling."

Which we did in due course, and when he saw it, looking up with the spotting scope I use to check the paint from the ground, he laughed and said, "That's marvelous! A little artistic joke. You have captured precisely my girl."

"You think she'll mind?"

"On the contrary, she'll be delighted."

"I thought she didn't like artistic jokes."

"That would depend on the joke and its context. Artistic jokes are amusing only against a serious background. Mozart wrote a musical joke, but Mozart is easily distinguishable from Spike Jones. This"— here he gestured upward—"is astounding. I see the paint is still fresh, but I would be hard-pressed not to call it the work of the master, and it's not merely the composition, which of course you had from the cartoons, it's the colors, that glorious shot-silk effect and the delicacy of the drawing in the details, that marvelous line he has. Or you have.

It is a consummate forgery. In fact, I believe it is, all told, the very best artistic forgery I have ever seen. And I have seen a few."

"Really? When?"

"Oh, it was something I did in my early career. I had the degree in art history, perfectly useless, I thought, for a diplomat—economics, political science far more the thing, and if history, one wants the history of rulers and their elaborate murders, wars and so forth—but someone in the ministry must have examined dossiers because I was picked to participate in the negotiations around returning artworks looted by the Third Reich. This was in, I believe, 1956. Of course, the great troves, the most famous works stolen by Göring and the big gangsters, had already been returned. But the scale of the looting was so vast . . . I mean, an enormous proportion of the cultured class in Germany and the conquered lands was despoiled, not to mention museums in places like the Netherlands and France and Poland. Not only the Jews, who of course lost everything, but liberals and socialists of every stripe. I mean to say, if you have a regime that is essentially lawless, anyone with a pretension to power can take anything he wants from anyone designated as an enemy of the state."

"So what did you do?"

"Well, the apologetic powers established an office in Paris and there someone would come, let us say a French Jew who survived, and place a claim: I had a Cézanne, I had a Rubens, and the Germans came and they're gone. And then the police, let us say, locate the Germans who were in this man's area, and they look, and sure enough former Hauptführer-SS Schultz has a Cézanne stashed away in his attic, the Frenchman's very Cézanne, or so it seems. But since this was an international body and very correct, it must make sure it is the same painting and that the Frenchman really owned it, and so forth, and for this they need an art-historical diplomat, and this is me. Now, Herr Schultz has done his time in prison, perhaps three years, because after all he only killed a hundred Jews instead of a hundred thousand, and he is participating in the German reconstruction and he wishes very much to hold on to the painting, which he intends to sell at some point to expand his business, and so he cleverly decides to hire some art student to copy it, and someone must be on hand to catch him at his tricks, and again this is me."

"Gosh, I didn't know any of this," I said. "Did this happen a lot?"

"No, because as I'm sure you know, forgery is difficult and these people were no great connoisseurs in the main. The efforts to deceive were generally quite childish." He smiled and jerked his thumb upward. "I'm grateful you were not in business at that time."

And now something made me think of the conversation I'd had with Mark about art forgery, maybe the word "business" triggered some neuron too, and I asked him, "Did you ever hear of someone in the art business named Krebs?"

At the mention of this name the familiar genial expression vanished from his face, and for a moment I saw replacing it the mask of the diplomat he'd probably worn to work for thirty years.

"You are referring to Horst Axel Krebs?"

I said, "No, I think his name is Werner."

"The son, then. Why do you ask?"

So I told him about Slotsky mentioning the connection between this fresco job and Krebs. He listened in silence and then said, "Let's take a walk. I want to take a look at the San Zaccaria Bellini again."

We left the palazzo and walked south on Corte Rotta in the chill rain that keeps the tourists scant in Venice's winter between Christmas and Carnival and makes the uneven streets reflect, canal-like, the colored stonework of the great facades. As we walked, he said, "So— let me tell you about Herr Krebs. First the father, Horst Axel Krebs. Like me and Hitler, a failed artist. He was young enough to miss the first war, and after a bohemian youth in Munich, he set up as an art dealer there in 1923. In 1928 he joined the Nazi party, and after the Nazis took power he was made a curator at the Alte Pinakothek in the place of a removed Jew. By this time he is married and has a son, Werner Horst, born 1933. In 1940, the Nazis organized the Einsatz-stab Reichsleiter Rosenberg. Do you know what that was?"

"No, but I'm guessing it wasn't devoted to increasing the sum total of human happiness."

"You would be correct. It was the bureaucracy assigned to loot the collections of France and Western Europe of any artworks of inter-est to the new rulers, especially the collections of Jews. Our Krebs is assigned to the Paris office, the richest lode of all, and here he special-izes in record keeping. He knows what has been looted from whom and where it is kept. So he goes on for four years, and then comes 1944, D-day. The Allies advance and the ERR pulls out of Paris with trainloads and truck convoys of artworks. Some of it was stopped by the French resistance, tons of it were found by the Allies, but a lot of it disappeared and remains lost to this day. In late 1945, Horst Axel Krebs was arrested by the British, tried at Nuremberg, and given a two-year sentence."

"That seems fairly light," I said.

"Yes, but at the time, as I suggested earlier, mass murderers were getting ten years or less, and he hadn't actually killed anyone as far as they knew. Just a thief was Horst Axel. So by 1949 he's back in Munich contributing to the economic miracle. He has a little gallery on the Kirchenstrasse where he sells harmless landscapes and flowers to burghers refurbishing their war-torn homes. Obviously he's poi-son to the legitimate art market; he's investigated up and down by the Allied occupation authorities, they have a whole dossier on him, but as far as anyone knows, he's clean, just a businessman. Well, time goes on, the anti-Nazi fervor fades away, everyone is just a good Ger-man trying to get by and be a bulwark against communism, et cetera, and meanwhile little Werner is all grown up, with a *diplom* from the Ludwig-Maximilians University in art history and conservation. He now settles in Frankfurt to get a little distance from the father in Munich, and also because Frankfurt is where all the money is. He's taking a hand in the family business, of course, but the real business, not the Kirchenstrasse gallery."

"What was the other business?" I asked.

"Well, you know, the remarkable thing about the Nazi looting is that they kept nearly impeccable records of everything they took. For example, at Nuremberg, at the trial of Alfred Rosenberg, the prosecution presented thirty-nine thick volumes that cataloged everything they'd confiscated, with photographs of the art. There were hundreds of such volumes in all. The Allies seized roomfuls of filing cabinets with tens of thousands of index cards: descriptions of the art, who they took it from, and so on.

"So let's say it's the middle of 1944, and you've been stealing art and making these very catalogs for four years, and you are a smart person and so you know that the Nazis are finished, and suppose you wanted to feather your nest after the war. You might contrive to search out a selection of valuable pieces, nothing too showy, and neglect to place these pieces in the catalogs, and naturally you would strip out the relevant index cards too. And you would choose just those things that belonged to Jews who had died in the camps and who left no survivors at all. For someone with Horst Krebs's old Nazi connections that information would be easy to get. And then you would use the excellent forging capabilities of the SS to generate phony bills of sale, so that instead of, say, a nice Pissaro being sold to a Jacques Bernstein of Paris in 1908, it was shown as being sold to a Kurt Langschweile of Geneva, Switzerland, same year. Then, after the war, Herr Langschweile's heirs supposedly sell the painting to the respectable firm W. H. Krebs, of Frankfurt. Yes, we know that the proprietor is the son of the notorious Horst Axel Krebs, but in the Federal Republic they do not look too closely at what your father did in the war, or else there'd be no business at all. Old Krebs died in his bed in seventy-nine, by the way, a pillar of the community."

"And he still does this?" I asked. "I mean Werner."

"Not anymore. And there has never been, to my knowledge, any solid evidence that he *ever* did it. As I said earlier, the Nazi hoard was so enormous and the artworks went through so many movements and changes of custody, and so many people had access to them during the crazy years, that countless pieces were lost track of. It is just a fact that the younger Krebs made his initial fortune selling small, well-chosen Impressionist and early-twentieth-century pieces he bought in Switzerland. Plenty of Jews shipped stuff out to Switzerland in pawn to raise money after they were stripped of their livelihoods during the thirties. Then they were murdered and the artworks belonged to the people they sold them to. The phony provenances were a nice added touch, a little insulation, and the SS forgers who did them for Krebs are deceased, most of them having been prisoners of various kinds, Jews and so forth. So there is nothing but hearsay against him, but there is a lot of it, and it is consistent."

By this time we were in the *campo* in front of the great white elevation of San Zacccaria, and we paused under the shallow portico to get out of the rain.

"Did you ever meet him? Krebs?" I asked.

"Only once. Krebs was offering for sale a Derain landscape that the French authorities spotted as the property of a Paris clothing manufacturer named Kamine. The man and his family had perished during the war, but a son had escaped to England, and it was his heirs who were making the official claim. Well, not to bore you with the details, but Krebs admitted he had made an error, that the provenance he had was a fake, and he handed over the painting with an apology."

"And . . ."

"Well, I looked at the painting and I had experts look at the painting. The experts said it was Derain. The paint was good, the canvas and frame . . . but all they had to go on was a faded black-and-white print. I thought it was a fake, but my opinion wasn't probative and so the return went through."

"So what happened to the original? I mean, if you were right. A buyer could never sell it on the open market."

"True enough, but you realize there's a substantial *closed* market for artwork. There are any number of people who want to own old masters and Impressionists, far more than the honest market can supply, because, obviously, most of the works are in museums already, and the old masters are, well, dead—there are no more in the pipeline."

"Interesting. What did you make of the man himself?"

"Charming. Cultivated. He knew a great deal about pictures, and not just as a dealer. He truly loved the work. One would think that the stories were true, that he had held on to the remainder of the Schloss paintings."

"Schloss? I never heard of him. Modern?"

"No, he was not a painter. Adolph Schloss was a broker for department stores and purveyor to the Russian imperial court. He was a fabulously wealthy Jew, a French citizen, who assembled what was probably the finest collection of Dutch old masters in private hands, back around the turn of the twentieth century, just the sort of paintings that Hitler and Göring liked best. To make a long story short, the Nazis seized the three-hundred-odd paintings in the collection and shipped them to Munich, and stored them in Nazi party buildings there. Hitler was planning a vast art museum in his hometown of Linz, and this depot was where they stored the things they were going to stock it with.

"In April 1945, the Allies entered Munich, by which time the collections had been thoroughly pillaged by various Germans with access to it, and later the Americans did some light pillaging of their own. The Schloss family eventually recovered one hundred and forty-nine of these paintings, with the rest scattered or lost. Evidence presented at the elder Krebs's trial showed that he worked at the Munich depository in the winter of 1944 and that he left the city with two vans and a military escort in January of 1945. We have no idea what happened to those vans or what was in them. Old Krebs never talked and young Krebs has always denied knowing anything about any stolen old masters. In fact, he always dealt in more modern pictures when he was becoming established."

Here he stopped and appeared about to say something else regarding Krebs, but what came out was, "But now let's look at the Bellini."

We entered the church and I found, almost without willing it, that I had dipped my finger in the marble stoup of holy water at the door and crossed myself.

We stood in silence in front of the altarpiece for a long time, until Maurice sighed deeply and said, "Quite aside from its quality as a work of art, this makes me feel better about my present decrepit age. He was seventy-five when he painted it, can you imagine? Do you know his *Nude with a Mirror?*"

"I saw it when I was a kid, in Vienna."

"His only nude, and he did it when he was *eighty*-five. Marvelous painting, and at eighty-five!"

"I guess he figured it was safe by then."

"Indeed. Sadly safe. But now this . . . how can one do that? To paint the very air around the figures. There is the whole of the Renaissance in one painting. You could with justice say that Giovanni Bellini started the Renaissance in this city, at least in painting, and carried it through decade after decade—incredible! He started painting like Giotto and ended like Titian, who of course was his pupil, as was

Giorgione. And always deep, deep thought from a lost age underlying the contemporary style. So he shows us the Virgin and Child all the way back at the rear of the niche, and no one is looking at them. The angel is sawing away at the viola and she and saints Peter and Jerome are facing us, not the Virgin, and saints Lucy and Catherine there in the middle distance are also lost in contemplation. Whatever was he thinking? In nearly every other altarpiece in the world, the Virgin is the center of attention for all the other figures, but not here."

"Maybe they're just thinking about her. It's a study of contemplation, an example to us who can't see the Virgin at all."

"Yes, that's a good reading. And the art-historical subtext is that if you're a true artist, like Bellini, you must keep at it and keep your spirit open and the art will feed you, if you let it. Lotte tells me you had some trouble in New York."

"What did she tell you?"

"Oh, no details, but she suggested that you might be wise to seek the services of a psychiatrist."

"And this is the reason you looked me up? To check out if I was really nuts?"

"Only partially," he said with a disarming smile. "And I shall be happy to report you seem perfectly sane. Are you doing any of your own painting, by the way?"

"I don't know, Maurice—sometimes I think, What's the point? What does work of my *own* mean anymore? I look at this thing and there's a whole coherent culture embodied in it. The illusionistic space; the theatricality, like a stage set; the atmosphere . . . like you said, he's learned how to paint air, and he can do it because the art and technique are in service of something greater than the artist. But now there's nothing greater than the artist—the artist is *it*. And the critics and the investment potential. If I did something like this, except as a parody, it would be called kitsch. And it would *be* kitsch.

We don't believe in the Virgin and the saints anymore, or at least not the way Bellini did. Our icons are blank and the only religion we see in the galleries is irony. I can do irony fine, but it makes me sick."

"Yes, but my dear man, there is a flourishing school of modern figurative painting, what Kitaj called the school of London—himself, Bacon, Lucien Freud, Auerbach. If you want to paint that way, why not do it?"

"But I *don't* want to paint that way. Gin up a little individual style and sell it to fools? I want to paint like *this*, I want to paint in a culture that *transcends* the art that expresses it. And all that's gone."

He nodded gravely. "Yes. I take your point. And I don't have an answer to your problem. Still, we're standing here and we are having a certain experience. Neither of us, I think, are believers in the sense that Bellini was, and yet we are at this moment under his spell. Is it only admiration for his bravura? Are we merely worshipping his art?"

"Or we're being drugged. You know what Duchamp said about art."

"Yes, 'As a drug it's probably useful for a number of people, very sedative, but as a religion it's not even as good as God.' An interesting man, Duchamp, probably the major influence on the art of the past century, after Cézanne, even though he produced very little work. I met him once, you know."

"Really?"

"Yes, in New York. I was in Greenwich Village and I wanted a coffee and the shop only had one free chair, so I asked the old man sitting there if I could use it. He had a chessboard in front of him, and he said I could sit there if I would give him a game, so I did. It was only after I sat down that I realized it was Duchamp."

"Did you win?"

"Of course not. He was an international grand master. We played three games, and he won the last while spotting me two rooks. We did not, unfortunately, discuss art. I talked about what I have just been telling you, my work in the art recovery effort, and when I told him that there were dozens of masterpieces that had gone missing, do you know what he said? 'They are the fortunate ones.' Everyone thought he'd given up painting entirely, but when he died they found he'd been working on the same painting, a representational nude, for the last twenty years of his life. One looks at it through a peephole."

"What did he think of his artistic progeny?"

"I wish I'd thought to ask him, but from what he wrote I gather he didn't have much use for pop or conceptual art. As I imagine these people, the Virgin and the saints, would not have had much use for what the Catholic Church became after their time. We are a bunch of silly monkeys after all, but what an astounding miracle it is that we can also make and enjoy things like this. After the kind of life I have led . . . you know, there are people who believe that after what Europe has done to itself in the twentieth century, that vast catastrophe, we can no longer have poetry, have art, that this is all meaningless *merde* because it leads to the death camps. They have a point, I suppose, but, as I was saying, after the kind of life I have led, here I am, in a church, looking at Bellini. Another kind of miracle, perhaps."

I didn't know what to say to that, and after a moment he plucked his sleeve back and looked at his watch.

"And now, unfortunately, I must go. I have a meeting at four—at the Gritti, of all places. It's part of the perpetual EU *pagaille* about how to save Venice and its treasures from the rising waters."

"I hope you succeed," I said.

"Perhaps we will, or perhaps one day there will be fishes swimming through here nibbling at the painted saints."

We went outside and found it had stopped raining. Winter sun struggled through the thinning clouds, lighting the facades of the church and the surrounding buildings with dramatic effect. Maurice looked about the *campo*, beaming in delight.

"Now we are in a Canaletto ourselves," he said, and we embraced. Then he held me by the shoulders at arm's length and looked me in the face.

"Chaz, I don't know the extent of your involvement with Herr Krebs, but I would urge you not to get in any further with him."

"Why? I thought you said he wasn't a crook."

"No, I said he had never been caught. It's not the same thing. But whatever his legal status at present, he is not a person you wish to know. Please take my word for this."

I finished the ceiling just before Christmas and Castelli threw a party for the unveiling of the work. My *patrono*, I found, looked just like one of those cutthroat condottieri who ran Italy in the quattrocento, a shark face in Armani, and came with an entourage of shady remoras and a blond sweetie twenty years younger who wasn't Mrs. C. Trailing discreetly along, and looking like he fit right in, was my old pal Mark Slotsky.

So, shitloads of champagne, and later a gigantic seven-course meal under my fresco, a couple dozen rich people, jeweled women, politicians, and so on, and business fascist types. Zuccone informed me that the real Venetians had been invited but declined; all those Golden Book families weren't going to show up to gaze on Castelli's fake Tiepolo. I wasn't invited either. They set up a table in a dusty room near the kitchen for the help, of which I was one, because it was a restoration; the *artist* was Tiepolo, and he was dead. I mean, you wouldn't expect the plasterers or the scaffold guy to be in there with the fucking *patrono*.

And you know, I didn't feel bad about it at all, I felt great, maybe for the first time in my life I felt I was where I belonged. Guys slapped me on the back and kissed me, all like that. We had a great time too, had the same food, and maybe better wine, courtesy of Zuccone, and got drunk and noisy. It was like the *Marriage of Figaro*: the real life, decency, honesty, was below the stairs.

Toward the end of the evening, Mark came in and went through an elaborate and, I thought, totally phony apology about how it was outrageous I hadn't been seated in the frescoed hall, and I was like, it's okay, Mark, I'm having a great time with the *paisans*, and then he kind of leaned close and said, "Castelli was real impressed with what you did, amazed really, he had no idea anyone could work like that, I mean it's fucking perfect, that fresco, you can't tell it from a Tiepolo except it's so fresh and clean."

And I said, "Does that mean I'm getting paid?"

He said, "Absolutely, the check's in my account as we speak. But listen, Chaz, this is just like the very beginning. Two hundred grand is chump change compared to what you could be pulling down with the right connections."

"Bigger ceilings?" I said.

"No, there're guys here tonight who—" And then he dropped his voice even lower, like there was anyone in the room who could speak English worth a damn, and he asked me, "How would you like to make a *million* bucks?"

Well, that got my attention. I said, "Who's going to pay me a million dollars? And for what?"

"Werner Krebs. He's here. He loves your work."

And here I thought about what Maurice had said about the guy, he's shady but loves art, something different from the usual art hag, and different also from a vulgarian semigangster like Castelli, and I decided that despite what Maurice had said, I *did* want to know him.

So I said, "Okay, let's go."

"No, not now—tomorrow. Have you got some decent clothes?"

I said no and asked again what Werner was going to pay me a million dollars for, but he said, "You'll talk to the man, we're on for tomorrow. But we need to get you cleaned up."

He actually bought me an outfit the next morning; we went down to San Marco, Armani for the clothes, shoes at Bottega Veneta, the works, and a barber near the Danieli Hotel who eyed me carefully, like a fresco guy checking a decayed ceiling, and gave me a haircut, face steam, and shave. Then we took the Hotel Cipriani's private launch over to Giudecca and Krebs's suite there. Mark had been doing nervous chatter all morning, but when he got onto the boat he clammed up. I thought he was seasick, but in retrospect I think he was just nervous. Or scared.

I was scared too, but not of Krebs.

While we were on the boat it happened again: I was looking out over the lagoon back to the city, enjoying the feeling of being out on the water again and the terrific if overdone view, and I sort of blinked and saw that the Riva degli Schiavoni was crammed with ships, caravels and cogs and lateen-sailed tartans, and the near distance was full of small craft, and there was black smoke making a smudged cloud over the Arsenale. And there was no engine sound anymore, and I'm on a galley, up on the poop under an embroidered awning, and I'm dressed in black with a ruff; there are other similarly dressed men standing around on the deck, and one of them is speaking to me, Don Gilberto de Peralta, the Spanish ambassador's majordomo, who is serving as my cicerone on this, my first visit to Venice, and we are not heading away from the city but toward it, toward the Molo in front of San Marco, and he's telling me about the Tintorettos and Veroneses in the Sala del Gran Consiglio. I am staring past him at the glittering pile I can just see through the masts of the ships, my heart soaring in my breast. I can barely believe I am in the city of Titian and the other masters; my eyes are hungry for the sights promised me. And now the galley touches gently against the quay and our party descends and assembles at the gangway; the smoke from censers burning to cover the stench of the slaves below blows heavily across our faces, but we can still smell them, the wretches. There is a delegation waiting for us, for I am traveling with Don Ambrogio Spinola, Marqués de los

Balbases, captain-general of the Catholic armies fighting the heretics in the Low Countries, who has been graciously kind to me throughout our voyage from Barcelona. And he steps off first, of course, and then some of his train, and then me, onto the soil of Venice at last.

And I did step onto a pier, but it was the Danieli Hotel's, and I staggered like a drunk and would've fallen if Mark hadn't grabbed my arm. He said, "Christ, man, you should've told me you got seasick. I would've slipped you a Dramamine patch."

"I never get seasick," I said.

"Then it's something. You're white as a sheet. Are you okay to do this?"

I lied that I was fine. I was the last thing from fine; I was thinking, It's been weeks since I had any salvinorin and now I have a salvinorin trip, and maybe I'll wake up in the Gorgeous Loft of Terror again and this whole Venice thing will have proved to be another psychotic break, and it was only with difficulty that I was able to put one foot in front of the other and walk with Mark into the lobby of the hotel.

Krebs had taken the Dogaressa suite. Pale, overstuffed furniture, Oriental carpets on the floor, a view through high, narrow windows of the tower of the Doge's Palace in St. Mark's. I've heard about this place, probably the most expensive room in Venice, three grand a night in euros or something like that, and here was the man himself, trim, dark suit, handmade shoes, five-hundred-dollar tie, a big cigar. He's got that tanned, slick, plastic skin you only see on really rich men, like a Kewpie doll, smooth, all the blemishes and sags of old age expertly removed—he was over seventy, I knew, but he looked fifteen years younger. Short, silvery hair in a fringe around a bald dome—he must've passed on the hair implants. Gave me a look, like a man buying a dog, up and down.

I looked at him the same way: the impression of power, ruthlessness, something you don't see in your average bond trader, and which

I recognized well, having just been in conversation with Captain-General Spinola, back in the seventeenth century. Our eyes met, and a smile formed on his face. A little shock now—he was genuinely glad to see me.

Introductions by Mark, a gentle, dry handshake, not a macho gripper, doesn't need to, obviously. I saw my old pal Franco was there; I thought he worked for Castelli, but no, unless it's a loan, like regular people lend tools: here's my muscle guy and driver, enjoy! We sat deep into the soft couch, he plopped into the armchair opposite, cigars offered, Mark takes one, a Cuban Cohiba, of course; I choose a glass of Dom P. served by Franco, a man of many skills, it seems. Mark starts a little chatter, pleasantries, how was the trip, what a nice room, etc., silenced by a look. He just wants to talk to me.

So—compliments on the Tiepolo, intelligent questions about how we did it, then the talk moves to art, the old masters, who do I like, their virtues and faults. What have I seen in Venice? Not much except Tiepolos, I've been busy. A shame, he says, and tells me what's worth seeing: the Veroneses in the palace, some things at the Franchetti Gallery in the Ca' D'oro, Titian's *Venus at Her Mirror*, don't miss the paintings in San Sebastiano, a good place to get away from the tourists. We talk about there being no major museums in Venice, because Venice *is* a museum, the old Venetians didn't buy pictures from anyone but the local boys, as a rule, and they kept them in their palazzi. He talked about this for a while and seemed to approve of my responses.

I was still a little rocky from my boat ride as Velázquez, but I was feeling the influence of the wine and the flattery. I don't have much experience with wealthy collectors praising my work and being interested in my views on art, so I was yakking away. The guy knew traditional painting up the ying-yang, just like Maurice described; he seemed to have seen practically every important painting in the world at least once, not only in museums but in all the major private collections too. Encyclopedic, really; he makes even Slotsky look like he just got out of Art History 101.

After a while he raised the subject of Velázquez. He said no one painted like Velázquez, incomparable, not the images so much, but the technique. So I talked about the technique, the palette, the brushwork. I said I thought it was because he didn't care, he didn't care about the painting, it wasn't work to him, his self-worth wasn't derived from it.

"How do you know that?" Krebs asked.

I said, "It's obvious. Look at his life: he spent all his real energy climbing the greasy pole, collecting offices, shouldering his way into the aristocracy. He had a great gift and he used it, but it was like he found a box of treasure somewhere, it flowed *through* him, but it wasn't him. And he wasn't driven, he had a sinecure for life, which was why he did fewer paintings than any artist of comparable stature besides Vermeer."

I saw something interesting then: his focus on me seemed to increase, his blue eyes got sharper and hotter, and I found I wasn't just spouting art history stuff, or even my own opinions, I was talking from direct knowledge, like I'd actually felt those feelings about Velázquez's art. Which, of course, I had, in the drug mania, but it was weird all the same that it came through and that he could spot it.

After I ran down on this theme a little, he stood up and said he'd like to show me something. I got up and so did Mark, but Krebs made it clear by a gesture that only I was invited. I followed him into the bedroom of the suite. There was a display easel set up there with a small painting on it, maybe thirty inches by a little less, and he asked me to take a look at it.

I looked: it was a portrait of a man in black velvet with a small ruff, fleshy face, mustache, and spade beard, his hand playing with a gold chain around his neck, a look of comfortable sensuality. The paint was thin, the fine canvas almost showing through, the brushwork free as a swallow in the skies, the palette simple, not more than five pigments. I'd never seen a Velázquez outside a museum. Nor had I ever seen a reproduction of this painting. It was a fucking *unknown* Velázquez, propped up on an easel in a guy's hotel room. Sweat popped out all over me.

So after a while he said, "What do you think?"

I said, "What do I think? I think it's a Velázquez, it looks contemporary with the ones of Cardinal Pamphili and the Pope, probably from the 1649 trip to Rome." He seemed to be waiting for something else, so I said, "I never saw it before."

He nodded and said, "That's because it's one of his lost paintings. It's a portrait of Don Gaspar Méndes de Haro, Marqués de Heliche. An interesting face, wouldn't you say? A man who gets what he wants."

I agreed and asked him how he'd gotten the painting. He didn't answer directly. Instead he asked me, did I like museums? I said I liked them fine, I'd spent hundreds, maybe thousands of hours in museums, that's how you got to look at originals.

"Yes," he said, "that's one way, but do you *like* them, do you enjoy that they're only open at certain hours, really for the convenience of the bureaucrats and the little stuffed men in their uniforms, do you enjoy the packs of whey-faced tourists shuffling endlessly through the halls, being exposed to art so they can say they saw something they can't possibly comprehend? Wouldn't you like to have all day to contemplate a painting, this painting perhaps, at any hour of the day, all by yourself? Like Don Gaspar did with this one, or as he did with Velázquez's *Venus*, or as Phillip the Fourth did with the other paintings this man did for him? Wouldn't that be fine?"

I agreed it would be fine, but that it was like wishing you could swim like a fish or fly like a bird, a useless desire, and then his eyes heated up and he said, "Not at all."

He pointed to the portrait. "Do you think *that* man would ever think of allowing his swineherds and scullery maids into his gallery to gawp at his *Venus and Cupid?*

I laughed and said, "Probably not, but he's long dead; things have changed."

"Not as much as you think, perhaps," he said. "There are still men like that, and I am obviously one of them, because this picture will never hang in a museum. As for the others, let's say that they are men of great wealth, power, and discrimination, with private collections of which the world knows nothing. These are the men I deal with, Wilmot, and I assure you it is very profitable to do so."

I didn't get what he meant, so I said, "You might be right. I wouldn't know, not being an art dealer."

"No, you are a painter, and a painter as gifted as Velázquez in your way. I mean to say, if I asked you to paint *me*, in just that style, I have every confidence that you could do it."

He gave me an inquiring look, and I said I probably could. He said, "When I saw that ceiling you painted, I was astounded. Because you know, it was *better* than Tiepolo, lusher, more lively, but still identifiable as his. Do you know, I have been following your work for many years."

"Really? That's strange, I haven't painted for the gallery trade in a long time."

"No, I meant the pastiches. The advertisements and magazine illustrations. I said to myself, this fellow, whyever is he wasting his time with this garbage? He really knows how to paint in the grand manner, and not the degraded form that has dominated that sort of painting for a hundred and fifty years—Landseer, Bouguereau, and so forth—but as the old masters painted, with penetration and density and passion. You seemed like a man born out of his time."

I felt a bubble of tension form in my belly and rise into my throat so that I had to swallow a lump, first, because since my breakdown this was the first independent, undeniable confirmation that the miserable life I recalled was real in some objective sense; and second, because for the first time in my adult life I'd found someone who really understood who I *was*.

I managed to say, "Well, thank you. I've often felt that way myself."

"I'm sure. I also am a man born outside of his time, so we have something in common, you and I. So when Castelli mentioned that he was repairing his palazzo and wished to hire an artist, I naturally thought of you and so he made the offer through Mark Slade."

"Well, then, thank you, again."

"Yes, but this is really nothing compared to what you are capable of, isn't it so? There you were copying an existing design, but of course, you can paint from your own imagination as well, as Velázquez did, as Rubens did, and so forth. Fate has brought us together, yes?" Here a smile, a charming one, we men of the world sharing a moment. Okay, to be honest, I was bowled over a little. Like I say, stuff like this doesn't happen to me on an average day in New York.

He led me back to the living room of the suite and had lunch served; waiters brought in a table and a whole spread, with wine and everything, and we ate convivially enough. Krebs pulled Mark out of the freezer, to which Mark responded like a toy poodle. I was a little loopy from all the wine and so it took a while for me to pick up that the conversation had swung around to me, that somehow an arrangement had been made that involved me doing something and that a million dollars was involved. Mark had neglected to tell me that I was part of some done deal.

So I said, "Excuse me, guys, I seem to be missing something. What am I supposed to do for my million?"

There fell a silence, and Krebs shot Mark a look that turned him moth-wing green. Krebs said, "I thought you had thoroughly briefed Wilmot on this project."

Mark spluttered some lame excuse, but Krebs shut him down. He gave me a look like a stainless steel rod, no smiles now. He said, "When Velázquez was in Rome, according to reliable testimony, he made four paintings of women in the nude, in all probability for Don Gaspar himself. As everyone knows, only one of them survives, the so-called *Rokeby Venus*. You're going to paint one of the others, in the same style and with the same skill. And, later, who knows? There may be other opportunities in that line."

Okay, so at first I figured this was the *Vanity Fair* job again, which was cool, but then I thought, Why so much money? I recalled Mark's crackpot scheme to sell real-fakes to the masters of the universe, and for a bit I thought this was the same on a larger scale. I asked about that, and he said, "No, I am not interested in decorations for the nouveau riche. I am interested in a painting that is stylistically and physically indistinguishable from a genuine Velázquez—accurate in every respect: the stretchers, the canvas, the pigments, all must be period. And that requires a certain skill, which I am willing to pay for."

So then—*duh!*—I got it.

I said, "You're going to sell it as genuine, aren't you? You're paying me a million bucks to forge a Velázquez."

The F-word, once out in the air, didn't seem to affect him at all. He said, "Call it what you like. You understand, Wilmot, there is an immense private demand for old masters, not to mention the attraction of the subject matter. Who would not want to have their own *Venus* by Velázquez? And this sort of thing has been going on for years. You go to a museum and you read the little tags and so you know, this is a Tintoretto, this is a Vermeer, and mostly that attribution is based on people like Duveen or Berenson or even your friend here, whose primary interest is in selling paintings for large sums. But the main thing is the quality of the painting, what it does to the eye and the heart. If the painting speaks to the eye and the heart, who cares if it came from the brush of Titian or from someone just as good?"

I pointed out that it was, like, still illegal, and that I preferred not to go to prison, because when any unknown old master painting showed up at auction, not to mention a Velázquez, people would ask questions, there were forensic tests . . . but he waved his hand in the air, brushing away flies.

"First of all," he said, "there is no question of any auctions. This will be a strictly private sale, for cash. And as far as forensics go, I have people who are experts in this, they will advise you. Besides this, there is no illegality without a complaint, and there will be no complaint. The clients will be happy, you will be happy, I will be happy, even Mr. Slade here will be happy. Happiness all around, what could be wrong with that?"

"Nothing, I guess. Look, no offense, but this is a little strange for me. Can I think about it a little before I decide?"

So Krebs kind of leans forward and makes a little tent with his hands, and now he has a different kind of smile.

He said, "My friend, you put me in something of an uncomfortable position. Arrangements have been made with various people on the understanding that you are agreed on this project. Monies have been advanced, and the kind of people who advance monies for such a thing are not the Deutsche Bank. Also, you are now privy to the plan. If I now go back to my people and say, well, Wilmot will not do it, then I am in big trouble and, I am very much afraid, so are you and so is your friend Mark. Here we are in beautiful Venice, the home of the oubliette, you know? The little hole in the floor where you drop the fellow who has become inconvenient? You wait for the right tide, of course, and all your errors are flushed away by the sea. I'm sad to say I have very unforgiving partners."

MICHAEL GRUBER

It was the kind of situation where you can't really believe it's happening to you, and I kind of chuckled, like he was a big kidder, and said, "Who are these partners?"

He kept smiling, as at an idiot child: no, we mustn't stick the fork in the wall socket, dear.

"They prefer to remain silent partners, very discreet people, these partners. In any case I urge you to reconsider your position. Really, it's a choice between being rich and happy or else all three of us floating out into the *laguna*."

"What about Franco? Is he going to float too?"

I looked at Franco, who was standing in the corner with his arms folded. He gave me a white-toothed smile too. Everyone was happy except Mark, who looked like a piece of old Gorgonzola.

Krebs said, "Oh, Franco! Franco will be fine. Franco doesn't work for me, you see. He is a representative of the interests I was just discussing. In fact, I believe he would actually participate in the disposals, should they become necessary. With great regret, I'm sure."

He clapped his hands; Mark jumped an inch off his cushion.

"But . . . why are we dwelling on hypothetical unpleasantness? You will do the job, yes?"

I nodded. "Now that you put it in those terms . . . I would be happy to."

He said, "Excellent!" and extended his hand, and we shook.

"And now you are in the great Venetian tradition of *contrafazzione*, in which I believe you have already begun with your marvelous Tiepolo. Wilmot, I don't think you have yet understood that now you have entered a completely different mode of being. Before this you belonged to the world of people who wait in lines like sheep, at the tram, at the airport, and scrabble for a living because there is never enough, and eat shit every day. You have before now wasted yourself making pictures for magazines and have had to wait in the anterooms of men who are not fit to clean your boots. And when you became ill, or your children became ill, then you also had to wait, wait for some doctor to give you a moment of his so valuable time. You have a sick child, yes? You have no idea of what it will now be like for you and this child. The finest care, the finest! Clinics in Switzerland . . . do you need organs? Expensive drugs? There is no question you will get what you require, and with a smile too, and with no delay."

I said something stupid about the forgery business having a good health care plan. He ignored me; he was in full flood and went on for quite a while about the difference between the proles and their masters, and all about how the masters deserved the art and the proles didn't, and how wonderful it was going to be for me, probably not a set of opinions you'd be likely to hear in New York society, but maybe I was wrong, maybe this was how these people talked all the time when people like me weren't around. It was an interesting change, anyway, from hanging around with rich liberals. And then he said something that really got to me.

He said, "You are a great artist, Wilmot, and now that we have discovered one another you will fulfill your destiny, you will be my Velázquez. This is what you have wanted your whole life—to paint like this and be rewarded for it, am I not right?"

And, you know, he was. That's what I wanted. That is what I'd always wanted, and never knew until that moment.

I said, "And you're the king of Spain."

He nodded and said, "Yes. I am the king of Spain." No irony. We were in an irony-free zone, which I also found strange and bracing.

And I said, "Okay, Your Majesty. Where do you want this painting done? Here in Venice?"

And he said, "No, in Rome, of course. It's all arranged."

S lotsky and I went out to the launch and boarded it, and as soon as we'd cleared the dock I turned to him and said, "Well, Mark, you really know how to show a girl a good time."

"Jesus Christ, Wilmot! Do you think I knew what that crazy fucker was going to propose? I just thought he was going to give you another restoration job. Do you think I like being threatened with fucking *death*? I'm an art dealer, for crying out loud! I thought I was going to crap in my pants there."

"Don't bullshit me, buddy. I think we're *way* the fuck out of the bullshitting regions now. I've heard a little about Herr Krebs from another source; he's not just your everyday old masters dealer, and if I knew it, so did you. You set this whole thing up, but you were too chickenshit to let me in on it before he proposed it and it was too late. Why? Because you knew goddamn well I would never have come if I'd known. So spill!"

He said, "I swear to *God* I didn't know he was talking about a forgery. I never would have gotten you into this if—"

I stepped closer to him, put my arm around his shoulders, and grabbed his near arm.

"Let me interrupt you here, Mark," I said, close to his ear. "I am angry. I'm a mild kind of guy, but like many mild guys, when I blow my top I'm out of control. I'm shaking from the adrenaline and I probably have the superhuman strength you read about, and so, my little man, if you don't fucking level with me about Krebs and this whole deal, I am going to pick you up and throw you over the side of this vessel."

And after a little struggle, out it came, because I really would have tossed him in the drink, and he knew it. I think it was the four-thousand-dollar suit and the five-hundred-dollar shoes more than the fear of actually drowning.

"Okay, here's the whole thing," he said. "First, what do you know about art theft?"

"Enough to know that ninety-five percent of it is bozos grabbing pictures off the wall and running out the door. Most museum security is a joke."

"Exactly. But here I'm talking about the other five percent. I'm talking well-known paintings that can never be sold openly. Assuming they're stolen by halfway smart thieves, what do they get out of it?"

"Ransom?"

"There's that, but the fact is that when professional thieves lift major works of art, they want them for purposes of collateral. Criminal enterprises need to raise money the same as legitimate ones, and obviously they can't go to legitimate sources of credit. A twenty-million-dollar painting is light, portable, easily hidden. I give you my painting, and you give me the five mil I need to buy heroin or armaments, and then when I've made my pile I pay you back plus your vig and you give me back my work of art. If the deal goes sour, you get to keep the painting. There are paintings we know of that've been used this way multiple times. It's better than drugs or cash because there's less possibility of pilferage, a little like commercial paper for bad guys."

"I thought those boys worked by shooting people if they didn't pay."

"Oh, they do, they do, but that doesn't do shit for their cash flow. With the artwork, they're covered."

"And where does our friend come into this?"

"I'll tell you where. Think about it: at any one time there are a couple of dozen major works of art floating around the underworld, and these guys are not usually connoisseurs. They got no use for a Renoir. After the need for collateral is over, or if the party who has it in pawn needs some ready cash, what does he do? He's got something worth twenty mil and he's got no fucking idea in the world how to realize it. That's what Krebs does."

"He sells stolen artworks for criminals. Terrific. Who does he sell them to?"

"The people he was talking about. Rich fuckers who don't give a damn."

"And let me guess—you find the rich fuckers for him."

"What're you, nuts? I'm a legitimate dealer, I can't be associated with the sale of stolen goods."

"So what's your end of the deal?"

"I'm a consultant."

I laughed in his face.

"Seriously," he said. "No kidding. He needs someone to talk to."

"Who, Krebs? Mark, with all due respect, Krebs doesn't need you to advise him about paintings."

"No, but he does need a legitimate dealer to get him close to the museums. Not that the big houses are above handling dodgy stuff, but Krebs is poison. So when the time comes, it turns out that some-one not to be named has offered Mark Slade Associates the stolen Renoir. Does the museum want it back? Of course they do, and so do the insurance companies who paid out. I arrange for the transfer and take a commission. The thief gets something, Krebs is insulated, the insurer cuts their loss, the picture's back on the wall. Everyone is happy."

"So you're a front. A beard."

"If you want to call it that. As far as the museum is concerned, I'm a hero. And this is all very discreet. I mean, you know me for years and you had no idea."

"But I'm sort of not surprised. Where do the cops figure in all this?"

"What cops? Some of this isn't even reported, and what is reported, well, most cops think there are better uses of their time, the guy who holds up liquor stores with a gun, drug gangs, rapists. They could care less, really, if some rich assholes lose a couple of paintings, especially if they get them back. They might get interested if an art theft led to a drug gang, or a big arms dealer, but if not, then not."

"Not even about forgery?"

"What're you talking *forgery?* Forgery is I steal some checks and draw money from your account. Forgery is a fake will, Auntie Agatha's money goes to the evil nephew and not the old cats' shelter. There's an injured party. Here, you're producing a work of art indistinguishable from an original. *Indistinguishable!* Where's the injury? The buyer looks at it and he's full of exactly the same pride and pleasure as he would be if the work came from some guy who died three hundred years ago. And like Krebs said, how the hell do we know if *anything* is genuine? Because a so-called scholar who was getting paid by a dealer said so? The whole attribution thing is horseshit from beginning to end."

"So we might as well get rich off the corruption."

"Damn straight! Look, you probably don't know any Wall Street types, bond traders, mergers and acquisitions guys, hedge fund managers, but I do. They're my best customers. Chaz, believe me, these guys are assholes. They know nothing. When the market's up they're geniuses, and when the market's down it's not their fault, and they walk away with billions. These are people who run up a fifteen-thousand-dollar bar bill in an evening and they don't even *think* about it. And you want me to be scrupulous about the authenticity of some *painting* I sell them?"

"It's a point of view."

"It's the only one that makes sense, given the world as it is. Look, Chaz, I *love* painting. That's something we have in common, me and Krebs. It's not just commodities or bragging rights for us. It's the only fucking *genuine* thing that's left. And I love your work. You're a wonderful artist, and over the years every time I'd see one of those things you'd done for some magazine, it'd stab me in the heart; I'd think, What a waste! And okay, you wouldn't show your work, I don't even want to ask why, but, honest to God, I always wanted to see you get out of that grungy world, busting your ass for three, four, five grand a pop, living in that shithole you're in, never having any leisure, none of the respect your work deserves, and when this opportunity came up—"

"How did it come up?"

"Well, like he said, he's a big fan."

"That wasn't bullshit?"

"No, and in fact that's how I was able to get close to him. I met him at a party at Castelli's. I'd sold him—I mean Castelli—a nice Correggio red chalk study of St. Mark, and I got introduced. This is like seven, eight years ago. Of course, I'd heard of Krebs, and we got to talking about painting, I mean contemporary stuff, and how we neither of us would hang on our own personal walls the work of anyone who couldn't draw, and we talked about who could and couldn't and he brought up your name. He'd seen that poster you did for the AIDS group, the Bosch? He thought it was amazing, and he was blown away when I told him you were like practically my best friend."

"Former best friend."

"Oh, come off it, Wilmot! I saw your eyes light up when he started talking about the money. Stop acting like a girl who just lost her cherry."

I gave him a hard look, or what was meant to be one, but I knew there was no moral force behind it, and so did he.

The boat touched, bounced; the deck man leaped off and secured the prow to a cleat. I said, "Yeah, well, why the hell not?"

Mark grinned and clapped me on the shoulder. We walked into Venice like regular people.

Back at my hotel there was an envelope waiting for me containing instructions for my trip to Rome. Interesting. Were they so sure I would agree, or did Krebs have agents ready to deliver such instructions at a moment's notice? I found I didn't care and that I was not offended. So they had my number? So what? In any case, there was a private jet leaving in the morning. I would get on it with Franco, but until then I was free.

Then out of the hotel, walking aimlessly in the direction of San Zaccaria. Man, I was scared to death but full of incredible energy, it was like waking up in Oz, intensified color, little shivers on my skin. I passed the San Zaccaria vaporetto stop, where a boat waited; I wandered aboard and thought it might possibly be my very last trip ever on public transportation. We putt-putted around the lagoon and I got off at San Basilio in the Dorsoduro. I recalled Krebs talking about San Sebastiano, and I thought I'd drop in and take a look. The *campo* there in front of the church and the Scuola dei Carmini is one of the few places in Venice with any trees, pretty neat, but the Scuola building was closed. I waved a fifty-euro note in the guard's face because I'm now one of the people who don't ever have to wait. Inside there were walls and walls and walls of Giambattista Tiepolo's work, which I liked but thought a bit too heavily influenced by that of Charles P. Wilmot, Jr.

Then I went to the church itself, which is entirely covered by Veronese paintings, except there's one by Rubens, one of the very few

Rubens paintings in Venice, *Esther Before Ahasuerus*. It was dark in there so I had to peer close, and then I noticed that the painting wasn't a Rubens at all but a Titian, *Danaë Receiving the Golden Rain*, and for a strange transitory second I thought, Boy, this is a funny painting for a church, that splayed white body, luscious, and I am in El Escorial and I am caught up in a strange emotion . . . fear, a little, but mainly joy, elation. It is one of the best days of my life, as great almost as when I was made painter to His Majesty's household, because next to me, listening respectfully to what I have to say, is Peter Paul Rubens, the greatest man in the whole world, save only His Majesty of Spain and the Pope.

He is telling me that I have to go to Italy, to see the classics and the great Italian painters, and although he is the most diplomatic of men, in fact a professional diplomat, still I am conscious of a tone, a suggestion that Madrid is not the center of the artistic universe, that being the painter to the king of Spain is perhaps not all that a painter can ask for, and I understand that yes, I must travel to Italy, and I begin to think how this can be arranged with the king, and with my lord the Count-Duke Olivares, who is my patron and besides has his hand on the purse.

So we talk about Titian some more and how he obtains his effects, how he can create motion out of controlling the eye of the viewer, and how this is done with color and composition, a technical problem that I wish to solve because he is suggesting that it is one thing I lack, that all Spanish painters of the present time lack: the figures are still, like tombstones; passion, yes, but not this Italian movement.

And then it's later, or another day, and he's copying one of His Majesty's Titians and I'm watching him paint, he's demonstrating something and just then one of the dwarfs comes trotting along, I can't recall its name, an ugly squat thing, and when it sees us it begins to tumble and makes faces, and not wishing to be distracted I snap at the thing and tell it to be off. And it goes scuttling away.

Rubens pauses and watches the creature pass. I am surprised when he asks, "What do you think of your king?"

So I make the conventional response, or start to, but he shakes his head, and says, "No, Don Diego, I wish to hear not the courtier but the man. I know he's been good to you and that you're a loyal subject, but were Philip not king by God's grace, then how would you judge him?"

I say, "As a painter he is not much," and he laughs and says, "Nor as a king, I think. He is a fool, a decent man enough, but not a brain in his head. And your Olivares is as bad. All Europe knows it. You think not?"

He points to the painting he is copying, Titian's *Charles the Fifth on Horseback*, and says, "When *he* ruled Spain, it was out of all question the mightiest realm upon earth, and now eighty years later you cannot beat the Dutch. Or the French, or the English. In that same time, you have brought from the Indies a mountain of gold and silver, a mountain! And gold and silver still land at Cádiz every year. Yet Castille and Aragon are among the poorest lands in Europe, miserable villages, miserable cities, miserable roads, rags and staring bones wherever you go. Flanders is rich, Holland is rich, England is rich, France is richest of all, yet Spain with all its gold is poor. How can this be?"

I say I don't know, I am ignorant of such things, but also that the magnificence of the palaces in Madrid belies his accusation.

Rubens says, "Yes, gold enough for palaces, if barely. His Majesty still owes me five hundred reales, and I doubt I shall have it before I leave. Now listen to me, sir. You are a fine painter and may be a great one someday. As great as him, perhaps"—he gestures grandly with his brush at the Titian—"or me. I have never seen anyone paint as you do.

I devise a painting in my mind, and think it out, and block it in, the bones of the piece, as it were, and perhaps I will do the faces, too, and let my people paint the rest. For as you know, I must earn my bread by my brush: I am not the painter to the king of Spain. But you, while you know little of composition and your figures are arranged anyhow and pressed together like a crowd in a tavern, still you have the gift of a living brush, the painting flies out of you like breath. But you must go to Italy, sir, Italy's the place to learn how to build a painting. And soon, while the king still has enough to pay your way."

And he laughed. We both laughed, although my laugh was a little forced.

"And another thing. You are a born painter and have made yourself a good courtier enough, but you will never make a diplomat, sir. It is your face, sir. While I was slighting your king and country just now, you had a look of murder on your face, and that is a look we diplomats can never wear. But you will do well; the king loves you, I have heard him say it. And I will say more, for I have known more kings than you, sir. They love us, yes, but they love us in the way they love their dwarfs and fools, like that little fellow just now, amusing for a moment and then got rid of with a kick and a curse. Never think otherwise, sir, however sweetly His Majesty praises you; they are none of them to be trusted."

And now I am in a room brightly lit with candles, speaking with my lord the Count-Duke of Olivares, the king's prime minister, about Italy, and he says they are sending General Spinola there, I can go with him. His Majesty will approve the voyage and will ask you to buy paintings for him, but for the love of God keep down the cost!

Then I am in a different place, walking down a narrow street, and everything is marble, old marble. Faces crumbled with time stare out of the architecture; there is a different smell and a different feel to the air, it is damp, and the women have a different look to them, bolder and more saucy, I think. I'm in Italy, in a crowded street, and I look around for my party, my servants, and there are some artists and officials of this city, I can't recall which one, Modena, Naples . . . ?

I move to push by some people. There is a bridge of some kind ahead that looks familiar, and someone says, "Mister, can you take a picture of us, please?" and sticks out her hand, and there's a digital camera in it.

I stared dumbly at her and her husband said, "Honey, he's a foreigner, he can't speak English," but the woman said, "Yes, he can. You're an American, aren't you?"

A middle-aged woman with a Midwestern accent, small, tanned, her husband huge by her in a yellow golf jacket; the color hurt my eyes. The bridge was the Rialto, and it took me a half minute or so to understand what the little silvery thing in my hand was. Oh, right, a camera; so I take the picture and give the camera back to her. Now her smile was uncertain; she thought I was some kind of maniac.

I just stood there like I was one of those poles they use to tie up the gondolas while the tourists swarmed around me, thinking, How the hell did I walk blind across half of Venice, from San Sebastiano in Dorsoduro all the way through San Polo and the Rialto without falling into the water?

Then I ducked into a bar and had a grappa, and then another, and then a beer. Watched the tourists for a while, and when a group of seventeenth-century folks strolled by I blinked and swallowed booze until they weren't there anymore.

Later I looked it up on the Web in an Internet café. It checked out: Velázquez and Rubens met when Rubens came to Madrid on a diplomatic mission and also to paint for the king. He did an equestrian portrait of Philip that got hung up in place of the one Velázquez did, which maybe was just politeness, but in any case the two painters got along okay. Rubens gave him some good advice, and Velázquez, age thirty, went off to Italy the next year. I had lived through his entrance into Venice the other day.

The funny part about this was that I was kind of glad to still be crazy in this way, because in having fantasies about being Velázquez I was still being who I was, if you get what I'm saying. The *me* Chaz Wilmot. The pasticheur, the coming forger. Not that other guy in New York who I didn't want to think about. A small plank to cling to in the whirlpool, but it was all I had. I left the café and returned to my hotel, where I packed and drank in a local bar until I was in the mood for sleep, and then slept and woke up.

A pang of terror upon awakening. I checked. Still me.

We took off in a private jet from Nicelli Airport, which is a small airport right on the Lido, just east of the city. A Gulfstream II, and I was trying to act cool, like I was used to this kind of travel, which I supposed I would have to learn to like from now on, although the only person to impress on the scene was Franco, who ignored me. I was alone with him in the cabin except for a pretty young woman who couldn't do enough for us. I drank a bottle of perfectly chilled Taittinger, in memory of Dad, and got a little looped, and wondered what would happen if I turned into Velázquez on an airplane. Would I go crazy? More than I am, I mean.

Franco drank only coffee, probably because he was on duty, and read an Italian sports magazine. Not a talkative fellow, Franco. I asked him who he worked for, and he said he worked for Signor Krebs, even though we both knew it wasn't true. Or maybe Krebs was lying, I thought. Maybe there was no Mr. Big behind all this, maybe he just said that to get me scared. But I wasn't scared, or at least not of the forgery business. As far as that went, he had me at the million dollars.

I recall studying Franco's head, a look like one of Masaccio's Romans, that handsome brutality without any hint of sadism. A button man, as they say, a professional. Would he kill me, if he were ordered to? No question. I found then that I didn't mind it as much as I probably would have if it had been presented to me beforehand as an option. Most of the great painters before the nineteenth century passed their lives rubbing shoulders with people who would've cut throats for a handful of coins. There was actually something terrifically baroque about it, the farthest thing from the art hags of Manhattan, invigorating as pure oxygen.

We landed in Rome and drove in a Mercedes to a house on the Via L. Santini, one of the little streets that run off the Piazza di S. Cosimato in Trastevere. We had the whole house. There was a furniture shop on the ground floor selling antiques they fake in the back; I had the *piano nobile* upstairs, a nice three-bedroom apartment, and my studio was one flight up. When we arrived, Franco turned me over to an old guy named Baldassare Tasso, who was going to help me with the work. Apparently he was the head forger. He showed me the studio where I was to paint and explained that the entire surface of the room, floors, ceiling, walls, had been stripped back to the seventeenth century or prior, the debris vacuumed and washed and vacuumed again. The windows were sealed shut and all the air intake came from a vent that led to a heat pump and a HEPA filtration system designed to catch and trap anything from the twenty-first century. I was supposed to enter the studio through an anteroom, in which I had to remove any clothing except for that made of leather, cotton, linen, and wool. I had to work in a natural fiber zone, for what a shame if after all my work there were fragments of nylon or polyethylene stuck to the paint! The room was furnished with an antique wooden easel, some old tables and chairs, and a couch, all vetted for period. The top floor was where the cook, Signora Daniello, and her daughter and her daughter's kid lived. Me and Franco and Tasso were in residence in the apartment. Everything was as jolly as hell, smiles all around.

After we moved in, Franco handed me an envelope containing a black Deutsche Bank MasterCard and an ATM card for my account, which I was not aware that I had ever applied for, but that's apparently how things got done in my new life. We had a lunch, which was a really terrific risotto; Sra. Daniello's daughter, whose name I didn't get, was the housemaid and waitress, and I think Franco had something going there or wanted to. After lunch and a small traditional nap I took a walk down the Viale di Trastevere until I found a bank, stuck my new card in the slot, got five hundred euros for walking-around money, and learned that I had an available balance of a hundred thousand euros.

I went back to the house sort of floating over the quaint cobblestones. Franco was standing outside the house looking anxious; he asked me where I'd been, and I told him and asked him whether there'd been a mistake in my account, so much money in it, and he said, no, Signor Krebs was very generous to those who work for him. And now a big smile. I got the sense that he was glad I was back, that he was supposed to watch me all the time.

So I figured I better get right to work, yes indeedy, and went up to the studio, where I found Baldassare taking the paper off a flat package. After he unwrapped it he set it on the easel. It was about fifty by seventy inches, a *Flight to Egypt* so dark and dirty you could just about make out what a talentless piece of shit it was, some Caravaggio wannabe who could barely draw.

"What do you think, signor?" he asked. I made the Italian choking gesture and he laughed. "Who's it by?" I asked him, and he said, "A name lost to art history, but it dates from around 1650, it was painted in Rome, and he used the same very-fine-weave linen canvas that Velázquez liked. So we will clean this shit off and you will paint on his good seventeenth-century glue-size primer."

"And the stretchers will be period perfect too," I added, and he got a funny, sneaky look on his face and said, "Yes, eventually." I had no idea what he meant until a good while later.

He spoke slowly in a mixture of Italian and English, and I could understand him pretty well. A scrawny bald guy, he must've been around seventy, little gold-framed glasses, a bald dome with liver spots all over his scalp and a fringe of white curls. He looked like Gepetto in the cartoon *Pinocchio*, complete to the bib apron and the rolled-up sleeves and the neck-cloth.

I asked him about paints and brushes and he led me over to one of the tables, where a group of bottles and jars was neatly arranged along with what looked like a bunch of used bristle brushes. With some pride in his voice he told me what I was looking at.

"Ground pigments, all exactly similar to the ones Velázquez used in 1650; we have calcite to add transparency to the glazes, naturally. For yellow, tin oxide; for the reds, vermillion of mercury, red lake, red iron oxide; for the blues you have smalt and azurite. We've oxidized the smalt so it's grayer than it would have been when it was supposedly painted on, so you'll have to take that into consideration when you use it. Then the browns—brown iron oxide, ochre, manganese oxide. No greens—he always made his greens, as I'm sure you know."

"Yeah, but what about the red lake? That's organic. It can be dated."

He grinned and nodded like he was acknowledging a dull but willing pupil. "Yes, that's true, and he used a lot of it. We were able to locate a store of very old red cloth, and we extracted the dyestuffs with alkali. Spectrographically they're from cochineal and lac, which is consistent with what your man used, and the carbon isotopes should give us no worries. The same for the blacks. We used charcoal from archaeological sites. They burned a lot of buildings in the Thirty Years' War, and a lot of people too. And they can date white too, you know."

I didn't know, except that you had to use lead, not zinc or titanium, I knew that much, and he said, "Yes, of course, we use lead white, the so-called flake white, but now they can analyze the ratio of various radioisotopes in the lead and can date when the lead was smelted from the galena ore. Therefore we have to make our flake white from seventeenth-century lead, which we have done. The museums of Europe are full of old bullets and the churches are roofed with old lead. It is not so difficult. In the cellar there is an earthenware vat where we corrode the lead with acetic acid to make lead carbonate. We use electric heaters instead of burying the vat in dung, but that should not affect the authenticity. The pigment is a little coarse, but you can use that to good effect, as Velázquez did. Extremely poisonous, of course, signor, you must not point your brushes in your mouth. And as for these brushes, I think you'll agree we have done well."

He held up a jar with a dozen or so brushes of all sizes. I'd never seen any like them before; the handles were heavy, dark wood, and the hairs were tied into the ferule with fine brass wire.

Baldassare said, "These are on loan from a museum in Munich. Genuine seventeenth century, in case a tiny hair should slip out into the painting—we don't want someone to say, oh, this badger died in 1994."

"On *loan*?" I said.

"In a manner of speaking, signor. They will be returned when we are done with them."

"Who did they belong to?"

"Attributed to Rubens, but who knows? Perhaps they are forgeries too." A big smile, just like Franco's, but with fewer teeth. Smiles all around this place, and it made me nervous.

He showed me the divan where I was going to pose my model, with the velvet draperies and bedclothes in the approximate Velázquez colors: red, a greeny gray, and white, all as naturally fibrous as could be. A heavy wood-framed rectangular mirror was standing against the wall.

"You have the model too," I said.

He shrugged. "We have Sophia. And her boy. We can get another, but we would prefer to keep all of this work in the house, as a matter of security."

So I asked, "Who's Sophia?" and he looked surprised and said, "She served you your risotto this afternoon."

"Oh, the waitress," I said, and I honestly couldn't recall what she looked like.

"Yes, she helps her mother, but she's an artist. Like you."

I said, "You mean a forger."

A nod, a smile, an Italian gesture of the hand. "A forger *is* an artist. She does antiquities and drawings, small things, very good quality. The boy will pose too, you know, with the mirror. The Cupid. Naturally, in the faces you will use your imagination, we don't want someone to say, you know, I saw that woman with that little boy on the Number Fourteen bus."

I agreed that would be embarrassing, and then for the rest of the afternoon I watched him rub out the crappy *Flight into Egypt*.

He used flame and turpentine—and not just any turps, he used the kind I'd be using for the painting, real Strasbourg turpentine made from the resin of the Tyrolian silver fir. Terrific smell, a little Pavlov in there; when it hit my nose I couldn't wait to get back to work. Fresco is neat but there's nothing like oil, just the feel of it down the brush to your hand and the way it shines, rich and sweaty, and of course that smell. Baldassare was talking about varnish, how we'd use real mastic from Pistaccia trees, the finest Chios grade, prepared with that same turpentine.

"How are we going to age it?" I asked him, and he stopped cleaning and made that gesture of the finger to the side of the nose, indicating a secret.

"You will see, but first we do the painting, okay?"

The cleaning and the drying of the canvas took a couple of days, during which I wandered around the city, on foot and by public transportation. Franco offered to drive me anyplace I wanted to go, but I preferred to mooch around the city myself. I hadn't been in Rome since I came with Dad at age ten. Obviously, it's changed, becoming more like everywhere else.

I looked at a lot of pictures but I kept coming back to the Doria Pamphili and Velázquez's Pope. Joshua Reynolds thought it was one of the best portraits in the world. Second that. The first time I ever saw it I was terrified and had nightmares about it for weeks afterward. "Innocent, my ass!" is what my father said, before giving me his usual close reading of the work. He was always going on about the inherent superiority of an oil portrait to a photograph, especially when the image was literally as large as life, as here. You don't see many life-size photographs, and even when you see actors on the screen, larger than life, as the saying goes, it's still not the same. There's something about the human scale that finds a trigger in our brains, and this painting has the usual legends attached to it, of servants coming into a room where it was hanging and mistaking it for the actual man, bowing and so forth.

But its power comes from a lot more than scale, because a life-size Kodachrome print would be a joke. It's not mere illusion, has nothing to do with those fussy little *nature mort* or trompe l'oeil paintings you see in the side rooms of museums, it's its own thing, the life of two men, artist and subject interpenetrated, coming alive, the vital loom of a life in a moment of time—no wonder the servants bowed. And technically, the handling of the satin of the *camauro* and the *manteletta* and the dense fall of the *rochetta*, white but made of every color but white, and the rendering of the damp flesh of a living man—you can look at it for hours and digitize the fucking brushstrokes and penetrate it with X-rays, yet still at its heart there's a mystery. All the balls he had to keep in the air at once, every brushstroke in balance with every other—and what strokes, exactly right, each one, and all perfectly free, loose, and graceful. I must be insane to pretend I can do this, is what I was thinking, to be absolutely honest, raving mad. And for gangsters too! I was starting to feel like the queen in Rumpelstiltskin: oh, sure, king, honey, I can spin straw into gold . . .

And at that point it struck me that the obscure names for his ecclesiastic garments had popped into my head as I studied them, and I was sure I had no idea what a *rochetta* was when I walked into the museum. I felt the hair stand up on my neck, and I left in a hurry, with a funny sense that something was on my heels.

I needed a drink after that and I found a café in the Corso and had a grappa. As I was drinking a beer to wash away the taste, I called Mark in New York and asked him to send the money from Castelli, minus commission and expenses, to Lotte. He said he would and he wanted to talk about what I was doing and how the you-know-what was turning out, but I didn't want to talk to Mark and I got off the phone as soon as I could.

Then I made the call I'd been putting off, my guilt call to Lotte at home. It was nine or so in the evening there and she sounded sleepy and irritable.

"So you finally decided to call us," she said. "Honestly, Chaz, what are you thinking?"

"I'm sorry," I said lamely. "I've been working really hard."

"Yes, that's always been your excuse. You think you can treat people any way you like and it will be all fine because you are being productive."

"I said I was sorry, Lotte."

"That's not enough. I have been worried sick about you. You have some kind of psychotic break, you are arrested and sent to Bellevue, and then, instead of getting help, you run away to Europe—"

"How are the kids?" I said, hoping to change the subject to the safer one of our mutual parenthood, a ploy that had often worked in the past.

"Oh, yes, the kids! Their father has disappeared without a word of good-bye, after they saw him with a bloody face in the *Post* being taken by the police—how do you think they are?"

And more in this line, and I listened without fighting back or interrupting, and at last she wore it out and I smoothed things over with the lie that I would seek psychiatric help in Europe. We eased back into our usual conversational mode and I asked about the children again, and this time she said, "Oh, well, we had a small crisis the other day. Rudolf is no more."

"Finally. He was old for a hamster. What did he die of?"

"Of *death*, as Rose says with great solemnity. She took it very well, I must say. We all dressed in black and had a funeral in the back garden. Milo played the march from *Saul* on his flutophone and Rose did a eulogy that would have made a cat laugh. It was amazing that Milo could keep playing. She described hamster heaven in some detail. Apparently Baby Jesus visits it every day, before his bedtime. She's constructed a shrine, with one of her shredder collages—Rudolf escorted into said heaven by St. Peter and the angels, with an altar cloth made of shredder waste. It's killingly funny, and Milo is under strict orders not to mock."

"How's he doing?"

"Fine, except the new drug makes him itch and he says he has no energy. I wish I trusted them more, but what can we do? At the end of the day our boy is a guinea pig, and that's what we must put up with to keep him alive."

I said, "You don't have to worry about money for a while anyway, because I just told Slotsky to send you the proceeds from my restoration job. It should come to a little under two hundred grand."

A small silence while she absorbed this, and then she said, "But, Chaz, what will you live on if you give us all of it?"

"Oh, that's what I'm calling about, really. It sounds funny when you actually say it, but I have a patron."

"A patron?"

"Yeah, like in the old days. A rich guy, a pal of the man I did the restoration for, he saw it and we got to talking and I sort of told him my sad story, and he said something like there's no reason for an artist of your ability to have to grub in the marketplace, and he had a studio I could use rent-free and he's promised to pay me a regular stipend and take everything I paint."

"Who is this man?" she asked me, suspicion in her voice, warranted obviously; can she really tell a porker over the telephone? But not really a lie when you think about it; Krebs really is a patron and possibly *less* of a gangster than the old kings of Europe, considering the kind of shit they pulled as a matter of course—Krebs never sent his boys to burn a city and rape its women and burn people at the stake.

"His name's Krebs," I said. "He's a German art dealer and collector. Mark set it up, but I'm not working through Mark. This is all directly for the collector."

"That's ridiculous. No one sells paintings like that. What will happen when your work is sold? Will you share in the proceeds?"

"Not clear, and I don't care. I'm getting paid top dollar to please a single connoisseur who loves my work. Every artist in Europe had that arrangement before the modern period. Lotte, I've been looking for this all my life. And you've been yelling at me for years to do the best work I can, not jokes, Lotte, no more jokes. And the money . . . the money is *fantastic*. It means a completely new life for us."

"As for example . . ."

"He's going to give me a million for the painting I'm doing now."

A longer pause here and a long, sad sigh. "Oh, Chaz," she said, "why do I even talk to you? I don't know what to do."

"What?"

"You are out of your mind, you are still in some kind of fantasy world. I'm sorry, I cannot do this—"

"Listen, it's *not* a fantasy, Krebs is real. Ask Mark."

"I don't trust Mark. He's perfectly capable of encouraging your insanity for his own purposes, and in any case, what you describe is impossible! No one could realize that much on your work in the market—"

"Lotte, there's no market. That's the *point*. He's an eccentric zillionaire. He's got private jets, private yachts, he can afford to have a private artist, just like Lorenzo the Magnificent and Ludovico Sforza and the rest of those guys."

A long silence, and at last she said, "Well. Then I congratulate you. Honestly . . . I'm sorry if I sound doubtful, but it all seems like . . . I don't know, some impossible and grandiose fantasy. You used to have them all the time when you were taking drugs, if you recall, so perhaps you'll forgive me if I am not just now breaking out the champagne. By the way, my father rang and said he'd seen you and that you looked well."

"So you know I'm not doping," I said, maybe a little acerbic tone there, because she said, "I didn't mean to imply any such thing. But, you know, it *is* my business—everyone is suspicious, the artists think they're being cheated, the customers think the same, haggling, always haggling. No one comes in the door and says, I love this work and here is a check for what it says on the card. It's always, if I buy two can I have twenty percent off? And I sell a work and then the artist sees it at auction and it sells for twice what he got, and he yells at me for undervaluing his work."

"So quit. We don't need the money for the gallery anymore."

"Yes, your new fortune. I tell you, Chaz, I would like to meet this man and see with my own eyes what you have gotten into. Then maybe I'll believe it."

"Blessed are those who have not seen and believed."

That got a laugh. "Well, if you quote the Bible I suppose I must become a little excited." She sighed. "Ah, if only it were true! There are clinics in Switzerland that have had wonderful successes with children like Milo, where a month costs what I take in, gross, in my best year."

"It's covered. I'm telling you, Lotte, it's a new world. Look, the other reason I called—I want you to come over here."

"What, to Venice?"

"No, I'm in Rome. That's where the studio is. I'll send you first-class tickets, you'll come, we'll stay in a swanky hotel. When was the last time we did something like that? Never is when."

"But the gallery. And the children—"

"The girl can handle the gallery for a few days and the kids'll be fine with Ewa. Come on, Lotte, you can spare four, five days."

And she agreed right away, which I thought was a little odd. Lotte's response to poverty is the classic French one of bitterness, self-denial, and also resenting the pleasure others get in expending money. We used to fight about that a lot: we couldn't ever go out for a nice meal, and when I did drag her out she always ordered the least expensive thing on the menu and drank a single glass of wine and sat like the chief mourner at a provincial funeral. She wasn't like that when I met her; no, she knew how to let the good times roll. It was the kid getting sick. Or me. Maybe I have a special charism for making women bitter.

Two days later Franco and I picked her up at the airport and drove to the San Francesco, which is not quite the Danieli in Venice but is the best hotel in Trastevere. She was quiet, a little withdrawn, which I guess I had to expect, and when we got out of the Merc at the hotel, she gave me a look. Lotte, being a diplomatic brat, is used to the top end of things—or was before she married me—and the look said, can you *really* afford a place like this? And so I whipped out my magic black card and handed it to the desk clerk.

Who took it with both hands and made a little bow and was all smiles. He was about to check us into the room I'd reserved when Lotte put a hand on my arm and drew me aside.

"I want my own room," she said.

"Why, you think I'm going to attack you in a frenzy of lust?"

"No, but I'm not here for a cozy holiday. A few months ago you were a raving maniac who pulled a knife on a gallery owner, and I would like to have at least one door between us if this maniac should happen to return."

"Fine. So what is this, a tour of inspection, like a sanitary commission?"

Now she was standing in combat position, with her arms folded across her breasts and her jaw thrust out, and at that moment more than anything I wanted to tell her the whole thing. But I did not. I was terrified that if I spilled it her face would take on a certain look, one I was more than familiar with from the terminal stages of our marriage, in which shock, pain, and bone-deep disappointment each played a part. The suspicious and canny face she was now showing was not a natural part of her expressive repertoire, I knew. It was me that put it there, as surely as if I'd painted it on with oils. My mom used to wear it often, as a matter of fact, and now I'd given it to my beloved forever. Life is just *so* wonderful.

"If you like," she said. "You say you have all this money, and I've seen some of it, but I want to be sure you are not in some insane delusion about the rest of it. It's about our child, Chaz, and about his future. You see why it's hard for me to trust you—"

"Sure. Okay, no problem. Two rooms. Can they be adjoining or do you have to be heavily isolated from the maniac?"

"Adjoining is fine," she said coolly, and I turned again to the desk.

An elderly porter with the manners of an ambassador ushered us up to our rooms and got a tip commensurate with his mien. When he'd gone, we agreed to meet in an hour and go out to dinner. I tossed my bag onto what would be my lonely bed and left for the bar on the roof of the hotel, where I drank a couple of Camparis and watched the sky go dark and the shadows creep up the ochre walls of the little convent across the street until they vanished into blackness.

When I returned and knocked on the door of Lotte's room, I found her ready to go, wearing a dress of just the rose pink that Fra Angelico used to clothe his angels in and a worn velvet jacket colored a sort of verdigris, very quattrocento. It suited her coloring, the dark blond hair, the dark eyes, an unusual combo, but one you see often in paintings from that period. From her Italian mother. And it's a habit of Lotte's to dress in colors, when everyone in her circles in New York wears black, as a sign, she says, of mourning for the death of art.

We walked down to the river and north and went to a restaurant I liked off the Piazza di Sta. Cecilia in Trastevere. Both of us had decided to forget about the big issues and the tension of the afternoon, and we had our usual out-of-marriage good time. After dinner we walked back slowly, arm in arm, and talked about light matters or were companionably silent for long stretches on the dark streets. In the hotel, we both went to our separate rooms, after a set of Euro-style cheek kisses, very civilized.

I was exhausted but couldn't sleep; I paced and watched Italian TV with the sound off for a while, and then found myself waggling the knob of the door to the next room. It was unlocked. Meaning what? She'd neglected to lock her side? Or maybe this is how they did it in Italian hotels when a couple opted for adjoining rooms.

I walked in and sat at the little desk and watched her sleep, and after a while I took a couple of sheets of hotel stationery and the short pencil they supplied for taking phone messages and made a drawing of Lotte as she slept, the rich spill of hair, her ear, the lovely strong lines of neck, jaw, cheekbone. Then I went and retrieved one of the boxes of Staedtler pens I'd bought as presents for the kids and added color, and I was soon caught up in the technical problem of how to get interesting effects with the unsubtle chemical tones they put in these things, and I found myself cruising down the old expressionist highway, pushing the color with lots of overlayering, and it got to be kind of fun.

After that I went back to my room and did a portrait from memory of the two of us sitting up in bed, kind of Kirchneresque, but with the anatomy correct and more detailed, stronger drawing, a Wilmot, in fact, and this made me feel good, although I kept slipping into those strange dreamlike states you fall into at such times and then jerking awake.

And thinking, I have not been sleeping well; I wake from unpleasant dreams in which there are roaring monsters on the canals and half-naked women riding on their backs. And almost every night, even when I do manage to sleep, I am awakened by shouts and gunfire. During my time here there have been outbursts throughout the city, day and night, some affray between the great families of Venice, and the ambassador gives me to understand that it is ever thus. Yet also, Venice plays a dangerous game between the Pope and the power of Spain and the Empire; it was explained to me, but I cannot understand it, something to do with the principality of Montferrat. Assassins prowl the streets; yesterday I saw them fish a body from the canal. My copy of the *Crucifixion of Our Lord* by Tintoretto is almost done, and after that I will copy his *Christ Giving Communion to the Disciples*. Now that I have seen the paintings that are here, I am ashamed of how I have composed my own, but I count it ignorance rather than lack of skill. Once you have seen it done scores of times, you say, of course, this is how to arrange figures.

I think the best thing I have seen is the altarpiece that Titian did for the Pesaro family; there is nothing like it in Spain. He commands your eye with masses of color, so that you see the different parts of the work in the order he prescribes. It is like a Mass in itself, one thing following another, and each wonderful—St. Peter and the Virgin and Child, and the banner and the captive Turk and St. Francis and the family of Pesaro, with that remarkable boy staring at an onlooker from out of the picture—that face alone would make a masterpiece, and the audacity of it! But I can do this as well.

Now I hear shots and cries from the direction of San Marco. I think I will leave as soon as I am done with my copies and go on to Rome.

Then I was wide awake, sweating, my heart going fast. I'd come to out in the street; somehow I'd pulled my pants and shoes on and got out there. Terrific! That must've been his first visit to Venice in 1629. I always liked that Pesaro Titian myself. Strangely, my memories of this hallucination include memories of dreams he'd been having, and it appeared that he was dreaming my twenty-first-century life. Or I was somehow recalling my life while I was being him. The whole thing was unspeakably terrifying and wonderful at the same time, if you can imagine that, like I suppose skydiving is, or would be if you dove through time rather than space, and the experience began all by itself.

Anyway, this little excursion into woo-woo knocked me out pretty good, and I went back into the hotel, getting an interested look from the night man, and returned to my own room. I slipped the drawings I'd done under the door to Lotte's room, fell into bed, and was instantly asleep. I woke up late the next morning, a little past ten. I cleaned up and dressed and tapped on the adjoining door. No answer. Then I noticed one of the drawings had been slid back onto my side. She'd folded a note onto the double portrait, on which she'd written: "!!!" and a heart with little electric lines around it, and "At breakfast, L."

I went up to the roof café and found Lotte. She was sitting at a table talking to Werner Krebs.

I was so startled that I froze at the entrance to the café and just watched them for a while. They seemed to be the best of friends, chatting away in French. Lotte had the look she has on whenever she's speaking her native tongue, a certain relaxed formal look, if that makes sense, as if it's taken her some effort to conform to the sloppy way that Americans hold their bodies and their faces and now she's snapped back into a persona that was, paradoxically, more natural.

It wasn't just surprise; it was like being knocked down by an unexpected wave at the beach, disorienting, you don't know which way is up, you can't breathe.

While I was standing there paralyzed, a waiter approached and asked whether I wanted a table. This caught their attention, and Lotte looked up and waved. I went to their table; Krebs rose, gave a little bow, and shook my hand. I was thinking about how he'd arranged this, about how he must be having me watched, and also dying to know what they'd been talking about.

I sat down at their table. It was a little chilly and the buildings across the street wore pale banners of mist, but the hotel had set up tall steel heaters, far more efficient than the pitch-soaked flaming

Christians that Nero had used in his own wintry Rome for the same purpose.

Krebs said, "This charming lady was just telling me that you spent the night drawing, with wonderful results."

Here he indicated the drawing of Lotte lying on the table before him. "This is quite remarkable, for a drawing on cheap paper with a hotel pencil and children's markers. No, actually, it would be remarkable in any medium—the energy of the lines and the colors combine to give a real sense of mass and living presence."

Lotte said, "He did another one that's even better."

"Really? I would like to see it."

"I'll go and get it, if you like," she said. "If you give me your key, Chaz."

Like a zombie I handed her the key and she walked off.

"What are you doing here?" I said, trying, perhaps unsuccessfully, to keep the hostility out of my voice.

"You seem surprised. I have a good deal of business in Rome and this hotel is convenient to the studio. Why should I not be here?"

"Having breakfast with my wife?"

A dismissive gesture. "Your ex-wife, I believe, was looking at your drawing, and I expressed appreciation, and then the whole coincidence emerged. And not only that: it is also the case that I know her father slightly, in the way of business."

"He was investigating you."

"That is a harsh way of putting it, I think. He was engaged in an official international investigatory commission, and I was happy to help with my expertise. A charming woman, if I may say so."

"Did you tell her about the forgery?"

"What forgery?"

"Oh, don't be cute! The Velázquez I'm faking down the road there."

"Wilmot, this becomes tedious. You seem to believe that I am some kind of criminal, but I am simply an art dealer who has hired a painter, you, to produce an artwork in the manner of Velázquez, using antique materials. If someone, some expert, wishes to identify it as an authentic Velázquez, that is none of my concern."

"Just like Luca Giordano."

He laughed and his face was transformed by delight. "In a manner of speaking, although given modern techniques of analysis, I think we must dispense with the signature under a layer of paint." He laughed again, and the situation was so crazy that I laughed too. I had no idea if it was self-deception on his part or if he was playing with me. It's a forgery, it's not a forgery—whatever you say, Majesty . . .

Then his faced changed, grew serious, a little menacing. "On the other hand, it would be extremely unfortunate if what you are doing became generally known. As I believe I have already stated, I am in business with people who don't share our sense of humor about these things. Do you understand me? We exist in parallel worlds, the world of artistic achievement and the world of tradable commodities and money. We consort with the new condottieri, like the painters of the quattrocento. They wish to realize their investment in this project, and anyone who might stand in their way, let us say a principled person who heard about the provenance of this supposed Velázquez from an unimpeachable source and talked about it in public, might be in considerable danger. Your ex-wife, for example. So, let us be very, very discreet, Wilmot. Am I perfectly clear?"

I nodded, because my throat had become too dry to generate speech, terrified, but also, strangely, glad that he was not going to spill any beans about what I was doing.

At this point Lotte reappeared, and she must have seen my face, because she asked, "What's the matter?"

Krebs said, "We were just discussing the discontents of the current art scene, a lamentable and depressing subject. But now let us turn to art itself." He took the drawing from Lotte and studied it. I took a drink of water.

"You're correct," said Krebs, "it's even better than the other, I think because of the energy flowing between the figures. Just wonderful! Tell me, Wilmot, have you been working in this style for long?"

"Yes, for about twenty minutes," I said. "It's known as my Magic Marker period."

He and Lotte shared a look, the kind parents wear when the indulged child has done something embarrassing; it made me want to throttle both of them.

"I would like to take these with me and have them matted and framed," he said.

I shrugged. "That's up to Lotte. I made them for her."

There was a heavy moment, which Krebs ended by saying, "Well, not to stand on a technicality, but as I was explaining to Lotte just before you arrived, I believe that our arrangement is that all your work is mine to dispose of."

"Even doodles?" I said, as in my head amazement struggled with relief, relief because he'd somehow gone with the patronage story I'd sold to Lotte, and so the happy fiction had been confirmed.

"Pardon me, but these are not doodles, and as I'm sure Lotte will tell you, the market price of works on paper has gone like a rocket in these past few years. I would be embarrassed to tell you what scrawls on napkins by Picasso fetch nowadays."

"But I'm not Picasso."

"Not yet, you're not. But you are certainly going to be rich, and I am a long-term investor." With that, he lifted a worn leather briefcase, opened it, removed a folder, slipped in the two drawings, and snapped it shut again. "I'm sorry to be so unforgivably crass," he said. "But, you know, when I see a beautiful thing, I want to snatch, snatch ..."

He illustrated this tendency with a grabbing motion of his right hand and contorted his face into a mime of feral avarice that I thought was rather more often its resting state than the avuncular one he had foisted off on my ex.

But we were all pals now, and so we both laughed politely at this display, and I had the waiter bring me biscotti and cappuccino, and the rest of the hour passed pleasantly enough in talk about painting and markets and what to see in Rome. Then Krebs had to leave for an appointment and avowed he was desolated that he could not ask us out to dinner, but he had to be in Stuttgart that evening. Another time, perhaps. He actually kissed Lotte's hand as he left.

"So what did you think?" I asked when he was gone.

"Well, what I think is that if his checks continue to clear at the banks, you are the luckiest painter of this age. He is in love with you. I have seen it before: a rich collector is ravished by an artist, he cannot do enough for this person, he courts, he buys . . . and it is wonderful for the artist while it lasts."

"Sometimes it doesn't last?"

"Sadly, yes. Artists change their styles, they explore new themes, and in these the lover is perhaps not so interested. But I think that your Herr Krebs will be faithful, as long as you produce. I think he will be impatient with, let us say, a low rate of production, just as, to extend the metaphor, a rich man with a beautiful mistress would become annoyed if this mistress did not allow him the freedom of her body."

"Gee, you make me sound like an old whore."

"Not at all. If you have truly begun to paint as you should, there is no question of your success, either with Krebs or without. I have told you this a thousand thousand times before, but me you don't believe and Krebs you do, only because he has the money. If he throws you out, for whatever reason, you will be very successful on the open market, especially if it becomes known that Herr Krebs is an important collector of your work."

There was something cold in the way she said this, and now that I was looking there was something odd about her expression as well. Lotte has a frank, fearless look—it's one of her signal features—but now it was hooded, the dark eyes sliding away from mine.

"You don't approve?"

"I have no right to approve or not. But if you really want to know, I resent you for giving the fucking commissions to Krebs and not to me!"

"I'm sorry."

"You're not in the least sorry. But I have no intention of fighting about it. We're in Rome. Take me to look at pictures!"

So we got up and went out. I have to say that even in our roughest periods, when we could barely get through a meal without fighting, we could always go and look at paintings. When a big show came to the Met or the Modern, that was a signal for a truce, and we would stroll through the crowded halls, and look, and be ravished, and be transported to the higher realms before returning to the heartbreak. And so it proved now, in a somewhat different context, because I thought there was a chance that we could return to something else, that I could convert the lie into solid ground.

I took her to the Doria Pamphili, and after we'd seen Memling take Christ down from the cross and Caravaggio show the repentant Magdalene, and the Breughels and the Raphael marvelous double portrait and the yards upon yards of filler, all those mannerist and Caravaggist patzers who make up the bulk of museum collections worldwide, we came to the Pope.

I wanted to stand next to it with Lotte, I can't really say why, maybe for some good juju, so that her faith in me might flow into my head and revive my spirit, and in fact I did start to feel better and thought, Yeah, I can do that, I might not have invented how to do it, but now that it's done I know how he did it, I can even sort of smell the turps off the surface of the thing, and then I'm standing there with a brush in my hand loaded with a flake-white mixture, and I'm painting the Pope's white *rochetta* and there's the high crimson silk *camauro* against the draperies and the throne, and there's the actual face, turned slightly away just now as a lackey delivers a message, and then the terrible eyes are turned back on me.

And I am frightened and also excited; this is the most important painting I've ever done, because if he likes it he will do for me what no one else in the world can do, ensure the accomplishment of what I chiefly desire.

The brush is flying almost without conscious thought as I lay in the shadows on the white cloth—not white in the painting, of course, because white is never white, only fools paint it so with actual white paint—and I have to lean hard on the stick in my left hand to keep my brush from trembling. Another man comes in and hands the Pope a paper; he reads, says a few words, shifts in his chair. He is getting restless. I put my palette aside, bow, anticipate him: Holiness, I can finish this without your presence. It is almost done.

He rises, walks around, and considers the painting on the easel.

"You are no flatterer, Don Diego."

"No, Holiness, I paint the truth as I see it. Truth is of God."

And I think, almost before the words slip out, Jesus Maria, I am ruined, did I dare instruct the Pope on religion?

For an instant there is a sharp look, and then, thank Christ, a small cat smile forms on his hideous face.

"It is *too* true," he says, "but still, it pleases me. And what is that paper I am holding?"

"It is my fancy, Holiness. A letter from myself, a petition."

"Yes? What sort of petition?"

"For your support, Holiness. I wish to make casts of the Belvedere statues and other sculptures belonging to the Holy See. It would please my master."

The Pope nods. "I will speak of this to the camerlengo. Your king is a well-beloved servant of the Holy Church."

He turns to go, and with my heart in my throat I say, "And Holiness, a petition on my own behalf, with your permission."

He turns, a little impatiently. "Yes?"

"I wish to become a knight of the military order of Santiago. In Spain, they still believe that painters, however noble their birth, cannot aspire to such honors. My family is of pure blood back to the most ancient times, and yet I fear my profession will undo me in this effort."

A pause. That sly smile again. "Then we must inform them that in our Italy such is not the case."

For a second I'm looking at the painting on the wall and the throne is empty, and then there's the portrait again and a guard is holding my elbow, asking me what I'm doing, not amused. Lotte is standing next to him, white faced.

I could barely stand. I asked him what was up and he told me I had been mumbling to myself and trotting around the museum bumping into people. He advised me to go home and sleep it off.

I faced Lotte and she was frantic, she said I'd started talking to myself, that I'd walked off like I was going somewhere without a word to her, and that the guard had been right, I'd been acting like a crazy person, and what was going on?

Stupidly, I said it was nothing, when it clearly wasn't, like that tired joke about the guy in bed with another woman and his wife's standing there and he goes, "Who're you going to believe, me or your own eyes?" And then she went into a whole thing about she couldn't stand it, I was sick, and I was going to screw up this new opportunity with Krebs, just like I'd screwed up the rest of my painting career, but she wasn't going to be an enabler, she was done with that, and I had to get professional help, I'd always been crazy, I'd destroyed myself because of my damned narcissism about my precious work, and how I'd let it destroy our marriage, oh, no, every great artist in the world had sold their work in galleries, but Chaz Wilmot was too good for that, I'd rather see our son dead, and she pitied me, and she swore she'd never speak to me again or let me see the kids until I was in a damned mental hospital where I belonged.

Nor was I silent while this was going on; I called her a money-grubbing bitch, I seem to recall, and we had a screaming match right there with the silly mannerist Virgins looking down on us, and the guards came and told us we had to leave. She ran out and I walked out, and when I got to the street she was gone. I hailed a cab of my own. The cabbie figured I was a rich tourist and took me on the scenic route back to the hotel, north and down through the crazy Vatican-area traffic, and I was too miserable to bitch. She'd left the hotel too, no note. I called her cell phone, but she declined to answer. When the message tone came on I couldn't think of anything to say.

So after that I checked out of the hotel and returned to the forger's nest. Sophia greeted me cheerfully when I passed her in the hall, as if I'd never left, but I suspected they knew pretty much what had gone down. I'm not paranoid or anything, but I do a lot of people-watching myself and I know that when you concentrate your attention on people they sooner or later get hip to it. I had been conscious of eyes on me for the past couple of days.

The odd thing was that I didn't sink into an orgy of self-contempt the way I would have previously when something like that happened. It was like my real life—Lotte and the kids and New York—had become just another alternative life, one of several now available, and so the rejection didn't sting the way it once had. Nothing is real, and nothing to get hung about, as the Beatles used to say. And the money, that universal balm. People also used to say love will get you through times of no money better than money will get you through times of no love, but that's only partially true. Money's not everything, sure, but neither is it nothing.

And the other thing was I really *liked* being Velázquez. I remembered vividly what it was like to paint like him, I'd actually *done* that portrait, and I thought if they could put *that* experience into powder form, no one would ever look at crack cocaine.

I spent the next morning staring at the cleaned canvas on the easel. Baldassare had changed the size a little, a couple of inches off each dimension, but I didn't bother to ask him why. Nor did I touch a brush; I just stared at the white. I'd been studying the radiographs published in Brown and Garrido and in various monographs to get some idea of what his underpainting was like. The problem with Velázquez in his mature period was that he was so good he barely did any preliminary work. Aside from a few questionable sketches of the Pope's portrait, there are no Velázquez sketches at all. None. The bastard just painted. He laid in the ground with a big brush or a palette knife in flake white and grays made with ochre and azurite, varying it according to the composition of the painting. When he had that right he drew in the figures directly, what they call *alla prima* painting, and then used diluted pigments to color them, so that the light ground and sometimes even the grain of the canvas showed through, a totally bravura technique, which is why nobody but an idiot tries to forge Velázquez.

All the confidence I'd felt briefly at the Doria in front of Innocent X had vanished with Lotte, as did my pleasure in my new wealth. Because in order to get that wealth, of course, I had to put paint on canvas, which just now I seemed disinclined to do. And as the good light faded I had plenty of time to consider the cowardice of Charles Wilmot, Jr., the Chaz of all my memories, the real reason why he wasn't really a million-dollars-a-painting guy, not the market, not the art appreciation business at all, just the pure funk, because now, when it really counted, the big leagues, an actual million-dollar commission, Chaz doesn't show up.

I blew a couple of days like that, just looking at the damned canvas. Baldassare came in once and told me he'd sized the old canvas with a secret water-soluble compound. The point of this was to fill the cracks in the seventeenth-century ground I'd be painting on, so that the new paint wouldn't sink into it. After the forgery was done and dried, he'd dip the whole thing in water and the sizing would dissolve out; with a little bending and shaking the surface would conform to the old cracks, and bingo! Instant craqueleur.

I asked him to give me a couple of new stretched canvases in the same dimensions and texture, because I figured I'd be better off easing into it, do a test run, as it were, get comfortable with the paint and the style. And the model. So I started looking at Sophia and she started looking at me, you know, a little discreet flirting around dinnertime, smiles, increasingly warmer, little jokes. It turned out Franco wasn't that interested, not that he would've kicked her out of bed—nor would I have—but not interested. That was all I needed now, given the thing with Lotte. I'd called her cell phone half a dozen times but she never called back.

Which pissed me off, and so I asked Sophia out for a drink after dinner, and she took me to a bar, Guido's, over by Santa Maria, full of local people now in winter with most of the tourists gone. She was known there, she chatted with friends in the Roman dialect that I could barely follow. We spoke to each other in English, mainly, and I got her story. She'd done art at La Sapienza; there was a guy, an Australian she'd gotten involved with; then she became pregnant and he split, and there she was with little Enrico, dropped out of school with no degree and no prospects for a job. She was working as a *madonnaro*, drawing holy pictures on the sidewalk in front of churches for tips. Then her mother had called Baldassare, a *cugine*, it turned out, and he'd brought her into the family business.

She did mainly seventeenth-century drawings—Cortona, the Caracci, Domenichino—and helped out with paintings on fake Italian provincial antiques. I asked her whether it bothered her, the faking, and she said no, why should it? Romans had been faking art for *bàbbioni* tourists since BC. She was good at it, used only the best materials, genuine paper from old books and the right inks, and she had the style down. She'd done a Cortona *Christ on the Cross* that'd fetched thirty thousand euros at a German auction, and that kind of wage certainly beat some low-end curatorial job at a provincial museum.

A little defensive there, I thought, but it turned out that she wasn't abashed at all, but envious. I was the big-time gunslinger brought in for this gigantic coup. Baldassare had told her all about it, but, she said, he doesn't think you can do it. I asked her if he'd actually told her that, and she said yeah, he said you don't have *le palle sfaccettate*. That's what you need in this business. You know what that means? I didn't. It means balls with hard edges, like a crystal.

I said, we'll see, and then I asked her if she ever modeled, and she said not really, but Baldassare thought that she'd be right for this picture and asked her if she'd do it, and of course, what could she say? And the boy too, he said they'd need a child. I said that was right and asked her why she thought she'd do for the figure, and she said, you want someone like the *Rokeby Venus*, don't you? With which she got up and walked slowly away and then back again and into her chair, grinning like a cat. *Bellesponde*, as they say. A narrow waist and a pear-shaped bottom, longish legs. Her face was what they call "interesting," the features a little over-large for real beauty, nose too long, chin a little small, but she had a mass of thick, dark hair with coppery highlights, and in any case I was going to make up the face, for obvious reasons.

We drank some more and then some friends of hers came by and started in with the Romano chatter, and I got my pad out and started futzing around, and then as usual they saw what I was doing and I made drawings of each of them. Everyone was impressed, as usual. If this didn't work out, I thought, I could always become a *madonnaro* myself.

We stayed late and got pretty oiled, and we walked back home through sleeping Trastevere in a light rain. When we got to the house it was clear that she was available, but I begged off, and that raised her eyebrow and produced a shrug. Whatever, *signor*. In fact, it was not Lotte mainly, but that whole thing seemed a little too planned, another way to inveigle me deeper into the circle of Krebs.

I told her I wanted to start in the morning; she said okay and went off to bed, and I did too. I woke up at first light. Or someone woke up, but it wasn't in the bed I'd gone to sleep in and it wasn't me.

I awaken in a different bed, a huge thing with four posts and heavy velvet hangings. I smell cooking and a kind of incense, and underneath a sweet, unpleasant smell, maybe sewage—that's what the world smells like. I have to piss, and I use the chamber pot I pull out of a little box by the bedside. I'm wearing a white embroidered nightshirt and a cap. I push the curtains aside.

A huge room with high, coffered ceilings and wall paintings, Zucchis mainly, the usual Roman unclothed nymphs; they make me irritable every time I see them. I have not slept well. I've dreamed again of being in hell, vast cliffs with eyes, iron streets populated with gargoyles, half-dressed harpies, and in the streets chariots going of themselves, spitting the stench of pitch and sulphur.

Servants attend me while I wash and dress. Pareja is sullen as usual, although I have permitted him to paint, in contravention to the codes, and why not? This is Rome, where everything is permitted, especially that which is prohibited.

I eat something—I forget what—in a large room overlooking the famous gardens. This is the Villa Medici. The duke allows me to stay here, as he did during my first visit, although as an honorary ambassador to His Holiness I should be lodged at the Vatican. I cannot bear to stay there, however; the food does not suit me—far too rich—and the meals formal and at set times. Here I can eat what I want, when I want, and I can work.

After my meal, I go down to the Trinitá to hear Mass, then return to my studio and work on a view I have made of a gate to the gardens. It is a small thing, but it gives me a particular pleasure, as it has no connection with a patron but is for myself alone, a landscape in the French manner, or the Dutch. I have never done such a thing before, and it makes a kind of cleansing after the Pope's portrait.

At noon I eat again, this time at a table with some of the other guests, all people of rank, and none of them think it disgraceful to dine with a painter.

Now I command Juan Pareja to call for a carriage, and we leave the villa for our appointment at the house of my lord Don Gaspar de Haro, Marqués de Heliche, a great man among the Spanish in Rome, who favors me above all others of my profession. During the journey I am much engaged with my pocket book, where I list all the worrying arrangements I must make to fulfill His Majesty's commission: gaining permission to make casts of famous sculptures, supervising the artisans making the casts, making sure they are properly crated, paying for the shipment, making sure the carters do not steal everything, viewing paintings for sale, making appointments for portraits of the notables who favor me and whose friendship is desired by His Majesty—never enough time and never, never enough money, the Titians alone cost over a thousand ducats and the majordomo at the embassy says there is no money. There is no money in all of Spain, it seems, or so I am told. Although it is the king's will that these treasures be bought, every petty clerk defies me. As they say, too much meat on to roast and some will be burnt.

At the palazzo I am announced and led to a hall full of paintings. The paintings are very fine, but I have no chance to study them, for here is my lord of Heliche and his train. They are merry and an odor of wine and perfume floats above them. They are Romans in the main, and of a type that my lord's father, far less his uncle the count-duke, would never have thought to entertain. I am introduced, I bow, they bow, the marqués takes my arm, and we go off privily to tour his gallery. We talk of paintings: he is passing knowledgeable, for one so young, and avid for more treasures; he condemns me for driving up the market by my visit and my gold from Madrid, although there is hardly any. We stop before a *Venus with a Mirror*, a copy after the Titian that hangs in the Alcázar. He says, I want one like that. A copy, my lord? No, a painting, a new painting. But we will speak of this further. First I wish to show you a prodigy. You will hardly believe this, Don Diego, there is nothing like it in Spain.

We move up a stair and down a hallway. There is a room from which issues a familiar odor. He signs to the footman to open the door without sound, and we stand in the doorway. Inside there is an easel and a man in a long smock and turban painting at it, and a model, a woman, sits holding a swaddled plaster baby. The man is painting rapidly, placing a blue glaze. A Venetian, I think, or one trained in their style.

My lord speaks low: "What do you think, Don Diego?"

I answer: "It is well enough done. The forms have some strength at least; the colors are clear and harmonious. A young man, I think, with little experience. The composition is not all it could be."

In the same low voice he says, slyly now, "You are entirely mistaken in this, I fear."

I say, "Then I bow to your superior knowledge of the painter's art, my lord."

"No, that's not what I meant," he says. "I meant it is not a young man. It is not a man at all!"

With that he cries out, "Leonora!" And the painter turns around, and I see it is a young woman. She stands frozen a moment, startled, brush in hand. The marqués strides into the room and embraces the woman in a most lascivious way, although he is married, and recently too, to a girl reputed to be the beauty of Italy, and rich. Still holding her to his body, he calls to me, "Is this not a prodigy, Don Diego, a woman who paints! Can you imagine what they would say in Spain? My treasure, this is Don Diego de Velázquez, the king's painter, come to Rome to buy every painting that can be bought and impoverish all us poor collectors. Don Diego, it is said that you allow your slave to paint, but I think I have you bested in this one: I have the honor to present to you Leonora di Cortona di Fortunati."

The woman smiles indulgently. The marqués bends to kiss her neck, and his hand slips between the buttons of her smock. The model looks away and blushes. I am thunderstruck myself.

The woman pushes him away; he resists, laughing; she taps him on the nose with her brush tip and his nose becomes bright lapis blue. He touches his nose, goggles at his hand. A look of anger starts on his face, but he turns it into a toothed grin like a carter's and lets free a bellow of laughter.

"Clean me!" he orders, and she does, with a rag dipped in turpentine.

"Pah!" he cries. "I will stink like a damned painter all day. Look here, Don Diego, this is what I want you to paint." He pointed at the woman.

"A Madonna and child, my lord?"

"No, of course not, God blast you! What would I do with yet another Madonna and child? No, her, Leonora, I want you to paint her as Venus with her mirror."

I look at the woman with the paint rag still in her hand, and she looks back at me. Her eyes are sea-gray; the wisp of hair that has escaped from her turban is auburn. She has a blunt, oval face with a high forehead, snub nose, and strong chin, the face of a sharp market woman, not a beauty; but there is the disturbing way she's staring into my eyes, slightly mocking, but also with a deeper complicity, as if we alone in that room understood some important secret. I have never been looked at like that by a woman, not my wife, not the women of the court. It unnerves me and even makes my voice shake a little when I say, "A Venus, my lord; do you mean unclothed?"

"Of course, unclothed! Nude. Naked, whatever you call it. There's a woman under that tent, you'll see. And, my man—you'll make haste, will you? I have other things I want you to do as well." With that he claps me on the shoulder and departs the room.

As soon as the door closes she dismisses the model, who takes her plaster baby and rushes out, and then my lady removes her smock right before me, not bothering to retire. Beneath is a dress of fine russet silk with a falling collar, good lace; a stomacher strung with gold cords; lace at the sleeves, but not much, and not cut as low at the bosom as some Roman ladies wear. They do not wear the *guardinfante* in Rome, preferring to round out their hips with petticoats. A remarkably thin waist. Off comes the turban and she shakes her ringlets out, they have red lights in them. Some bracelets of amber, some of gilt, no jewels that I can see. I think of what the marqués said of her body; I have never heard a woman spoken to so, except a whore, and this is no whore. These Romans are blind to honor. In this city I have heard men use words and make gestures to one another that would have earned a fight in Seville, perhaps a coffin too.

She moves to her painting and speaks.

"Alas, you are entirely correct about my work, Don Diego. I can draw well enough, I can mix colors, and my perspective is true, but I cannot find the balance of the forms, or not very well. It is something that must be taught, I think, and no one will teach me."

"No one taught me," I say. "When I was your age I knew as little as you. Don Pedro Rubens advised me to go to Italy and look at paintings, and I did, and so learned the art of composition and how to make solid forms appear on a flat plane."

"Yes," she says with a laugh, "but unfortunately I am in Italy already, and I am not Velázquez. So, tell me, do you too think it scandalous that a woman paints?"

"Not scandalous," I say. "Futile, maybe, as if you were learning to fight with a sword. I am surprised your husband permits it."

A sour face, and she says, "My husband is a Roman count with a great deal of money and no chin. He collects enamels and boys, and if he does not mind that I lie in the bed of the marqués de Heliche, do you think he cares spit about my painting, as long as I don't publicly acknowledge my sad little commissions and drag down his ancient name? Or piss on the altar at St. Peter's during the Pope's Mass— that would be nearly as scandalous. I am sorry, sir, I have shocked you, a fine Spanish gentleman such as yourself, but this is how we Roman courtesans learn to speak. Anyway, no one bothers to stop me from painting. Heliche thinks it amusing, like a monkey taught to dance for a grape."

I ask, "Then why do you do it?"

"Because I love it. It gives me pleasure to make a world appear upon a white canvas, which I can order as I will. You must understand this."

"Must I?"

"Of course. Painting as you do, you must love to paint."

I said, "I love my honor, my kin, my king and my church, and as for painting, I paint as I breathe and eat. It is how I live and make my place in the world. Had I been born a marqués, I might never have lifted a brush."

She stared at me as if I had said something coarse.

"That is remarkable. I know many painters and sculptors. Bernini, Poussin, Gentileschi—"

"I know Gentileschi's work," I said. "The best of the Caravaggisti, I think."

"That is the father. I was speaking of the daughter, also a painter, quite aged now, but I knew her when I was a girl. She helped corrupt my mind, as my husband tells me. In any case, it is common for painters to seek to outdo one another. They bring passion to their desire to excel in their art, to confound their rivals. And have you none of this passion, Don Diego?"

"I have no rivals," I say, and she laughs and says, "Forgive me, sir, I forgot for a moment you are Spanish. Don't we in Italy send our perfumers to Spain to collect your night soil? It would not dare to stink of anything but violets."

"The señora will have her joke," I say, "but I do not care to be the butt of it. I wish you good day, señora." I make to bow out, but she gives a little "oh!" and dashes forward and places her hand on my sleeve. I can feel the warmth of it through the cloth.

"Please, please," she cries out, "let us not part so. Of all the men now in Rome, you are the one I most wished to meet, and now I have spoiled all. Oh, Madonna! You have no idea, sir. When your painting of the black man was on display at the Pantheon I went every day. I wished to fall on my knees and worship it, as they did in ancient times when the Pantheon was a temple of the pagans. It is the greatest portrait ever seen, sir, every painter who saw it desired to cut your throat, and you just brought it into being out of . . . what? Pure spirit? Any cardinal in Rome would have weighed you out in gold for such a promise of immortal fame, and you did it for a *slave*? It is the greatest stroke of bravura this age."

Her hand still on my arm, and I wish to go now, but I also wish her to leave her hand there. And now I recall what the marqués has demanded and I almost tremble. I do tremble as I say, "You are kind, señora, but we have arrangements to make, I believe."

"Yes," she says, "my painting. Obviously, my face cannot be seen, or it must be disguised. Is Venus ever masked?"

"I have never seen her so depicted, but we will arrange something, I am sure."

"Certainly. You are at the Villa Medici, are you not? Perhaps the second hour after noon would be the most discreet. All Rome is sleeping then. Let us start tomorrow."

I think of my pocket book and all my tasks and appointments. Impossible! "Not tomorrow, señora, nor the next day, I'm afraid. A week from tomorrow, perhaps?"

"No, it must be now," she says. "Heliche is like a great baby, and now his mind is set on this Venus of me. He is dismissing me, or will in the next few weeks; as you will observe when we descend to the salon in a moment, he is besotted with the Contessa Emilia Odescalchi, who is more beautiful than I am and more stupid, both desirable traits in a mistress. He will palm me off on one of his train, to salve his conscience, but before that he wishes a souvenir of our liaison, and this is your painting. And don't imagine that it will be just one painting. So you must begin now, nor should you suppose he will accept excuses. Heliche is vicious, but he is not a fool, and you will not want to displease him, for you are not a fool either. You do not need his enmity in the courts of Madrid."

I cannot recall the remainder of that day. I attended my lord for some time at his palazzo and drank more wine than I am used to. I returned to my rooms and slept badly, more dreams of Rome transformed into hell. Thank God I can remember little of it but the roaring and the stench, or else I would paint like that Flamenco the late king favored, Geronimo Bosco, who they say was driven mad by his visions of eternal torment.

The next day I send boys out with letters to those I cannot see at the time I have appointed, yet I must go out myself to the foundry shop where they are casting my Laocoön, such begging I did to gain permission from His Holiness and the camerlengo, the bribes dispensed . . . I must be there to ensure it is done correctly, and then I must rush to return in time to meet this accursed woman, driving as fast as we dare through a cold rain; this Roman winter makes my bones ache. The bells are striking twice as I enter the villa; the place is silent as a tomb for the siesta.

I set up my easel and prepare my paints; there is no time to fetch a proper gilt mirror, so I have Pareja bring the plain one from the room the servants use and then dismiss him and the other boys, arrange a red drape behind the couch, and cover it with a linen sheet. There is a canvas already primed that I was going to use for another view of the gardens, but it will do. When all is ready I wait, for of course the woman is late—who can count on a woman to be anywhere at the hour!

Then a knock and she is here, dressed in a heavy black velvet cloak to the floor, hooded and masked, a silk scarf of pale green about her neck. She removes the mask, throws back her hood. She has tied up her hair on top of her head in imitation of the Venuses of Titian and Caracci and of the Medici Venus, I mean the famous statue that is the root of all art devoted to the female form. We speak a little, the weather, the cold; she apologizes for her lateness and then we stand dumb. I have never painted a woman of rank, nude, from the life. There is no precedent, manners are no guide.

She gestures to the couch. "Shall I be a reclining Venus, there?"

"If you please, señora," I say, "and there is your mirror."

She walks over and looks at it. "Not a mirror for a goddess, I think. And it is a wall mirror. How am I to gaze at my beauty while reclining on your couch?"

I am ashamed I have not thought of this and I am mute with embarrassment.

She says, "If you had a cupid holding it at her feet, propped up on the couch, she could lie on her back and gaze. You could paint in the child later."

I agree this is worth trying; I croak, in fact, my throat is so dry. I say, "You may undress behind that screen."

"I don't need your screen," she says, and takes off her cloak. Beneath it she is all alabaster skin, not a stitch on her.

"May I spread my cloak and lie on it? It is cold in this room. Will it spoil your colors?"

"No, please," I say, stammering. I turn my back to take up my palette and brushes, and when I again look to the couch she is lying on her back, relaxed, her thighs lolling open, revealing the dark curls at her groin and a tiny sliver of pink sex.

"How shall I arrange my limbs, Don Diego? Shall I have my hand here like Titian's Venus, covering myself modestly? And the other behind my head, like this?"

"Yes," I say, "that's good. Turn your head a little, toward the mirror."

Some adjustments of that damned mirror follow; leaning over her I can smell her, some dense perfume. I am sweating like a Seville porter. When I pick up brush and palette my hand shakes. I begin to block in the forms in gray-ochre; I can see her looking at me in the mirror, amusement in her eyes, the mocking whore!

I stop and put down the palette.

"What is wrong, Don Diego?"

"The pose. It's awkward with you on your back like that, the line of your neck is clumsy . . ." And similar nonsense, but the fact is that I can neither bear to stare at her sex nor ask her to close her legs, and so I say, "Roll on your right side."

"You wish to take me from the back, then?"

I ignore the coarse wit and say, "Yes, there is a statue I like, an antique hermaphrodite at the Villa Borghese—I am having it cast in bronze for His Majesty—which shows the back very well, and there is Annibale Caracci's *Venus with Satyrs*, which shows the woman from the back as well. I think it would suit in this case . . ."

And similar babble, until she rolls slowly over and I adjust the black cloak, and the white linen showing through on both sides of this, and also a wisp of her green chiffon scarf. And now I need not stare at her breasts and their brown buds stiff with the chill, and the darker pink of her clam, and I can paint the line of her back, with just a little more adjustment. If it were a boy or a man I would simply shift the limbs or head with my hands, but now it is like painting the king, I must ask for small, important movements, the lower leg thrust a little forward so the mass of her upper ham falls naturally and the lower is compressed, and between them the light just striking that thin fold of flesh; yes, my lord the marqués will like that, I'll make sure that shows, a tiny carmine lamp at the gates to paradise.

It is winter; there is little light left, and at four or so we stop and she wraps herself in the cloak again. She sits on the couch with her knees up like a little girl; the woman has no shame at all and yet is not degraded by it. We agree to meet tomorrow, but earlier this time, so as to catch the light.

But she does not come, instead sends a message that she was out late with the marqués, and I have to scurry to fill my day, uncanceling meetings and rushing about the city. I manage to arrange a final sitting with Cardinal Pamphili; his silly face is done and I can finish the rest here, his gown and the background and so on. But I am uneasy all the day and have the same unpleasant dreams, rooms full of strange light that shows the faces of people glowing like rotted corpses, yet no candle or fire to give it, and those people crying out in a language I don't know.

She comes early, just after dawn, in the same black cloak, again naked beneath it.

"You must not think, Don Diego, that I travel through the city of Rome like this ordinarily," she tells me, "but if I am dressed I must bring a woman along to undress me, and dress me again, my stays and laces and the rest—it is a disability of us women—and we wish to keep this painting our secret. Unless you would care to do that service?"

She sees my face and laughs. "I observe that it would not please you to serve me so. Therefore, let me take my pose."

She does so and I paint. In the morning light her skin glows like pearl, and I brush in thin tints of lake mixed with flake white, always thin so that the white of the underpainting shows through, and plenty of calcite for transparency, tiny blended strokes so that the surface is perfectly smooth, as it would be to the hand's touch. My fancy is that the light comes from within her, and I paint in the image in the glass, her face plain enough, and then I darken it and change it so that it could be any girl on the couch.

I work without stopping—I have lost count of the bells—until she complains of stiffness and the need to use the jakes. The figure is nearly done, and I say, a moment longer, I say, a few more strokes then, a little more modeling on the upper thigh, a bluish-gray, very thin. I put my brush down and gesture to her that she can move. She rises, groans, laughs, and with the cloak about her shoulders, she comes around and looks at the canvas.

"That arm is out of the drawing," she says, "but I see why you did it, yes, the line of the back is made bolder, a desperate move, but it works. Look how thin the paint, the fabric shows through, what a miser you are! There is almost nothing there, but also everything, you compel the eye itself to make up the difference. Yes, my narrow waist, I am as proud as Satan of it, yet she is not much of a goddess, I think, but a mortal woman. I thank you for disguising my face, but you have my big *culo* to the life, and I believe some men would recognize me from that alone. Oh, Madonna, I am speaking like a whore again, I offend your Spanish sensibilities."

She looks me in the face, smiling, showing her teeth like a peasant. She says, "I do it only because I hate you. This, seeing this work, makes me want to break my brushes. I would give my soul to be able to make flesh shine like that. Heliche will die when he sees it; it is just the kind of thing he likes. I imagine he will find some way of looking at it while he enjoys his new mistress."

"Are you sure he has one?"

"Oh, yes, in that realm I am an expert, as you are as a painter."

"And have you been fobbed off upon one of his train, as you foretold?"

"Indeed, I have," she says.

"Who is it?" I ask, stupidly.

"Why, it is you, Velázquez," she says. "Who else?"

She slips out of her cloak and comes to me, pressing her hot body against me, her mouth against my mouth, her tongue darting in like a little fish.

"And what do you think of love, Velázquez?" she says between kisses. "Do you think it is an art, like painting, or a mere craft that any churl or whore may accomplish well enough, or is it even less, a spasm of the flesh, akin to what the beasts do, that we inherit from the sin of Eve?"

I don't know what to answer. I am dizzy. My knees shake. We fall upon the couch. She is upon me now, naked, her skin giving off a heat

I can feel on my face, as from a brazier. She plucks at my clothes, her hands under my shirt, sliding down my body. I should try to break free, I know, but I have no strength in my hands or limbs.

"But let us suppose," she continues, "that such an art exists, and that it is as far above the coupling of the mass of mankind as your art is above a painted sign hanging before an inn, or the music of the divine Palestrina above a street boy's whistle. Do you think it possible? Let us now explore this interesting question."

So was I taught about love, but I did not love the learning. Never before had I been imprisoned by my own flesh, and I found therein a harsh jailer, one who never slept, whose eye was always on me, whose hot goad was crueler than the instruments of the Holy Office, for they were used for the gaining of hell rather than heaven. What tricks she had of finger and mouth, and she gave me potions and salves so that I was as a boy of eighteen upon the couch—not that I ever did thus even as a boy of eighteen. She was like a cat in season, on me everywhere, in my studio, in my apartments, in hallways, in carriages, in the fields and amid the ruins of old Rome, in her house at Trastevere all night long. And still I had my duty to do, the buying, the shipping, the meetings with notables, my painting.

I painted her again, two more Venuses, as my lord of Heliche demanded, one standing in the pose of Medici's Venus and another with Mars discovered by Vulcan. I aged ten years in that year.

In bed, in her passion, she called me Velázquez, and I told her no one calls me that and she must not either. She asked, then, "What do they call you in Spain?"

I answered, "They call me El Sevilliano, or Señor de Silva, or Don Diego."

"Even your wife?"

"What my wife calls me is not for you to know," I say, "but not Velázquez, at any rate. That is my name in painting."

"I know," she says, "and that is why I call you Velázquez in my bed, for were you not Velázquez you would not be there." And starts her damned caresses again.

I think that she believed in nothing but painting, certainly not honor, nor station, nor the truths of our Holy Faith, or but a little. She treated me sometimes as a god for this reason, and other times as a slave. I was a slave with her, I admit, and a god too.

I will say she knew paintings. She would look at what I bought with a keen eye and inform me about what paintings were to come on the market, or which cardinal would part with some prize to curry favor with my king. I showed her once an Annibale Caracci I was thinking of buying, a *Venus Adorned by Graces,* and she laughed and said, "That is no Caracci. It is that wretched boy in Naples again, at his tricks. He is very good."

"What boy?" I asked.

"Old Giordano's son, Luca. The father is a nothing, a sign painter, but the boy is a prodigy, another Giotto perhaps, if he can stop his crimes to make a style for himself."

"And why is this forger not brought to book?" I asked.

"Because he signs his work with his own name and paints it over. Look," she says, and goes to my table and soaks a rag in turpentine. She rubs at a corner and there is a signature revealed. We both laugh at that. I think I have not laughed so much in my life as when I was with her. And we fought too.

Once she took me to Santa Maria in Trastevere to the porch of the basilica where the cripples gather, the deformed and the naturals, to seek alms, and she asked me if I wanted to paint these as I had painted the royal dwarfs and fools.

"Why should I?" I answered. "Those I painted because they were in the king's service and part of his household. I painted his dogs too."

This answer I saw did not please her, and she asked me, "Does the king love you?"

And I replied, "Assuredly he does, for he gives me honor and appoints me to noble posts in his house."

She said, "Well might he honor you, for you do him honor with your brush and paint the magnificence of his daughters so they may be married off to kings and emperors. But does he love you as *Velázquez*, as I love you? Or are you a sport of nature, as are these miserable ones? The infantas of Spain have dwarfs around them so that their beauty is magnified by comparison, and so the king has the greatest painter in Europe by him, to magnify his own glory. It is all they care about, the kings of the earth."

"The king loves me," I said again. "He has said he will make me a knight of Santiago when I return."

I had not meant to say this, for to boast to a woman of such things is not my way, but she vexed me, and I thought about how I had spoken with Rubens on the same subject and how he had slighted my king.

"Ribbons are cheap," she said. "It is like giving a sweetmeat to a fool or a scrap to a dog."

I grew angry then, for she was not Rubens, and I said, "You know nothing of such matters, you, the daughter of a merchant and a stranger to honor."

"Am I so?" she said in a loud voice, so that the crowd turned and stared. "Do you think that? Yes, my mother married a merchant to keep from starving, but she descended from the Colonnas and before that from the Aurelii. We were great in Rome when Madrid was a mud village. And what of your blood, Sr. Sevilliano, you from a city swarming with half-Jews and quasi-Moors and every sort of mongrel cur!"

And she strode away back to her house and I was laughed at in the street.

We fought like that many times. She had no idea of how a woman should behave. Many times I stayed away and many times she did too, but always her witchcraft drew me back, this madness, destroying all honor and duty as an oiled rag wipes through the paint and makes all dull mud.

I painted her once more, toward the end of my stay in Rome. The king had commanded me back to Spain, each letter more importunate, and yet I could not leave. She was with child, she said, mine, and I believed her. Her husband barred her from his house and cut her off entirely, and she took a mean apartment near the river by the Pope's bridge. I said I would acknowledge the child and see it bred, but this did not seem to please her as it should. She knew I was going; of course I was going! What did she imagine, that I would stay with her there or drag a concubine back to the Alcázar? She drank. She had always drunk deeply of wine, but now she began to take brandy and Holland spirits. It made her madder and even more abandoned in lust. And dragged me down with her.

So, upon an afternoon in spring, we had exhausted ourselves upon the couch in my studio, and as it happened that same mirror was propped up upon a high chest, and as we lay there our reflections shone out from the dusty glass and she said, "That would be a painting, Velázquez, a Venus as the world has not yet seen her, fucked into insensibility by her Adonis. But you would never do a thing like that. Your Holy Office and your Spanish court would never approve. Or no, I believe that such a painting is beyond even your art, to capture us as we are now and perhaps will never be again. No, not even you."

"I can paint anything," I said, "even this."

"Then do it! There are the paints, here am I. You can paint our little kitchen-boy Cupid in later."

I got up from the couch and placed a primed canvas on my easel and painted her as she was. I worked all afternoon, and when the figure was done I turned it to the wall and would not let her look, though she snarled at me like a vixen. Later I found the boy we'd used in the first painting, the one of her back, and painted him in, and then the rest, the draperies and so on, and when I was done I hid it in my closet where I keep my funds and my accounts and where no one goes but me.

I showed it to her later, the last time we were together. I was packed, with my casts and paintings all sent ahead; we were to leave for the ship at Genoa within the week.

She laughed like a crow when she saw it. "Oh, Velázquez, we would burn for this if anyone saw it, you and I, our smokes would mingle above the Campo dei Fiori; it is the worst thing ever painted. Give it to the Pope as a parting gift, I beg you, and let us die together."

"No one burns for a painting anymore," I said.

"You are quite right, nor have I taught you wit in all these long months or to know when I speak in jest. But, my love, it is still enough to ruin you. Whatever possessed you to put your face and my face in it?"

"I was drunk," I said.

"That will not do when they drag you before the Inquisition. There are only two things to be done with it. You can sell it to Heliche. He will value it and keep it close."

"I do not sell paintings," I said. "I am not in trade."

"Oh, pardon me, Don Diego de Silva y Velázquez, I had forgotten," she said, "but in that case a brushload of flake white will do."

"I had thought you could take it. I had planned to give it to you."

"Oh, did you!" she cried. "What generosity! So that in my misery I could be daily reminded of the great passion of my whole life? Velázquez, my dear love, you are an ass. I will paint it over this minute. I will paint over it and paint something else on top of it, a religious subject in the Venetian manner, and give it to a church. Then may God forgive me."

So I left her and returned to my apartments, and I was busy with my leaving and thought of her not at all. Until that night, in my bed, when I considered that never again would she share it, nor would I ever again experience those pleasures she knew how to draw from me. Then I felt bereft and sleep would not come, and I called for hot wine and so achieved the oblivion I sought.

And awoke in terror of the light that shone from a glass with no flame and the noises from the street outside and sounds from a small box as if a demon were captive inside, and my first thought was, I have died in the night and I have awakened in hell, this is my punishment. A sound of roaring, like a torrent, and a gurgling noise from a room nearby, and then to my extreme horror through the door walked a naked woman I had never seen before, and I screamed and slid from the bed and crouched in a corner, covering myself and crying prayers, begging forgiveness. And the woman came closer with a look of consternation on her face, trying to embrace me and speaking a language like the Romans speak, but I could not make out one word in five. When she saw I would not be tempted into lust she wrapped herself in a robe and left, and I pulled the blanket over my head and wept for my damnation.

So this must be like trying to describe sex to a child or religious exaltation to an atheist; it's something you have to experience to know about. I was having those thoughts and feelings, Velázquez in torment, and at the same time, like a carrot in a boiling stewpot, there floated into my consciousness bit by bit the pattern of memories and learned behaviors that constituted the personality of Charles Wilmot, Jr. That's not a box of demons, that's a clock radio playing. Those noises are early automobile traffic through the piazza. That's a lightbulb.

Then the enormity of what had just happened to me struck me in the vitals. I was lucky I now recalled where the bathroom was and what it was for, because I barely reached the toilet in time. They found me that way, all retched out and shivering, and Franco got me into the shower and cleaned off and Sophia put me to bed and stayed, trying to find out what was wrong with me, and the odd thing now was she was speaking Roman dialect and expecting me to understand, and finally I asked her to speak English and, with a puzzled look on her face, she switched languages.

She wanted to know what was up with me, naturally, and I made something up. I said that something must have gone wrong with my brain during the night, maybe a tiny stroke, because when I woke up I didn't know who I was or where I was. And there was something wrong with my memory, some kind of amnesia.

This alarmed her. She squeezed my hand and put her other hand to the hollow of her throat. "Yes, but you remember *us*."

"No, I don't," I said. "My last memory is us going to that little bar and talking with your friends and me drawing a bunch of people."

"Chaz! That first time at Guido's was months ago! How could you not remember?"

"What's the date, Sophia? Today's date."

"It's the third of March."

"Okay, then everything from mid-December onward is a complete blank."

"But, you will see doctors . . . it will come back, yes?"

"It could," I said, carefully, not believing it at all. "You could help me if you sort of told me what I was like, what I've been like, how we got together and all, what I've been doing."

It took some prodding, because amnesia is so terribly threatening. Our lives are constructed so much of shared memories that we tend to panic when our partners in these refuse to confirm our own. But in a little while, when she saw I wasn't going to suddenly remember, she began to tell me her tale. She'd started to pose the day after we'd gone out to Guido's. It was pleasant enough. We'd talked as I worked, just chat at first, but later I'd told her something about my life and she'd told me something about hers, her family, her lovers, her ambitions for herself and the boy. We worked in the morning and then had lunch with the ménage. She related anecdotes: Baldassare and his liver, and the home remedies he'd marshaled in its support; about Franco and his vanity and his women and his dark past; about little Enrico and his teachers and friends. A domestic life in all its Italianate richness. It had apparently been a happy time.

And I'd told her about my family in the States, how I was still more or less carrying a torch for my wife. She knew it was a long shot, but she'd liked me. She thought I was gentle, a decent man, a genius with paint. She admired me. She didn't care that I was hung up on another woman. Any man worth having had other women in his life, but I was here now and she had a feeling for me, one she hadn't felt in a long time. And so it happened. One day, when the light had gone, she'd risen naked from the couch and embraced me, and I was hesitant, like a young girl, which she found charming, but in the end I'd fallen back on the couch with her, and we'd made love and it was wonderful. And so on, for the next months, and she liked how I was with Enrico, he'd opened up so much, was always asking if Chaz was to be his new *babbo*.

At that point she was crying, searching my face for some sign that I'd shared this life, but there was none. I mean, I wasn't being callous, there was just nothing there—she was a nice woman with whom I'd had one date, and so I steered the conversation as gently as I could to the painting.

"Oh, yes," she said, "you did your painting. You don't remember that either?"

"No. But I'd like to see it now. Maybe it would snap me back or something."

"It's not here," she said. "Baldassare has taken it to the laboratory on Via Portina, an industrial area, you understand? He needs high vacuums and ovens, special equipments for this work, the aging."

"What's the painting like?"

"What is it like? It is like Velázquez. It *is* Velázquez, the most astonishing thing I have ever seen. Baldassare says it is a miracle."

And she told me what I had painted, and I recalled it well, having just finished it a few weeks ago in subjective time, in Rome, in 1650. Painting's not just in the eye and the head, it's in the body too, like a dance—the hand, the arm, the back, the way you lean forward and sideways to check out a passage, the standing away and moving close. So when you look at something you've done, you have all the intimate body memory, and in this case I had a whole other set of memories, the feel and scent of this particular woman's skin, the density of Leonora's living flesh in my hand and under me and on top of me, the squirming damp reality of it. And more than that—this is even harder to explain or even to think about—I had the sense memories of somebody *else*, somebody else doing the painting. The brain fucks with your head, but the body never lies, or so I'd thought.

For the next week I was a complete wreck, afraid to go to sleep, afraid I might wake up again not me. I spent most of these first days after my return wandering along the river, up to Castel Sant'Angelo and down to Ponte Testaccio, exhausting myself, drinking in a bar before returning home. Most of me was still in 1650: I could recall dozens, hundreds of details, more than I could recollect of the last year of my so-called real life. Maybe the seventeenth century made for a denser, more vivid existence: I mean street scenes, talking to cardinals, servants, what I ate at banquets, the talk at diplomatic receptions, being with Leonora.

Yeah, her. My body, my mind, my heart, if you want to call it that, was burdened with a relationship that I never had, with a woman who died over three hundred years ago. So what was the real story?

Obviously, an unprecedented reaction to salvinorin, combined with amnesia, also drug related. My brain was damaged, we already knew that, and since the only deep emotional attachment I've ever had was to Lotte, somehow I conflated all that with thinking about Velázquez and came up with this imagined life, and there you had it, an explanation that Shelly Zubkoff would swallow without gagging.

Another reason for staying out of the house was that Sophia started crying nearly every time she looked at me, and it freaked me out, because she'd had a love affair with a ghost, a demon lover, while I'd been making love to Leonora three centuries ago.

One day she wasn't there and her mother told me she'd gone with the kid to visit friends in Bologna. The *signora* had been crying too, I could see, and through the barrier of language she let me know that I had been a complete shitbag.

You have to understand that part of the problem here was my complete isolation. I'd checked my cell phone after coming out of the past and learned that there were no messages at all on it. Not one. Jackie Moreau was dead; Mark was, well, Mark, not a sympathetic ear; Charlie was God knew where in Africa, and Lotte was incommunicado. It was like I'd been jailed by the secret police.

So I called my ex-wife one evening, and as soon as she heard my voice she said, "The only thing I want to hear from you is that you're getting psychiatric help."

I said, "Hey, I'm planning to, honestly, but look—I've, um, been painting like mad and Krebs is coming tomorrow to check out the work and if he likes it, that's a million bucks to me. Lotte, imagine what we're going to do with—"

But she wouldn't listen. She said, "You know, it makes no sense to talk to a maniac, and it hurts me to hear you rave like this. Call me when you are getting the medical help you need."

And she hung up. Isolation complete, then. Yes, good thing I didn't tell her about what I'd been doing, or imagining I was doing, for the last three months. She might've *really* been annoyed. So, okay, I was crazy, but you know, just then I didn't *feel* crazy. I mean, I was functional as an artist, because apparently I had pulled off this huge coup of a forgery. I felt crazy in New York, but now I didn't. And frankly I was dazzled by the money and the promise of more. It's the rule that if you're rich enough you can't be that crazy. So I really looked forward to Krebs coming for that reason, and also because, now that I thought about it, he was my only remaining friend.

Now came the big day. That morning Baldassare went out and brought my picture back from the secret forgery lab. He set it up on a display easel in the parlor, covered with a black velvet cloth, and he was guarding it like a dragon, wouldn't let anyone have a peek before Krebs arrived. Franco drove to the airport to meet him, and while he did that I got fed up with the tension in the house and went out to take a long walk, east to the Tiber and along the Ripa and back through the Porta Portese in the ruins of the old walls. It wasn't quite warm yet but spring was happening in Rome; you could smell the river and the trees on the boulevards were greening up and blossoming, if they were that kind of tree.

When I returned to the house on Santini I saw that the Mercedes was already parked outside and I hurried in. Krebs was there, in the parlor, with Franco and Baldassare and a man I didn't recognize, a small, stout, olive-skinned guy with dark-rimmed glasses and the air of an academic. They were all standing around drinking Prosecco, and I saw that the drape was still on the painting.

Krebs hailed me as I came in, embraced me warmly, and said that he'd insisted they wait until I came back for the unveiling. He introduced the stranger as Dr. Vicencio de Salinas, a curator from the Palacio de Livia, the private collection of the duchess of Alba, which kind of puzzled me at the time, because I thought, Hey, isn't this a little premature, showing the thing to an expert before the boss even had a look?

Then Baldassare pulled the drape off with a flourish and there were gasps all around. All three of us—Krebs, Salinas, and me—surged forward to look at it more closely and bumped shoulders, and I kind of pulled back and let them get the best look. They were the customers. But I'd seen enough to understand that Baldassare had worked a wonder. Oil paint takes years to really cure up and dry, and it changes its appearance during that time; even the things I'd done as a kid still looked like the contemporary objects they in fact were. But this son of a bitch looked *old*, and it had the palpable authority that old things have. It looked cracked and heavy with age, like every painting from the seventeenth century you see in museums, and I had a brief moment of temporal vertigo, as if I'd painted it in the seventeenth century for real.

The Spaniard inspected the painting at various distances for what seemed a long time. At last he turned to Krebs with a small smile, nodding his head—reluctantly, it seemed to me.

"Well? You said it couldn't be done," said Krebs. "What do you think now?"

Salinas shrugged and answered, "Frankly, I admit to being astounded. The brushwork, the colors, that glow on the skin are all entirely true to the *Rokeby Venus*. And the . . . the preparation is also very fine; the craqueleur seems flawless on initial inspection."

Krebs clapped Baldassare heartily on the back. "Yes! Bravo Signor Baldassare!"

And Salinas went on, "Subject, as I say, to technical examination, the pigments and so forth, I would have no trouble in passing this as genuine."

I stood there amid the smiles, and no one looked at me or patted me on the back, and I figured it was something like what went down with Castelli's faked Tiepolo—they were practicing pretending that it was real. I couldn't study it closely myself. When I tried to a pain started across my eyes and my vision blurred a little and I had to sit down.

I looked up at Krebs again and he was talking with Salinas, something about the exact dimensions of the painting, and Krebs assured him that it was right to a tenth of a millimeter and told him to get on with taking his samples, because he had to get back to Madrid as soon as possible so as not to be missed at the museum.

Salinas opened a briefcase from which he removed a set of binocular goggles, a high-intensity headlamp, and a small black container about the size of an eyeglass case. He put on the goggles and the lamp, switched it on, turning himself into something like ET on a spelunking expedition. He approached the painting and from his little case drew a shiny small tool.

"He's taking a core to analyze the paint layers," Krebs said. "Tiny, and virtually invisible. He'll check the pigments and the ground for age and anachronism. Which of course he will not find."

"I hope not. What was all that about exact dimensions?"

"Well, obviously whatever connoisseurship and technical analysis may say, the thing is worthless without an impeccable provenance. Now, with a drawing, or some minor Corot, or even a Rubens, this is easily handled, as I'm sure you know. It's nothing to prepare a seventeenth-century bill of sale—old Baldassare can do it in his sleep—and there are thousands of dusty garrets in Europe and ancient families who will attest, for a consideration, that their ancestor the count bought the thing in sixteen whatever. But for something like this, such dodges will not do, not at all."

Salinas seemed to be finished at the painting. He switched off his lamp, removed his goggles, and held up a small vial as if it were the cure for cancer.

"I have it," he said, and placed the vial into his little box.

"Excellent," said Krebs. "Franco will drive you to the Ciampino airport; the jet you came on is fueled and waiting and you should be back at your desk in Madrid"—he checked his wristwatch—"no more than four hours after you left. A long siesta, but not unknown in Madrid, I believe."

Salinas smiled and shook hands with both of us, with the usual assurances of goodwill, not entirely hiding what I saw, close up now, was extreme terror; he packed up his things and departed in something of a rush. I heard the Mercedes start up outside.

"A useful little man, that," said Krebs reflectively as the sounds of the car receded. "And a bitter man: well trained, but without the flair needed in a museum director nowadays. He was passed over for promotion as director of collections, and this is his revenge. And his prosperous retirement."

"He's going to buy the painting for the Livia?"

Krebs gave me an unbelieving look and laughed. "Of course not. His job is to give us a flawless provenance."

"How?"

"That you will see with your own eyes, perhaps as soon as next week, when we go to Madrid."

"We?"

"Yes, of course." He looked at his watch again. "You know, it's past one. Aren't you famished? I am."

With that we left the house and walked down the street and across the Piazza San Cosimato to a little restaurant where they apparently knew Krebs and were very glad to see him. They gave us a table by the window, and when we were settled with a plate of dried anchovies and one of whitebait fritters, and a bottle of Krug, he said, "Wilmot, I realize you are an artist and thus not entirely of this world, but I must press upon you that from now until however long it takes you must keep yourself under almost military discipline. No wandering off and no unauthorized calls. When we return I will ask you to surrender your cellular phone. It's not me who makes these rules."

"Who does then?"

"Our friends. My partners in this venture."

"You mean you're mobbed up?" I said, or rather the wine said.

"Excuse me?"

"Mobbed up. You're working for the Mafia."

He seemed to find this amusing, and while he was chuckling the waiter came and we ordered food. The waiter said the *scampi Casino di Venezia* was very good and Krebs said we had to have it in honor of the city where we began our association, so I said, okay, I'll have that too, and he ordered a bottle of Procanico to go with it. When the man had gone he continued, "Mobbed up—I must remember that expression. But let us not confuse things. The Mafia is about whores and drugs and corrupt contracts for poured concrete. We are talking about an entirely different level of enterprise."

"Criminal enterprise. Whatever happened to letting the experts come to their own conclusions? Whatever happened to Giordano Luca? You're planning a major fraud."

He looked at me with what seemed like amused pity. "Ah, Wilmot, did you ever actually think it would be anything else? Really?"

And I had to admit to myself that he was right. I do have a habit of believing my own lies. I took a breath, drank some more wine, and asked, "So when do I get my money? Or was that another thing, like those crummy sketches you raved about, that I should have realized was too good to be true?"

"Good God, do you think I intend to cheat you?" he said, with what seemed to be genuine amazement. "That's the last thing in the world I would ever do. Wilmot, I have been searching most of my life for someone like you, someone with your incredible facility with the styles of the past. You are, to my present knowledge, unique in the world. I would have to be insane to treat you with anything but the greatest respect."

"That's terrific, but on the other hand I have to ask you if I can make a phone call."

"I told you, I don't make those rules. But when the operation is complete, and the surveillance is lifted, you may call anyone you like. Always being discreet, of course. Because, you understand me, there is no—how shall I put it?—statutes of limitations on art forgery. That is, until the actual witnesses are deceased, the authenticity of the painting is always at risk. With one careless word an object worth many tens, hundreds, of millions becomes a mere pastiche and worth nothing, and then the buyers look to get their money back. They go to the dealer and of course he talks, and then the cord that holds it all together unravels. Then it is either prison for all of us or a worse fate, if in any way the gentlemen I referred to earlier are in the least implicated. Not a happy prospect. Especially not for you. Or for your family."

When he said that I almost lost a mouthful of whitebait, but I managed to get it down and asked him, "What're you talking about? My family?"

"Well, only as a means of controlling you. While you remain alive."

"Excuse me?"

"Yes, well, I speak loosely of witnesses, but in affairs like this one, there is only one witness who counts. I mean, Baldassare knows, and Franco, and that girl who posed, but no one cares about them. Anyone can cry forgery and the interests that wish for the painting to be original can always shout them down. It happens all the time. But one witness can never be shouted down." He paused and inclined his head toward me and snapped a bit of fish from his fork.

"The forger himself," I said.

"Just so. Now don't be downhearted, Wilmot, I beg you. As I keep saying, this is a new life you are in now. Danger, yes, but when has real art not been associated with a certain danger? Quattrocento Florence was a violent place, and art's greatest patrons have always been violent men."

"Like the Nazis?" A little dig there, but he didn't blink.

"I was thinking of the robber barons of America or the aristocrats of Europe. And the artists themselves have always been freebooters, living on the edges of society. When art becomes domesticated into a branch of show business, it becomes flaccid and dull, as now."

"Sorry, but that's nonsense, like Harry Lime's remark about Switzerland and the cuckoo clock in *The Third Man*. Velázquez had a steady job—"

"Yes, and in his lifetime he did fewer than one hundred fifty paintings. Rembrandt, living on the edge of life, did over five hundred."

"And Vermeer, who was even more on the edge, did forty. I'm sorry, it won't wash, Krebs. You can't generalize about what kind of temperament and what social conditions produce great painting. It's a mystery."

I could see he was starting to get a little steamed to have his pet theories exploded like this, but it's always gotten *me* steamed to hear theories about how art happens dumped on my head by people who never handled a brush. But then he shrugged, and smiled, and said, "Well, perhaps you're right. It is a life I am used to, and we all tell ourselves stories to justify ourselves to ourselves and others, because we wish to have some company in these little scenarios. But I see it is not to be, you have a head as hard as mine. And really, it does not matter in the least, as long as you do not forget that the sword that hangs over us is harder than both our heads. Ah, good, here is our meal."

The food was excellent, but I had acid on my tongue and could hardly taste it. I drank more than my share of the wine, however, and got enough of a buzz to keep me in my seat instead of running out of the place screaming hysterically. Krebs chewed away on his scampi and I wondered how he'd ever gotten used to this kind of life. I mean, he seemed like an ordinary guy, no more ruthless—in fact, maybe less ruthless—than the typical high-end New York gallery magnate.

I wanted to jab him some more, though, so I said, "Is it true, by the way, that you got your start selling pictures stolen from murdered Jews?"

"Yes," he said blandly, "perfectly true. But as I'm sure you know, there was no question of returning these things to the rightful owners. It would be like trying to return a carving to an Assyrian or an Aztec. They were dead. I sincerely wish they hadn't died, but I didn't kill them. I was thirteen when the war ended. So what was I supposed to do, leave them in a Swiss vault forever?"

"An interesting moral point."

"Yes, and I'll tell you another one, as long as you've brought up the subject. My father was a Nazi and I was raised as a Nazi. Everyone of my generation was. As a boy I could not wait to be old enough to join the forces and fight for the Reich. I believed every lie they told me, as I imagine you believed the lies your country told you. Tell me, were you in Vietnam?"

"No, I was exempt. I had a kid."

"Lucky you. According to the Vietnamese your country killed three million of their people, most of them civilians. I'm not excusing what the Nazis did, of course, just pointing out that Germany is not alone in slaughtering innocents, and for a long time the Americans supported that war. Now I will tell you an amusing story. In December of 1944 my whole family was back in Munich and the city was being bombed day and night. My father was naturally concerned for the safety of his family, and so he pulled strings and got us out of there, to a place that had never been bombed and which was considered quite safe. Do you know where this was? It was Dresden. We were there in February when the Allies burnt the city to the ground. I survived; my mother did not. I hid in the sewers."

Here he drank some wine and let loose a small sigh.

"After the bombing I went back to where our house had been and there was nothing but ash. My mother had turned into a little black manikin one meter long. We scraped her off the cellar wall with pieces of a smashed toilet. And then the war was over and we learned the full story of our shame, and so we were not allowed to voice the suffering we had experienced. This destruction, this slaughter of children, these thousands of rapes we endured could not be acknowledged. It was our just recompense, our nemesis. And so most of my generation picked ourselves up and went on with life and rebuilt our country."

He paused and I said, "What does that have to do with—"

He held up his fork. "Wait, be patient, I will get to that. So we all participated in rebuilding the country, but there were scars that could never be mentioned. Some of us never recovered from the disillusion, this massive betrayal, this nursery of lies in which we were raised. We were forever cut off from our fellow citizens, because any idea of a shared culture, our *heimat*, had been poisoned. The Nazis were very clever: they understood that to create a great evil you must pervert a great good, and this was our love of nation and family and culture.

"And when I asked my father what he had done in the war, he answered me honestly, and when I heard of it, I was not shocked, I did not reject him, because I knew in my heart I was no better than him, and I did not join the self-righteous of my generation, the ones who supposed they would have behaved so much more nobly than their parents in the same situation. So I became the person I am today. After my art studies were complete, I went to Switzerland and forged provenances and sold the paintings of the dead Jews without a single qualm. I said to myself that I was returning beauty to the world. Perhaps a self-serving lie, but, as I have suggested already, who does not tell themselves such lies? Yet the beauty is real, perhaps the only real thing there is. It does not save us, but it is better, I think, for there to be beauty than not. You have created a thing of great beauty, deep beauty, a thing that will last for as long as there are men to see it, and they will love it the more if they think it came from the hand of Diego Velázquez. This is foolishness, of course—the thing is the thing—yet who shall blame us if we profit from this foolishness? What legitimate business does not?"

"Well, gosh, you convinced me," I said. "Now I can't wait to forge again," and he laughed and slapped the table.

"That is why I like you, Wilmot. One needs a sense of humor in this business, and also a certain cynicism. I tell you the most painful moments of my life, with Germanic seriousness and *weltschmerz*, and you make a joke of it. But one thing I cannot let slip, and that is the accusation that I am not a patron of your own work. In fact, I am. I believe that once you are freed from the necessity of whoring for the galleries and the commercial arts you will truly blossom as a painter. Those two little drawings prove it, and it will give me a great deal of personal satisfaction to see you do this."

"You don't think it's too late?"

"Of course not! Who knew of Joseph Cornell until he was older than you? Even Cézanne sold hardly a painting until he was your age. And nowadays, with enough resources, one can secure a reputation. You would be surprised at how entirely corruptible is the world of art criticism. And you are good besides. I could make reputations for painters who do not have the talent that is in your little finger."

He put down his fork and looked at the empty scampi shells with satisfaction. Mine remained half finished, and when the waiter came by I told him to take it away.

Krebs said, "I hope what I have been saying has not affected your appetite. No? Good, then perhaps we might now speak of this drug you have taken and the illusion that you are living the life of Velázquez."

Well, obviously he'd gotten the story from Mark, I mean the early experiences in New York, and I told him the rest, about how I'd spent 1650 in Rome, while we enjoyed dishes of wild strawberries *capriccio dio Wanda*, cups of espresso, and a finale of grappa. The bottle was left at the table, and I had several.

When I'd finished talking, he said, "Well, I wouldn't have believed it if I had not heard it from your own lips."

"I still don't believe it, and it happened to me."

"Yes, and let me say, better you than me, Wilmot. I would not take such a drug for any consideration."

"Why not? You could end up Holbein."

"Yes, or Bosch. Or standing up to my nose in shit in a Dresden sewer for ten hours. Again." He shuddered. "In any case, an interesting phenomenon. You ingest a drug and you experience events outside the bounds of rational explanation. Tell me, are you familiar with the theory that we have five bodies?"

"No," I said, "but I'm not sure I want to know about it, if it's going to scare me worse than I am already."

He smiled like the mad scientist in a bad movie, mock sadistically, or maybe not that mock. "Yes, so first we have the body that science and medicine deal with, the meat, the nerves and chemicals and so on. Then we have the second, the representation of the body in the mind, which does not always match the reality of the first—phantom limbs and so on—plus the sense of ourselves and the recognition that this thing also exists in others, as when we feel the loom of another person close to us or look into another's eyes."

He looked into my eyes and grinned.

"Third we have the unconscious body, the source of dreams and, we think, also of creativity. It is the task of the mystics to merge the second with the third body to find the soul, as they would put it. Those who accomplish this are the only ones who are truly awake— everyone else is a robot enslaved to the mass mind, as pumped out by the media or established by social norms. Then fourth is the magical body, by which adepts can be in two places at once or walk through walls or heal the sick or curse their enemies. Finally there is the spiritual body, which Hegel called the zeitgeist. The one who can control all the other bodies and also controls history."

"You believe all this?"

He shrugged. "It's just a theory. But it does explain some things. It explains how you could become Velázquez. It helps to explain why the most cultivated and educated nation in Europe should have submitted itself happily and enthusiastically to the absolute power of an ill-bred corporal. I can tell you, Wilmot, I was there, just a boy perhaps, but I was *there*. I felt the power. For my first years of conscious life I was living entirely in someone else's dream, and my father, who is no fool, was the same. Even now, it is hard for me to believe that such power was entirely of this world. And when it was over, as soon as he blew out his brains, I felt a sense of release, of waking out of a long dream, and every German who was conscious at the time will tell you the same story. We looked around at the ruins and asked ourselves, how did this happen? How did ordinary Germans do such terrible things? Some people have argued that Germans are naturally brutal and undemocratic, at your knees or at your throat, as they say, but this is unsatisfying. The French terrified Europe for far longer than the Germans ever did, and they are always held up as the model of civilization, and the Scandinavians were monsters of destruction for three centuries and are all lambs up there now and don't hurt a fly. And besides that, if we are naturally so awful, how come we are today the least militaristic nation on earth? So my point is that, if such a mysterious and unexpected thing could happen to a whole nation, I think that when a man tells me he is living for periods in a different time and having the thoughts of a man long dead, I say, why not?"

"Yeah, easy for you to say."

"I appreciate your difficulty, my friend. But on the other hand, even without, let us say, artificial means of enhancement, you would still be a dweller in mystery. You remember what Duchamp said about art: 'Only one thing in art is valid—that which cannot be explained.' I think even your Dr. Zubkoff would agree that the creative capacities of the human mind remain beyond human explanation. And I'll tell you this, Wilmot. I am a very successful man—that is, I have as much money as I require, and my family, such as remains, is well provided for. I have enough experience with men who have vastly more wealth to convince me that I am not this type, I am not interested in accumulating more money than I can possibly spend in a lifetime. I do not dream of the Werner Krebs Museum or the Krebs Trust doing the good works. I scheme and deal, I buy and sell—this is for more years than you have been alive, I think— and I confess, life becomes a little dull, and in my secret thoughts I say to myself, maybe I shall grow careless and end up in prison or dead. This is exciting for some time, but even this fades, and really, I would rather not be imprisoned or dead. So what shall I do? I don't know. And then, as from nowhere, comes Charles P. Wilmot, Jr., into my life, and suddenly I am as a boy again selling my first stolen painting."

I said, "I'm glad you're happy, Mr. Krebs." And I was. I had a pretty good idea about what it was like if Krebs was not happy with you.

"I am. I tell you what is most remarkable about you, Wilmot. You are a genius, but you are not a son of a bitch. I have dealt with these before now and it is no fun. But I *like* you, I really do. And we are going to have fun, a *lot* of fun, you and I. There is something I have been longing to do for over fifty years that I believe you can help me accomplish, but . . . excuse me, I believe I must take this call."

A little tune had played, Bach's *Toccata in D* on a harpsichord, and

Krebs pulled a cell phone from his inner pocket. He turned slightly away from me and spoke rapidly in German.

I finished my grappa, conscious of a strange feeling after this speech from Krebs, thinking about what Lotte had said about collectors falling in love with artists, and also about the doomed little girl that Frankenstein falls for, and also about Fay Wray and Kong. Lotte always used to quote a saying of La Rochefoucauld's that there were some situations in life that you have to be half crazy to escape from. If that were really true, I thought then, I should be just fine.

Two days later we moved to Madrid, occupying a couple of suites at the Villa Real. Our party was made up of the king (Krebs), the First Murderer (Franco), the Fool (me), and a new guy, the Second Murderer (Kellermann), who met us at the Madrid airport in the usual gangster Mercedes limo. I gathered he was an employee at Krebs's secret mountain hideout in Bavaria, a large, polite blondie with nice teeth. Franco had nice teeth too, which you usually don't see on Europeans. I asked him about it once and he told me that Herr Krebs insists on good dental care for all his staff, pays for it out of his own pocket. An unashamed patron is Herr Krebs, and it wouldn't surprise me much to learn he arranged their marriages too.

All in all it was kind of neat to be part of Herr Krebs's little court. The life of an international criminal is not a strenuous one, which is why it's so popular. We rose late, ate well; Krebs and I toured the galleries and museums, strolled the temperate plazas at night, and ate tapas and heard music and discussed art on a high level.

Yes, nice indeed to be driven in a limo everywhere and to stay in this really snazzy hotel and never have to wonder about where you're going. It was not that great being an American in Spain since the Iraq shit started and the Madrid metro bombings, and I detected dirty looks, subtle rudenesses, and obscene comments behind the backs of the Americans I saw strolling obliviously around this hotel.

Which was five-star, naturally, old on the outside, sleek as a fighter jet on the inside, furnished in leather and brushed steel, wired to the gills. Krebs told me I couldn't make phone calls without permission, and I haven't, but he didn't say anything about e-mail. We had Wi-Fi in our suite and I was able to cruise the Web (all those sites about memory and craziness, although there does not seem to be an organization devoted to fixing what's wrong with me) and communicate with my children, chatty e-mails from Milo with links to cool websites and videos, and from Rose I got, "hEllo DadDDy I am FIIN" with little drawing-program pictures attached. Lotte didn't answer the ones I sent her.

And then one night we drove out to the west end of the city, to a commercial street on the other side of Bailén. In a vacant loft, lit bright as day by big portable worklights, we found a couple of familiar faces, Baldassare and Salinas from the Palacio de Livia museum. Salinas informed us that the tests of the paint samples had been perfect; the little scrape was chemically indistinguishable from similar ones taken from undoubted Velázquez paintings. He seemed sad when he said this—maybe he was having second thoughts, or maybe it was his curatorial faith in technology receiving a deadly blow. Anyway, we were obviously on to the next phase.

On a couple of big glass-topped tables pushed together I saw my *Venus* and another painting, just the same size, that looked a lot like *The Miraculous Draught of Fishes* by Jacopo Bassano, which hangs in the National Gallery in D.C. Both paintings had been taken off their stretchers and were laid flat on the tables, the Bassano weighted taut with small leather shot bags. I noticed that the fake Velázquez had been adhered in some way to a thick glass sheet somewhat larger than the painting. The air in the loft was close and smelled of old building, turps, and some chemical I couldn't identify.

"What's going on, Werner?" I asked.

"Well, you see we have your wonderful painting, but, as I've told you, however wonderful it is, it will not pass as genuine unless it has a flawless provenance. What do you think of the other painting?"

"It looks like a Bassano," I said.

"Yes, but which one? He had four sons, all painters, and the work from their hands is not nearly as valuable as the father's."

"The story of my life," I said, "but this one looks a lot like the one in Washington. It's a nice painting. How do you tell the various Bassanos apart anyway?"

"It's almost impossible without evidence from provenance. But this particular painting was in fact sold as a Jacopo to the duke of Alba in 1687. It's been in the family's possession ever since, and so its provenance is as good as any provenance can be."

"Yeah, but what does that have to do with the Velázquez?" I said, and then I yelled.

Baldassare had taken a wide brush full of thick white paint and wiped a line right across my fake *Venus*, and a second later I realized why he'd done it and why we were all there. Baldassare gave me a smirk and continued to paint over the nude.

"You're going to lift the Bassano and adhere it on top of the *Venus*," I said, and the sweat popped out all over my face and scalp. Now at last this was the thing itself, the patent act of fraud, no more horseshit about indistinguishable works of art and buyer beware and who are we hurting. And that's why we all had to be there, the same reason why a junior mafioso has to make his bones before he becomes a made guy. I had to get dirty.

"Yes, we are," Krebs said. "Only it's not a Bassano at all."

"It's not?"

"No, it's the work of your most illustrious predecessor, Luca Giordano. Underneath the surface is his signature. The duke was fooled, and this time Luca did not confess. The thing has been hanging as a Bassano for three hundred years, until Salinas here had it cleaned and

X-rayed as a matter of routine. He saw the signature of the faker and called me."

"Why?" I asked. I was watching Baldassare obliterate my painting with what I presumed was the finest seventeenth-century flake white.

"Because of the provenance. Our curator here has just discovered that a painting worth perhaps a quarter of a million euros is now worth no more than twenty thousand. This happens in museums all the time. Sometimes they continue to hang the painting with a revised attribution, school of so-and-so, for example. Sometimes they sell it. Salinas decided that the painting should be sold. Now, he conspires to commit a little fraud of his own, this naughty man, with the connivance of his superiors at the museum, of course. Suppose that he puts the painting on the market discreetly as a Jacopo Bassano. Americans love old masters, and one of them is sure to want this one. So Salinas calls our friend Mark Slade."

"Who else?"

"Yes, and if an American can be gulled, so much the better. Who likes Americans nowadays? Perhaps you have noticed this, eh? Yes, very sad. And Mark is a good choice in another way. He specializes in very private sales to rich Yankees by museums in need of cash. All museums have too many pictures to show, second-rate pieces cluttering the basement, and they don't like going to the auction houses because they don't want to be accused of selling off the national patrimony or the endowed collection of some rich fool. So discretion is very important."

Baldassare had by this time sprayed the surface of the Bassano with a clear substance. He carefully flipped it over facedown on a large plate of thin glass, a few inches larger on all sides than the painting, and reweighted it. Now he brushed the back of the canvas with a chemical whose scent I did not recognize but that had to be some kind of sophisticated solvent. Then we waited.

I wandered out of the glare and found that they'd supplied the forgery headquarters with a number of leather lounge chairs, a low table, and a large cooler full of beer and cold tapas. The furniture was all brand-new, down to the price stickers, and the refreshments were first class. I recalled what Krebs had said about the investment of his silent partners: someone was spending money without stint on this one.

Baldassare laid out the spread of food and drink and then dragged one of the chairs into the shadows and lay down. Krebs and Salinas were conversing quietly in Spanish, a conversation to which I was clearly not invited, and it was equally clear that Baldassare did not want to chat with me. I brought out my sketchbook and drew the scene, a less dramatic version of *Vulcan's Forge* by Velázquez, and wondered what would happen if the cops burst in instead of Apollo.

Which didn't happen. After a couple of hours a little alarm buzzed on Baldassare's watch and we all got up to check out the tables. Baldassare and Salinas donned surgical gloves, and with steel spatulas the two men slowly pried the old canvas up from the paint layer of the Bassano. It took a while. Except for brief exchanges between the two men at work, all was silent. When the canvas was at last peeled away I could see only the bottom layer of the underpainting—the image was facedown on the glass sheet. Baldassare picked this up by its edges, rotated it, and then, with painstaking care, let it down on the damp layer of flake white covering the forgery. Jesus and the startled fishermen shone out through the glass. He then clamped the edges of the two glass sheets together with small steel clips.

"What do you think?" Krebs asked Baldassare.

"It's good. I will squirt some solvent in there to release the glass over the top painting, then a few days in the oven, a little chemical treatment, a little wash, and you will have a wonderful sandwich. Then we take the bottom glass off and I'll nail it to the original Bassano stretchers. Not more than four or five days."

Handshakes all around, and we left Baldassare in the loft. In the street there was a car waiting for Salinas. When he'd gone and I was in our car with Krebs, I asked him, "So what's the plan now?"

"The next phase is moving our painting to market, obviously. Salinas will call Mark. He will show him the painting as a genuine Jacopo of flawless provenance. Mark will ask for an X-ray analysis. In the presence of witnesses, Salinas will object."

"But he *did* X-ray it."

"Yes, but with a single, highly corruptible technician. There is no record of this X-ray and the technician will not talk. To resume: Salinas will have explained to his management that he did not X-ray it because his curatorial eye told him it was probably a Luca forgery, but as long as this was mere suspicion he had decided to see if he could get a Bassano price out of it. His objection to having it X-rayed will be on record."

"I'm not getting this," I said. "Salinas knows the fake Bassano is a Velázquez. His superiors think it's just a fake Bassano, and that they're ripping off a stupid American by charging him the full Bassano price. So why does Slotsky go along with not doing an X-ray after he's made a big deal about asking for one?"

"Oh, he relents, I'm afraid. After the argument, he apologizes to Salinas for doubting the word of a Spanish gentleman and writes out a check for the full Bassano price on the spot. This is also a much-witnessed transaction. The museum board laughs all the way to the bank. Obviously, once he has taken possession and has it back in the States, he decides to X-ray it, again with reliable witnesses, and discovers the hidden Velázquez. This is announced to the world, the process of technical and curatorial examination confirms the authenticity of the work and we go to auction. The Liria is furious of course, but what can they do except fire poor Salinas?"

"Wait a minute—*auction*? You told me this was going to be one of your discreet sales to a billionaire."

He smiled and shrugged. "I lied. No, that is not exactly true. Frankly, I had not expected the work to be so very good, and so I assumed that a private sale would have been required. But not for our *Venus*, no, this one will go through the rooms to the highest bidder."

On the following day I got up early and went down to the lobby of the hotel. We usually breakfast off room service, but today I didn't feel like eating with Krebs and his two boys, so I said I wanted to eat early and hit the museums. The three big ones—the Prado, the Reina Sophía, and the Thyssen—are within walking distance of the hotel, and I wanted to look at pictures that were probably not all fakes. Krebs waved me off and said, "Franco will go with you. We are going out at two this afternoon."

"Where to?"

"You'll see," he said. "There are some people who want to meet you."

"What people?"

He smiled and exchanged a glance with Franco. "Have a nice time at the museum," he said with a dismissive wave.

We went to the Thyssen-Bornemisza museum, which was the nearest. It's the collection of a Dutch-born Swiss citizen with a Hungarian title who lived most of his life in Spain and was one of the great art collectors of the last century. He liked German expressionists and picked a lot of them up cheap in the thirties when the Nazis (whom his cousin Fritz was helping to finance) cleaned them out of German galleries as degenerate. A nice small collection of post-impressionists and the lesser impressionists and a handful of old masters, among which I was happy to see a Luca Giordano that he broke down and signed with his own name. It's a *Judgment of Solomon*. There's the great king got up in gilded breastplates and blond, just like Alexander the Great—funny, he doesn't look Jewish—and there are the two contentious women and the executioner holding the live baby uncomfortably by one foot, while he reaches for his sword. It's a little Rubensy and a little Rembrandty, a typical piece of late-Baroque wallpaper, beautifully drawn, but the expressions are waxworks and the paint surface dreary. The only exception is over to the left, the face of a little dwarf, a marvelous grotesque portrait that wouldn't have been out of place in a Goya capriccio. The Bassano forgery was a lot better as a painting, the poor bastard.

Back in my room, a little depressed now, I had a drink or two from the minibar and watched Bayern play Arsenal on the television, and at a little past noon there came a knock on the door that connected my room to Krebs's suite and an anouncement that lunch was served. I dined with Krebs, a fish soup and a platter of cold meats, a white wine and beer available.

That day the German papers were full of the uncovering of yet another terrorist plot; we talked about that and I told him about Bosco's 9/11 installation and the ensuing riot, and he said he would have liked to have seen it. He was firmly on Bosco's side and said he thought the typical American attitude to the terror attack inane and infantile. Less than three thousand dead and two office buildings destroyed in a nation of three hundred million? It was a joke, and a joke was the appropriate artistic response. Our grotesque reaction was the laughing-stock of the world, although people were too polite or too frightened to voice it. Try seven hundred thousand civilian dead in a nation of sixty million, which was what the Germans lost from the Allied bombing, and nearly *every* building destroyed in some places!

And no artistic response at all—no poetry, no art, no dramas. About the Nazis and the Jews there is plenty, we must never forget and all that, but about the destruction of German urban life not a whisper. We started it, and deserved it, and that was that. But the Americans were innocent, Americans never did anything bad, even to suggest there was a connection between an aggressive foreign policy, a continuous violent interference in the affairs of other nations, and this event, oh, no, that was off the table entirely.

The funny thing about this attitude was that Lotte shared it, despite having been in lower Manhattan when the planes hit the towers and despite having a kid who went blue when there was any dust in the air. Lotte thought that the right response to terror was bravery. You cleaned up the mess, mourned the dead for a particular limited period, and then moved on. I shared this with Krebs and then we talked about art, and how art dealt with the various horrors the world was heir to, and I said that I never felt a need to deal with that aspect of life in what I did, and did that make me some kind of pussy. Easel painting in oils while the world burned? And he asked what was the worst century in European history before the twentieth. It was the fourteenth century. The Black Death, half the population dead, devastating famines, and still they hardly paused the continual wars. Yet they didn't stop making art—Giotto, van Eyck, van der Goes.

"So we're saved by beauty?" I said. "I thought beauty was passé. I thought the concept was king now."

"No, saving or not saving is hardly the point, as I believe I've already said. Although I often think that God, if there really is such a being, only holds his hand from destroying us all because we create beauty for his amusement. And also I think submitting ourselves to the terror of beauty, the ravishment of it, prevents us from giving vent to the kind of despair that would lead to the absolute destruction of our kind. Do you know Rilke?"

He recited some German in that portentous way that people always recite poetry, and then translated, "'For beauty's only the beginning of terror we're still just able to bear. And the reason we adore it so is that it serenely disdains to destroy us.' So, Wilmot, you are a terrorist also, just like your friend Bosco, but more subtle. They don't riot against you, but maybe they should."

"Yeah, but the Nazis were supposed to be big art lovers and it didn't do much for their destructiveness."

"Not so. The Nazis—we Nazis?—were simple looters by and large. They wanted the things that indicated imperial power, and their taste was uniformly bad. *Kitschmenschen* almost to a man."

"Although Hitler was a painter," I said. "That always makes me feel terrific about my profession."

"A very bad painter," he said, "and an ignoramus. He went to his grave, I believe, under the impression that Michelangelo Merisi—Caravaggio—and Michelangelo Buonarroti were the same person."

Okay, fun talking about art, and in fact it did make me feel better a little, mainly because it reminded me of the safe haven I had with Lotte when things went sour with us—we could always talk about art. Maybe *that's* its true purpose. But I figured I'd take advantage of the casual discussion to mine some information. I said, "So—these people we're going to see. Since you're being so mysterious, I'm going to presume they're your gangster partners. Or sponsors. Cronies?"

"Yes. They are what you might call representatives of the consortium that set up this project."

"And they're like the Nazis? Murderers and art lovers in the same package?"

He gave me a stern look for a moment and then grinned. "Wilmot, you persist in being curious. I beg you, please, please do not be curious this afternoon! All right, I understand that you wish to know something about our friends. Very well. In general, only."

He poured a glass of wine and drank some of it. "We look at the world today and we see interesting things. We say we are living in a global village, which is true enough, but what is not so often observed is that it is a village of feudal times. Legitimacy—the empire, let us say—has collapsed. Religious fanaticism is widespread, of course. Art is simply loot, with no transcendent purposes or value. On the one hand, in the so-called democracies, we see a political class composed of vapid hypocrites, beauty queens, and thugs, placed in office by propaganda and money. In the other former empire, we observe the expropriation of state property by simple gangsters. The rest of the world is ruled as it always has been, by tribal chieftains. So we observe vast masses of new wealth being seized by people who are largely amoral brutes—on a larger scale, just what happened in the original dark ages or in Germany in the thirties. Essentially, therefore, much of the world is controlled by a kind of condottiere. But unlike the originals, these men like to dwell in the shadows. I am speaking, you understand, not about the figureheads, the leaders we see on the television, but the henchmen—the corrupt company officers, the fixers, Central American and African looters. And this class blends into actual gangsters, the more respectable drug lords and arms dealers, the Asian triads, the yakuzas, and so forth. And because they dwell in the shadows they desire symbols of their status, so they can look every day and know they are somebody, and this is why art is stolen from museums and collections."

"Yeah, but that has nothing to do with forgery. Why are these guys getting involved in this particular operation?"

"Ordinarily they would not; art forgery, as I'm sure you know, has historically been a petty affair. But in recent years all this has changed. The market value of paintings by the noble dead has increased by orders of magnitude. Hundred-million-dollar auctions are not unknown. And this kind of money can attract the sort of people we are talking about. Now, since I have been selling such people paintings for a while, when they think art they naturally come to Krebs. They say, Krebs, can this be done? And I say no, at first, the technical foolery we can do, of course, but really, forging a major work by an old master, who could possibly do this?"

Then he smiled broadly and reached over and patted my hand. He said, "And then I found you."

"You assumed I could do this from looking at magazine covers and ads?"

"Of course not. That is, I was interested in you, but it was not until Mark sent me those paintings, the one of the movie star as Maria of Austria and the incomplete *Los Borrachos*, that I understood what you were capable of. When Mark told me you were hallucinating that you were Velázquez under the influence of some drug, it sounded insane, a fantasy, and yet there were the paintings. So I made my contacts and, as you Americans put it, I pitched the deal, and got the clearance and backing I needed."

"So that's why he paid me ten grand for half a copy of a painting."

"Ten only? He charged me thirty-five for it." Krebs laughed and added, "And well worth it at any price. And of course it is not a copy in any real sense. You recreated it *as* Velázquez, although I don't pretend to understand how this can be."

"Join the club."

"Yes, but why and wherefore hardly matters at this point." He clapped his hands briskly, ending that line of conversation. "So—I have described our masters to you. Shortly you will meet them for yourself." He finished his wine, dabbed his mouth, tossed the napkin on his plate. "We should begin to prepare now. Bathe, shave, wear your best clothes. Do you need anything? Shoes, shirts, whatever?"

"No, I'm fine. So what is this, like a job interview?"

"Not exactly. They wish to personally certify the existence of Charles Wilmot. They wish to see the body."

An hour later Franco drove me and Krebs to a hotel near Barajas Airport, all three of us dressed as for an important funeral, a head of state maybe, and we ascended to the top floor and past a small platoon of gentlemen in dark suits who made sure we weren't carrying anything lethal, polite but thorough, and then we went into the suite. Three guys were sitting there, an Asian, someone who looked French or Italian, and a bald guy with the ice eyes and high cheekbones of a Slav. I wasn't introduced and no one used names. The French guy did almost all the talking, and the conversation was in English. I was sitting in a side chair, a little behind the action, which was being conducted around a teak table in the center of the room. I tried not to listen, but I gathered they were talking about particular artworks loose on the secret market. After about twenty minutes of this, Krebs motioned me to come to the table.

All three of the men looked at me, but as you'd expect, given what they did for a living, their faces were perfectly unreadable: I might have been the view out the window of an airplane. The maybe-French guy said, "So you are the artist. We have heard great things about you."

I said, "Thank you."

He said, "Let's see what you can do, then. Draw me."

"Excuse me?" I said.

"I want you to draw a portrait of me. Here, use this!"

He slid across the table a single sheet of 150-pound drawing paper, 10 x 14. He assumed, correctly, that I had a drawing implement on me.

I had a pencil, but I figured this guy would be impressed by bravura, and so I used my fountain pen. Interesting face anyway, maybe in his early fifties, that French kind of nose, a long downward-sloping bridge with a little blob on the end, wide mouth with full lips, small dark eyes with generous pouches, oval chin, thick neck, hair dark, coarse like horsehair, a little gray at the sides, the face of a corrupt cardinal in the reign of the Sun King.

So—pen held vertically out at arm's length, a cliché, but you really use it to transfer the proportions from life to the paper: the general shape of the face, the triangle formed by the eyes, and the mouth has to be perfect or you won't get a likeness; start with those three dots and then four more to mark the top of the head, the sides, the chin, then the tip of the nose, another dot, and then the edges of the eyes and the mouth. You grow the drawing on the page, the eyes, the mouth, then the shadows formed by the mass of the nose and the lips. I worked for about half an hour, using a wetted finger to smear in the gray tones, and when I reached the point where any further potching around would've wrecked it, I slid the paper across the table.

He looked, he showed it to his partners, there was the usual release of tension you get when a likeness works. Magic, a little scary. It looked like him, cool and brutal; I hadn't made it pretty and I could see he liked it and was irritated by it at the same time. Yes, that's me, but who are you, you little pisser, to see *me*?

He slid the sheet into a leather portfolio on the table without the pretense of asking for it, nor did I object. And that was the meeting. A few more minutes, mainly pleasantries of a sort, and we were out of there. Back in the car, I asked Krebs why he'd done that, made me draw.

"Because, as I have told you earlier, they wanted to see you. And they wished to be certain you were really this marvelous artist. If you were really Charles Wilmot."

"They wouldn't take your word for it?"

"No. These are men who survive by being sure. Suppose I had brought along an imposter?"

"Why would you've done that, for God's sake?"

"Oh, perhaps to preserve the real Wilmot for my own purposes," he said casually, "and therefore to identify a valueless person as the artist. A dummy. Now, however, in case they decide to get rid of you, they know who you are."

S ome days followed on this event—three, ten? I can't recall how many; people who don't have schedules have that problem. Where did the week go? The way we lived cut us off from the rhythms of daily life, plus in my particular case my time sense has been ripped out of my brain, trampled on the ground, and stuck back in my skull upside down and crossways. I had no cell phone anymore, so I was as isolated as a man living in the seventeenth century. I could theoretically have made a call from the hotel phone, but I had been told not to in the strongest terms, and of course they'd know if I did.

The larger conspiracy continued. According to Krebs, Mark had duly "discovered" the hidden Velázquez and quietly summoned experts from Yale, from Berkeley; learned heads were put together, and tests were made. As we'd expected, the forensic tests checked out, the thing was deemed of seventeenth-century origin. The provenance, of course, was flawless. The Palacio Liria cried foul, but what could they do? The painting was bought in good faith as a Bassano, the museum knew it was a fake Bassano, and the fact that there was a real Velázquez hiding under it meant that they'd been hoist by their own petard, the swindler swindled. And the learned heads had looked at the art itself, the brushwork and so on, and concluded that yes, it must be so, this was Velázquez indeed, hooray.

There were objectors, of course, there always are, but mainly because they couldn't swallow the subject: the dour Don Diego could not have painted so naughty a picture. Such people, we understood, would be looking for any hint of scandal, any hint of forgery, and so now was the most vulnerable hour, both for the *Venus* and for me. Krebs seemed to want to preserve my life for reasons of his own, and I was more than willing to play along with that, although I was kind of curious why.

One morning Franco and I set out for the Prado, nice day, spring in Madrid, not too hot, flowers blooming in the boulevard planters, pleasant scents abroad in the air from the botanical garden nearby. Stood for a couple of minutes in contemplation by the big blackened bronze statue of my guy that sits in front of the museum, wanted him to get down off his chair, fling his arm over my shoulder, and give me some fatherly advice, and for a second my head got all wobbly, smeared vision, and the bulk of the museum became vague, and I was looking through the park to the palace of Buen Retiro as it'd been in the seventeenth century, just for a second there, and—something I never did before—I kind of put my foot on the brake and came back to now. A new skill? Useful.

I avoided Velázquez's paintings that day and spent my time on the top floor with the Goyas. Okay, here's a guy came up the hard way, hustling commissions from crappy little convents and provincial churches, spent years doing cartoons for a tapestry workshop, comes to Madrid, gets named painter to the king, studies Velázquez, figures, oh, this is perfection, the perfect realization of a baroque world still intact—honor, glory, nobility, all that—and so he says, screw it, he's going to paint the shattered world we see in dreams and also the world in his time, the bleeding subject of the nightmares brought forth by the dreams of reason. Here's his portrait of the royal family, the polar opposite of *Las Meninas*, silly marionettes in a glass case, no air, their feet barely touch the ground. And his *majas*, they're dolls, no one ever painted a nude so badly: the arms are wrong, the tits are insane, the head's skewed on the neck, and yet this doll made up of spare parts has an incredible erotic authority. The pubic hair helps, the first real crotch in the history of European art. A mystery, but it works.

Franco, discreetly accompanying me, stared long at this one; it's his favorite, obviously, and why not?

What was I thinking here? Death and madness, my Goyesque period, utter loneliness; about Lotte, she'd save me if she could, if I let her, the realest thing I know, her and the kids; and also about my dad—always when I think about Goya—about what he could've been, how he saw the war, why he didn't harness that rage and bitterness into art, an exact contemporary of Francis Bacon, that's who he should've been. Instead he decided to be almost as famous as Norman Rockwell.

And there I was in front of Goya's *Cronus Eating One of His Sons*, the mad glare, bulging eyeballs, as he bites his victim's head off, nothing else like it in art, the putrid yellow flesh of the titan in a light cast from hell, and then a moment of disembodiment and I'm gone, out of the Prado and back to my father's studio, age ten or so. I'm not supposed to be back in the racks where he keeps all his old stuff, but I'm at the curious age; I want to know who is this titan controlling my world. Smell of paper and canvas and glue, top note of his cigars and turps from the studio on the other side of the closed door.

On tiptoe I reach and pull down a set of sketchbooks tied with twine. They're exciting, secret, they have a history, beat up, the covers scored and dirty, one's been in the water, rippled and stained. I open the twine and there's his war, Okinawa, planes, ships, tanks, all the beautiful death machines, faces of young marines caught in unmanly terror, landscapes with shell craters, dressing stations lit by battle lanterns, the masked surgeons looking like figures from Bosch as they probe the ruined youths. And page after page of the dead, American and Japanese, lovingly rendered in watercolor, all the wonderful ways that high explosive, fast-flying metal, and flame can turn mankind into garbage: eviscerated bodies; exposed coils of gut, impossibly long, stretched out on the earth; smashed faces, eyeballs hanging from bloody stalks; the peculiar arty black forms, hideously "modern," created when human beings incinerate, things I'd never imagined. No one ever sees this stuff, it's like feces, it can't be shown in public; you have to be there.

I loved it, of course, nasty little boy that I was, and I swiped the sketchbooks and took them back to my room, my little "studio" with my kid-sized easel and my first-class paints, and I started to copy. Being Goya to Velázquez, I wanted to learn how to do that, stroke, lick, smear, and there was a skinned traumatic amputation, a jawless face, solid, brilliant, puke making. I went through sheet after sheet of expensive Arches paper—never any lack of art supplies, he used to buy it all by the ton—and after a while, it took weeks, I had it down, I could do the glisten of naked bone against riven flesh, and one evening he found me at it, with the sketchbooks strewn around my room and the painting there on the block, and he bit my head off.

It wasn't just the usual keep your hands off my things; he was enraged, insane, way more than he would've been if I'd tried to copy one of his *Post* covers or a corporate portrait; no, he'd buried this and I'd dug it up, and not only that, I'd *seen* it. And I wanted it, not the slick shit, I'd instinctively wanted the real thing, the entombed Goya he was, and not only *that*, I could *do* it too, at eight years old.

He just beat the shit out of me, practically the only time he ever did. I remember the beating and I stuck it away in the slot of don't touch Daddy's stuff, but not the rest; the underpainting was wiped away, leaving only the slick and meaningless surface.

I have a photo from around that time, Charlie must've snapped it: I'm on the floor of our sunroom with my sketchbook, drawing, and he's in a wicker easy chair with a drink in his hand, and he's looking at me, and he's got the strangest expression on his face, not paternal pride at all, but doubt and fear, and I just figured that out, there in the Prado. I always thought, Hey, he was a son of a bitch in a lot of ways, and a shit to my mother, but at least he encouraged me as an artist, he was proud of my talent, but now I saw that wasn't true, the opposite was true, all those drawing lessons, painting lessons—now I can *really* recall them, because I was ten-year-old me just a few minutes ago, and I know what he did, the subtle warping, the criticism. He wanted me to be just like him, a locked box, a successful mediocrity. And I thought again of that gorgeous loft on Hudson Street and the painting in it, and I felt like I'd been socked in the belly; I literally could not breathe for a long minute.

"Are you okay?"

Franco was looking into my face and he was all blurred. I'm going blind now, hysterical blindness, I was thinking, maybe a mercy, and I said, "Yeah, I'm fine. Why?" and he said, "You're crying." And I laughed (hysterically) and said, "I'm not crying, it's the pollen. I have hay fever"—a lie, just like my life. And what the fuck am I supposed to do with it now, this revelation, this understanding? Someone once said understanding was the booby prize, and oh, it's true.

At that point I couldn't stand to look at any more pictures, and we exited out to the Paseo, the wide boulevard that runs in front of the museum, and waited in a crowd of tourists at the crosswalk for the light to change—they wait in Madrid, unlike Rome, where no one waits for traffic. I was right by the curb, under a putrid cloud of self-pity, when something slammed me hard in the back and threw me right into the path of a city bus.

I was down on my knees and the bus was almost on top of me—I saw a band of red paint and above it the reflecting windshield of the monster—and then I was heaved into the air with a force that nearly yanked my arm from its socket, and the edge of the bus's bumper smacked into my heel, ripping my sneaker from my foot as the air brakes screeched.

I found myself lying face-up on top of Franco, who also lay face-up on the sidewalk, the pair of us like a couple of lounge chairs stacked poolside. He'd pulled me so hard he'd fallen down on his back. He scooted out from under me and stood scanning the crowd, but whoever had done it had vanished. He helped me to my feet, or foot, because the left one was out of action. According to Franco, the guy had snaked in through the crowd and hit me from the right. Neither of us thought it'd been an accident or a maniac.

We hobbled back to the hotel, which fortunately was only about a hundred yards distant. I thanked him for saving my life, and he shrugged and said, "No problem."

When we got back to the suite he tended me like a mommy, fetching ice for my wounded heel, ordering new sneakers from the concierge, pouring me a scotch. Yeah, he was just doing his job, but it was nice anyway, a sere form of human contact, but better than the howling waste of isolation into which I had fallen. Somebody just tried to kill me, but I was more terrified of life than of imminent death; it left me strangely, unnaturally calm. I have a feeling that's what my dad was like on Okinawa, or he wouldn't have been able to see what he saw and make it into art.

Krebs had been out somewhere with Kellermann, but when he came back and got the story of the attempted murder he immediately turned our lazy and louche little ménage into the Afrika Korps: orders snapped out, scurrying of the foot soldiers. Within an hour of his return, we were en route to the airport.

"Where are we going?" I asked him when we were in the car. I'd asked before but no one had bothered to answer me.

"We'll fly to Munich," he said. "I've arranged a jet."

"What's in Munich?"

"Many cultural wonders, but we're not going to stay in Munich. It's the nearest major airport to my home."

"You're taking me home?"

"Yes. I believe it's the only place I can guarantee your safety until this thing is finished and the picture has been sold and my associates are paid off."

"Your associates just tried to kill me," I said. I guess I was a little irritated that he hadn't made more of a fuss, oh, my dear Chaz, can you forgive me, I'm sorry, are you all right? And like that, but nothing: he listened to Franco's report of the incident and barely looked at me while we were getting ready to leave.

He patted my leg and said, "Cheer up, Wilmot. Imagine that you are Caravaggio, fleeing a charge of murder, or Michelangelo defying the Pope, or Veronese under the thumb of the Inquisition."

"I never wanted to be any of those guys."

"No, you wanted to be Velázquez, with an honorable sinecure in the royal household, a liveried coat, and a bag of golden reales every quarter."

"Yeah, and I thought that's what I was getting."

"So you shall, but you know even Velázquez had to go to dangerous Italy twice in his life, and not only to look at pictures. And didn't he plunge into a risky affair with that woman, as you yourself have recounted, and didn't he paint those wonderful nudes?"

I stared at him. "That was a fantasy. That was the drug screwing with my head."

And now he turned and looked at me, and it was uncanny, like he'd turned into a different person or like I was seeing him properly for the first time. The slightly manic air he usually had was gone, and he looked tired, and older, and somehow more caring. I have no idea how he did it. He looked at me this way for what seemed like a long time. Then he said, "Was it really? You spend a good deal of time in a fantasy world, don't you? Perhaps this idea that you forged a Velázquez accepted by the whole world as genuine was also a fantasy. Perhaps it really is genuine after all. How could you tell?"

"What do you mean, how could I tell? I remember every fucking brushstroke on that thing."

"Yes, and your memory is full of things that did not in fact happen to you, as you yourself confess. So this is not an impressive claim."

"But the painting is real. I saw it. I saw Salinas test it. I saw you phony it up with that Bassano fake."

"Did you? Tell me, do you actually know who I am?"

"Yes, of course I know who you are. You're Werner Krebs, art dealer and criminal mastermind, and for some reason you're trying to fuck with my brain."

"My friend, your brain is, as you put it, fucked up beyond my poor power to add or reduce. And why would I do that, if I am such a criminal? Perhaps I am actually trying to bring a brilliant but psychotic artist back to reality. Perhaps I am a psychiatrist hired by your family to take you to my clinic in rural Bavaria."

"Oh, right. But I don't have the kind of family that shells out for Bavarian clinics, remember? Lotte can barely pay her rent, I have a sick kid, and my son from my first marriage wouldn't pay a nickel to save my life."

"Yes, but perhaps that is the case only in your paranoid ideation. Suppose, however, that in truth you are a well-known and famous artist, whose work routinely sells in the six figures, and that all these memories of failure and frustration are part of the psychosis."

And now that whole New York thing, which I had been repressing all this time, came snarling out of its box and started tearing big chunks out of my sense of who I was. The result was paralyzing terror. What did I know? Montaigne's question, and I couldn't answer it. I shook. I sweated. I shut down: the traffic sounds and Krebs's voice seemed to come through thick insulation.

"Wilmot," he said, in that same calm professional voice, "believe me when I say that although you are a brilliant painter, you have no way of distinguishing what is real from what is the product of your afflicted brain and of the drug you were given."

"We went to see those gangsters," I said dully. "I was pushed in front of a bus. I remember that."

"Yes, this is how you interpret your appearance before, let us say, a mental health commitment board—international gangsters. And you *jumped* in front of the bus, Wilmot. This is why Franco must follow you everywhere. You could have been badly injured. Well, in any case, here we are at the airport."

"I'm not talking to you anymore," I said.

He smiled. "I'm sorry to hear that," he said, "but we shall see what happens. It is early days yet in our relationship."

They led me out of the car and onto a plane; I did as I was told, without will, moving slowly like one of those sad brain-damaged vets you see in the documentaries, and we flew out of Spain on an elegant little thing, a six-passenger job carrying me, Krebs, Franco, and Kellermann. Kellermann slept in the rear the whole way, snoring; Franco was next to me and Krebs was up front talking on his cell phone in German.

"Franco," I said when we were up in cloudland, "tell me, did you get a look at the guy who pushed me in front of the bus?"

"What guy?" he answered. "You jumped."

Stupid to ask, really, Franco a faithful servant of the king. Although Krebs had said he wasn't, that he worked for the bad guys. Who knew? Was that the first mirror in the hall of mirrors? Were there bad guys at all?

I reclined my seat and tried not to think about anything. It's harder than it sounds, although apparently the holy men do it all the time. It must be very restful, not to think.

We landed, we got in a big Mercedes, just me and Krebs and Franco—Kellermann had been assigned some errand—and we drove north on the A9 autobahn. It's nice to drive in a powerful car on the German autobahn: there are no speed limits and the peasants are wise enough to keep out of the left lane. I got a kick out of the big blue signs that read *Ausfahrt Dachau*; gotta love the Germans—they're sorry, but not *that* sorry, not sorry enough to change the name of a town that's a curse in every other civilized country. I mentioned this to Krebs, who gave me the kind of look you give to kids who mention poo-poo at the dinner table, and then he started talking about where we were going, a part of Bavaria known as the Fränkische Alb, a real beauty spot apparently, quite isolated even in crowded Germany. His father had bought the house just after the war, along with a substantial area of surrounding land. Much of the neighborhood was a nature preserve, but he had fishing and hunting rights on his own land. Did I like to fish? To hunt?

I said I did, and was this part of my therapy?

"Of course," he said genially. "Everything is part of therapy. But I think the best thing will be if you have your family around you. I have been in contact with your ex-wife and she has agreed to visit. I am truly looking forward to meeting your children."

At which point I started to cry.

I sat in that car, slumped in a corner with my temple against the cool glass, watching the sweat and tears flow down the window, thinking, Oh, yeah, I bet he was looking forward to meeting my kids, then he'd have total control over me, the master manipulator. Who did I think he was—right, the question Jesus asked his disciples, but in my case no answer came. Rolling through the possibilities in my mind, logic a comfort, a sign that the brain's still functioning. No, actually, maniacs are flawlessly logical, it's their premises that are false. Dredging up memories, my Cartesian theater lit up and roaring, all the crap jobs I'd done, the details of the paintings, my loft, the meals I'd eaten, cubic yards of Chinese food and pizza, the children in the loft, the move to Brooklyn, the furniture of our house, my life with Lotte, the agony of our divorce . . . Yeah, it was there in my head, solid, reliable, visuals, audio, even smells, twenty years of life.

And then I recalled my life as Velázquez and it was the same: grinding pigments; laying on the paint; my wife, Juana; talking with my teacher and father-in-law, Pacheco; walking with the king in the gardens of Buen Retiro, painting him, his ugly, gentle face, all just as real. Besides that, I have the same vivid memories of a whole year that never happened to me, and no memories at all of three months that did, apparently. And I knew it couldn't be real, so what good was memory? It was no good at all, and without that existential confidence, I was *nothing*, I was in there with the Man Who Mistook His Wife for a Hat, deep brain malfunction, like those people who think their wives are robots sent from the CIA.

Other explanations? A gigantic conspiracy? Terrific, that's not just schizophrenia, that's *paranoid* schizophrenia. Paranoia's related to memory, that's clear, Alzheimer's patients attacking their kids, becoming suspicious, who are all these strangers pretending to love me? Happening to me too, inevitable. And Shelly Zubkoff—did *that* really happen at all, or was that a fantasy too, an excuse to retreat from reality, like the CIA rays that make necessary the wearing of tinfoil helmets?

Why would Krebs do such a thing? If he's Krebs the criminal, why am I still with him? He's got the painting. A handshake and good-bye for Wilmot would be more to the point, or a knock on the head—thinking of Eric Hebborn, greatest faker of the last century, besides me, had his head cracked open in Rome, murder never solved. How would someone like Krebs handle forgers who've outlived their usefulness? He's planning to kill me in his secret mountain laboratory? No, Franco saved me, and Franco works for Krebs. Unless Franco *pushed* me and then pretended to save me, so that I'd be scared, so that I'd stick with Krebs, a docile tool, and get my family into his clutches. Again, if true, why? And then, why rig up this dark legion of background heavies, that interview, maybe it was a setup entirely, a show with actors, so that I'd see Krebs as my protector instead of my persecutor—but why go through all that trouble, like I wouldn't do what he wants out of simple fear? I *would*, I admit it, I'm a total chicken.

But all this is just what a paranoid maniac *would* think, the desperate attempt of a mind unhinged to seek some rational explanation that doesn't involve the One Big Fact: that everything I remember about the last few decades of my life is false. That I'm Someone Else. So my thoughts go around and around, Krebs sitting next to me; I'm a silk-wrapped fly in his web. I can't look at him.

Meanwhile, underneath all these thoughts, like a suppurating ulcer you can't stand to look at, was what happened in New York, those paintings. That was real all right, and an insinuating voice in my head was saying, Oh, Chaz, come back, come back to your real and only life.

Right, shit, it's easy to sit here and recount or try to recount what went through my head on that fucking car ride, but it's a lot harder to recapture the feelings, the hamster in a wire wheel spinning, the car on black ice out of control. What I did eventually was breathe slow and deep and contemplate the glories of nature. Not all that glorious on the autobahn, mainly a blur, but we turned off onto a secondary road south of Ingolstadt and drove on west into the sun. The day had begun cloudy but cleared up later in the afternoon, a spring day in the ancient heart of Europe, forests of dark spruce and beech just coming into leaf, that ravishing pale green hard to get with paint, too easy to make it acid, chloriney, tube colors no good, you have to use a very pale gray undercoat and work it in with greens you make out of ultramarine and chrome yellow, thin washes over the off-white, marvelous against the almost blacky green of the spruces, and there were fields of intense violent yellow rapeseed, and other fields just greening up with grain, and the shadows of the clouds flying over them a different light show every minute.

Every so often we slid through a town, old squares lined by half-timbered houses with overhanging roofs, and the churches of the local stone with their clocked steeples mosaicked with stones of different colors, some wonderful anonymous artists of the baroque, and it made me feel good to see that. Later the towns came more infrequently and the land rose a thousand feet or so; the forest closed in on the road, and we turned in to the forest itself, dark with shafts of light shooting down through the trees, reddening as the sun got lower, the kind of effect that was transcendent in the baroque and kitsch in the late nineteenth century, acres of Teutonic landscapes stuffing third-rate museums. Then down an *allée* of beeches entwined overhead, and at last the house.

I suppose I had imagined a Dracula castle, black sweating stone with Gothic turrets and gargoyles, but this was just a large, three-story Bavarian house, with the usual sharply peaked, hipped roof and half-timbering. I wanted it to exude an air of menace, but it just sat there, clumsy and plain as pumpernickel. It might have originally been the manor house of a substantial estate. There were some outbuildings in a more modern style clustered around it; one was a garage. Franco stopped the car in front of it and we all got out.

Just like on *Masterpiece Theater*, I was glad to see, the staff gathered at the front door to greet the returning master. Two middle-aged people, Herr and Frau Bieneke, she the housekeeper, he the majordomo, butler, whatever you call it, plain and competent looking; a couple of young housemaids, Liesl and Gerda, goggling at me shyly; the cook, Frau Bonner, in apron, red and damp faced; and two men, Revich and Macek, Slavic in appearance, whose duties were not defined but who were obviously the muscle. Krebs made the intros with seigneurial graciousness; the staff nodded, smiled; I nodded, smiled. Everyone had very good teeth. We went inside, and Krebs left me in the hands of Herr Bieneke to show me my rooms and the layout.

We went through the entrance foyer into what seemed to be the main hall, and here my imagination was at last satisfied: flagged floors with scattered Oriental rugs, heavy black furnishings with studded red leather upholstery, a stone fireplace, deer antlers up and down the walls with a couple of boars' heads mounted among them, a full suit of armor standing in one corner, and over the fireplace a vast trophy, a shield with a coat of arms on it and a dozen or so swords and pole-arms. A bearskin with snarling head lay in front of the fireplace to complete the Teutonic splendorama.

I got the whole tour. Top floor servants' quarters, Bieneke and the frau live in a farmhouse on the property. The master has his suite, office, bedroom, study, on the ground floor; I was shown the door, but not the inside. At the back of the house, a wonder, a huge artist's studio; the man tells me that Herr Krebs's father added it to the house. A wall of windows connecting to a skylight two floors above, a professional easel, the usual worktables, cabinets. Signs of long-ago painting, faded spatters, but no sniff of turps, no one has used this room in a long time. I ask. The old man painted a little, and Herr Krebs when young, but not recently. Interesting.

Below the main floor are the kitchen, storerooms, the usual, and a door in the back leading to the basement. We descend the stairs. All old stonework, original, must be seventeenth century at least, arches and niches suitable for hogsheads of wine and beer, now filled with wine racks and central heating equipment. In a corner I see a small ironbound door, low, set into the wall, looks original to the house.

What's down there? Nothing, sir, an old well, dangerous, kept locked at all times. Aha, there's the secret, I thought, the Bluebeard room, where the dead wives are kept, the Nazi memorabilia, the crates of gold coins.

Then up a staircase with heavy carved banisters to the second floor and down a hall to a room, mine. Nice room, simply furnished: a wooden bed with posts, checked bedspread, goosefeather pillows, a desk, chair, the usual lamps, a door to a bathroom, fortunately the latest, not at all what you'd expect, obviously a great deal of expensive renovations in the recent past.

Dinner was me and Krebs, served by the two girls, decent heavy food, soup, chops, spaetzle, a rich cake. Conversation sputtered a little; I was almost mute, because if you're no one, you don't have much to say. So he gave me a history of the house, it dated from 1694, the country seat of a servant of the Bavarian monarchy. Extensively modified, of course. He went on about the delights of the country-side, the seasons. He hunts boar and will take me if I like, if I am still here in the fall. Or there is a river, we can catch trout. I didn't object to his assumption that I would be an indefinite guest. No more talk about psychiatry. We're pals now. The wine helped. I drank most of a bottle of Rhône.

After dinner, he invited me to his end of the house for a cigar, a cognac. More comfortable there, he said, and yes it was, a large room that looked like a museum of modern design. The walls were oyster; the furniture was all leather, brushed steel, glass, marble, and rare woods, beautiful designs, the best studio stuff, all handmade and ferociously expensive: a desk, a comfortable-looking sling chair, an elegant couch, of the type a wealthy psychiatric patient might be expected to lie in and tell Herr Dr. Krebs about early trauma. The ceiling was high and one wall was entirely glass, looking out into the night, a moonlit meadow, black woodlands beyond. There was a wall of books, mostly gigantic treatises on various artists, and several shelves of medical tomes in many different European languages, plus a tropical marine fish tank built into the wall and swimming with clownfish and a variety of other colorful creatures. An elaborate sound system in dull gray steel looked custom-made and was softly playing a Mozart violin concerto. Above the sound system, rank on rank, were framed awards and diplomas. Their language was Latin but I could make out on each the name of Werner Krebs.

Three paintings hung on the remaining pale wall: a Cézanne view of Mt. St. Victoire, a Matisse odalisque in a pink room, and in the center, a large gilt-framed altarpiece, a Virgin with child and donors by some Flemish master.

Krebs handed me a balloon glass charged with cognac and asked me if I could identify the altarpiece.

I sipped cognac and said, "It looks like a van der Goes."

"Yes. An early work, but already he shows the sympathy for the ordinary man for which he was famous. Obviously the Virgin and the angel are at the center, but observe the servants staring longingly in at the window, their care-worn faces. A very van der Goes touch. He was a member of the Brethren of the Common Life, you know, almost a monk. He went mad from the conflict between his growing fame as a painter and the demands he made on himself to be humble. A sad case."

"Is it real?"

"Does it matter? The technique is there, the iconography is correct, the religious fervor shines from every corner of the panel. You feel it, I feel it. If a spectrograph showed titanium white in it, would those qualities, those feelings vanish?"

"A nice point, but I also think you wouldn't hang a fake in your study. Where did you get it? Nazi swag?"

"As a matter of fact, yes," he said agreeably. "As are the others. I couldn't bear to part with them. A vice of all art dealers, I'm afraid."

"So your old dad really did get away with the Schloss paintings."

He gave me a strange look, surprise, a brief irritation, then amusement. "Alas, no, he did not."

"What about those two vans out of Munich?"

He smiled now. "Excellent, you have been studying my history. Very commendable. As it happens, however, we were only able to move one of the vans into Switzerland; the other was caught in the Dresden bombing, and this contained the Schloss material. A great pity that so much beauty should be permanently lost to the world. But would you like to see something of more particular interest?"

Now I was drunk; the wine and the cognac had loosened me up. The craziness was still boiling underneath, but the supposed real me had recovered a little nerve. I said, "Does that mean pornography, Doctor?"

"Of a type," he said, and walked to the far end of the room. He opened a door and motioned me through. It was his bedroom, a lot larger than mine and furnished like a television starship. There were several small paintings on the walls but I had eyes only for one.

"Where the hell did you get *that*?" I said.

"It turned up in London some years ago, an auction at Christie's. Remarkable, isn't it?"

Yeah, it was. A small oil, maybe twenty-five by thirty inches; in the left foreground a couple of teenage marines were standing, one lighting a cigarette, the other looking out at us with the usual thousand-yard stare. In the center of the picture lay a Japanese soldier writhing in flames, ignored, his crisped hand reaching up to uncaring heaven, and behind him was a marine with a flamethrower, the obvious cause of this event, and in the same plane a group of other marines hanging around, smoking, talking to each other, taking a break. Above, a dirty early-evening sky; behind, a scorched and pocked hillside and the mouth of a cave smoking like the gates to hell. The thing had been painted with the authority and bravura brushwork of *The Surrender of Breda* by Velázquez. It seemed to me to be a historical painting of similar quality, and you could tell that the artist was thinking of that earlier painting when he did it: this is what war's like now, folks: gormless, brutalized farm boys having a human barbeque, and note the absence of courtly gentlemen bowing to one another on the field of honor. Signed with my dad's familiar monogram and the date, 1945.

Krebs studied my face as I looked at the painting and asked, "You find it depressing?"

"Not the subject matter so much as the waste. How he could do this and then have the life he had."

"You might ask yourself the very same question."

"I might and I do. Is this part of my therapy, Doctor?"

"If you want it to be."

"What I want is for you to tell me why you're doing this, the fake psychiatrist routine."

"Is it a fake? You seem to be particularly interested in fakes, Wilmot. I wonder why. Come with me, I want to show you something else."

We left the bedroom and went back to the study. Krebs reached up to a bookshelf and took down a large-format art book. He motioned me to sit down on one of his delicious leather chairs and laid it on my lap. It had a realistic painting of a beautiful red-haired woman on the cover. She was reclining in a plush purple chair and holding to her crotch a wooden hand mirror, in which was reflected a penis. In large block letters a title: WILMOT. Soft covers, but expensively printed. My eyes blurred; I blinked. Pressure began in my temples and the dense German dinner began to stir in my belly.

"What the hell is this?" I asked.

"It's a catalog raisonée of your show at the Whitney, a few years ago," said Krebs.

I ignored the text and paged through the plates. I recognized some of the work from my first and only gallery show, and the others were just like the paintings in the Enso Gallery and the thing on the easel in the Hudson Street loft. I didn't know what to say, couldn't really have said anything, my mouth so dry, my speech centers shut down for the night.

"Take it," said Krebs. "Study it. Maybe it will bring some memory—"

I shot to my feet, flinging the book away from me like some loathsome insect that had crawled unseen onto my lap, and dashed out of the room without another word. I walked through the house, not knowing where I was going, my brain frozen.

I ended up in the studio. All dark, of course; I scrabbled at the walls until I found a light switch. Why here? Good place for a suicide, lots of toxic solvents in a studio. There was a balcony too, throw a rope around the rail up there, stand on a stool, jump off.

An immense canvas set up on the easel. Smell of turpentine became stronger, someone's been painting pictures. Not me, though.

Sound of steps coming closer, and the light's changed too, not the harsh glare of fluorescents, but gray daylight filtering through a tall window. High ceilings in a large room with its walls covered in paintings, a mirror on one wall, coffered doors.

She says, "Are you ready for me now, sir?"

I see that I am, my palette set with colors; she's wearing the dark blue velvet dress I asked for, the one with the silver trim.

"Yes, I am. If you please, stand over by the window, in the light. Chin up. Hold your hand so. Higher. Good."

The underpainting is already done, and this is the final layer. I'm using smalt with calcite on the dress, touches of lapis on the collar and in the folds. I want transparency and speed; I'm working with the paint thinned to a milky liquid, a few back-and-forth swashes of the large brush lays in her face. His Majesty has asked for a group portrait of himself with his family for his private rooms, and I have been thinking about this and working on it for many weeks. He asks me often when it will be finished, and I say, soon, Majesty, and he smiles; I am well known as a phlegmatic, it is a joke of the court.

I paint in the highlights and features of her hideous face, her lank brown hair. I will have another dwarf there and a dog as well. The cuffs, the surface glitter of the gown. That is enough. I put my palette on the table.

"May I see the painting, Don Diego?"

"If you like."

Maribárbola waddles around the easel and looks up at the canvas. After some minutes, she says, "I have never seen anything like this picture."

I say, "There *is* nothing like this picture."

"No. You have made my face as it might be seen through a misted glass. Why is that?"

"A fancy. I wish to direct the eye toward the center of the painting, and so the figures on the edges are indistinct."

"Yes, toward the infanta and the *meninas*. And for another reason too: when we see something ugly we squint our eyes so as to make it blur. Yet you have made Their Majesties the most indistinct of all, there in that dusty mirror. They are ugly as well. Perhaps you have grown tired of painting them. But you know, the true center of the picture is not at all the infanta. It is you, the painter. That's very clever. It is a clever painting. Do you think His Majesty will like it?"

"He likes all my paintings."

"Yes. It is unusual that such a stupid man as our king should allow such cleverness in a servant, and him not a freak of nature. Cleverness is suspect in Spain, don't you think? It suggests Jewish blood."

"There is no Jew in my line back to the remotest antiquity."

"Yes, so you are always saying, always, and His Majesty pretends to believe it, and therefore so must we all. You will get your knight's cross, Don Diego, never fear. You paint the truth cleverly, as we fools speak it, and as I say, our king prizes the truth, but only from such as we."

"I am not a freak of nature."

"Oh, but you are, Don Diego, you are; there is no one like you in the world. I am common as bread compared to you. I am the twin sister of the infanta compared to you. However, our masters, being the greater fools, don't comprehend it, for you have the figure of a man and not a dwarf. I assure you that if you looked like El Primo you might paint just as you do, but you would not be a chamberlain. In fact, El Primo is the cleverest man at court, or near to it, but because his head is only a yard above his feet, no one bothers about what is inside it. If I have your leave, sir, I must go now and entertain the infanta. I will somersault and play tunes upon my whistle, and hope the stupid child, whom may God bless, has not been naughty again, and if she has, that someone other than me will have the whipping. I bid you good day, sir."

She leaves. I call for my servant, who comes to clean my painting things. I return to my apartments and change my clothes. I meet this morning with contractors and decorators to plan the celebrations for the queen's name day. It is a weakness of mine to converse seriously with fools. And yet who else is there? One cannot speak to servants of anything consequential, my equals are all rivals, and those above me have nothing to say. If I had a son . . . but I do not, and my son-in-law, while a perfectly worthy fellow, has neither cultivation nor much talent with the brush. Such is my fate, to be alone in the world.

B ut I *have* a son. This was my first thought when I awoke. I have a son. Or do I? Maybe Milo is another fantasy. And Rose, and Lotte. I've been painting *Las Meninas* and talking to Maribárbola, the dwarf in the lower right. That's as real to me as any memory of my supposed family. And now . . . there's always a moment when you wake up, usually brief, when you don't quite know who you are or where you are, accentuated when you're traveling, awaking in a strange room and so on, and then whatever brain system brings you up out of unconsciousness reboots and there you are, yourself again.

But not this morning. Or night, because it was dark in the room. I had no idea who I was. There were possibilities, I had those, and I ran through the Rolodex, flipping through. I might be Chaz Wilmot, hack artist, forger of a painting now hailed as one of the great works of Velázquez, hiding out from criminals. I might be Chaz Wilmot, successful New York painter, now insane and under treatment, with a load of false memories, just as false as that conversation with a baroque dwarf. Or I might be Diego Velázquez, caught in a nightmare. Or some combination. Or someone else entirely. Or maybe this was hell itself. How would I tell?

So I just lay there, breathing, trying to control my pounding heart. No point in getting up, no point in any action at all. There are people in mental hospitals with perfectly intact brains and bodies who haven't made a volitional movement in decades. Now I could see why.

After a while my bladder informed me that it wanted to be emptied. I knew I should get up and find either a seventeenth-century chamber pot or a toilet, but that would mean moving, and that was hard to contemplate. I could see why the people in the locked wards preferred to lie in their own filth all day. You could get used to lying in filth but never to the terror involved in deciding to move in a world that was implacably hostile and alien. Your feet could break off. Why not? Or if you moved, the Eaters could get you, if such monsters featured in your particular madness. Or you could turn into someone else. Best to stay still. I pissed in the bed.

I could see something now, grayness and shapes, a light source very faint. I was in the room in Krebs's house. Maybe. I could be in China, or in Dr. Zubkoff's laboratory. It looked like my bedroom at Krebs's, but looks are deceiving, oh yes. Painters deceive you all the time, or used to.

I didn't sleep as the daylight penetrated the room. I tried not to think, but thoughts came. Time passed. People came into the room and out again, I was cleaned and put back into a fresh bed. A woman tried to spoon food into my mouth, but I kept my jaws clenched and struck out at her and screamed until some men came in and tied my hands to the bed frame. That was fine with me. I wasn't going anywhere.

A tapping on the door, or so it seemed. I lay very, very still and hoped it would go away. No, another tap and a voice. It said, "Chaz?" A familiar voice? How could I tell?

Sound of a door opening, and a click and the room was flooded with hideous light—I could see everything! I squirmed down under the covers to hide my face. A weight on the bed next to me, tugging at the quilt, a voice. It was Lotte's voice, should have been comforting, I missed her so much, or somebody missed her, although it may have been someone else. She wanted me to get up, she pleaded, the children are upset. How long have they been here? I wondered. Are they really here at all?

She exposed my face and I didn't try to hide it. Best to be completely passive. She looked a lot like Lotte my wife, but her face was blurry, not in focus, like the face of the dwarf in my painting. She touched my face. She said, "Oh, Chaz, what has happened to you?"

I'd like to know that too, I really would.

I didn't know what to say to her. I didn't want to ask her. I didn't want to know who she'd been married to.

She said, "I have been so worried. Krebs said you had had a relapse, you were incoherent, raving. I came as soon as I could."

I rummaged around for a while until I found my voice, one that sounded strange in my ears. I said, "I was painting the royal family. I am the greatest painter of the age."

"Look at me," she ordered. "You know who I am."

I said, "You look like Lotte. Is this real?" and I laughed, a horrible sound. Lunatics are always depicted as laughing; we speak of maniacal laughter, and this is why. When the ground of reality is stripped away, when meaning itself takes a walk, what's left is this monstrous hilarity.

And tears. I wept and she held me, and perhaps the reality of the familiar body, the smell of her hair, her perfume, worked on a brain level below the one that was screwed up so badly, and I calmed a little. She spoke slowly and gently as she often did to the children, about being summoned, about Krebs arranging everything, how he thought the presence of my family would help get me through this crisis.

And into my mind then, in the midst of the most extreme existential terror, came the thought that now my only course was to cleave to the wisdom of the sages and the bumper stickers and simply abandon all memory as unreliable, to discard the past and the future and simply try to exist moment to moment and see what happened. So, whoever this nice woman was, I was not going to ask her to confirm or deny anything about my past or about who Krebs was; I was just going to let her take the lead, and follow.

I said, "My memory is all scrambled."

"But you remember *me*, yes? And the children?"

"Yes. How are the kids?"

"Oh, you know, all excited, the plane ride, this place. It's quite lovely. There's a little farm attached to it. They were down there all morning, ducks and goats and so on. Did I tell you, I've found a marvelous clinic in Geneva for Milo? They think they can really do something for him."

I said that sounded great, I said I was fine, not to worry. So, I made myself move like one of those robots controlled by a little remote, press one button for out of bed, another for the shower, and so on. I got dressed, greeted the world, and life, of a sort, resumed.

It was my daughter, Rose, who made the difference. I fell upon her with an intensity that amazed both of us, hugs and kisses and foolish talk. I spent unaccustomed hours with her over the next days, I'm not busy anymore, all the time in the world. She was the only person in my life who didn't think I was crazy, she accepted me at face value, not caring for what the world thought. Could build your life on a kid, many people do, although it's unfair as hell to the kid—they're supposed to build on you. We walked through the woodlands, dabbled in streams, did little art projects. She found a shredder somewhere and made a big sheet of collage, the farm and its animals, but didn't have enough pink for the pigs.

We were much at the farm, always accompanied by Franco. It's where the Bienekes live, and there are some workers who actually do the farm work, very feudal arrangements hereabouts, the guys actually wearing lederhosen. This time of year we have young animals; Rose is entranced, it's like her Richard Scarry animal book coming to life. Fine weather, fluffy clouds, a Constable painting, felicity surrounds us, except for our son dying in his room, but here's the great part of being in the now: it doesn't matter what's *going* to happen or what *has* happened.

I believe I was as pleasant to others as I have ever been, a little shallow maybe, but no one seemed to mind. Lotte treated me very gently, like a live bomb, or no, more like she's always treated Milo, like somebody who might disappear at any moment. Milo himself was stiff and formal with me, he's at the age when insanity in a parent is particularly distressing. For my part, I avoided him as much as I could. I couldn't bear the expression on his face when he looked at me.

At the farm one morning Rose brought me a little duckling and I was able to focus my full attention on the squirming golden ball, and on my girl's delight in the duck, and on the day, which seemed to last an amazingly long time, like summer days in childhood. Rose was able to drag me uncomplaining around the farm like a large rolling toy.

We entered the sheep barn. There were young lambs. As we inspected them, I knelt and said softly to my daughter, "Could I ask you a question?"

"Yes. Is this a game?"

"Uh-huh. I'm pretending I don't know anything and you have to tell me stuff, okay?"

"What stuff?"

"Like what's my name?"

"It's Chaz. That's a shortcut for Charles."

"Very good! And where do I live?"

"In your loft."

"And where do you and Mommy and Milo live?"

"In our house. It's 134 Congress Street, Brooklyn, New York. I know our phone number too."

I hugged her tight. "I bet you do, honey. Thank you."

"Is this all of the game?"

"Yes, for now," I said.

What a wonderful day!

It got better. We had lunch at the farm with the workers, big sweaty blondes who made much of my daughter and wife in German. Rose is bilingual in French and was delighted to discover that there was another language in which people can be sweet to her, and she was able to communicate a little, with Lotte supplying phrases both amusing and useful. Such hearty laughter!

But after lunch it occurred to me that I might have hallucinated Rose's answers. I was angry with myself for even thinking of such a stupid ploy, and in this mood I slipped down to the kitchen, chatted with the girls and Frau Bonner. They were making cakes, and busy, and I had no problem easing a six-inch chef's knife out of a drawer and up my sleeve. It was old and black and the wooden handle was cracked, so they probably don't use it much and won't miss it. Still razor sharp, though. It made me feel good to have a weapon. I thought that if I ever figured out who my real enemies were I would use it on them. I tested it on my own wrists too, just scratches. That was also a possibility that came to mind.

That evening we were having dinner with his excellency the evil magician, and we were asked to dress for it. Lotte thought it was a lovely idea, to dress up for dinner. I wore my Venice suit; she fetched out a wonderful sheath dress in a Naples-yellow fabric that sparkled. She looked terrific in the formal dining room too, along with the crystal and the polished mahogany and the silver champagne bucket and Krebs smiling in his white dinner jacket like Reichsmarschal Göring, but not as fat.

A nice dinner too, or would've been if I hadn't had so much to drink. I'd forgotten that booze knocked you out of that state of just being, which is why drunks are always going on about the past and making promises about the future, and why AA is always preaching one day at a time. Anyway, we'd just finished the boar with red cabbage, and Krebs and Lotte were deep in a conversation about what was showing in New York, and Lotte was telling him about Rudolf Stingel, who apparently uses chipped Styrofoam panels and linoleum and industrial carpeting distressed in various ways and hung on the wall to make people forget beauty and really experience the fact that everything is just total shit, and who was having his one-man at the Whitney, and Lotte turned to Krebs and said in a clear voice something about my own one-man show at the Whitney.

Krebs listened affably to this while my blood chilled, and then Lotte looked me right in the eye with a hesitant half smile and said, "It was a wonderful show."

Yes, my Lotte.

Before anyone could stop me, I jumped up and ran out of the dining room and down the hall to Krebs's office, where I entered and locked the door behind me. I started searching, I'm not sure for what, some *evidence*, some physical object that I could use to defend my memories of my life as an impoverished commercial hack, and funny, isn't it, I hated it while I was living it, but in retrospect it seemed to be the most precious thing in the world; how we love what we take to be our true selves. And so much did I *not* want to be the painter of those sexy Teflon nudes that I looked for such an item. I looked a little roughly, I have to say; I think I broke some nice things in there. I used my knife on some of Krebs's possessions.

Keys were rattling in the lock as I ran out through the French windows, around the house, and in through the kitchen door. There was a wall phone there, and I grabbed it and punched in my sister's number, the number of her organization, surely there'd be someone there who would take an emergency message, get it to her in Africa, please, your brother doesn't know who he is, could you tell him? But what I heard was "The number you have reached is not a working number, please try again," which I didn't have time to do, because they were coming through the house after me, so I ran up the back stairs. I had to find Rose, because she was the only one now, because maybe I'd made up Charlie too. If I could get to Rose and ask her a few questions again I'd be all right.

She was standing in the hallway holding her pink blanket. I dropped to my knees in front of her.

"Rosie! What are you doing out of bed?"

"I was scared, Daddy. I heard people shouting." Indeed people were shouting, in German. Footsteps pounded below.

"It's okay, Rose," I said. "Look, I'm going to take you to bed again, but first I want to play that game again, okay? Just tell me where I live and where you live and I'll take you to bed and tell you a story and it'll be all right."

"I don't want to, Daddy. I'm scared."

"Come on, Rosie—where does Daddy live?" I knew it was wrong, just like I knew blowing a grand's worth of coke a week was wrong, but I'd done that too. I thought. Anyway, I had to hear it, I had to have that information that instant or die.

I can imagine what my face looked like at that moment, because I could see the terror in her eyes. She started to blubber. I grabbed her by the shoulder and shook her. "Tell me, damn it!" I yelled. Rose cried out and I heard Lotte scream behind me, as who would not on see-ing a maniac poised over a little girl brandishing a knife? And then I was jerked backward by an arm around my throat and the knife went flying and Franco and one of the Slavs held me down, screaming, and then Krebs came up and yanked down my pants and shot me up with something that switched off my brain.

I came to in a small white room, tied with soft restraints to a hos-pital bed, my mouth parched, foul tasting, and dry as old news-papers. I croaked a little and someone must've heard me, because a nurse (or someone posing as a nurse) came in and took my pulse and gave me a cup of water and a straw to sip from. She said what I sup-posed were soothing things in German, and shortly thereafter a brisk young man appeared in my field of view. He had on a white lab coat and those fashionable slit-type black eyeglasses, and he said his name was Schick and that he was the psychiatrist in charge of my case.

I said, "The world is whatever is the case."

He blinked, then smiled. "Ah, yes, Wittgenstein. Do you study him?"

"No," I said. "It's just a bit that floated up."

"Ah! Well, no matter. Do you know where you are, Mr. Wilmot?"

"A hospital?"

"Yes, it is a small hospital near Ingolstadt, and this is the psychiatric ward. Do you know why you are here?"

"I'm crazy?"

He smiled again. "Well, you have had a breakdown of some kind, delusions and amnesia, and so forth. In such cases, where there is no history and rapid onset, we look for organic causes, and I am happy to tell you that we have found none. You were given a CAT scan while you were unconscious, and your brain is perfectly normal in all respects."

"That's nice," I said.

"Yes. And could you tell me what is this implant you have? It showed up on the scan."

"I don't have an implant."

"Oh, yes. Very small, at the back of your left arm."

"I have no idea what you're talking about."

"Well, this may be part of your amnesia, yes? In any case we will have it out and then we shall see what is what. Now, tell me, do you know now who you are?"

I didn't, but I told him the story I thought he wanted to hear, successful painter goes berserk, thinks he's an unsuccessful painter, and as we talked it suddenly made a lot of sense. What a strange thing to have concocted, I thought then, fantasizing myself as a bitter failure instead of the prosperous painter I clearly was. I felt calmer than I'd been for a long time. They had me on some drug, obviously, and it was working. The implant? Well, I was sure there was some explanation, some necessary medical procedure that had slipped my mind. I hadn't been myself lately, and so I might have forgotten I'd had it put in. Really, nothing seemed worth getting excited about. When he saw how calm I was he released the restraints. Quite a pleasant talk with Dr. Schick, and then he went away.

I had lunch and a pill and dozed for a while, and a nurse came in and shot some local anesthetic into my arm and did something with an instrument and went away. I asked her if I could see what she took out of me, but I couldn't make myself understood, or maybe it wasn't allowed. In a little while I fell asleep again.

When I awakened it was dark, darker than a hospital usually is, and that hospital smell was gone. I rose from my bed and walked out of the room to find myself in a wide hallway, high ceilinged, the walls covered in tapestries, with an occasional large painting. By the dim yellow light from candles set in wall sconces I see there are people there too, guards with helmets and halberds, and men and women dressed in black, with lace collars. None of them pay me any attention. There is a room from which comes the sound of weeping and muttered prayer. I go in and pass through several rooms, all richly furnished and lit with many candles, and at last to a bedroom, and a deathbed. There I see the soon-to-be widow, and the daughter and the son-in-law, and the priests, and those who have come to pay their last respects, and on the high draped bed is the dying man. The air is heavy with the scent of cloves.

I stand at the foot of this bed and stare at the wan, exhausted face, and the man opens his eyes and sees me.

He says, "You! I know you. I've dreamed about you in my dreams of hell. Are you a demon?"

"No," I say, "just a painter like you. And it wasn't hell you dreamed of, it was the future."

"Am I dreaming still, then?"

"Perhaps. Perhaps I am dreaming you. No one else here can see me and this is real, at least to you."

He closes his eyes and shakes his head. "Then go away. I am sick."

"You are dying, Don Diego. This is your last day on earth."

"Then why are you tormenting me? Leave me in peace!"

"I had no choice in the matter," I say. "I took a drug that comes from the Indies and the drug brought me to you. I can't explain it, even though in the future we are more clever about these things than they were in your time. In any case, here I am, and I would like to ask you a question."

He opens his eyes, waiting.

I say, "What became of the last portrait you painted of Leonora Fortunati, the one with your own portrait in the mirror?"

"You know about that?" he says, and his sunken eyes grow wide.

"I know everything, Don Diego. I know about you chasing the seller of red carnations when you were a child and how the priest brought you home, and how you learned to paint, and your visit to Madrid, when you were rejected, and how you went another time and became the king's painter and how you felt when he first touched you, and your conversations with Rubens and your voyages to Italy, the first and the second, and I know about Leonora, how you painted her for Heliche and how she taught you about the art of love."

It is a while before he speaks again, nor am I sure that he speaks at all. Perhaps it is a more subtle communication. "She died," he says. "The plague struck in Rome and the boy died and she became sick as well and she wrote to me. She said she burnt it. I burnt her letter."

I say, "This may be so, but the painting lives again. I've seen it with my own eyes."

"Well, since I am conversing with a phantom, which is impossible, then I suppose that it is also possible that a burnt painting can come back to life. It was a wicked painting, but a good one. What you saw, however, was a forgery. The woman did not lie, I think, not when she saw the marks of death on her body."

He pauses, perhaps lost for a moment in memory. Then he says, "You said you were a painter—do they paint, then, in your future?"

"Yes, after a fashion. Not as you did."

"No one painted as I did, even in my own time. Tell me, do the kings of Spain still keep my paintings and admire them?"

"Yes, they do, and so does all the world. In a few years from now Luca Giordano will stand before your portrait of the royal family and call it the theology of painting. A thousand painters have gone to school before it."

A faint smile forms on the dry lips. "That Neapolitan boy—how we laughed about him!" He lets out a long sigh and says, "And now, Sir Phantom, I must, as you say, be about the business of dying, and I wish to turn my thoughts to God and away from things that happened long ago, that I regret."

"But it was a wonderful painting."

"Yes, wonderful," he says, and perhaps he does not mean the painting, or not entirely.

I say, "Farewell, Velázquez," and he says, "Go with God, Sir Phantom, if you are not a devil."

What to make of this, I thought, lying in my madhouse bed, later on that long night. A vivid dream is the easiest explanation, a kind of tying up of the whole thing, now that I'm officially on the mend. But I sniffed the sleeves of my bathrobe and got a whiff of cloves. Or did I imagine that too? Like my little game with Rose. Did I imagine her giving the failed artist Chaz's address when I asked her in the barn? I felt so bad about frightening her in the hall at Krebs's house, but only in a vague and distant way, like it had happened long ago to someone else. It was sweet not to have any of it matter under these wonderful drugs.

I slept then, deep and dreamless, and in the morning when I passed my door on the way to the toilet, I happened to look out the little window, and who should I see but Krebs. He was in deep consultation with Dr. Schick and another man, one whose face I knew well, because I'd drawn a portrait of it in Madrid. Dr. Schick seemed to be explaining something to him, and he was nodding. Well, then, as Krebs suggested, he must be some kind of mental health guy. Although he still had the face of a gangster.

About an hour later, after breakfast, Dr. Schick came in and I had a long session with him. I gave him the life story, and how I felt about painting, and especially about the paintings I was doing, the slick nudes, I meant, and why I should imagine myself an impoverished though principled hack, rather than a wealthy and fashionable painter. He had a lot of good things to say about the fragility of the mind, and how it sometimes cracked under the strain of contrary urges and desires. Not at all unusual, he said, even among highly successful people. I told him about the salvinorin, and he wiggled his eyebrows and said, "Well, no wonder!"

I asked him what was in the implant that they removed, and he said they didn't know. It was empty.

"What could it have been?" I asked.

"I would have to guess there," he said, "for of course I have no medical records here for you. But people have had good success with such devices for dispensing antipsychotics. You know, many of those suffering from forms of schizophrenia refuse to take their medications, and this is one way to fix that."

I agreed that this was a possible explanation, and we chatted some more about controlling my symptoms. He gave me a prescription for more calming drugs and also for Haldol, which he thought I'd do well on, almost an ideal Haldol patient, he said.

I must have been, because a few days later I was discharged. I sat out on a bench in the sun outside the hospital. I was trying to recall painting those Wilmot nudes I'd seen, and the events that went with that life, and you know, it started to come back to me. My shows, mingling with the rich and famous, doing the paintings, and bit by bit I assembled memories of that life. It's amazing what the mind can do. After a while a Mercedes pulled up on the drive with Franco at the wheel, and I got in and he drove me back to the Krebs establishment.

I did wonder why Lotte hadn't come to see me at the hospital, but I found that she'd left to bring Milo to his Swiss clinic, taking Rose with her. That was fine by me. It's embarrassing to be crazy, especially the kind of crazy I was, where you've forgotten the life you lived with another person. Were we really still married in this life? I hadn't asked.

A few days passed. Not a bad existence, I had to admit. Responsibilities were few, one never wanted for company, and I had the run of the place except for Krebs's office. Time just flowed on by. I did not pick up a brush or a pencil after returning from the nuthouse, but I knew I eventually would, maybe as an outsider artist, like those brilliant schizophrenics who cover acres of paper with their obsessions, or maybe I will cleave more closely to the mainstream and turn my craziness into real money, like van Gogh, and Cornell, and Munch. Or go back to the pricey nudes.

I detected a certain tension in the house. It was because the auction of the *Venus* had been scheduled in New York. D-day was, I believe, just three days away, and the worlds of art and high finance (is there a difference?) were churning like baskets of eels. I saw a copy of *Der Spiegel* lying around with the painting spread over the cover, with the blurb stating that the painting would go on the block with a reserve price of a hundred and ten million dollars. I didn't get a chance to read the article. They restricted my access to media: doctor's orders.

Later that day, Kellermann handed me a cell phone, and it was Lotte from Geneva. She said the special rich-people clinic had poked Milo and examined his insides and declared that yeah, they can make him good as new for about a million bucks, more or less; a few new organs required, but it turns out that for these we don't have to go on no stinkin' list, they're ready more or less when we are. Milo does look a little less peaky, she says. Maybe it's the hope.

To her great credit, Lotte asked about the source of the putative organs, and the man didn't quite get why she was asking. She said she didn't want them to, like, come from people especially murdered to provide them, and the guy was shocked she would have thought such a thing, this being Switzerland and very correct. No, they have deals with people in high-risk professions, money up front and we get your good parts when the parachute doesn't open, and also they'll pay for the education of a cohort of kids, and should they drown some summer, the families let them take a cut, so to speak. Very rational and actuarial, something like dairy farming, ever a Swiss specialty. Whether it's legal in the strict sense she didn't ask.

I had a discussion with Krebs about the money end of this plan. It seemed that a million dollars was at that moment sitting in a Swiss account for me, in payment of all the paintings he'd sold from my vast output, which he'd been representing for years. Sorry you don't recall that, Wilmot, sorry you recall something that didn't happen and sorry you don't recall something that did, but, hey, you're crazy! I took this in calmly, or the Haldol did. The fact is, I can't help liking him and I think he genuinely likes me.

That evening I wandered into the room Rose had occupied, wondering when I'd get to see the kids again, if ever, and I saw, taped to

the wall, one of her shredder-strip pasteups. It was of two fat pig-
gies in a green field. Clearly she'd found a supply of pink. Well, you
know, I really have a good eye for color, and a very good memory for
color, if not for much else, and something about the strips of pink
paper she was using to construct the pigs made a connection in my
head: many of her strips had on them small sections of an intense
rose madder.

I poked around the room, looking for the source, and after a while
I found it, stuck in the back of a bureau drawer, a clear plastic bag
full of shredder waste, mainly pink. I took it back to my room and
dumped the strips onto the floor. I was lucky that it was a strip shredder and not the confetti kind, because you can do a pretty good job of
reconstruction on that kind of strip. After the Iranian students took
over the Tehran embassy back in '79 they had teams of women recon-
struct a lot of CIA secrets from the shredder waste, and I sat there
all night and did the same thing, using a glue stick. It wasn't perfect
when I got through, but you could see what it was.

When I was done I sat through the dawn and the early morning thinking about what had been done to me, and also about why I
wasn't angrier. I wasn't really angry at all, just sad. Relieved? A little,
but mainly sad. How could she have? But I knew the answer to that.

There was a little stone terrace on the east side of the house, with
a table and an umbrella set up on it, and there Krebs liked to
take his breakfast alone, read half a dozen newspapers, and, I suppose, plot his next crimes. No one is supposed to interrupt him there,
but I figured this was a special occasion.

I walked out into the early sunlight and held my pasteup in front
of his face.

He looked at it for a moment, sighed, and said, "That Liesl!

Honestly, she has been told a hundred times to attend to the burn bags before she does anything else."

He gestured to a chair. "Sit down, Wilmot. Tell me, what do you think you have there?"

I said, "I have there a Photoshop printout of an unfinished fake painting I last saw in a loft I was supposedly living in on Greenwich Street in New York. I was so rattled that I didn't look at it closely enough, or I would have seen it was a huge ink-jet image printed onto canvas, then artfully gone over with a brush, and then glazed. I assume the images in that phony gallery were made in the same way."

He didn't say anything, just sat there with an amused look on his face.

I said, "The gallery, and the loft, and changing my door and my locks, and that ringer in Bosco's place. And you got to Lotte too. It's . . . I don't know what to call it—insane? And how did you know the drug would affect me in that way? I mean the Velázquez connection. You couldn't have planned it."

He said nothing.

"No, of course not," I continued. "It was just taking advantage of a preexisting fact. I was hallucinating Velázquez, and those paintings I did proved I had the skill. So of course, you had to forge a Velázquez."

"Go on. This is fascinating."

"And you implanted that slow-release thing in me so I'd keep having the experience even after I wasn't getting the drug from Shelly."

"It could certainly have been done that way, yes. Low-level American health care personnel are shockingly ill paid. It could have been done in that mental hospital in New York."

"Zubkoff was in on it too."

"I think you will find him perfectly innocent. If such a series of events actually transpired, then Mark Slade would have had to have been the instigator of the whole New York endeavor. You should be more careful about your confidantes in future."

"But *why?* Why did you go through all that incredible trouble and expense?"

"Well, if I were to humor you in this conjecture," he said, "I would have to say it was because of what happened to Jackie Moreau."

The name came as a shock. "He's dead," I said inanely.

"Yes. Murdered. He did a very nice Pissarro for us, and a Monet. And he wouldn't keep his mouth shut. I tried to protect him, but I was overruled. So I was not going to take a chance with you. Because in something like this, as I have tried to explain to you, the forger always talks in the end, forgers can't help it. And the people who deal in forgeries at this level understand that. But no one listens to a madman. I believe your madness has saved your life."

"And you thought driving me crazy was the solution? Why in hell didn't you come to me like a man and tell me the straight story and ask me to pretend to be crazy?"

He shook his head. "Assuming for a moment that you are right, no such imposture would have worked. You are an artist, not an actor. Do you imagine that the gentleman who asked you to draw him that day in Madrid would be taken in for a moment by an imposture? No, you had to be genuinely mad, mad before witnesses, certified mad by doctors of unimpeachable reputation. And mad you must remain for all your days, if you want to live."

"That was why that guy was talking to Schick in the hospital," I said. "He was checking up that I was really around the bend."

He shrugged. "If you like."

"So you're agreeing I'm not a succesful gallery painter and that I did paint that fake Velázquez?"

"I'm not agreeing to anything of the sort. Wait here a moment and I'll show you something."

He got up and left me staring at his empty chair. After a short while he returned, holding what looked like a leather-bound photo album. He handed it to me and I opened it. Every right-hand page held a color photograph of a painting affixed to the thick black paper with old-fashioned corner mounts, and on each facing page was pasted a typed provenance, in German. There were twenty-eight in all: several Rembrandts, a Vermeer, two Franz Hals, and the rest good-quality Dutch masters of the seventeenth century, with two exceptions. One was a Breughel of a skating party on a canal, and the other was the van der Goes altarpiece I'd seen in Krebs's office that time. Besides that, all of them were unfamiliar to me.

"What is this?" I asked him.

"Well, you'll recall the story I told you of the van that was consumed in Dresden. These were the paintings in that van."

"Except for the van der Goes."

"Yes, that had been removed and placed in the other van for reasons now obscure. But these paintings in the album are assuredly gone. Now, you may have noticed during your tour of this house a small door in the cellar that is always locked. Behind it is a bricked-up well. It was bricked up in 1948. Now, suppose I wished to remove the bricks for some reason and hired a respectable firm of builders to do the job, and suppose that behind the bricks we found all these paintings. Wouldn't that be wonderful!"

It took me a few seconds to get it, and it was so absurd that I had to laugh. "You want me to forge twenty-seven paintings."

He laughed too. "Yes. Marvelous, isn't it?"

"But you'd never be able to sell them. The Schloss family and the international authorities—"

He waved his hand. "No, no, not a public sale. I've explained this to you. There is an immense private market for high-value paintings. To dispose of these would be quite easy, once news of the discovery was made available to a particular subset of the market. People have been wondering about the lost Schloss paintings since the war, and of course it is known that my father had access to them. They would sell like pancakes."

"That's an interesting offer," I said.

"Isn't it? And of course it would more than fund your own work and any expenses you might have in connection with your son's treatment."

"Yes, that," I said, and thought of Lotte and my old pal Mark, and how they'd both contributed to the plot. I said, "I'm curious. How did you rope Mark and Lotte into this thing?"

"Speaking hypothetically, you mean?"

"If it makes you happy."

"Then it was money, of course. Mark will realize a colossal commission from the Velázquez. And he does not seem to like you very much. He was quite gleeful to be, as he put it, fucking with your head."

"And Lotte. Doesn't she like me either?"

"On the contrary, she loves you very much. She agreed to help us so as to blast you forever out of your ridiculous and miserable existence as a commercial artist and also to obtain adequate medical care for your son, which you were never going to be able to do. There is no deeper love than this, you know, than to surrender the loved one so that he can become what he was meant to be."

"I was meant to be an insane forger?"

"I wouldn't put it that way, Wilmot. Yes, you *are* insane, as planned. I mean to say, you imagine you are Diego Velázquez! What could be more clear evidence of madness than that? It is textbook diagnosis. You have long fits of amnesia during which you believe you have painted old masters. And so forth."

For a long moment I stared at him, literally gaping. It was like a movie, a bad melodrama in which the villain explains to the helpless James Bond how he's going to blow up the city. But Krebs wasn't looking villainous at all, no malicious glee, just a concerned and paternal expression like Dad has when he breaks it to little Virginia that there's no Santa.

There was no juice of outrage in me. I managed to say, "That's pretty fucking arrogant, Krebs, to do that to someone, don't you think?"

"Well, yes, I am an arrogant bastard. It is my nature and of course our national vice as well. But consider, Wilmot, that you have always been crazy, and with no help from me. When we started this you were a neurotically constricted artist incapable of doing decent work and slaving for workman's wages producing shit for advertising or whatever. For an artist of your capability, that is the true insanity. Now, on the other hand, you have money and freedom to do what you like."

"As long as what I like is forging paintings for you."

"It will not take up too much of your time, I think. You no longer have the excuse of having to struggle to support your family, and you will have to face the white canvas without that crutch. You can paint for yourself. Perhaps you will flourish as never before, and perhaps not. I hope for the former, of course. Maybe you will be the one to rescue easel painting for another thousand years."

"Oh, yeah, lay *that* on me!" I said, and then we both smiled. I couldn't help it.

"And another thing," he said. "I think that also in your heart of hearts you do not despise this idea of forgery. You wished to add beauty to the world, and the art establishment has no taste for it anymore; this is a way to do it and also to give them one in the eye. And this is my desire too. The Schloss paintings, which were destroyed through my father's doing and the wickedness of my country, will live again. And no one will ever know the difference."

"You could give them back to the Schloss family."

"I could. And perhaps I will—some of them. But, you know, I have my expenses, and patronage is a costly proposition. I must keep Charles Wilmot happy, after all."

"You must. I notice you've abandoned the pretense that I was a successful figurative painter with a Whitney retrospective."

"I haven't abandoned anything," he said. "It's you who are unfortunately incapable of keeping your story straight, or even of recalling what has been said to you from one minute to the next. For example, I have no idea what you think we have just been discussing. I myself recall a conversation about the watercolors of Winslow Homer."

I stared at him for a second, and then I had to laugh; it just came bubbling up from inside me and it went on for a long time. He was absolutely right. We might have been discussing anything. My clever pasteup might not even exist. In fact, after I had finished wiping my eyes and caught my breath, I found that it had somehow vanished from the table. And where was that tiny implant? Who knew?

"I am happy you are amused," he said, and I thought he was just a little uneasy when he said it. I mean, he wanted me crazy, but not that crazy.

"Yeah, now I know why they always depict madmen as laughing. You know, Werner, this is a pleasant spot, but I think I'll take my lunatic ass back to New York. Unless I'm still a prisoner."

"You've never been a prisoner, except of yourself. What will you do in New York?"

"Oh, you know, tie up my affairs. Take a look at that painting you say I didn't do."

"You didn't. Salinas discovered the lost Velázquez in the bowels of the Alba's vast holdings, don't ask me how. All of Mark's machinations with it were merely to help Salinas smuggle it out of Spain. It truly had a fake Bassano painted on top of it. Perhaps Leonora

Fortunati herself had this done to protect herself and her famous lover. As you have yourself described to me."

"It makes a good story anyway. Werner, don't you *ever* tell the truth?"

"I *always* tell the truth, after a fashion," he said, and stood and shook my hand. "I'll be in touch," he said, and walked back into the house.

The next day Franco drove me to Munich, and I caught a flight out to London and then to New York. I checked into the midtown Hilton and called Mark, and we had a nice chat, with no mention of the various betrayals he'd engineered, although he did seem a little nervous on the line. He invited me to his celebration and mentioned in passing that you'd be there, and I accepted.

After I stop talking I'm going to download all the sound files you've just heard onto a CD and go to Mark's party and hand this CD to you. Why you? I don't know, you've always seemed a kind of neutral observer to me, and I'm curious about what you make of it. Maybe there's some clue you could point me at that'll make more sense of the whole affair than I could. You might want to study the painting too, if you can get close enough. You might find it particularly interesting.

It was four in the morning when I finished playing the last file, and then I fell into bed half dressed and slept until almost noon, slept right through the alarm and the buzzing on my cell phone, my secretary going a little batty trying to reach me. I called the front desk, but no Chaz Wilmot had shown up or called, which I thought odd. I thought the whole point of the CD was to meet and discuss it. When I checked my messages there was one from Mark Slade inviting me to attend the auction that afternoon and asking me if I'd heard anything from Chaz.

I'd planned to go back to Stamford, I had a meeting at one, but I called the office and had it rescheduled—I was still somewhat under the spell of Chaz's weird tale and didn't feel up to discussing the details of theme park reinsurance. I screwed around for a few hours, making some calls and trying to do paperwork and e-mails and such, to no great effect, and then I cleaned myself up, dressed, and caught a cab uptown to Sotheby's.

I wasn't in the room for more than a few minutes before Mark pulled himself away from a group of prosperous-looking gentlemen and steered me to a corner. He was full of himself that day, and full of the prospect of the killing he was going to make. The billionaire boys' club was there in strength apparently, from Europe, Japan, the Middle East, Latin America, because this was a unique chance to snag a Velázquez. The last painting by the artist to go on sale had been the Juan de Pareja portrait that the Met had bought at Christie's in 1970 for four and a half million, and there would not be another in the foreseeable future. I asked him whether the Met would get this one too, and he said not a chance, it's way out of their range now. Who then? He pointed to a woman wearing a severe gray suit standing in the rear of the room by the phones that off-site bidders used to communicate with their agents at the auction. She had black hair parted in the middle and done up in a bun, scarlet lipstick, and nail polish the same color. Olive skin. Green eyes. That's Spain, Mark said.

"You mean the Prado?"

"No, I mean the fucking kingdom of Spain. You should watch her on the phone."

And then he turned the conversation to Chaz and asked me again if I'd spoken to him at the party, and I said I had, and he asked me right out if Chaz had claimed to have painted the Velázquez, and I said yeah, he had. I didn't mention the CD. Mark said he was afraid of that, poor bastard. You know he had a nervous breakdown? I said I hadn't heard but that he had seemed a little flaky. A little! Mark said, the guy's a refugee from the funny farm, I wonder why they let him walk around, and he went on to tell me the story of how he had gotten Chaz this commission in Europe and how he'd gone off the rails there and started accusing people of drugging him, and how he thought he could travel back through time and be Velázquez and paint his works, including this one, and that he'd blanked out big chunks of his real life. I said that was awful, and he said, yeah, but it's going to do wonders for his sales, if he'd produce something; people love crazy artist stories, look at Pollock, look at Munch, look at van Gogh.

So that was Mark's tale, and after he'd delivered it, he dropped me in favor of a couple of guys in suits and spade beards who looked like sons of the desert, and I went to sit down. The auction started with half a dozen teaser items, which went quickly, and then the boys in white gloves rolled out the Velázquez, and there was a stir. The auctioneer said this is the *Venus with Self-Portrait* by Diego Velázquez, also called the *Alba Venus*, and he said a little about its history and then announced that the bidding would start at one hundred million. There were four serious bidders as the bids raced up the ladder in half-million-dollar jumps, and after each round the auctioneer looked to the back of the room and got a nod from the lady of Spain, and then one by one the others dropped out and the Prado had it for 210 million, the highest price ever recorded for a single painting. Thus the barons of our age learned the lesson that the kings of the age of Velázquez had taught their own barons—it doesn't matter how rich you are, you can't compete with the sovereign, and what we were seeing here was Spain herself bringing back her purloined treasure. No one else had ever had a chance.

What was that, two, two and a half years ago? During that time Chaz Wilmot dropped completely out of sight. I'd always thought it would've taken a nuclear detonation to get him out of that loft, but apparently he'd cleaned out whatever he wanted and walked away from the rest. This I got from the girl at Lotte Rothschild's gallery. Lotte was still in business, doing rather better than before, to judge from her prices. I didn't stick around to see her. Well, I thought then, bye-bye Chaz, not that he was ever a very important part of my life. I figured he was being maintained in some Swiss clinic.

But it happened that I was called to Barcelona for a meeting with a European consortium building a gigantic amusement park near that city. I had one meeting that lasted all day, and the one scheduled for the next day was moved to the following day in Madrid, so I got a free day in the town, which is one of my favorite cities, as lovely as Paris, but without the attitude. The Catalans even like Americans, probably because the Spaniards don't very much nowadays. It was a pretty day, warm but not hot, with a breeze that blew away the usual smog, so I took a cab up to Parc Güell to wander through the mosaics, sit on the terrace, and ogle the tourists ogling Gaudí.

And there, on the middle path, among the line of Africans selling cheap sunglasses, crafts, and souvenirs, was a fellow with an easel doing aquarelle portraits of tourists at ten euros a pop. I thought that was a pretty good deal, so I waited my turn and sat down on the little chair provided. The artist, in a straw hat and sunglasses, was darkly tanned and wore a bushy gray-flecked beard. He got right to work without a word. It took about ten or twelve minutes and then he snapped it off his easel and handed it to me.

There I was in all my stony glory. He'd put me in the clothing of a Spanish grandee of the seventeenth century, just like Velázquez used to do, and just as good as the one he'd done of me twenty-five years before.

I said, "Let's get a drink, Chaz," and he grinned at me, a little sheepishly, I thought, and asked one of the Africans to watch his stuff. We went over to that little café they have there and sat under a beer-company umbrella.

He said, "You weren't looking for me, by any chance?"

I said, "No, it was just luck. Why, are you in hiding?"

We ordered *claras*, and when the waiter left he said, "Not really. It's just I like to stay kind of private."

"Well, you've succeeded," I said. "So what've you been doing all this time? Sidewalk portraits for ten euros?"

"Among other things. What do you think of your portrait?"

I studied it again. "It's terrific. Full of life. More of me than I like to see revealed, frankly. And incredible that you can work in watercolors instead of pastels like the other sidewalk guys. Do your customers appreciate this kind of work?"

"Some do. Some *really* do. And a small percentage think they're crap, not pretty enough."

"Just like real life," I said. "But you can't possibly make a living from this."

"No. I have other sources of income." Our drinks came, and Chaz engaged in some rapid-fire repartee in Spanish with the waiter that I didn't get. The man laughed and went away.

"Then why do it?" I asked.

"I enjoy it. It's perfectly non-commoditized art, anonymous, and a pure gift of pleasure to those who can see, and even those who can't see might come to appreciate their portraits after a while. Artists used to live like that in Europe all the time, back in the Middle Ages. Besides that, I have a studio. I paint a lot."

"What do you paint?"

He grinned a sly grin. "Oh, you know, slick, witty nudes, just like before. It's amusing. And I do other stuff too."

The tone here was purposely vague, and I rose to the bait.

"You're working for Krebs," I said. "You're putting together that collection that got burned in Dresden."

"I might be. Although you can't really trust anything I say. I mean, I'm a crazy person doing sidewalk portraits for small change."

"But you're not crazy. You proved that. The whole thing was a scam."

"Was it? Maybe I made that up too."

"Yeah, but come on, Chaz. Hundreds of people knew you, there are records, tax returns . . . I mean, you may have had some issues with memory, but you also had a verifiable life."

"No!" he said with some heat. "No one has a verifiable life. A little lump in your brain growing in the wrong place and you're not you anymore, and all the records in the world won't change that. If you can't trust your memory—and I can't—then the record of your life, the witness of others, is meaningless. If I presented you with a shitload of records and the testimony of dozens of people telling you that you were, I don't know, a plumber from Arkansas, would you believe it? If your supposed wife Lulubelle and your five kids swore on a stack of Bibles that you were Elmer Gudge of Texarkana, would you say, gosh, well, I had a fantasy that I was an insurance guy from Connecticut, but that's all over now, hand me my pipe wrench? Of course you wouldn't, because your memory's intact. But what if your memory became unreliable, and what if your actual wife, say, looked at you and went, who's he?"

This line of talk was making me uncomfortable, so I said, "That must've been tough, Lotte shafting you like that. I assume you don't see her anymore."

"Why would you assume that?"

"Well, she betrayed you, didn't she? She must have been involved in the scam from the beginning, supplying photos and whatnot, and she betrayed you to your face, just before you went berserk. Unless you've forgiven her."

"There was nothing to forgive, and she didn't betray me. I betrayed myself. She just made me see it. I'm sort of grateful to her for that. And if I don't see much of her, it's not because of what she did—it's the shame."

"What do you mean?"

"You know how you look through a kaleidoscope and you tap it, and the same little pieces of glass snap into a completely different pattern? That's what happened. I left Mark's party that night and took a cab to my loft. And when I went in it was like an alien place, and full of horrible vibes, like an ancient tomb with evil spirits inhabiting it, and even though I'd lived there and worked there for years, it was like I was there for the first time. I couldn't find stuff, I didn't recognize the things that were there, as if another me had been there all those years. And I started to freak out bad, and then this revelation—the kaleidoscope clicked, and I saw it. I saw that there was really no difference at all between me and Suzanne."

He stared at me in a way that seemed to require a response, so I said, "That's ridiculous. Her problem is she has no talent and wants to be recognized. You have a lot of talent."

He said, "Yeah, you don't get it either. It's the *same fucking thing*!

Having talent and not putting it on the line is just like not having it and desperately wanting to be recognized. It's the same kind of pathetic. It's not noble. It's not elevated to use the techniques of Velázquez on a perfume ad and laugh secretly at the customer for not catching the nuances. It's a life made of shit, and I'm positively grateful to Lotte and Krebs for getting me out of it."

"By making you crazy."

"No, just crazy in a different way," he said, and smiled the smile of a contented man.

I had no idea what he was talking about.

"I don't buy it," I said after a bit. "I can't understand why you didn't just call your sister. Surely she would've blown the whole plot to pieces."

"Oh, right, Charlie. Yes, sure, but Charlie was nowhere to be found during the period in question. Some anonymous donor gave her a bunch of money to set up a field hospital in Chad, immediate departure a requirement, and you'll recall I didn't have a phone. She was incommunicado for six weeks, and so when I called her the night I went berserk I got a no-such-number message, although there should have been people at her organization. For a while I thought I'd made her up too."

"You were using Krebs's phone. Maybe they messed with it somehow."

"Yes, and they arranged for Charlie to be gone, and everything else that drove me nuts. A secretive international organization with tentacles everywhere. Don't you realize how crazy that sounds?"

It did sound crazy, so I changed the subject. "So Charlie's back from there?"

"Oh, yeah. In fact she lives with me in . . . wherever I live. She's in and out on missions of mercy, but we have a nice setup."

"Just like your boyhood dream."

"Just." Again, that annoying smile.

"And Milo? I presume he survived."

"Yeah. He had his transplant, he's flourishing. A teenager, which we never thought we'd see. The fruits of my wickedness."

"Speaking of which, did you ever figure out if you did that Velázquez *Venus*?"

"Does it matter? You've got all the information. What do *you* think?"

"What I think is that you're a terrific painter, but you're not Velázquez."

This was a little cruel, I admit, but something about how this had all turned out irritated me. It was like when someone accosts you on the street with a problem and you start to respond in a civilized way, to be of service, let's say, and after a few minutes you pick up that the fellow is crazy and you feel like you've wasted your time and your concern.

"You're right, I'm not," he said. "But did you ever get a chance to take a close look at it? The real thing, I mean, not the poster."

"No, but I'll be in Madrid tomorrow. I intend to see it then. And I assume you haven't had anymore whatever you call them—visions. Where you think you're him."

"No," he said, with a tone of regret in his voice, "not since I saw him die. I seem to have enough trouble keeping up with me."

"And you have no interest in finding out the truth?"

"'What is truth? said jesting Pilate; and would not stay for an answer.' You must remember that from Humanities 102. Bacon's *On Truth*? Look around you, my friend. Truth has left the building. Everything is manipulable now, even photography, and art is a lie to begin with. Picasso said so, and so say I. We all tell lies, even the stories we tell ourselves about our lives, even in the intimate depths of our private thoughts. But somehow, I don't know how, maybe through what my sister calls grace, these lies occasionally produce something we all recognize as true. And when I paint I wait for those miracles."

I didn't know what to say to that, and the conversation subsequently ran down a little. We talked about other things, the cities of Europe and what was going on in the world, and we parted amicably enough.

The next day I was in Madrid and spent the morning in a meeting discussing how to assess the risks of terrorism and sabotage on the proposed amusement venue, which is a growth area among the actuarial set, and I had lunch with my colleagues, then walked over to the Prado. They'd placed it in Room Twelve on the wall to the right of *Las Meninas*, which was quite the compliment, I thought; not many paintings can stand the comparison.

A little throng had gathered around the Most Expensive Painting in the World, the irresistible tugs of sex and money working together there, and a guard was standing by to make sure people didn't stay too long and hog the view. I waited until it was my turn, and as I got to the front I was conscious of the little sighs people were making, as if to say, ah, if only love could be like that, sex could be like that, always. There she lay, obviously the same model who had posed for the *Rokeby Venus*, except now she lay on her back, with her hand covering her crotch, not palm-down, modestly, but palm-up, a joke, offering it, not to us, but to the sweat-soaked man reflected in the black-framed mirror, the same fellow you could see with his palette in hand in the center of the great painting to the left.

You know, I think every man with some experience at love has in his heart the image of the girl who got away, the one who pops into your mind at idle moments, about whom the inevitable longing centers, no matter how content you are with spouse and home. That was the appeal of this painting, I thought; he'd painted, in some wonderful and mysterious way, That Girl. But in my own case, literally, because when I finally got a chance to see the *Alba Venus* close up I saw that the body the artist had painted was one I'd known intimately, but too fleetingly, some decades ago. I remember in particular a small black beauty mark just below the navel, to the right of the midline. I only got to see it on two occasions, unfortunately, before my old pal Chaz Wilmot swept into that reunion party and yanked Lotte Rothschild out of my life.

Probably for the best, actually; Diana is a much more suitable wife for someone like me. And maybe I am confabulating this too in my mind, a mere black dot—who could recall its exact placement after all these years? Although it's the kind of thing Chaz would do, the sly bastard.

And then I had to move on, and I circled around behind the crowd and stood for a moment in front of the greatest painting in the world, *The Maids of Honor* by Velázquez, and thought about what it would be like to be him, really be him, and I couldn't deal with it, and I left and reentered the long, gray sanity of my life.

A NOTE TO THE READER

This is a work of fiction, but Diego Rodríguez de Silva y Velázquez was, of course, a real painter. The details of his life as provided here are consistent with the historical record, as far as that goes; he was a very private man. Scholars differ on where Velázquez did the painting known as the *Rokeby Venus*, now in London's National Gallery. Some say Madrid, some say during his second trip to Rome, in 1650. I've opted for the latter, to increase the fun. The identity of the woman who posed for it is lost to history. Velázquez may have painted it for the Marqués de Heliche, who was, in fact, a notorious libertine, and there is some evidence that Velázquez painted other nudes at that time, which have vanished.

The Palacio Livia is a real museum in Madrid, and as far as I know it is of sterling reputation and would never try to pass off a doubtful painting on an American.

Salvinorin A is a real drug and is derived from the plant known as *Salvia divinorum*, which is used in shamanic rituals by the Mazotec Indians of Mexico. The time-traveling effects described here have been recorded in the extensive literature on the drug by some of its aficionados. It remains a legal drug but has never become a popular recreational substance, for obvious reasons.

BOOKS BY MICHAEL GRUBER

THE FORGERY OF VENUS
A Novel
ISBN 978-0-06-087449-0 (hc)

"A tour-de-force combination of suspense and characterization, as well as a primer on the world of art and art forgery." —*Seattle Times*

THE BOOK OF AIR AND SHADOWS
ISBN 978-0-06-145657-2 (pb)

A *NEW YORK TIMES* BESTSELLER

"Breathlessly engaging . . . incredibly smart . . . unpredictable." —*USA Today*

• THE JIMMY PAZ SERIES •

TROPIC OF NIGHT
ISBN 978-0-06-050955-2 (mm) • ISBN 978-0-06-165073-4 (pb)

"A blockbuster. As unsettling as it is exciting." —*People*

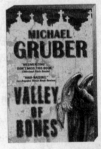

VALLEY OF BONES
ISBN 978-0-06-057767-4 (mm) • ISBN 978-0-06-075930-8 (cd)

"Dazzling, literate, and downright scary."
—*Cleveland Plain Dealer*

NIGHT OF THE JAGUAR
A Novel
ISBN 978-0-06-057769-8 (mm)

"An astonishing piece of fiction." —*Washington Post*

Visit www.AuthorTracker.com
for exclusive information on your favorite HarperCollins authors.

Available wherever books are sold, or call 1-800-331-3761 to order.